FREEDOM—OR SLAVERY

This is the brilliant and disturbingly accurate novel of
Europe in the mid-century, gripped by the fear that it
will be enslaved by totalitarian aggression. The scene is
Paris, and the characters are the menacing enemy agents
and the pathetically bewildered members of the glamorous international society who anxiously await an unknown future.

Symbolizing the struggle between the forces of freedom and slavery is the passionate and abortive love
affair between a sophisticated American girl and a Communist official. Hydie is wealthy and cultivated, convent-
educated but disillusioned with religion, and embittered
by an unhappy marriage. She longs for something in
which to believe and thinks she has found it when she
meets Fedya at a lavish party.

Fedya, product of revolution and perfect model of
the totalitarian mind, is a cold and ruthless man who
long ago has erased any humanitarian feelings for others
or for himself. Attracted by Hydie's passionate acquies-
cence, he betrays her in a humiliating and debasing episode which finally makes her recognize the corruptness
of a faith based on destruction.

Many critics have called this powerful novel about
the spiritual and political crisis of our time Koestler's
best book. "Koestler is a superb writer . . . and here
he provides both sex and humor in some quantity, the
humor contributing most of the sharpness in his outlines
of the Communist mind."—*Combat Forces Journal*
"*The Age of Longing* is at once complex, powerful and
terrifying . . . it has the power of one of those night-
mares from which the sleeper wakes sweating in mental
agony."—Harrison Smith, *Saturday Review.*

Other SIGNET and MENTOR Books
You Will Enjoy

DARKNESS AT NOON *by Arthur Koestler*
The dramatic novel about a man who could no longer survive in a society which does not recognize the rights of the individual. (Signet #671—25c)

1984 *by George Orwell*
The tyrannical, terrifying world of 1984—the end product of forces at work today. (Signet #798—25c)

NEW WORLD WRITING
Second Mentor Selection
The second volume of the exciting new publication that includes selections from forthcoming novels, plus short stories, poems, criticism and articles. There are contributions by Shirley Jackson, Norman Mailer, Dylan Thomas, and many lesser-known Americans, as well as by writers from Italy, India, Poland, Greece, and other countries. (Mentor #Ms 79—50c)

A WORLD APART *by Gustav Herling*
A vivid, absorbing account of a Russian slave labor camp by a man who was imprisoned there. (Mentor #M75—35c)

A HERO OF OUR TIME *by Vasco Pratolini*
An engrossing novel about a brutal youth and a woman bound to him with a perverse and irresistible love. (Signet #969—25c)

TO OUR READERS

We welcome your comments about Signet or Mentor Books, as well as your suggestions for new reprints. If your dealer does not have the books you want, you may order them by mail, enclosing the list price plus 5c a copy to cover mailing costs. Send for a copy of our complete catalogue. The New American Library of World Literature, Inc., 501 Madison Avenue, New York 22, N. Y.

THE AGE OF
LONGING

by ARTHUR KOESTLER

A SIGNET BOOK

Published by THE NEW AMERICAN LIBRARY

Published as a SIGNET BOOK
By Arrangement with The Macmillan Company

FIRST PRINTING, JANUARY, 1953

SIGNET BOOKS are published by
The New American Library of World Literature, Inc.
501 Madison Avenue, New York 22, New York

PRINTED IN THE UNITED STATES OF AMERICA

To JAMES PUTNAM

The characters in this book are fictitious, and the events described in it have not yet taken place.

Yet it is not a visionary tale of the future; it merely carries the present one step further in time—to the middle nineteen-fifties.

The Interlude between Parts One and Two may be regarded as a chapter from an as yet unwritten history book on the fall of pre-Puberterian man.

A. K.   Fontaine le Port, July 1950

CONTENTS

PART ONE

1

BASTILLE DAY, 195...

THE Colonel had drunk so much wine that when he heard the swish of the rocket he almost took cover behind the parapet of the balcony. His hands gripped the sooty iron railing, his eyes were closed, his body swayed a little amidst the dense row of guests. Presently he felt his daughter's smooth arm press excitedly against his shoulder, and he opened his eyes. He saw the rocket thrust like a golden comet across the stars, then silently explode into a shower of green and purple drops. A Roman candle burst somewhere above the Louvre, a Bengal light on the Pont Neuf set the Seine on fire with blue flames. From the quays below rose the enchanted murmur of the crowd; his daughter Hydie's hair brushed the Colonel's cheek like a warm summer breeze.

The river, the dark sky, the island below, tilted away and back as during the landing of an aeroplane, then stood still. Colonel Anderson felt abruptly sobered up and happy. He put his arm round his daughter's shoulder which was almost level with his—a slim column flanking a massive Roman portal.

"For a moment I felt quite drunk," he said deliberately, in case she had noticed it. "No honest man can stand up to four different wines during dinner. I wonder how the French do it . . ."

"They just drink one glass or less of each," said Hydie, absorbed in the fireworks. "And they have no ulcers."

"But it's such damn' good stuff. And they keep filling your glass up," he said piteously.

Six revolving Catherine wheels were spluttering fire of six different colours from the balustrades of the Pont Royal. Hydie stared at them, colour-drunk and dizzy. Then a girandole of some fifty sky-rockets, released at the same time, ripped into the dark tissue of the firmament; and as they exploded, an enormous luminous peacock tail spread from the mansards of the Cité up to the moon.

The crowd down on the quays yelled in a frenzy. The guests on the balcony gave out a long voluptuous a-ah; several young women screamed with delight like children on a roller coaster.

Hydie, with a cry, swerved round to point her arm at three tour billions spiralling upwards with trails of flame from the Sacré Coeur; and as the man on her other side happened at the same time to bend forward, her bare elbow hit him with full force in the face. Her arm retained the sensation of contact with alien skin, hot and glabrous with hard bone underneath; she had hit the man on the saddle of the nose. The physical sensation was the more unpleasant as her unknown neighbour had, at a fleeting glance a little while ago, filled her with unaccountable discomfort.

Hydie made an embarrassed apology. Her victim bowed stiffly but with a certain bodily grace; and as he bowed a dark drop of blood left the cavity of his nostril and began to slide across the shaven surface of his upper lip. He was between thirty-five and forty, a little under medium height, and wore a blue flannel suit of a slightly too vivid colour which looked outlandish and mass-produced. His face was open and pleasant, but equally outlandish and mass-produced. It was a Slavonic face with its round skull and shock of stiff, blond hair, cropped close in military fashion. Between the wide temples and wide cheekbones there was a marked stricture like the waist of an hour-glass, which gave his features a slightly Mongolic touch. His full lips seemed inclined to smile, but were now compressed in embarrassment. In the light of the spluttering Catherine wheels all faces looked bluish-green as under neon tubes; and the drop of blood, slowly sliding down the upper lip, glistened in a viscous purple. For a moment Hydie had an almost irresistible impulse to lick that drop off with her tongue. It seemed such a natural thing to do that she only just checked herself in time, and her aversion against the stranger became even more pronounced.

"But you are bleeding," she cried, gripping his arm. It was a hard, unyielding arm under the somewhat coarse fabric of the sleeve.

"It is nothing," the man said with an annoyed smile, while he wiped the blood away with the back of his hand.

"Have you no handkerchief?" exclaimed Hydie, fumbling in her bag. A moment later she wanted to bite her tongue off because she saw that the man had blushed; in the queer light his face appeared a deeper blue. Stiffly he took a handkerchief from his breast pocket, wiped the back of his hand, then with another ridiculously formal bow, made to turn away from her; his manner indicating that the incident, and with it their acquaintance, had come to an end. It made Hydie feel that she had added insult to injury; to turn her back and watch the fireworks, ignoring her neighbour, had now become impossible.

"But you are still bleeding," she cried, for indeed a steady trickle of blood now ran like a rivulet across his shaven upper lip. Instead of dabbing at it with his handkerchief he pretended not to notice it.

"You must go and bathe it in cold water," exclaimed Hydie in despair. "Do you know your way in the house? Come, I will show you." Again she gripped the stiff fabric of the sleeve, the unyielding arm, pulling at it. For a second she thought that he would wrench himself free; then, obviously realising that the scene was becoming ridiculous, he gave in and followed her across the french window into Monsieur Anatole's salon. The other five or six guests on the balcony were too absorbed in the fireworks to pay attention to them. The Colonel had witnessed the scene with embarrassment; now he found that the only tactful thing to do was to turn his back and watch the tourbillions.

Inside, Monsieur Anatole was sitting with his back to the fireplace, his crutches leaning against the two sides of his armchair. It was the only comfortable chair in the vast, decorous and desolate Louis XV salon, with its fragile congeries of curved and gilded legs, faded silk covers and tufts of stuffing sprouting from divans like hair from old men's ears and nostrils. Flanked by his son and daughter, who stood by the crutches like sentries or caryatids, Monsieur Anatole was holding forth to a small circle of admirers. As Hydie entered, followed by her reluctant victim, Monsieur Anatole's vivacious jackdaw eyes turned toward her; and so did all the other eyes in the salon—the son's and daughter's last.

"Tiens!" said Monsieur Anatole. "Citizen Nikitin, the belated victim of the storming of the Bastille. The blood of the Third Estate is still being shed—I beg your pardon, I mean the Fourth, the revolutionary proletariat, as you call it."

He broke off; everybody stared curiously at Hydie and Nikitin. "An accident," said Hydie, flushing; "I inadvertently punched his nose with my elbow." She knew it sounded unconvincing: nobody would believe her. Monsieur Anatole cackled. "So it has started," he said. "The overture to the next world war. It always starts with little incidents like this . . ."

The daughter advanced towards Nikitin. She was a colourless, moth-like being of indeterminable age; it was known that she had refused to marry for her invalid father's sake. "I will show you to the bathroom," she said in a toneless voice.

"It is nothing," said Nikitin. He spoke with a strong foreign accent, softened by a pleasant baritone voice, which carried with unexpected force across the silent salon. This seemed to embarrass him even more; his full mouth set in a sullen pout. He bowed stiffly to Monsieur Anatole. "I am very thankful for your hospitality, but now I must leave."

"You cannot leave with your jacket soiled with blood," said Mademoiselle Agnès, the daughter. "The blots will disappear with warm water, but it must be done before they dry. Please give it to me." With the authority of a hospital nurse, she got hold of the collar of his jacket. Nikitin looked very annoyed; he glanced at the spots on his new flannel suit—his yellow calf-leather shoes were also new and creaking—and for a moment he gave the impression of a schoolboy on the point of bursting into a rage. It was evidently a situation unforeseen in the careful training he had received before being sent abroad; and as Mademoiselle Agnès pulled at the collar of his jacket to help him out of it—gently but firmly, as she was used to dealing with her reluctant patient, the naughty boy who was her father—Nikitin's bodily frame momentarily lost its natural grace of movement in the throes of a kind of panic, and Hydie, overcome with pity, again grabbed his sleeve.

"But look," she said, "all the men are in their shirtsleeves." The heat of the Paris July night was suffocating.

"That's right," crowed Monsieur Anatole, "roll up your sleeves and let us fight it out." He lifted a crutch and waved its rubber end towards Nikitin. Nikitin shook Hydie's arm off almost rudely, and looking at her with undisguised dislike, yielded his jacket to Mademoiselle Agnès.

"Come on," cried Monsieur Anatole, waving his crutch. His arms were still powerful, and so was his chest—the barrelled torso of old men who in their youth have practised fencing and fought duels in the Bois de Boulogne. "Come on and let's have it out. We stormed our Bastille two centuries ago—now you keep building new ones to the tune of revolutionary songs. Is all our work to be undone? Come closer and tell us."

Nikitin bowed. He had regained his composure and gave Monsieur Anatole a polite smile. "The people of my country are admirers of the French Revolution," he said with careful precision. "They are continuing its work to complete it."

In his shirt, which brought out his straight muscular shoulders, he was very good-looking. His face had a simple directness, a simplicity without guile; only his slightly slanting grey eyes were markedly expressionless—one-way pupils that took the light in, gave nothing out. While he was talking to Monsieur Anatole and turning his back to Hydie, she saw that there was a broad scar across the shaven back of his skull. Mademoiselle Agnès glided soundlessly out of the room with the jacket over her arm; and out of the breast pocket of the jacket, which was upside down, slid Nikitin's notebook and fell soundlessly on the carpet. They were all talking, standing round Monsieur Anatole's armchair, except Hydie who was left out of the circle, alone with her guilty conscience. She picked up the notebook and moved towards the others to hand it back to Nikitin. He had now completely regained his poise and was giving short, precise answers to Monsieur Anatole in his pleasant voice with the harsh foreign accent. Should she once more pull his sleeve to hand back his notebook? With his back turned on her, he seemed completely unapproachable. He had been very rude to her; and a moment ago he had shaken her hand off his arm and had looked at her with frank disgust, as if she were a leper. For a second Hydie stood undecided on the fringe of Monsieur Anatole's lively circle; then with a shrug she stepped out to the balcony, let the notebook drop into her little silk bag, and took her father's arm.

The fireworks were nearing their end, and the Catherine wheels, gerbes and lances, the pastilles, maroons and girandoles were fighting a losing battle against the first fat drops of rain. As the rain gathered momentum, the flame and colour gradually went out of the sky and gave way first to a dusty afterglow, with a smell of gunpowder, then to the normal darkness of night. The last attraction was to be an elaborate pyrotechnical model of the Bastille going up in flames, to be replaced by a lettered design featuring the three words which expressed the creed of the Revolution. But it got only as far as LIB . . . ; the rest of the letters, together with the fixed suns, fountains and waterfalls, were smothered by the cloudburst.

"Oh, but don't go, don't go yet, my dear," cried Monsieur Anatole, half bullyingly, half piteously. "No, I won't let go of your hand. What a lovely soft little hand—twitching like a young bird in the claws of an old hawk. Stay on for a little while, now that the others have gone; your father, the Colonel, is here to protect you and I am only an old man with one foot in the grave—though the other is still kicking . . ."

Monsieur Anatole, who suffered from insomnia, hated to let the last guests leave, though most of those who came to his weekly Friday gatherings bored and exasperated him. His life had become wedged into an ever narrowing margin between the boredom of gregariousness and the terror of loneliness. He knew that at his deathbed the two would finally meet: surrounded by relatives and friends, a spivvy son and an insipid daughter, the widowed sister waiting for the legacy and the devoted friend for some memorable last words to be put into his memoirs, he would have to meet the ultimate ordeal as a gladiator waits for the ceremonious *coup de grâce* in the middle of the circus. So he clutched Hydie's hand in both of his, drawing on its warmth. They were not hawk-like, though; they were long and delicate hands, but the nails had become discoloured and the skin almost transparent, dotted with pale freckles, which made Hydie shiver in revulsion. Embarrassed, she left him her hand as Abishag had lent the warmth of her limbs to the dying David. She was standing in front of him, on her father's arm, frozen in the position in which they had started to take their leave. Mademoiselle Agnès had gone to bed and Gaston, the son, had taken over the watch; he stood near his father's chair against the fireplace, politely bored. Monsieur Anatole had meant him to take over the publishing firm, but at twenty Gaston, a handsome and spoilt victim of his father's tyrannical crutches, had become a semiprofessional dancer and near-gigolo; his allowance only just enabled him to retain a precarious amateur status. He was now engaged in a second-hand sports-car racket and occasionally took part in a motor race. Cross-legged on the carpet, blissfully swaying with a glass of brandy and water in her hand, sat his present mistress, a slightly over-ripe but extremely presentable woman. She was American like Hydie, but of a different generation and type—the type who after the first world war had populated the cafés on Montparnasse, after the second, those of St. Germain des Prés, and who would later be seen, after the third, picking their way in high-heeled shoes among the rubble of the former boulevards, haunting the improvised absinthe shelters. The only other guest still present was Count Boris, a protégé of Mademoiselle Agnès. He was a refugee from the East, very tall and thin, with a gaunt face and a high-pitched voice, who suffered from a complicated form of tuberculosis, acquired as a deportee in the Arctic lumber camps.

"Don't go, my dear," repeated Monsieur Anatole, patting Hydie's limp hand. The Colonel, resigned to seeing his daughter a prisoner nailed by courtesy to the space in front of the old man's armchair, lowered himself carefully onto a frail settee and lit a cigar. He was used to accepting any ordeal which befell him through Hydie.

"Your daughter, Colonel," Monsieur Anatole pursued, "has delighted us all by the discomfiture she caused to the Neander-thaler in our midst."

"Who the hell was that character anyway?" asked the American woman, who seemed to wake from a blissful haze.

"A Neanderthal beau," repeated Monsieur Anatole. "In other words, an envoy from Neo-Byzantium."

Gaston, among whose filial duties it was to interpret Monsieur Anatole's more obscure pronouncements, explained politely:

"Fyodor Nikitin is one of the cultural attachés at the Free Commonwealth Embassy."[1]

"Cultural attaché!" exclaimed Boris, sitting up with a jerk which made the fragile chair creak under him. "You mean he is working for the . . ." As he pronounced the fateful initials whose sound at that time filled millions with an almost mystical horror, his high-pitched voice broke like an adolescent's.

Dear Lord, here they are off again, thought Hydie, whose legs were going to sleep from standing bolt upright in front of Monsieur Anatole. By a cunning manœuvre she managed to sit down cross-legged on the carpet, at the same time trying to withdraw her hand gently from Monsieur Anatole's grip. But he held her as in a vice; by now the surface where their skins were in contact was hot and moist, but Hydie no longer minded it. She had let the old man draw bodily heat from her, and now it was she who felt a current of a different kind of warmth flow back into her.

"But no, you must not leave," Monsieur Anatole repeated softly. "You young people on your young continent must learn to give, give, give, and to expect no return. For two great centuries it was France who gave to the rest of the world; now it is your turn. Your hand, my child, is on lend-lease to

---

[1] The official change of name from "Union of Socialist Soviet Republics" to "Commonwealth of Freedomloving People" (or "Free Commonwealth" for short), foreshadowed by similar changes in official terminology, was decreed by the Marshal of Peace in the early nineteen-fifties.

a vicious old man; it is my recovery grant, or whatever you call it. Your father watches us with benevolence, we are old friends."

"Beware, Hydie," said the Colonel. "Monsieur Anatole is an old wolf in sheep's clothes."

"Don't listen to him," said Monsieur Anatole delightedly. "He is jealous of a dying man. Ask my daughter if you don't believe me: she will tell you about the cirrhosis of the liver, and the swollen prostate and the blood pressure and this and that. The income tax you pay for your vices gets ever higher as the years pass, and in the end there is no income, only tax—then the ruthless collector attacks the capital and squeezes the last drop out of your reserves . . . Yes, I am condemned to death—but so are you, my lovely child, and your father and my good-for-nothing son. We are caught in the trap, members of a doomed civilisation, dancers on the darkening stage across which the shadow of Neanderthal is settling . . ."

Monsieur Anatole was off on one of his celebrated monologues. The public monologue at the end of his Friday receptions was the solution of his dilemma, the method by which he contrived to escape both the boredom of conversation and the terrors of silence. He was seventy-five, and for the last quarter of a century he had not listened to anybody's voice except his own. When somebody had once asked him whether this was not becoming tiresome, he had answered that on the contrary, he was getting on fine: he had heard all that there was to hear by the time he was fifty. Besides, he had added, most famous people such as actors, poets and statesmen, lived by the same principle: after fifty they did all the talking themselves, and when it was absolutely necessary to let the other person talk, they thought of their livers and of little girls.

At any rate, Monsieur Anatole enjoyed talking as much as others did listening to him. As he leant back in his armchair, with his black skull-cap, white silky eyebrows and yellow goatee, he gave the impression of a malicious and melancholy lemur who pretends to be amused while he languishes for his native climate—in Monsieur Anatole's case the Paris of Barrès and of the Goncourts, of Michelet and of the barricades of 1848, of Louis XIV and Mansard, and above all of Chateaubriand and Henry IV. But even when his monologue became lyrical in content, his diction never lost its precision, the histrionic eloquence of a French lawyer addressing the court.

". . . Ah, my dear," he continued, patting Hydie's hand,

"there is no doubt a certain consolation in the idea that one is not the only one condemned to the knacker's yard, that our whole civilisation is affected by sclerosis of the arteries and high blood pressure and hardening of the collective glands . . ." He cackled. "The inflamed prostate of Europe—the twitching face of the Occident between two strokes. . . . It is after all a consolation when one has reached the absurd age where desire survives virility and the only remaining pleasure is to sample a certain kind of picture-postcard for amateurs . . ."

"Gee, have you got some?" purred Gaston's girl-friend from the carpet. "I wish we could see them . . ."

"But on the other hand," pursued Monsieur Anatole, ignoring her, "on the other hand. . . . Don't smile, my child," he said irritably. "What are you smiling at? The postcards? An old man's solitary pleasures? Wait until you get to that age; we Latins are more frank about these matters . . . And what about your politicians quoting the Gettysburg speech and Jefferson and the Constitution?" he shot at her triumphantly.

"I don't follow the parallel," complained Hydie.

"It is the same thing," explained Monsieur Anatole. "Your democracy is debauched and impotent, and when your politicians quote Lincoln and Jefferson, they get the same kick out of it as old lechers gloating over performances of youthful virility, which they are no longer able to imitate. 'We hold it to be self-evident that all men'—Liberté, Egalité, Fraternité— the barricades of March '48—the Communist Manifesto— the Fourteen Points, the Four Freedoms, the 32 positions of love—it is always the same impotent exultation, the gloating over the past, the false pretence that it still exists. Vote for our candidate, for justice, progress and socialism, feelthy postcards, feelthy postcards! . . ."

He had worked himself into genuine indignation, thumping the carpet with his crutch; his sad lemur eyes were red with pain and anger.

"So there," he said, sighing, in a calmer voice. "Whatever they tell you, my child, don't believe it. Revolutions, reforms, programs, parties—they are always selling you the same picture: 'A glimpse of Paradise,' 'What the Maid saw through the Keyhole'; and it's always the same old harlot and the same old pimp who pose for 'Flames of Passion.' And yet, though the only comfort, somebody has said, for a man walking to the electric chair would be for him to learn that a comet was approaching and that at the very moment when the current is turned on, the whole planet will be destroyed; and yet, to know that this world which, for better or worse, was our world, is nearing its end, like Pompeii, like the Roman Empire, like the France of the Fifteenth Louis—it is an idea more painful than the twitches in my liver; and a cirrhosed liver is very painful, my child."

"If you think that everything is rotten and believe in nothing, I don't see why you mind," said Hydie, who, though she was in one of her humble moods, resented being treated at twenty-three as a child, and having her hand patted all the time.

"Who told you that I believe in nothing?" exclaimed Monsieur Anatole, genuinely shocked. "I don't know what you are, my child, a Catholic or a Communist or a Suffragette, it does not matter—at your age and with your lovely looks, beliefs are a luxury. But if an old cynic still believes in something, it is like a parched plant's belief in the soil from which its roots draw their scant nourishment. It is not a conviction or a dogma; it is the substance on which he lives."

"And what is it you believe in?" asked Hydie avidly, but already apprehensive of disappointment.

"It can be told in one word," said Monsieur Anatole. He paused, then, scanning out each syllable with his crutch but in a quiet voice, he said: "Con-ti-nu-ity."

"You mean: tradition?" asked Hydie, disappointed, as she had known she would be.

"I mean: con-ti-nu-ity. Tradition is based on inertia. Con-ti-nu-ity means to be conscious of the past but as the past, not as the present or future. To imitate the past and to abolish the past are equal sins against life. Therefore all reactionaries suffer from constipation and all revolutionaries from diarrhoea."

"Is that a fact?" asked the Colonel, who believed in statistics.

"It must be," declared Monsieur Anatole, "for it can be logically deduced."

With a sigh and a grunt, he lifted himself on to his crutches, aided by Gaston. He hobbled out to the balcony with surprising agility, and made a sign to his guests to follow him. The rain had ceased and the stars had reappeared, looking as if they had been freshly polished; they seemed to have decided to give a gala performance in honour of Bastille Day. The red and green lights from the bridges were reflected in the still water; from the direction of the Place St. Michel, where the crowd was still dancing in the streets, came the long-drawn notes of an accordion.

"Have a good look—fill your eyes to the brim," said Monsieur Anatole, "for all this will not last much longer; and if you survive, you will be able to tell your grandchildren that you have seen Paris when it still stood."

Leaning on his son's shoulder, Monsieur Anatole propped his right-hand crutch on the railing and moved its pointing end slowly from the silhouette of Notre Dame in the East toward the forest of gas-lights which was the Place de la Concorde.

"This panorama is the best example of what I mean by con-ti-nu-ity," he explained. "Do you know what the people of Paris did with the stones of the Bastile, after they had demolished it? They built out of them the upper part of the Pont de la Concorde. Do you know how long it took to make the Place de la Concorde into that miracle of townscape planning that it is? Three centuries, my friends. It was begun by Gabriel under the Fourteenth Louis, continued by the Fifteenth, carried on by the Revolution, continued by Napoleon, completed by Louis-Philippe. And it was one plan, one vision, which continued to materialise through the centuries, regardless of political upheavals, fires, famines, wars and plagues. You should not think that I am being sentimental; I have a disgust for sentimentality. No, I am talking to you of a visible example of the phenomenon of continuity. And you must understand me correctly. It is quite common that a building, like a cathedral or a palace, is being restored, reshaped and so on, for three centuries or more. But the Concorde is not a building, it is a square. It is an expanse of organised space. And when you stand on it, you see that the space has been organised around it for a mile to the West up to the Arch of Triumph, and half a mile to the North up to the Madeleine, and across the Seine to the Palais-Bourbon. If you look northward, you see two seventeenth century palazzi and between them, receding in a perfect flight of perspective, a Greek temple built in the early nineteenth. An abominable idea! But the effect is one of perfect beauty, because the detail dissolves in the whole, and the various periods fuse in harmonious con-ti-nu-ity. And if you look to the South, across the bridge built out of the slabs of a dungeon, you see another antique façade, on the Palais-Bourbon, made to match that to the North. But the joke is that the Bourbon Palace faces the other way, and this façade was stuck on its buttocks two hundred years after it was built. Another abomination! And to the West, the Champs-Elysées with that monstrous triumphal arch at its end! Yet the effect of the whole is perfection itself. But to build perfection out of so much ugly detail, you must have a vision which embraces centuries, which digests the past and makes the future grow out of it; in other words, you must have con-ti-nu-ity . . ."

From the crowd below came laughter in shrieks, and the rhythmic shuffle of dancing feet. In spite of the recent cloudburst the heat was still stifling. Light filtered through many of the mansard windows; they looked like the attics of a dolls' town lit by tiny candles. Apparently nobody was going to sleep tonight.

"Who knows," said Monsieur Anatole, "it may be our last Bastille Day before the advent of Neanderthal. Or the last-but-one, the last-but-two; what is the difference? The people of Pompeii were lucky: they did not know beforehand. Take an eyeful, my friends, before it is too late. Look at the island, Paris-Cité, where Europe started. It has an oval shape, like a fertilised mother cell, and out of it the rest has grown—not like modern towns which grow like a cancer, but grown like a crystal, like a living organism. Just before you, on the square in front of Notre Dame, is the exact spot where the spermatozoon entered the egg: it was here that the ancient road from Rome to the North pierced the water-way of the Seine. Here the North was fertilised by the Mediterranean, and everything that has happened since is a continuation of that event. For the fascination of Paris is its unique synthesis of the Mediterranean life with its open-air cafés and markets and *urinoires* on the one hand, and of Nordic, urban civilisation on the other. Here the Gothic married the Renaissance; imagine the whole of Paris cut by a horizontal plane about the height of this balcony, some fifty feet above ground; then underneath this plane you would have the Renaissance and the Baroque and the modern, but above your eye level you would behold a Gothic town with its maze of attics and chimneys and gables. The façades have evolved with time; but as the new houses went up, they did not trample the Middle Ages down, they lifted them on their shoulders toward the sky; and there, between the roofs, in the gabled mansard windows, they are resting still . . ."

An aged manservant, who looked like a popular edition of his master, appeared with a tray and handed round glasses of champagne. Monsieur Anatole's was only half filled. He muttered a feeble protest, more for form's sake, knowing that neither rage nor supplication would get him more; leaning on Gaston's shoulder, he avidly drank his glass like a frail, starving child its milk. "It is finished," he announced, leaving it open whether he meant his glass or the town. "Finished and accomplished and consummated. Now the continuity is going to be cut, the synthesis is breaking down like a delicately balanced organic compound under the action of a destructive acid. For it was this delicate balance of Nordic industry and diligence with the relaxed hedonism and sloth of the South which made the civilisation of the Seine valley a model to the rest of the world, and taught it the greatest of all arts: the art of living . . ."

In the momentary silence which followed Monsieur Anatole's monologue, one could hear Hydie swallow abruptly and then say:

"Why did you not teach us the art of dying also?"

"Dying? It is a necessity, not an art, my child."

"How do you know?" Hydie said belligerently. After the shock of the incident with Nikitin, and the college-girl part which Monsieur Anatole had forced her to play, she was beginning to recover. "How do you know?" she repeated hotly. "The art of dying of Socrates and Christ and St. Francis is greater than your art of living. But you have destroyed that art with your Enlightenment and your Republic of Reason. Nowhere do people die harder and more squalidly than in France—like mangy dogs. I have been to the Salpêtrière—oh, it was unspeakable . . ."

The Colonel gently pressed her arm to make her shut up. Monsieur Anatole looked at her in slight bewilderment. "What an extraordinary child," he tittered, patting his little black skull-cap into place. "Are all American virgins like that?"

"I am not a virgin," said Hydie indignantly.

Monsieur Anatole was shocked to the core. "Oh, *pardon* . . ." he muttered.

"My daughter," the Colonel interposed hastily, "married at nineteen and was divorced some time ago. She was brought up in a convent in England. What she meant before was that . . . that there is little dignity in death without faith . . ."

"Ah—so you are a Catholic," exclaimed Monsieur Anatole; Hydie felt that he was on the point of embarking on a monologue of enlightenment.

"No," she said, her nerves on edge. "But I was one at sixteen . . ." and she fell silent.

Fortunately the pause was filled in by a new wave of drifting accordion music. Everybody felt suddenly tired—including Monsieur Anatole, who seemed to shrink to even smaller size, clutching the shoulder of his bored son. When his guests after a little while took their leave, he no longer protested. His hand in Hydie's felt cold and limp, like a sick monkey's; he thought that with three pills, or maybe four, he might obtain a few hours' sleep after all—a small advance instalment of the void which waited for him

Fedya Nikitin pushed his way through the crowd in search of a taxi. There was perhaps still a chance that he had left the notebook in his room when he had laid out the contents of his pockets to change into the new suit. For the tenth or fifteenth time he went through every move he had made during the last few hours. Before going to Monsieur Anatole's party, he had dined, alone, in the little restaurant not far from the hostel. The fool there was indifferent and the waitress unfriendly, but it was a reliable place, recommended by the Service; it was advisable to have one's meals there as often as possible, to demonstrate that one had no inclination to "go to Capua." In Capua, Hannibal's army had gone soft by abandoning itself to the temptations of an older, refined and decadent civilisation; and from time to time it happened, despite the careful methods of selection, that somebody sent out on a mission deserted the Service and "went to Capua." It was like a physical disease, a sudden rash or outbreak of madness —and it befell as a rule those of whom one would have least expected it; the most reliable, puritan, disciplined types. Fedya knew that it would not happen to him. He was no puritan, and took whatever pleasure Capua had to offer, but never forgetting that it was Capua who offered it. The correct approach to the devil was to sup with him and let him pay the bill.

His complacency faded as his thoughts returned to the chronology of the evening. From the restaurant he had gone back to the hostel to change into his party suit and party shoes. In his thoughts he always referred to his abode as the "hostel," though officially it was an ordinary Paris hotel; in fact it was run by French Service personnel. He had taken his jacket off to shave when Smyrnov, who lived in the next room, had come in for a cigarette. So, with apparent casualness, he had put on his jacket again, for Smyrnov was of considerably superior rank, and though they were on friendly terms, this courtesy was due to him. But the question was: had he put the things which he had taken out of his pockets back into the jacket again—knowing that as soon as Smyrnov was gone he would change? He had given Smyrnov a light with his own lighter—he remembered it because it was a new lighter bought in Paris, and Smyrnov had casually remarked on it, mentioning that he preferred lighters manufactured at home. Whereupon Fedya had answered that he too thought the lighters from home superior but had bought this one for comparison's sake to test the efficiency of the French commodities' industries. . . . However, as he always carried the lighter in his trouser pocket, the incident proved nothing, for quite conceivably he might have emptied the pockets of his jacket, leaving those of his trousers for later. If he could only remember whether his fountain-pen had been in his breast pocket while he had talked to Smyrnov, the problem would be decided. But at this point his mind went blank. It was an obstinate kind of blankness, hard like a wall. He had once been present at an interrogation conducted by his friend Gletkin, in the course of which the suspect had actually run with his head against the wall. Gletkin had not interfered, he had merely watched, motionless behind his desk; but later on he had explained to Fedya that nobody could hurt himself seriously that way, except in fictional literature. Fedya felt a sudden, hard craving for his desk at home.

There was no taxi to be seen anywhere, only people dancing on the pavement, kissing, yelling, and having a jolly time. It was the petite-bourgeoisie of Paris celebrating the bourgeois revolution of two hundred years ago. But what had they been doing since? Resting on their laurels, producing a few decadent writers and painters, and losing one war after another—except when they were rescued in the last moment by the Americans, worried by the threatened loss of an export market. They were the devil at celebrating, but one only had to compare their Bastille Day with the imposing parades on May Day at home to know which way the wind of History was blowing.

Three little shop-girls, arm in arm, ran towards Fedya. He tried to avoid a collision, but they were intent on running him down and dancing with him. They laughed, called him "my little cabbage"—funny words of endearment they had. Who would think at home of calling one's sweetheart "my borsht"? —and tugged at his jacket, still slightly damp where the blood-stains had been. He shook them off, grinning good-humoured-ly, and they kept giggling; the least pretty of the three stuck her tongue out at him. He smiled, showing his white teeth, but could not help thinking how uncultured they were despite their pretty dresses. Perhaps they were prostitutes, one couldn't be sure. He wouldn't have minded picking up one of them, un-der different circumstances. Once more the craving for his desk at home hit him like a blow on his chest.

Smyrnov? Again the suspicion rose in him, and again he dis-missed it. Smyrnov worked in a different branch; it was just possible that he had been ordered to keep a check on Fedya, as a sideline; but even so, what possible motive could he have for engineering one's ruin? To leave a notebook lying on one's table for a few minutes in a senior colleague's presence could hardly be construed as criminal negligence. But perhaps it could—who knows? The claims of revolutionary vigilance were unlimited, and Smyrnov was the pedantic type: see his remark about the lighter. In this case Smyrnov would have taken the notebook to prove one's carelessness. But again only if he had a motive or grudge; and what grudge could Smyrnov have against him? He, Fedya, held no grudge against anybody. Or, Smyrnov might have wanted to play a prank. But it would be a deadly prank—entailing at least demotion and recall; and possibly the Arctic Circle. His mind went blank again.

Only a few people were still dancing in a desultory way out-side the café on the Boulevard St. Germain. The Colonel had gone home on leaving Monsieur Anatole's party. Hydie and the other American woman and the Pole named Boris had wandered from one café to another, drinking brandies with water and watching the people dance in the street, until the American woman felt sick and had to be bundled off in a taxi. Hydie and the Pole had stayed on in the café, victims of that sudden embarrassment which befalls strangers who have met at a party, and on leaving find themselves together in the street. Somebody at Monsieur Anatole's had told Hydie that Count Boris had been deported to some Arctic lumber camp, where he had lost the use of one lung and a half. She had a healthy horror of refugees; they always made one feel guilty. The poor were supposed to do that in sentimental stories; in fact charwomen and night porters had a style of life of their own which made it look silly to pity them. But refugees had no style of their own and no pattern of life, except shame-faced concealment. They formed an international slum population—even those who lived in luxury hotels.

This Pole was a tall, lean man with a sunken chest and jerky movements. His features were haggard and not at all Slavonic. He looked rather like an Indian army sergeant half consumed by malaria.

"I suppose it is time to go home," said Hydie, breaking the silence.

"If you must," said Count Boris. "Since I have become unable to fall asleep before three I can't understand why other people waste their lives by going to bed early." His voice became excited: "I even despise them. I know it is stupid, but I cannot help it. I also despise all people who do not hate the Commonwealth. But that is less stupid . . ." He lost the thread, then found it again:

"What I mean to say—about not going to bed—when one has acquired a perversion, one always despises the normal, I suppose. It is the same with illness. Particularly with illness of the chest. Have you read 'The Magic Mountain'? That is good, because if you had not read it I could probably not talk to you. Do you remember the Half-Lung Club in the book? All ill people are a club. And all people who were sent to the Arctic are also a club. You, for instance, are a pretty woman and probably very clever, but you are not of the Club. Even if you were to marry me, you would remain a stranger, one who is not of the Club. It is stimulating to talk to a stranger, but in the end it is always—frustrating . . ." His excitement fell as suddenly as it had risen. He added in a dull voice: "Because in fact there is no common language."

Hydie had drunk too much to feel embarrassed.

"What do you usually do until three if you can't sleep?" she asked.

"Oh—sit in cafés and talk. The café is the refugee's home. That is why all emigrations have always tended toward Paris. Cafés are excellent. They are not really homes but waiting-rooms. The normal people wait there until it is time for lunch or dinner or to go back to the office or to sleep. We, the members of the Club, just wait for something to happen. Of course nothing ever happens and we know it, but this knowledge is easier to bear in a café than anywhere else."

Hydie sipped at her glass. Here was another man living in his own portable glass cage. Most people she knew did. Each one inside a kind of invisible telephone box. They did not talk to you directly but through a wire. Their voices came through distorted and mostly they talked to the wrong number, even when they lay in bed with you. And yet her craving to smash the glass between the cages had come back again. If cafés were the home of those who had lost their country, bed was the sanctuary of those who had lost their faith. How pathetic he looked with his bitter lips, the taste of leather. With a clear, untroubled glance, she undressed the stooping figure across the table. She knew that men did that to women almost automatically, so she had acquired the same habit. For a short second she saw the unhealthy white skin of his torso stretched over protruding ribs, the useless flat nipples like ugly moles, the caving abdomen, the sparse coppice of his sex incongruously attached to the haggard figure as on sculptures of Christ. And how badly cut his suit was around the shoulders.

"You are just like Monsieur Anatole—you don't believe in anything," she said. The phrase had again come in that college-girl voice. She wanted to bite her tongue for it.

"Believe in anything?" he repeated absent-mindedly. "I was never interested in politics, if that is what you mean. I believe in the usual things: that my country should be left alone by others and that people should be left alone to live their lives. But all that has become a fantasy—a hashish dream. Another year, or another five years at the most, and there will be no Europe left, nothing. Click"—he made an ugly noise with his tongue and passed his hand savagely across his throat— "click—finished."

"How can you be so sure?" asked Hydie irritably.

"How can one be sure when gangrene has eaten a man's leg that it won't stop at the knee? Once you have seen it you know; and I have seen it, so I know. I have seen the living flesh of my nation turn black and rot in stench. But I know you don't believe me. You think I exaggerate or that I am hysterical. Everybody here believes that; that is how I know that they are lost. They will wait patiently for the gangrene to creep up their legs; or they will fumble with quack cures . . ."

His bony hands were folded on the table; he seemed to try

to pull them apart without succeeding; only the white knuckles cracked.

"That is the worst of it," he said, "to know and to be unable to convince. Greek mythology is full of horrors, but they forgot to invent the worst: Cassandra stricken dumb at the critical moment. She hears her own warning shriek, but she alone hears it: no sound comes out of her mouth. I knew a doctor who said that every illness has a mental cause. For a year and a half I slept in clothes stiff with my own frozen sweat, without a blanket, and was not ill. Then I came here and my lungs went. Maybe what busted them was this cry which couldn't come out—that choking feeling of being unable to make people listen."

He lifted his glass and put it down again without drinking; a funny idea seemed to have struck him.

"I once saw a comic film. A long line of people were queuing in front of some shop—I don't remember what sort of shop, but it promised to give goods away for nothing. As each customer entered, the poker-faced shop-keeper quietly hit him over the head with a club and his helpers dragged the victim out by his feet through a back door, and then the next one entered beaming and was hit on the head, and the next one, and so on. . . . That's what has been happening to one country after another in my part of the world, and the people here are still queuing to get into the shop. If you warn them that it is a bad place, they get angry with you because they can't bear to part with their illusions . . ."

Hydie felt bored. The fireworks, Monsieur Anatole, the people of Paris dancing round the accordions, all faded like a spook at the shrill crowing of the cock. She was back in the slums of reality. What the Pole had said, and what he was still going to say, was familiar to her from countless discussions between her father and his colleagues. Colonel Anderson was attached to some military mission which was studying the possibilities of standardising European armaments. After the second dry Martini all these well-meaning Americans slumming in Europe began to talk like the Pole: they all felt like Cassandra stricken with dumbness. Whenever Hydie went to cocktail parties given by her countrymen attached to this and that Europe-saving mission, she had the feeling of being surrounded by a crowd of jaunty athletes who know that they are impotent. The more conscientious and sensitive they were, the more the knowledge of their impotence made them suffer, even to the point of affecting their physical countenance.

But Boris obviously wanted to go on talking about himself, and Hydie resigned herself to listening. "What did you use to do before it all happened?" she asked.

"Before what happened?" Boris asked, startled out of his gloom. "Oh, I did some farming, and was an officer in the reserve. My wife, Maria, used to paint a little. She was very young when I married her . . ."

Lord, thought Hydie, here we go . . .

"Eighteen," said Boris. "She looked the opposite of you: blonde, small and fragile. I married her straight from the convent school."

"Which Order?" asked Hydie.

"The Order of the Holy Virgin."

"But I went to school at the same Order," exclaimed Hydie, "in England."

"Did you?" said Boris indifferently. "Some people said her painting was quite good. There was a still life: mimosas in a blue vase. The vase was a wedding gift from an aunt. . . . We had a little girl too: Dunyasha." In pronouncing the Slavonic name with the long vowels, his voice became melodious; then relapsed into rasping French. "She was pretty too, but we were worried because her teeth grew a little wide apart. The dentist suggested a good brace, but we couldn't make up our minds. Though she would only have had to wear it until she was eight or nine . . ."

"What happened to them?" asked Hydie.

"Click"—the Pole made the same ugly noise with his tongue as before, and passed his hand across his throat. "They were sent elsewhere—families must always be separated on deportation, you know. I went to the Arctic, they were sent to Kasakhstan. Of course we were not allowed to know where the other was. I only found out afterwards, by pure chance, that both had died of dysentery. . . . But all this is very boring to you. We must talk of something else. Do you like playing tennis? And bridge? Or do you prefer going to the movies . . ."

Why has all this made him so nasty and quarrelsome? thought Hydie. What about the famous purifying effect of suffering? Some people suffer and become saints. Others, by the same experience, are turned into brutes thirsting for vengeance. Others, just into neurotics. To draw spiritual nourishment from suffering, one must be endowed with the right kind of digestive system. Otherwise suffering turns sour on one. It was bad policy on the part of God to inflict suffering indiscriminately. It was like ordering laxatives for every kind of disease.

"Ah—here come friends of mine," said Boris with obvious relief. "I thought they would turn up. They are part of the Club. We are a triumvirate. It is called the Three Ravens Nevermore."

One of Boris' friends was short with stumpy legs and a dark, ugly, sharp-featured face. He was introduced as Professor Vardi; he shook Hydie's hand with the self-conscious ceremoniousness of very short men, while his eyes behind the rimless thick-lensed glasses gave her a fierce look of appraisal. The third member of the triumvirate, Julien Delattre, was a poet who had enjoyed a considerable vogue in the nineteen-thirties. He had a slight limp, was of slender build, fairly tall, and was wearing a polo sweater without a jacket. He had rather short-sighted eyes and a high forehead, on which a blue vein could occasionally be seen pulsing. The upper half of his face thus gave an impression of elegant frailness—but this was contradicted by the bitter curve of the mouth, and the cigarette perpetually stuck to his upper lip, which gave him a vaguely disreputable touch.

There was a pause as the two new arrivals drew their chairs up, not knowing what to make of Hydie. Boris apparently could not be bothered to explain who she was or where he had picked her up; he had withdrawn into an ill-tempered silence. Hydie felt like an intruder. The Professor took in every detail of her appearance with his sharp glance, but when their eyes met he looked away with a show of indifference. Delattre smiled at her without saying anything. Only now did Hydie notice a large, wine-coloured burnt patch of skin on one side of his face, which disfigured the larger part of the cheek. He had, however, developed such skill in showing himself in profile and turning the "good" half of his face towards the person he was talking to, that the disfigurement was only visible occasionally.

The silence became embarrassing; Hydie racked her brain to recall what work of Julien Delattre's she had read, but did not succeed.

"I have read a volume of your poems," she said at last to him, "but to be honest, it was five or six years ago and I can't remember the title."

To her surprise Delattre blushed, blinking through the smoke of his cigarette which he seemed to use as a protective screen. "Never mind," he said. "It's just as well forgotten." The Professor cut in:

"You mean 'Ode to the Cheka,' " he reminded her sharply and with a bellicose glance which said "any objections?"

The Pole gave a short laugh. " 'Ode to the Cheka,' " he repeated with a cough. "What fools you all made of yourselves —and it was only ten years ago."

"Not everybody is born infallible like you," snapped Vardi.

"Now it is all coming back," exclaimed Hydie. " 'Elegy on the Death of a Tractor.' And 'The Rape of Surplus Value— an Oratorio.' "

"I wish," said Julien, "people would forget other people's past asininities as they forget their own."

"Why?" said Vardi, turning on him. "It is cowardice to be ashamed of one's past mistakes. Who is going to cast the first stone and pretend that, in the concrete circumstances of the period, it was a mistake to believe in the international revolution and dedicate one's life to it? I admit that our belief was based on an illusion but I maintain that it was an honourable illusion, an error nearer the truth than the Philistines' rancid phrases about liberalism, democracy and the rest. The Philistines have been proved right, but one can be right for the wrong reasons, and we have been proved wrong, but one can be wrong for the right reasons."

"Oh, shut up," said Julien.

Boris woke up from his acid meditation: "What you say is simply that there is more rejoicing in heaven at a repentant sinner than at ten righteous men. I am hanged if I know why it should be so. I can see the ten righteous men who all their lives have tried to be honest, decent and reasonable—then suddenly there is a commotion in heaven and a sinister type like Julien, who wrote odes to the Cheka, is ushered in; he becomes the guest of honour and the decent people must make way for him. The repentant sinner sounds good and pious, but the fact is that while you wrote odes to a certain institution, that same institution caused my wife and daughter to die in their blood and excrement . . . I beg your pardon, I did not mean to offend your sensibilities," he said to Hydie, withdrawing his leathery lip from his upper teeth in a rodent smile.

"Oh Lord," said Hydie, "why are you always picking on me?"

"Picking?" repeated Boris, wonderingly. "Yes, I suppose I am behaving badly. Probably because you look so intact. . . . I am sorry," he said formally, reverting to his old-world gentry manners. His shoulders sagged and all vitality seemed to have run out of him.

The Professor cleared his throat. "Personal tragedies are beside the point," he said. "We all understand, but they don't prove anything . . ." He spoke both aggressively and with a certain rabbinical unction. Hydie thought that it was probably the most charitable attitude to treat Boris harshly, but it was obvious that this kind of charity, which to a priest came only at the end of a long and bitter training in self-discipline, came to this little man all too naturally. The most dubious charity was after all the surgeon's. ". . . Anything," repeated Vardi, with a clipped horizontal gesture of his podgy hand. "We can only achieve a constructive attitude if we rid ourselves of fallacious guilt-feelings about the past. During the first hopeful period of the Revolution only the reactionaries were on the other side of the barricades."

"That's right—reactionaries like me," said Boris. "People with a few acres to farm, and with a wife and a baby daughter to defend, instead of doctrines."

Hydie thought that Boris was talking of that wife and girl of his as the Jews about their pogromed grandfathers—making political capital out of the dead. But did not the Church with her cult of the martyrs do the same? And the French with their Joan and the British with their few who saved the many? Everybody with an axe to grind ground it in oil pressed from corpses; the dead were never left alone. She felt suddenly tired and weary, her whole body sagging, even her breasts. She squinted down her blouse for reassurance.

"*You* of course were never wrong," she heard Vardi say with venom to the Pole. "You and your caste always knew. A cousin of mine died in your prison at Brest-Litovsk, and when they buried him, half his face had been eaten by rats. He was not even a revolutionary, only an honest-to-God social democrat. If I have to choose between your rats and theirs— or between the juke box and the 'Pravda'—I still don't know."

"Don't you?" Julien asked, blinking across the smoke of his cigarette.

"If you don't know, why are you here and not over there?" said Boris to the Professor. "Because here you can quarrel and lecture us in a café. Over there you could only lecture the rats in the Lubianka—and sotto voce, for even the rats might denounce you."

"Vardi wouldn't mind that as long as they were leftist rats. Their bite has a more familiar flavour to him," said Julien.

"So it has," Vardi said, unperturbed. "And so it has for you, however cynically you act. Boris happens to be in the same boat with us just now, but there is nevertheless a world of difference between his attitude and ours."

"That is true, Professor," said Boris. "The difference is that you have worked in libraries, and I have worked in the Arctic mines."

"You are being unfair, Boris," said Julien. "Whatever happened to Vardi, he would stick to his rusty guns." He smiled at Hydie and recited in English:

" 'For Right is Right and Left is Left, and never the twain shall meet . . .'

"Except," he continued in French again, "that there is of course no longer any meaning left in either word."

"Isn't there?" said Vardi fiercely. "To my mind they are still the only signposts in the chaos, and as meaningful as the words Future and Past, Progress and Decay. If it were not so, why did you go to Spain and get yourself shot up and burnt?"

Julien's face twitched slightly round the eyes. "It could as well have happened in the War of the Roses," he said. "Lancaster and York, Jansenists and Jesuits, Girondins and Jacobins, Darwinism and Lamarckism, Right and Left, Socialism and Capitalism—they all looked once like signposts in the chaos. Every period has its specific dilemma which seems all-important, until history passes over it with a shrug; and afterwards people wonder what they were so excited about."

"What you mean," said Vardi, "is simply the dialectical movement from thesis to antithesis to synthesis."

"To hell with the dialectic. Catholic fought Protestant for generations, but where is the synthesis? The great disputes of history usually end in a stalemate, and then some new problem crops up, of a quite different kind, which absorbs all passions and drains the old controversy of its meaning. . . . People lost interest in waging wars of religion when national consciousness began to dawn on them; they stopped bothering about Monarchy or Republic when economic problems became all-important. Now we are again in a deadlock—

until some new mutation of consciousness occurs on the next higher level, with a shift of emphasis to quite different values. When that happens, the signposts and battle cries of the economic age will appear as anachronistic and silly as the question on which side to break the egg for which the Lilliputians fought their wars . . ."

"Bravo, bravo," cried Boris. "You will sit and wait for your mutation, and if meanwhile the Antichrist tears the guts out of your friends and family, so much the worse for them."

"Don't be an ass," said Julien. "I take it for granted that one must fight in self-defence, and in defence of the minimum decencies of life, and so on. I merely wish to point out that this has nothing to do with Vardi's signposts and dialectics and with leftism, rightism, capitalism, and socialism or any other idea or ism. When I hear those words, I smell the sewers."

"You mustn't take him seriously," the Professor said to Hydie. "He is only happy when he can fight, like in Spain, and at the same time explain to himself that the fight is absolutely meaningless."

Boris seemed to wake up from one of his periodic absences. He stared at the others with a frown, and at last Hydie discovered what was so disturbing about his face: all the lines on it ran vertically—down the hollow temples, the caved-in cheeks, the pointed chin.

"Words, words," he said in a curiously absent-minded voice. "I told you before, there is a simple solution . . ."

"We have heard your simple solution," said Vardi. "Political assassination is the panacea of all dilettantes. Shoot the villain in the piece and all will be well. In fact all historical evidence goes to show that changes of regime cannot be brought about by individual terror, only by the organised action of the masses."

"Words, words, words," said Boris. "Books, books, books. Go and lecture the rats in the Lubianka."

"Rats of the world unite," said Julien. "You have nothing to lose but your traps." He made a sweeping gesture with his hand which upset his brandy glass on the table. The brandy, yellow and sticky, expanded slowly into a Rorschach blotch on the marble surface. The puddle in the centre was shaped like Nikitin's skull, with rivulets like tentacles growing slowly out of it. "I must go home," said Hydie, rising.

"I'll get you a taxi," said Julien. He paid and limped towards the door. Boris and the Professor had resumed their argument. They hardly nodded when Hydie, like a good girl, politely said goodnight.

Outside, the street was grey with the rising dawn; a few lonely sweepers had begun to clear away the litter left behind by the eve of Bastille Day.

They got into a taxi and Julien fidgeted for a while until he got his lame leg into the right position.

"What did you think of our Zoo?" he asked after Hydie had given her address to the driver. "We are called the Three Ravens Nevermore," he continued in English—a careful, precise English which reminded Hydie of a certain French nun in her school with whom she had once been in love. ". . . Do you remember 'The Possessed'? They were an enviable crowd of maniacs. We are the dispossessed—the dispossessed of faith; the physically or spiritually homeless. A burning fanatic is dangerous; a burnt-out fanatic is abject. Boris hankers for revenge—but he doesn't believe in it any longer, he knows he is defeated. Vardi likes to prove that though he was wrong, he was right to be wrong. I . . . you are a good listener," he said in a changed tone.

"Because I am one of the dispossessed," said Hydie.

"Were you in the Movement?" Julien asked hopefully.

"No—not in yours. I have come from another parish."

"Never mind," said Julien. "Whatever your church or temple was, it comes to the same. All ruins look alike—have you noticed that? That is what holds our triumvirate together. I should like to write a story or a poem called 'Crusaders Return.' Young fellow, anno domini eleven ninety-one, has left home to conquer the New Jerusalem, build the Kingdom of Heaven and all that. He has been led up the garden path like the rest. He has raped and robbed and put Moors to the sword and contracted the pox, and fattened the purse of Philip Augustus. Now he is back—one man back out of ten. And the honest souls in his parish are still going to church and buying indulgences and making donations for the next crusade . . ."

"What does he do?"

"That doesn't matter. Perhaps he tries to tell them what it was really like, and is burnt as a heretic. Or he keeps his trap shut and is devoured by the pox. What really matters is the song of the Crusader's Return. It is the song of the dispossessed of faith, of the pox-ridden idealist who knows that he lives in a dying world but has no inkling of the new world which will replace it."

"Why don't you write it?" asked Hydie.

"Because I can write no more," said Julien. "Goodnight."

The taxi had come to halt in front of the block of flats where Hydie lived. "Goodnight," she echoed, scurrying out of the taxi in unseemly haste. As she pressed the button of the gate and turned to wave goodbye—it was, she thought, the least to be expected from a well-behaved Alice in Wonderland—she saw him leaning back in his seat, his lame leg stretched out, his head against the window pane, with the patient driver sitting immobile in front.

The Colonel was still up; the thin streak of yellow light under his door looked to Hydie like a plank of security. She had only to step over it and enter the haven. But to do that, she had to open the door and then the plank became a whole brightly lit room, and her father was no longer a remote idea of consolation but a figure with greying hair, bent over his desk, engrossed in the report he was writing. He turned though, and his smile was welcoming. "What have you been up to?" he asked.

She flung herself on the couch and told him abstractedly about Count Boris and the Three Ravens Nevermore. From time to time the Colonel and his daughter made a brave effort at intimacy and intellectual companionship, though they both knew it would end in frustration. In his thoughts, the Colonel called Hydie sentimentally his dark nymph, while Hydie thought of her father as the "perplexed Liberal"; but such was their mutual shyness that even the idea of pronouncing these words made each of them blush in their separate glass cages.

"That poor guy," said the Colonel, passing his hand across his forehead which was pink and unwrinkled in spite of his grey temples. "To lose one's wife and kid that way. And to think that there are now millions in the same boat."

"But that isn't the point," Hydie said impatiently. "The dreadful thing is not the suffering itself, but the pointlessness of it."

"Well, I don't know about that," said the Colonel. "I don't know whether there is ever any point in spitting one's lungs out. Anyway, all that's only the beginning. Once the real show starts . . ."

"Lord," said Hydie. "There we go again. Can't you lay off it even for a minute?"

The Colonel looked at her wearily. "Look, I shouldn't say this, but the news is alarming."

"That's good," said Hydie. "Each time there is a crisis it is followed by a lull. I only get frightened during the lulls."

"Yes," said the Colonel. "But this time it's a bit different." He hesitated. "Look—I really shouldn't say this. But I guess you are a special case. Though I also guess each time there is a security leak it's due to a special case."

"I don't want to be told anything," said Hydie. She wished she were in her room, in her bed, with her eyes shut tight.

"But I want you to know—God knows why," said the Colonel. Hydie now realised that he had been waiting for her to come back, waiting to tell her. It was quite unlike her father, and she felt even more apprehensive. The last time he had insisted on unburdening himself to her, against her wish, was many years ago. She had been almost a child then—fourteen, thirteen? Her mother had seemed no more drunk and terrifying than usual, and Hydie did not know who the men were who led her away with such expert gentleness—nor where. But her father had insisted on telling her, in a neutral, far-off voice, the exact reasons why it had been necessary to have her mother taken to a mental hospital.

"It's like this," said the Colonel. "When you came in, I was writing a report, more exactly a list. A list of twenty Frenchmen selected among those with whom my job has brought me into contact. These twenty—no more than twenty, mind you, and preferably less—are to be put on a flying Noah's Ark when the floods get going and we have to clear out. I guess a number of our people in various missions over here got similar orders to draw up similar lists. Let's say a hundred. That makes two thousand passengers for Noah's air convoy. The remaining forty odd million just have to hope for the best."

"What about the families of the people on your list?"

The Colonel shrugged, fingering his papers. "It says: 'The problem of relatives is still under consideration.' But the idea seems to be that the people on the lists should consider themselves sort of called up for service abroad, the nucleus of the future liberation army and liberation government." He slumped back heavily into his chair. "I wish we would all stop liberating each other," he said.

"Why did you insist on telling me about it?" asked Hydie.

"Why?" The Colonel again passed his palm over his forehead. "For some reason I thought you should know in case we have to clear out in a day or two."

"You thought we could do it with a calmer conscience after you have submitted your list."

"I guess so . . ." the Colonel said wearily. "Though I don't see where conscience comes in. Hell—*we* haven't invented Europe—nor Asia."

"But didn't we make ourselves strong with guarantees and defence pacts and what nots?"

"I guess so. If we hadn't done it, they would have called us selfish and isolationist. Now that we have done it they will say we have meddled and left them in the lurch."

"Is the thing that matters what they say—or what will happen to them?" Hydie asked in a soft, provocative voice. Of his daughter's several voices this was the one which the Colonel disliked most.

"I guess you are right," he said drily. "And maybe if you have a plan of what else we can do, you will communicate it to Mr. President."

Hydie got up: "Sorry—I was just talking. I always keep talking when I don't know what to say." She kissed him lightly and left the room. The Colonel thought that her self-accusations sounded even more arrogant than her denunciations of the wickedness of the world. It had all started in her convent days; since then, Hydie had become in the Colonel's eyes a jigsaw puzzle with an expressionist picture on it which he couldn't fit together as he never knew whether the bit with the nose on it should go into the head or under the navel.

He sighed and turned back to his list. The fact was, they had both wanted a boy.

Hydie undressed slowly. Naked, she paid herself the usual evening visit in the mirror. "When are you going to grow up?" she asked her image. Her breath dimmed a small area of the mirror, blurring her face. "That's right," she said. "No face, no personality. That is, too many." She had behaved like a gauche adolescent with the Russian, like an innocent virgin toward Monsieur Anatole, an understanding elder sister to Boris. And yet she had not been acting—she had, as always, just automatically fallen into the role which others imposed on her. The lady who was a chameleon. No core, no faith, no fixed values. How right that Russian had been to look at her with such disgust.

She looked herself up and down in the mirror. However expensively she dressed, there was always something wrong with her appearance. Now, without clothes there was the same incongruity. The main trouble of course was her legs—heavy and rather shapeless. They seemed to contradict the slim shoulders and slender waistline. And though her oval face with the smooth chestnut hair parted in the middle and the bright chestnut-coloured eyes was undeniably pretty, there was, she thought, something incongruous about it too. It did not fit her body from the hips downward. Or rather, there was something about her face which betrayed the legs even in a long evening dress. Hydie could always tell whether a woman was pregnant by a mere glance at her face; in the same way she had found that there was always something, a rather touching, disarming quality in the face of a beautiful woman with the wrong legs or some other hidden deformity. The beauty of such faces had an apologetic touch. But her own expression was, on the contrary, rather defiant, as if it were pointedly refusing to apologise for the legs. It must have something to do with over-compensation, or what psychiatrists called the "masculine protest." But why then did one feel at the same time such a sham, always falling into the part which people expected one to play? Another of those hopeless incongruities.

She put her nightgown on and knelt down on the worn priedieu; she had carried it with her ever since she had left the convent. She folded her fingers tightly, closed her eyes and took two deep breaths. She said aloud, slowly: LET ME BELIEVE IN SOMETHING. Then she slipped into bed, reached for her handbag, and fumbled in it for the tube of aspirins. Her fingers touched Nikitin's notebook, and she took it out with a thrill of curiosity. Now that she opened it, she knew that it had been all the time at the back of her mind.

It was not the diary type of notebook divided into days; it only contained simple, lined pages. Some of them were empty, some covered with a tidy, small handwriting in a foreign alphabet. It looked as if these pages contained poems, for they were all covered with vertical columns of words with blank margins on both sides. But there were only two, at most three words to each line, and at the end of some of these lines there were tiny signs—a plus or a minus sign, a query, or an exclamation mark. Some of the cyrillic letters were identical with latin ones, and by the sound of the half-formed words she suddenly understood that the columns were lists of names— probably of people whom Monsieur Nikitin met at parties to which he went. He must be a thorough man to write them all down; but then, somebody had said that he was a cultural attaché, so it was obviously part of his job. The signs after people's names probably indicated whether Monsieur Nikitin liked them or not, or their political views, or which of the men he should ask for lunch, and which of the girls looked likely for bed. It was rather disgusting—and most disgusting was she herself, prying into that stranger's sordid little human catalogue. Tomorrow she must find some means of getting it back to him.

Or was Nikitin perhaps one of those sinister spies? Such things happened. But her common-sense told her that spies don't walk around with the list of their agents written out in full in their pockets. There were dozens of names on these lists, and she could make out a number of "Jeans" and "Pierres" and "Maximes." The very last name on the last page was unmistakably "Boris"—which proved that Nikitin jotted people's names down as he met them. She wondered whether her own name was there too, but couldn't find any word which even faintly resembled it. She would have liked to know, though, what mark Nikitin would give her—an exclamation mark perhaps? More likely a cross—wishing that she were dead and buried . . .

She put the notebook back into the bag, turned the light off and settled down to sleep, with the familiar feeling of gnawing emptiness inside her.

2

AN INVITATION TO THE OPERA

THE next morning Hydie rang up Monsieur Anatole's, obtained Nikitin's number from Mademoiselle Agnès, and telephoned his hotel. The ill-tempered concierge made her spell out Nikitin's name three times, and then her own. She had to wait several minutes. At last a husky voice, whose foreign accent was emphasized by the wire, said at the other end:

"Yes?"

Hydie announced her name. "Do you remember me?" she asked.

There was a short pause, then the voice at the other end said in the same flat tone:

"Yes."

"I rang up to tell you," said Hydie, "that I have found your notebook. Or maybe you don't even know that you've lost it? It fell out of your pocket when your jacket was taken away to be cleaned and I put it into my bag. I am really very sorry—it was all my fault."

She paused and waited. The voice at the other end said:

"Yes."

"Do you want it back?"

"Yes."

"I would have sent it on, but they did not have your address at Monsieur Anatole's, only your phone number. Would you tell me where I should send it—or would you rather meet me somewhere?" she added as an afterthought. It was the least she could do, she told herself, having caused all this mess.

There was again a slight pause, then Nikitin's voice said: "I will meet you."

Even among all those Parisian women Hydie looked strikingly pretty; Fedya Nikitin asked himself how it was possible that he had not noticed it yesterday. With her oval-shaped dark glasses she reminded one of some elusive coquette with a satin mask at a Venetian carnival.

Nikitin wore the same slightly too blue suit as at Monsieur Anatole's; he sauntered into the terrace at Weber's with a careless gait, seeming to look for nobody in particular. But though his unsmiling face showed no sign of recognition, he must have picked Hydie out immediately in the crowd, for he advanced straight towards her table. To Hydie's surprise he kissed her hand stiffly, then sat down next to her, having kicked the chair back with his leg. There was an odd contrast between this unceremonious gesture and the ceremonious hand-kiss, which made Hydie laugh.

"Where did you pick up that habit?" she asked.

"Which habit?" he asked back politely.

"Hand-kissing. We don't do it, and I thought you didn't do it either, since the Revolution."

"The French like it," he said guardedly, as if careful to avoid a trap. "One should adapt oneself to a country's customs."

"It's frightfully unhygienic," said Hydie.

"Yes."

There was a pause. His face remained neutral, unsmiling. Hydie wondered whether she should hand him back the notebook at once. But this seemed such a crude, businesslike procedure; and the only possibility left after that would be to get up and say goodbye.

"Have the blots come out of your jacket?" she asked, her glance travelling down his lapel. She saw that he wore a preposterous tie, newly bought.

"Oh, that is nothing," he said. But he too gave the jacket a quick glance, for the sake of reassurance.

"I am most frightfully sorry," she said.

"It is nothing," he repeated.

Hydie thought he sounded like a sulking boy, but found this rather endearing. "Well, I brought your notebook along," she said, hoping that this would cheer him up. She started to fumble in her bag. To her surprise he put his hand out and closed her bag with a snap.

"Not here," he said. "When I shall accompany you in a taxi."

"But why?" asked Hydie, startled. She noted with curiosity the shape of his hand: it was the large hand of a farm boy, with faint black rims under the carefully manicured nails.

He did not answer her question. Instead, looking for the first time fully into her eyes, he asked:

"Why did you take it?"

His voice was even, almost casual, but his glance was not. His grey eyes were set wide apart, level with that slight stricture between temples and cheek bones. They gazed at her with a naked directness which brushed aside the polite small talk, disposed of all formalities in the same manner as he had kicked the chair back.

"I don't know," said Hydie. She felt herself go slightly pale under the sun-tan make-up. "I picked it up as it slipped out of the pocket and was going to give it back to you—but you were talking to Monsieur Anatole, so I put it into my bag and forgot about it . . ."

"You forgot about it," he repeated ironically, and with an insolent smile.

"I guess so . . ." Having gone pale a moment ago, she now felt herself blush like a young girl caught out on a lie.

"To whom did you show it?" he asked in a voice almost brutal.

"Show it?" Her eyebrows went up in an arch; she stared at him helplessly. "Why, you are crazy . . ."

He looked at her steadily and, seeing her obvious bewilderment, a gradual change came over him. His body seemed to relax with an inaudible sigh, his gaze lost its tenseness, let go of her, travelled for a second down her neck, circled briefly round her shoulders and breasts, came back with a gently mocking smile.

"So it was just curiosity—eh?" he asked.

"I suppose so . . ." she admitted guiltily.

"You looked at it?" His eyes were again slightly tense.

"Yes—when I was in bed." What has that detail got to do with it, she asked herself furiously—knowing at the same time that the more of a fraud she felt, the more angelic she looked. Daddy's dark nymph, she thought with an inward sneer. Once as a child she had overheard his murmured words of endearment, pretending to be asleep.

"Can you read the cyrillic alphabet?" asked Nikitin.

"No. But I guessed it's all names of people you met at parties. You seem to go to lots of parties."

His expression relaxed again into good-humoured mockery. "I am attached to our cultural mission."

"What do those little signs after the names mean?" she asked curiously.

"Guess. You are such an intelligent young lady."

His insolence was quite incredible; even more incredible was that she permitted it. Serves you right, she told herself. Aloud she said, with the smile of a bright pupil:

"I thought you gave everybody marks for niceness, or political sympathies, or sex appeal, or what not. Am I right?"

He kept smiling at her with amiable mockery.

"Yes. We all like playing those secret little games, eh?"

"But I think it's a horrid game—putting people into categories."

"Yes? Why is that horrible?" He seemed genuinely surprised at her remark.

"Why—it's like sorting out cattle or marking sheep—or marking trees for cutting down."

"But why is that wrong? You must distinguish categories, no?"

She shrugged and gave up. "Won't you buy me a drink after all I have been through because of you?"

He lifted a stumpy finger into the air, and as if by magic it at once caught the overworked waiter's eye. The waiter started wending his way towards them through the maze of tables on the terrace. Hydie was impressed.

"If I also kept a list, I would give you an exclamation mark for this," she said.

"For what?" Each time he failed to get the meaning of one of her remarks, his face reverted to that guarded, distrustful, almost aggressive expression of a sullen adolescent.

"For catching the waiter's eye," Hydie explained. "It's a kind of test to a woman."

"Oh, I understand. To have authority, eh?" He smiled, apparently impressed by so much feminine subtlety.

The waiter arrived and Hydie ordered a Pernod. Fedya looked at her with admiration. "You drink that?"

"I love it," said Hydie.

"It is very powerful. If one drinks too much of it one becomes blind, and . . ."

"Impotent?" Hydie suggested helpfully.

For the second time he gave her that naked, direct stare which made her hold her breath. He remained silent, and Hydie searched desperately for something to say. She took a plunge.

"Are you all such prudes back in your country?"

But it was like a plunge into tepid water, a swimming pool defiled by crowds of bathers since the beginning of time.

"Prudes? At home we talk about natural things naturally."

"Then why were you so shocked when I made that natural remark about the supposed effects of Pernod?"

He smiled, and said with unexpected gentleness:

"You don't talk naturally. You talk—frivolously."

The waiter arrived with the drinks. While she watched the yellow liquid in her glass go cloudy around the ice cube, she caught herself chewing her lip. A bad sign. Fedya waved the waiter with the water carafe aside and tilted the neat Pernod down in one gulp. "Two more," he said to the startled waiter.

"Lord," cried Hydie. "You can't do that with Pernod."

"But why?" He smiled at her amiably, showing his teeth. "This is how we drink at home."

"But this isn't vodka."

"No. It is parfumé."

He set his glass down placidly. Even their drinks are perfumed, he thought with amusement. Perfidious Capua. The sun shone down pleasantly, warming the wicker-chairs on the terrace with all those pretty women wondering with whom they should go to bed next. There was a traffic jam down at the Concorde caused by some Bastille Day parade, and all the taxis and cars were hooting with uncultured impatience. He wondered how long the waiter would be with the second drink; his craving for it was all that remained of the after-effects of last night's shock. To think that only five minutes before he had been called to the telephone he had still been wondering whether his fate would be Karaganda or the Arctic Circle. And all this because of this young female with the face of an angel on heat.

"Will you come with me to the Opera?" he asked with a stiff little bow, reverting to his ceremonious manner.

The question came so abruptly that she almost started. She had been wondering why she had let herself in for all this and how to get out of it, and whether she wanted to get out of it.

"Do you like opera?" she asked, uncertainly.

"Of course. It is the most democratic music, second only to vocal choirs."

"What do you mean by democratic?"

"When you are tired of the music you can watch the stage. When you are tired of watching you can listen to the music In this way the uneducated masses get accustomed to music. If you take the workers of a collective farm to a symphony concert, they fall asleep."

"Must one look at everything from such an educational angle?"

"Of course. Even the aristocrat Leo Tolstoi said so, and also the Greek, Plato. Only your decadents call the purposeful organisation of art tyranny and regimentation. Let them."

When he tried to explain things to her he spoke with a gentle, warm voice, like a patient teacher to a rather backward pupil. Also, when talking about abstract subjects his French at once became more precise, as is often the case with people who have learned a language from books.

"But is it not dreadful for a poet or a composer to work under censorship?"

He smiled at her indulgently. "Censorship has always existed. Only its forms change with the class-structure of society. Dante and Cervantes and Dostoyevsky worked under censorship. Literature and also philosophy has always been regimented, as you say, by churches or princes or laws or the reactionary prejudices of society."

"What about Greece?" said Hydie, for want of a better example.

"What happened to Socrates, eh? We use much more cultured methods with people who teach bad philosophy."

He tilted his second Pernod down, smiling at her. He seemed a completely different person from the one he had appeared the day before. What an extraordinary mixture of contradictions, Hydie thought. But whatever he said had the simplicity of absolute conviction—therein resided his superiority over her. He had faith, she thought with hungry envy, something to believe in. That was what made him so fascinating and unlike all the people she usually met— so unlike her father or herself, not to mention the Three Ravens Nevermore. At last somebody who did not live in a glass cage.

In the taxi in which he took her home she gave him his notebook back. He slipped it carelessly into his pocket. "Why didn't you want me to give it to you in the cafe?" she asked.

"But because," he said, smiling at her with his light-grey eyes, "then I would have had no time to invite you to the Opera."

At home she was told that Monsieur Julien Delattre had rung up and left his telephone number.

3

THE LONGING OF THE FLESH

ONE of Hydie's earliest memories was being woken up by her mother, wearing a beautiful white silk evening dress. She has left the door of the nursery open, and the noise of the gramophone downstairs, of people talking and laughing, floats into the room. Julia Anderson stands propped with one hand against the Donald Duck strip painted on the nursery wall, as if trying to push the wall back, and her body is swaying in a curious way as people did on the big boat when Hydie was sick. She looks down at Hydie in her cot, and Hydie sees that the pink pulpy mass in the corner of her mother's eyes has expanded as in a St. Bernard dog's. This pink pulp also forms a kind of rim between the upper lid and the white of the eye.

Sleep-drunk and frightened, Hydie begins to cry. Her mother, her eyes fixed on Hydie, lurches across the room, one hand all the time pushing the wall back. She smiles at Hydie, but with all that pink pulp in her eyes the smile is a leer. She whispers something which Hydie cannot understand, interrupted by giggles and hiccoughs. Her breath has a terrible smell. Hydie recoils against the wall, but her mother's fingers, with the pointed enamelled nails, pluck and tug at her. At last Hydie understands that her mother wants her to ride pick-a-back.

"I am the horse—like Daddy—like Daddy," Julia repeats urgently, and suddenly lets herself fall down on her hands and knees, rending her beautiful silk dress. She begins to crawl in circles on the floor, giggling, and her dress keeps getting under her knees and is being torn to shreds. She stops beside the cot and starts again tugging at Hydie: Come on, love, we will ride down the stairs. Then, with sudden force she drags Hydie out of the cot onto her back: Oh, why aren't you a boy, love, then you could ride properly. They crawl along the floor, then there is a tilt and a lurch and Hydie feels herself falling, then all goes black. When she wakes up, her father is sitting beside her cot: It is all right, Hydie, your mother is ill, in bed with migraine.

There are long stretches when her mother is away in hospital having a cure for her migraine; and others when she is having a cure at home and wanders about the house, grey-faced, silent, restless, frequently in tears, hardly ever touching food, rising abruptly in the middle of a meal. The servants have to walk on tiptoe; the whole household plays on muted strings. Hydie knows that she must keep out of her mother's way because she bores and upsets her; and she knows it is all her own fault because she isn't a boy. She is paralyzed by the strain of trying to be inaudible and invisible. It is like being smoothed under an eiderdown.

In between these stretches there are short intervals when the house is full of people, the gramophone blaring for hours, her mother feverishly gay. But each of these intervals ends in some lurid scene footlighted in her memory. One Sunday afternoon, when the servants are out, she finds her mother half undressed on the couch in the sitting-room and a man trying to do something horrid to her. One evening Julia is brought home by two men in evening dress and is sick over the carpet. Another night Hydie is woken up again by Julia who insists that they should have a real long talk about Hydie's inner life:

"We see so little of each other, love. You must be dying to confess all your little secrets. Just tell your mother everything, all the shameful little secrets—everything . . ."

Hydie squirms with embarrassment: this is even more horrible than riding pick-a-back. When in later years she is tempted to talk about her inner life, this scene comes back and freezes up; the glass cage has begun to form around her.

Hydie was fourteen when her mother disappeared from home and from her life, more abruptly and finally than if she had died, for there was a taboo on memories and a taboo on tears owing to the fact that Julia was still alive somewhere, a trembling, giggling stranger with the turned lids of a St. Bernard. The day after her mother had been taken away, the child entered on her first menstrual cycle, and the two events became linked together. There was nobody to whom she could turn for advice; though she consulted the medical dictionary she felt soiled, hiding her shameful secret, the unclean daughter of an unclean mother. At that time, in her omnivorous reading, she came across a passage in the First Epistle to the Corinthians: *It is sown in corruption, it is raised in incorruption; it is sown in dishonour, it is raised in glory; it is sown in weakness, it is raised in power.*

The words struck into her like lightning. There was a sudden flash of illumination followed by a strange feeling of peace, like the tender patter of rain after thunder. But it did not last long, and for some months Hydie had a recurring dream of riding pick-a-back on her mother's shoulders and falling off, sailing through darkness. She was woken up by her own imagined scream but found that she had uttered no sound; the scream had been stifled in a kind of icebox in her chest, and stored up with the dust of her dehydrated tears. During the day, under her worried father's eyes, she carried a veneer of brittle cheerfulness like enamel make-up. She had her first petting experiences, mostly on her own initiative, and always going through them with a cold, detached air. When an exasperated college boy asked her: "If you don't get anything out of this, why the hell did you start it?" she answered with innocent sincerity: "To prove to myself that I am clean."

When she was fifteen, the Colonel was sent to England as a military attaché and Hydie was put, at her own wish, into a

boarding school attached to a covent of the Order of the Holy
Virgin, where Julia's sister was Mother Superior. On Hydie's
birth Julia had insisted that the child be baptised in the
Catholic faith; but there Julia's interest in the matter and Hydie's religious education had ended. Now, between the old
stone walls of the convent in the Cotswolds a new world
opened to her, as remote, cool and calm as she had imagined
life on the moon to be. Even the smell of incense was new to
her. Its sweet, pure vapours seemed to penetrate the pores of
her skin, to cleanse her of all dross like a heavenly cosmetic.
Wrapped up in that newly gained serenity, she kept at a friendly distance from the girls of her class. Most of them were
English and both physically and mentally less developed than
Hydie; they made her feel old and experienced.

During her first month at the school Hydie developed a
Schwärmerei for the French teacher, a pretty, rotund and robust young nun from Périgord—and was promptly and almost
rudely told off by her. Sister Boutillot was walking alone
through the park when Hydie waylaid her after a hockey
game—the little French nun was captain of the team—and
grasping the nun's hand, said to her breathlessly: "You played
divinely—oh, I love you so." The nun stopped abruptly,
wrenched her hand free and flushed with indignation as if
Hydie had uttered some obscene insult. In her strong French
accent which sounded to Hydie infinitely moving and which
lent to the English words an unknown sweetness, she said:

"The adjective 'divine' apper-tains to God but not to hockey
games." They were standing in a sheltered alley of lime trees,
in front of a weathered stone bench which faced a primitive
crucifix of painted wood. "And if you have such a surplus of
love at your disposi-tion, better turn it to him." She pointed
at the sagging figure on the cross and turned to continue on her
way, when she saw tears welling up in Hydie's eyes. She hesitated, then added in a gentler voice:

"It is the best *méthode* . . . You have such beautiful trans-
lations of the psalms in English." Forming the words with careful precision, she recited: *"My soul thirsteth for thee, my flesh
also longeth for thee in a dry and weary land, where no water
is* . . . You should meditate on this." Her pretty lips, young
but already the colour of fading rose leaves, formed the faint-
est smile: "It is the best *méthode* . . ." She nodded to the girl,
turned and left her standing in the alley.

Hydie turned to the wooden image. It was very old, the

wood on the drooping skull of the crucified figure had cracked; it looked like a hideous gash, another wound to add to the body's torment. As Hydie contemplated the figure, it seemed to her that at any moment the hands might be torn from the nails by its weight and the whole body crash to the earth among the rotting autumn leaves. Actually the wood of the palms had decayed where the nails penetrated them, as if gangrene had set in the wounds. The fingers were not flattened and stylised; they were bent, clawing the air in furious pain. The face bore an expression of hopeless, unending torment. Hydie felt her inside convulsed by an insufferable spasm of pity—pity for the sheer physical pain exposed to her. The glass cage around her seemed to melt away in the scorching heat of that pity, and in a moment's space she had two visions of almost hallucinatory sharpness. The first was of a scene during a spring-cleaning in the sitting-room at home years ago. The maid had pulled the chintz cover off the sofa thus suddenly exposing the dilapidated fabric underneath with its cuts and rents and the horsehair protruding through the gashes; Hydie had felt such pity for the old sofa in its nakedness that she had begun to cry. The second vision was of that night when her mother had suddenly dropped on her hands and knees beside her cot and had ripped the white silk dress from knee to hip, exposing a patch of the sallow, slightly hairy skin of her thigh. At that time Hydie had only known that she was frightened; now she realised that what she had experienced then was horror mingled with an even more violent pity for her mother's bared, sickly flesh.

The two visions passed quickly away, and only the feeling of pity remained; but it had now become mellower, a loving-pain which was more and more delicious to feel—not unlike self-pity, but purer, cleaner. At the same time she knew that she had made a discovery of tremendous importance, yet impossible to put into words. It had something to do with the scene in the sitting-room. As she looked round her, it seemed indeed that the trees, the stone bench and the receding figure of Sister Boutillot had undergone a curious change: the dust-covers had been lifted from them. All things visible looked different in this curious, indefinable way: their protective covering, a kind of skin which had always been round them without being noticed, had peeled off, revealing their raw flesh to the eye. Thus exposed, they all seemed to share the same suffering, and it became suddenly obvious that they had an unexpected quality of belonging together, of being mere bits in a planned coherence—of which Hydie was so completely a part that she felt her own self dissolve in a melting pain-delight. She must have been blind and dumb not to have discovered the simple truth before. *My soul thirsteth for thee, my flesh also longeth for thee*—oh, but it was so simple, how could people fail to see the secret? They all lived in a dry and weary land, encased in their barren suffering, deprived of grace because deprived of pity. For pity was the only force which held the living world together and gave it coherence, just as gravity kept the planets in their orbits—without pity the world of men would disintegrate like an exploding star.

She looked again at the sagging figure on the cross, the gangrened hands, the clawing fingers, the crack in the drooping skull. She wondered how people could talk so much nonsense about religion when everything was so clear and obvious. His mission had been to teach mankind pity, that and nothing else; and he had achieved that in the simplest and most direct way, by submitting himself to bitter physical torture for the only purpose that men should learn to pity by looking at his image, even in a thousand years. It was obviously nonsense to say that his suffering had redeemed the sins of mankind. She had never understood how the fact that a man had died so many years ago in a certain place could have any bearing on the forgiveness or otherwise of her sins. It was all a silly misunderstanding. The only relation between that far-off event and her present condition was that by looking at his image, an echo of his pain was evoked in her across the immense distance in space and time—just as the tides were moved and her womb was made to bleed by the pale and distant pull of the moon. Clearly, the same must have happened to millions of other people by looking at the image on the cross. They were moved by the tide of pity, and thus carried to a vague comprehension of the togetherness of all beings, and thereby to love. For love, with its pain-delight, sprang from pity—only desire was pitiless, an impure itch, the curse of the original sin committed by some amoebic ancestor and perpetuated ever since. Plants shed their dry pollen, it travelled with the wind, settled on the fragrant stigma—only beasts copulated in the slimy pit, inter faeces et urinam. Her thoughts became blurred, went blank, and a guarded look came into her eyes—not unlike the expression on Fedya's face when he was unable to follow a remark. But the cloud went as fast as it

had come, and only the consciousness of her tremendous discovery remained—and that blissful state of peace, like the
pattering of rain after thunder, which she had first experienced
as a child while reading the words "it is sown in corruption,
it is raised in glory."

Though there were relapses, caused by the exuberant ap-
petites and itches of her young body, she succeeded each time
in recapturing her inner peace, that radiant stillness of the
flesh and mind which to hold securely seemed to her the only
joy and purpose of life. Because it was nourished by the
sources of both emotion and intellect, her faith was absolute,
and its content seemed so self-evident to her that she soon lost
the capacity to understand people who did not share it, or her
own state of mind before her conversion. She followed the
curriculum of her class without effort, but without the curiosity
and passion of her former studies. Algebraic equations and
chemical formulas, the cavalcade of princes and battles in
history still occasionally caught her imagination, but merely
in the manner a jigsaw puzzle or play of Chinese shadows may
divert the mind for a short while; they had no bearing on
ultimate reality, on the essence of her interests. She did not
devote more time to prayer than her classmates, for petition-
ary prayer she shunned, and to induce contemplative stillness
of the mind she only had to sit alone on the stone bench in
the alley and look at the wooden figure in front of her. Then
soon a wave of tenderness surged along the alley like the autumn breeze which swept the leaves towards her feet; the
wave traversed her and travelled sedately on, carrying away
all impurity and the very notion of her separate self.

She tried to read the writings of the mystics, but did not
respond; the words, grown trite and threadbare by wear, stood
between her and the experience. She saw no reason to doubt
that Teresa of Avila had the gift of levitation and floated sometimes unawares up to the ceiling, like a bubble in a glass; but
to judge by the words in which she described her ecstasies,
poor Teresa seemed to walk on trodden heels. For a time
Hydie was obsessed with the problem of sainthood; she imagined she perceived signs of her being called, fasted, unno-
ticed as she thought, for several days, and conceived the wild
idea that if she was really chosen, the menstrual curse would
be lifted from her. Once it was actually delayed by more than
a week, a week of rapture during which, despite her outward
self-control, she caught her classmates glancing at her with

curiosity and the nuns with silent disapproval, and then the event befell her during one of her rare walks with Sister Boutillot in her favourite alley. She ran back to the house, crying with rage and humiliation; but after she had confessed it all and had thought she detected a touch of amused irony in the priest's voice, she realised the monstrousness of her presumption and emerged from the episode more balanced and mature.

She knew now not only that sainthood was an end infinitely remote, but that even her chances of being admitted to the Order were feeble unless she used great cunning and dissimulation. She knew that the set policy of the Order was to discourage any tendency among the pupils in that direction—partly to test the determination and calling of possible candidates, partly because the reputation and very existence of the school depended on its vigorous abstention from soul-fishing. Sister Boutillot had driven this home with that malice which she seemed to reserve specially for Hydie. "You will never make a good catho-lique, little one," she told her. "Good catho-liques do not grow in sky-scrapers. They grow only in Latin countries, among the vineyards."

"But what about the Irish?" protested Hydie. "I am half Irish myself, you know."

She was several inches taller than the French nun; walking together, they gave the impression that Hydie was a slim page or youthful hidalgo, gallantly escorting a prim and somewhat dumpy damzelle. Only the sturdy legs of the page did not quite fit into the picture.

"Oh, the Irish are Celts—almost Gauls," said Sister Boutillot. "They come from the Mediterranean. But look at the Bavarians! They pretend to be Catho-liques but they are *boches*—savages with goiters who drink beer out of clay mugs by the litre. Catholicism does not go with beer, which is a Protestant drink—tasteless, *fade* and insipid. As for you, little one, you will be a drinker of cocktails—fie!" She wrinkled her short snub nose in a grimace. Hydie knew that the little nun was teasing her for reasons which she dimly guessed, but she went pale, and without any warning sob or conscious pain, her eyes suddenly overflowed.

"There—you want to be a Catho-lique and cannot even take a joke," said Sister Boutillot contemptuously.

Hydie walked on in sulky silence; then, after a few steps she said: "My mother was an alcoholic"—and immediately wanted to bite her tongue off. She had only meant to excuse her childish tears of a moment ago; but even while she spoke the words she realised that they were an abject means of wheedling sympathy from Sister Boutillot. At any rate they missed entirely their effect. The little nun looked at her coldly: "Quel horreur! But why do you talk about it?" she said matter-of-factly; and walked away with her quick vigorous steps down the alley, as was her habit.

Though none of the other nuns treated her in the caustic manner of Sister Boutillot, Hydie soon learned to dissimulate her aspirations and even the depth and intensity of her religious feeling. She knew that if she were frank, her aunt the Mother Superior—a tall, bony, forbidding martinet who treated Hydie with icy formality—would regard it as her duty to inform her father, and that the probable outcome of this would be her removal from the school. Prompted by instinct, Hydie developed a technique of dissimulation which soon grew into a protective, automatic habit. She appeared gay, more interested in her studies, less dreamy and introspective. As she could not be herself, her personality was difficult to get into focus, seemed to have no proper core, lacking a centre of gravity. Without conscious effort she always managed to fall into the part which in a given relationship was expected from her. She was the young page with an invisible sword on his side during her walks with Sister Boutillot; a blushing adolescent with downcast eyes when talking to Mother Superior, while to her classmates she appeared as the typical American flapper converted from morbid brooding to a passion for hockey. The paradox of her situation she found summed up in an anecdote which a girl of Jewish descent told one night in the dormitory.

"As you may or may not know," the girl, whose name was Miriam Rosenberg, explained to her audience after the lights had gone out, "it is the custom in Jewish communities that on high religious festivals access to the Synagogue is not free—the seats on the pews are sold by tickets at prices varying according to the distance from the altar. . . . In a way it is a quite sensible system: the money goes into the community's charity funds and the poor benefit by it.

"Now one day, on Atonement Day, which is the highest of the Jewish festivals, the synagogue in the little town where my grandfather came from was packed to bursting with bearded Jews, hitting their chests with their fists and confessing their sins in a wailing chorus. This is the most solemn moment in the whole service, and just at that moment a seamy individual came to the synagogue door and asked to talk to my grandfather who had a seat in the first row from the altar. 'Have you got a ticket?' the verger asked suspiciously.

" 'No,' the man said, 'but I only want to talk to Moses Rosenberg, and it is very, very urgent.'

"So the verger looked at him and said: 'I know these tricks, you rascal—you want to pray' . . ."

There was a moment's silence and then a subdued burst of laughter. Hydie couldn't stop giggling for a long time; she had to bite her handkerchief and almost had hysterics.

As the months passed, her faith underwent a gradual change. Almost imperceptibly its texture was shaped and trimmed to her environment by the routine of the observations, by her father confessor and by her rare but always wounding talks with Sister Boutillot. At the beginning, her mind had revolted against the acceptance of dogma, had desperately resisted the pinning down of her fluid emotional experience to an arbitrary sequence of events fixed at a given date and geographical site. She also guessed that, in spite of all her caution, her teachers knew exactly where she stood. One day she could not resist making an ironic remark to Sister Boutillot about the absurdity of the crude dogmatic form of belief. They were walking near a little pond at the end of Hydie's favourite alley, and after a silence Sister Boutillot said:

"How clever-clever you are, little one, are you not? So you have invented the real religion, like that man in a far-away village in Russia who invented the bi-cyclette all by himself in 1936 . . ."

Hydie blushed. They walked on in silence, Hydie biting her lip, a sulking, sturdy-legged page; but she carried her slim shoulders still slightly bent in a protective way towards short Sister Boutillot. They arrived at the little pond, where the nun halted and said:

"The contemplation—the meditation—the mystic sentiment —you think that is all one needs. But the sentiment is liquid —now it fills you, now it runs out of you through a puncture made by a small, sharp temptation, a little sin, an angriness like the prick of a needle. You are in peace, you are perhaps in a state of grace—of friendship with God as we say—and then there is that little puncture, this laceration, and the peace is finished, the grace is finished, the sentiment runs out—

glub, glub—you are left empty and dry. But there is this pond, there are the water lilies, it is also liquid, but why is it always full and still? Because the pond is held together by its banks, by limi-tations with a hard and definite form. Without these limi-tations, the rigid *dogmatisme* of the banks, the liquid could not keep its fullness and stillness. *Voilà . . .*"

She paused, then with a little smile on her fading lips, which were the only ageing part in her young face, she added:

"*D'ailleurs,* when you have accepted that there must be a bank, when you have accepted a single feature of the bank, you will find that the shape of the pond cannot be different from what it is. *Il n'y a que le premier pas qui coûte*—the rest must follow by itself, as you will see. You can accept it, you can reject it, but you can not alter it . . ." The irony of her smile deepened, while her voice became gentler than usual: "As it happens you are ripe for accepting it—and it is still the best *métho-de*. . . . To go on inventing the bicycle all over again is tiring even for very clever little ones, is it not?"

Sister Boutillot was right, as usual. Once, as a child, Hydie had been greatly impressed by the description in a novel by Jules Verne of a lake that did not freeze despite the intense cold, until a boy threw a pebble into it whose ripples trans-formed the whole surface into ice within a few seconds. This process, known to chemists as "inoculation," was the nearest simile she could think of to describe how, during the next few weeks, her faith became suddenly crystallised, developed a rigid, elaborate frame and structure. When on her next visit to London her father, after beating about the bush for a while, asked her with a kind of embarrassed diffidence why and on what grounds she accepted the doctrine of the Church, Hydie answered promptly, smiling at the naïveté of his question: "But simply because it happens to be true." The Colonel did not insist; he understood that he had already lost her, and lost her through his own guilt—for he had never ceased to regard Julia's defection as his own responsibility.

At seventeen, two years after her entry into the school, Hydie felt reasonably certain that she had won the first round of the contest. There was an undefinable change in the attitude of the nuns towards her—excluding Sister Boutillot but in-cluding the Mother Superior. She still had to go wary under their quiet, all-observant eyes which registered without react-ing, but she was less afraid now of their vigilant scrutiny. She had long known that not only her minutest actions were duly taken note of, but even her unconsummated impulses and un-spoken thoughts. How naïve she had been to imagine that she could deceive them! At times this constant, unobtrusive, ubi-quitous surveillance filled her with a panic comparable to what she imagined to be the state of mind of a citizen under a police regime. But gradually—as her faith adapted itself to the moulding pressure of her environment—her fears diminished, and she became more reassured, basking in the knowledge of the silent approval of her superiors. How far were now the days when she had presumed to experience faith in her own fashion, to proclaim, though only to herself, that compassion was the essence of Christianity, and the mission of Jesus to teach mankind pity and nothing else! She knew now that such beliefs were inspired by pantheistic, or at best deistic heresy, the more dangerous because of the spontaneity of the emo-tions which they released—that pain-delight and rapture which now appeared to her in retrospect as a self-indulgence almost as obscene as the merely cruder indulgences of the flesh.

If Sister Boutillot had once compared Hydie's faith to a volatile fluid, it had now become more like a crystal with a hard but brittle surface, carefully protected against damage and chipping by elastic cushions. If some experience never-theless succeeded in penetrating these protective zones of her mind, she was upset for days. Quite innocent-looking causes would unexpectedly release a minor crisis, like a passage from Donne:

> *Now thou art lifted up, draw me to thee,*
> *And at thy death giving such liberall dole,*
> *Moyst, with one drop of thy blood, my drye soule . . .*

which, for reasons unknown but dimly and desperately guessed, threw her into a violent crying fit. Now, however, the nuns were sympathetic and helpful; accesses of doubt were in their eyes a matter of routine, and so were the methods of coping with them. Once again, just as during the first stage of her conversion, she was quite unable to understand her previous state of mind, and looked back at her former self as on a stranger whose sight inspired violent revulsion and contempt. Gradually the same intolerance which she had for her own past began to permeate her attitude to others. They lived in a state of that ignorance and smug presumption which she knew only too well, had shared herself until its abjectness

and futility had been revealed to her. They perpetuated a
stage of development which she had long overcome, stubbornly clinging to its glaring errors, repeating like parrots the
same cheap, trite, clever-clever arguments which made her
want to bite her tongue off for having once used them herself. She smiled with polite indulgence, but they made her
writhe with exasperation—as adults are made to blush by the
silly behaviour of adolescents which reflects like a distorting
mirror the imbecilities of their own past. Try as she might,
she had no patience with them; it stood to reason that only
drastic methods offered a chance of saving those blind and
deaf to truth.

In one of those sudden flashes of insight which succeeded
each other more and more frequently (how right Sister Boutillot had been when she had said that the first step alone was
difficult), the profound wisdom of the Church militant of bygone ages became revealed to her. Oh, the fatuousness of all
the superficial talk about the Inquisition! She read several
works on the subject, and she gasped with shame at her own
stupidity. How could she not have seen the facts in their
proper light before, how could she for so long have been
blinded by the exaggerations and malicious distortions from
the enemy camp? She could hardly wait to bring up the matter
on her next walk with Sister Boutillot, though she knew that
the French nun would have some wounding retort ready—or
just because she knew it. And sure enough Hydie's remarks,
though they were made in a carefully restrained, almost casual
tone, were greeted by the familiar malicious smile.

"What a pity that Torquemada and Loyola were all men—
isn't it, little one? There is of course Jeanne d'Arc—but the
English have so little appreciation for maidens in armour.
Ah, if you were a man now . . ."

It hurt, but such hurts no longer much disturbed her; they
were absorbed by the elastic defences of her mind, could not
reach the crystalline core of her faith. Impressions from the
outside world, things which she read and heard, could only
attain to this perceptive core after passing through a series of
protective filters or prisms which aligned them on a single
wavelength as it were; for true faith draws confirmation from
every experience, as the leaves of the plant transform all colours of light into green. And in exchange, a hard, brilliant
radiance began to emanate from that inmost core through her

eyes, voice and gestures, which not even strangers could fail to notice.

When Hydie took her first vows, she was a young woman just over eighteen, obviously designed for a remarkable career in the Order. During his only interview in all these years with his sister-in-law, the Mother Superior, the Colonel had asked with wistful resignation: "Is my daughter going to be a saint?"

"She would make a rotten saint," the Mother Superior had remarked drily, "and we have taken care to drive that idea out of her head. What we need are crusaders, not saints, and fortunately that is more in my niece Clodagh's line." She always referred to the girl by her second, Irish name.

Hydie was happy as never before or after in her life. Only rarely, as if by a sudden eruption of a black sun-spot, was the radiance of her mind marred by an unexpected stab of panic, the short turbulent fear that it was all too good to be true, and that one day she would be relegated back into the outer darkness where the parched souls writhed in the agony of their thirst.

4

ATOMS AND MONKEYS

GRANDFATHER Arin came from Turkish Armenia. On Christmas Day, anno domini 1895, twelve hundred Armenians, men, women and children, were burnt alive in the Cathedral of Urfa. Grandfather Arin escaped by a miracle, but his wife and six children died in the flames. A burning beam crashed down on him and broke his back. But to kill Arin, at least the whole dome would have had to fall on top of him. His body remained slightly bent from the hip upward for the rest of his life, like a tree struck by lightning, but he was not a cripple. He was very tall, and the angle which the upper part of his body formed with the lower gave him a peculiar air of distinction, as if he were bending, out of sheer courtesy, toward the people to whom he talked. He had slim but powerful shoulders, a long neck and the head of an old hawk which he kept rigidly erect, thus giving the lie to his stoop.

For a week or so Arin lay in a ditch; the Turkish soldiers took him for dead. Then some missionaries picked him up and hid him until he could walk again. "What are you going to do now, unfortunate man?" the missionary's wife asked him tearfully. He lifted his head, looked at her fiercely with his black, close-set eyes, and said: "I shall find another wife and have another six children, but this time they will all be boys."

He was a cobbler by trade, and though illiterate he had been a member of Hunchagist, the secret society which aimed at the resurrection of a free, independent Armenia. Several of the society's members had studied or traded in Russia and even in Germany, and through them Arin became acquainted with modern European ideas. These, many years later, he handed on to his grandchild, Fedya. "The secret of life," he told Fedya, "is the atom. There is no God: He was an old man and died long ago of a broken heart. Everything now depends on the atoms, the little devils." Rocking the orphaned boy on his knees, he explained to him the origin of man: "Adam was a monkey. At that time, very long ago, the monkeys ruled the world. They fought, and the monkey with the strongest atoms became a man. One could tell at once that he was a man, because he had dignity." When the boy became a little older, Grandfather Arin expanded further on this question, on which he had his own theories: "Monkeys," he explained, "copulate back to belly. But Adam turned his wife over and kissed her between her eyes as he went into her. Thus he acquired dignity and thus he became a man."

After his recovery at the mission, Arin made his way across the Armenian vilayets of Turkey to Erivan in Russia. He earned his living on the road as an ambulant cobbler and by telling the villagers stories about atoms, monkeys, and the dignity of man. He was looking for a new wife, but the Armenians who had survived the massacres were few, and their daughters had all been dishonoured by the Turkish soldiery; besides, he wanted to get to Russia, whose Tsar was said to protect the Armenians and to have promised them independence.

Erivan, however, was a disappointment. In the narrow, dusty lanes between the mud-huts camped hundreds of miserable refugee families with their children and chattels; and the very day Arin arrived a company of Russian soldiers rounded half of them up and marched them off towards the Turkish frontier, back to the country of death from which they came. It appeared that the Tsar of the Russians was no better than the Emperor of the Turks, and soldiers remained soldiers whatever uniform they wore. So the same day Arin continued his journey across the mountains of the Little Kaukasus to Tiflis. There, in that big, gay, cosmopolitan town he felt that he had at last put enough distance between himself and his memories. The screams, the smoke, the smell of burning hair no longer haunted him. On passing a shoemaker's shop in a narrow street he saw a girl with fierce eyes standing in the door. He entered the shop, asked for a job, said he did not care how much he was paid, and was accepted. The girl's name was Tamar; his boss, Tamar's father, was an old Georgian and hence an enemy of Armenia—but like Arin he was an atheist, believed in atoms and was a member of a secret society which fought for the freedom and independence of Georgia. This society was called Dashnak, Arin's had been called Hunchagist, but what was the difference? They were branches on the same tree of man's progress towards dignity and enlightenment.

After three months Arin married the girl with the fierce look and after a further six months she bore him a child. But his trials had not come to an end yet; the atoms were against him. Though he had promised himself to have six sons, the child was a girl; and three days after its birth, its mother died of septic fever.

The little girl, and their common bereavement, were an even stronger tie between the two men than their respective secret societies. They sat all day, bent over their work, in the little shop in the Georgian bazaar which had no front-wall to the street, drove at a leisurely rate wooden tacks into old slippers and talked, while the little girl was playing under their feet. She had been named Tamar, after her mother, and had her mother's fine, long features, her taciturn nature and fierce eyes. Arin and Niko, the old Georgian, often discussed the causes of their bereavement in a philosophical manner. They agreed that it was due neither to the will of God, nor the cruelty of nature, but to the filth and carelessness of the midwife and the fact that there were no doctors in Tiflis for the poor. Such tragedies occurred daily in the bazaar; a father could call himself lucky if out of his five children two survived. This was a very stupid state of affairs; but how could it be remedied? The Dashnaks and Hunchagist talked about freedom and independence, but to this question of poverty which killed, they seemed to know no satisfactory answer. Freedom was necessary like the air one breathed, but it was not enough to fill one's belly. They talked about this many times, inventing wild remedies and rejecting them. They were both thoughtful men, and suffering had invested them with wisdom and dignity. But they were both illiterate; they knew there must be an answer, but could not find it.

The answer only reached them some years later, after the turn of the century. It came in the shape of a young lad named Grisha, who worked in the oil refineries of the Nobel Brothers in Baku. He was rather short, with a sunburnt, round, freckled face, a skull like a billiard ball, and loose, springy limbs which seemed specially designed for the Kaukasian heel-dance.

Grisha came into the shop one late afternoon in 1905, the year of the Russo-Japanese war and of the first abortive revolution. Rumours of it had penetrated into the bazaar of Tiflis, but the two illiterate cobblers could make neither head nor tail of them. It seemed that the trouble was mainly caused by the Jews in the Ukraine and by spies of the Mikado who had staged mutinies and incited the sailors of the Black Sea fleet to revolt. Once or twice, mad-looking youngsters distributed leaflets in the bazaars, but they were arrested and beaten up fearfully, and so were those who were found in possession of such leaflets, even if they could not read them. Arin and old Niko had for months lived in a state of great agitation; they knew that the answer they were looking for was within their reach, that things of the utmost importance were happening around them, but these events somehow eluded their little shop in the bazaar as storms and earthquakes elude the realm of the sleeping beauty.

It was little Tamar, then aged nine, who had first noticed the strange lad. He seemed to be loitering aimlessly in the street, peeping into several shops and looking for nothing in particular. Something about him seemed to fascinate the little girl—maybe his high kneeboots, or the mop of sandy, close-cropped hair over the round, freckled face. She said nothing, but after a while her father's and grandfather's eyes followed the direction of her stare. Grisha Nikitin came up to them in a hesitating way, then entered the shop. For a while he said nothing, but his eyes, which were very light and had a calm, deliberate look in contrast to the usually humorous expression of his face, glanced quickly from the aging to the old man, then to the little girl. "Can you repair this boot while I wait here?" he asked. Old Niko nodded silently, and Grisha sat down on the stool reserved for clients and visiting neighbours, and pulled his right boot off. Underneath he wore a cotton sock which was stiff with sweat and the dried blood of torn blisters. Niko carefully examined the boot, then said: "This boot is whole and needs no repairing." "No," said Grisha, and then asked on the same level tone: "Can you hide me overnight in this shop? I come from Baku and the police are after me."

Arin slowly lifted his head from the glue-pot. The two cobblers looked at the young man with apparently calm and reserved scrutiny, but their hearts were fluttering with the excitement of two old spinsters who have discovered a foundling at their door step. They knew at once that here was the answer they had been praying for, the light to disperse the darkness of their ignorance. "Are you a thief?" old Niko asked, to save his own self-respect. "No," said Grisha, trying to force his foot back into the boot, and grimacing with pain. He merely added, as if this explained everything: "I told you I come from Baku."

Tamar's eyes had never left the stranger's face since they had settled on him in the street. Without a word she took the boot from Grisha's hand and lit the primus-stove to prepare hot water. When she brought the bowl and knelt down in front of him to wash the bloodcrusts from his feet, Grisha stroked her head like a kitten's and pulled at her long, black tresses. "She will be good at carrying messages, and maybe even leaflets," he said as if everything had been settled between them to everybody's satisfaction.

The shop had a single, windowless back room, where the two men slept on their mats with the child's straw mattress between them. There was just enough space to fit the guest in along the wall toward which the feet of the three of them were pointing. During the years which followed, each time when he came on business to Tiflis, Grisha slept stretched out on the mudfloor at their feet like a big watchdog. They were happy years for all of them. Grisha was a member of the majority caucus in the Baku Committee of the revolutionary movement. When he started on the political education of his hosts, his first explanations were devoted to the essential difference between Majoritarians and Minoritarians. Apparently there had been a quarrel between these two groups some years ago at a Party Conference in London, England, and now they hated each other more than they hated the common enemy, the Tsar. Grisha, who was almost always in good humour and of a level mind, grew only furious when he talked about the Minoritarians—for, to complicate matters, in the Baku Committee, those Minoritarians held the majority. Neither Arin nor old Niko succeeded in really grasping the difference between the two factions, until one day Tamar, breaking her usual silence in an impatient outburst, explained to them: "Grisha's people want everything, the others want only half of the things, so they will get nothing." Grisha patted her head approvingly. In recent times he had taken to winding and unwinding her tresses round his hands while he talked and she sat at his feet and the two elders hammered away at their boots. It was tacitly understood that they would get married as soon as Tamar reached the age of fifteen.

A year before that, old Niko died peacefully of a stroke. Arin and his daughter now only lived for Grisha's visits, which had become rarer. Things were going badly for Grisha's party. They seemed to be quarrelling constantly among themselves, and their leaders, most of whom had been deported after the defeat of the 1905 revolution, continued their quarrels in exile.

Though Grisha never talked about himself, Arin and the girl knew that he now played a leading part in the organisation at the Baku oilfields. Sometimes he brought a copy of a newspaper called "The Baku Proletarian" which was printed secretly by his friends, and read out an article aloud. Old Arin, who in all these years had not learned to speak Russian properly, understood only half of it; but the girl seemed to drink in every word, less through her ears than through her dark, wide-open eyes, which were immutably fixed on Grisha. Grisha was teaching her to read and to write, and sometimes sent her on errands to deliver messages or to collect a manuscript from somebody, which was to be printed in the Baku paper.

One day he sent her on such an errand to the other end of the town. "Don't go past the Governor's building," he told her, and he indicated a long detour which she was to follow. Tamar nodded silently; she never questioned anything Grisha told her. While she was away, Grisha seemed restless—a rare thing with him, for as a rule if he had to stay in the shop he dropped down at once on the floor of the back-room, reading a pamphlet or a book, deaf and blind to the world. After a while Arin asked him whether anything special was the matter. "You will hear soon enough," said Grisha morosely. An hour later the news spread through the bazaar that terrorists had thrown a bomb in front of the Governor's Palace, killed a dozen or so people and made off with an enormous sum of money which a heavily guarded mailcoach had been delivering. These outrages were fairly frequent in those days and Arin disapproved of them. "Such methods," he said to Grisha, "are not in keeping with the dignity of the People's fight." "I agree with you," said Grisha bluntly. "Most of us are against it. But the others argue that the Party needs funds, that the end justifies the means, and for the time being they are backed by the leadership. At any rate, all this terrorism is only a temporary measure. When things brighten up a bit, we won't have to use such methods."

Arin was only half convinced but he did not have the words to argue with Grisha.

One night, in the dark back-room where the three of them slept, Arin heard a small, stifled cry and quick breathing. He knew that the inevitable had happened. He had been prepared for it for a long time and he also knew that the honour of his family would not suffer. In a few months Tamar would be fifteen and though the atoms did not care for sacraments, the two would get married, to satisfy custom and tradition. And maybe his grandsons—for he had promised himself to have six grandsons at least—would see the dawn of the new world, when the last heritage of the greedy monkey was shred and all men would live in peace and dignity.

A few weeks later the young people got married and Tamar went to live with Grisha in Baku. Arin remained alone in the shop; it was the loneliest time in his life, even lonelier than the time of his wanderings from Urfa to Erivan. But it was understood that he would sell the shop as soon as a buyer could be found, and then follow after.

Fedya, by his full name Fyodor Grigorevich Nikitin, was born in 1912, in a dark, dank basement in the Black Town of Baku. Grisha was now a foreman in the refineries. The earliest memories of Fedya were all soaked in the all-pervading odour of petrol. The room and the streets smelled of it, the bread smelled of it and his father smelled of it. When Grisha returned from the factory, he stood in a tin-tub, singing, and tried to get some of the smell out of his pores by means of a hard brush and liquid soap. It was an unheard-of thing to do and Tamar never got accustomed to it. She squatted in the corner of the room with Fedya on her lap, her face to the wall, to hide them both from the immoral sight of Grisha standing and splashing in the tub, naked and blond all over. She thought nothing of letting her husband take her while the child was lying at arm's length from them on the rug, sleeping or pretending to sleep, as long as it was dark; her modesty was entirely confined to the sense of vision. Most of the oil-workers in the Black Town were Moslem Tartars whose womenfolk were only seen swathed in the black veil; though Tamar, who had been brought up in the Georgian faith; wore no veil, she felt embarrassed by belonging to the minority of women who showed their naked faces in the streets. Grisha often joked about her prudishness, and the child, long before he understood what it was about, sided with the joker. He felt that his mother enjoyed, in a warm, obscure way, being teased by him as she was teased by his father; it was the child's way of making love to her.

After the tub-ceremony Grisha usually went off to a meeting; but sometimes when he was down with a bout of malaria, his comrades came to visit him. They were earnest and kind men, as direct in their manner as Grisha; they were gentle to Fedya without making a fuss over him, and talked to him as if he were grown up. One of them was a doctor with a beard, one a lawyer with a pince-nez, one a singer in the Baku Opera with a double chin, and the others were workers from the oil-fields. Fedya was always hoping that Grisha would go down for a while with malaria so that the men would come and sit on the mats and talk and fill the room with the blue mists of mahorka-smoke. He himself never caught malaria, nor the Egyptian disease which caused most of the children in the Black Town to have sticky, running eyes like sick puppies. They also had curiously big heads and bloated bellies carried on thin bowed legs, which made their walk wobbly and uncertain. Fedya, who was a sturdy child, liked them because they were weaker and accepted his leadership. But his father said that soon everything would change and then all the children would become as strong and healthy as Fedya was. This prospect filled Fedya with some apprehension, but it was outweighed by his curiosity and impatience to see the great change of which his father and the other men talked incessantly, though he himself was not allowed to talk about it to anybody outside the house. He kept the secret, however difficult it was at times, for he knew that if he talked the men would never come again, and his father would be taken away by the soldiers. But this secrecy only made the impending change more mysterious and marvellous. Every morning when he woke up, he ran to the window to see whether the change had already occurred, for he was convinced that it would transform the look of everything: the sky would be red instead of grey, the houses of brick and mud would be changed into palaces of polished marble, soft to the touch like his mother's cheek; and the air would smell like the bunch of tiny white flowers which his father had brought home shamefacedly on one of his crazy days, and which had made his mother cry with happiness and anger at the expense.

But as yet there was no change. The black snow from the oil-towers and the huge chimneys of the refineries drizzled day and night out of the grey sky, so that even the dust was black in the steep, narrow streets, and the spittle of the sick men was black in the dust, and the stuff which one poked out of one's nose was also black. Beyond the Black Town lay Byeligorod, the White Town, which was also black; and around them lay the great belt of the oilfields. Each of them had a beautiful name: Surakhany, Balakhany, Baladshary, Biby Eibat; Fedya's father had once said that if he were driven blindfolded across them, he would recognise each field by its particular smell, just as the winegrowers in the Kaukasus were said to be able to guess from which vineyard a bottle came by merely sniffing its flower. The belt of oilfields formed a kind of sinister forest round the town where the drill-towers stood for trees, the undergrowth of twisting pipelines replaced the lianas and climbing plants; where instead of green moss, one trod through slimy clay, and instead of the murmur of brooks one heard the bubbling of mud-volcanoes and the hissing of gas escaping through cracks in the earth. From close to, however, the drill-towers no longer looked like trees, but like a swarm of giant mosquitos, standing on their high, spidery legs and sucking through their long proboscies the black blood of the earth. From even closer each tower was different from the next: there were towers of wood and towers of metal, towers which had merely a skeleton-frame and towers that were panelled in from all sides; brand-new towers which hovered over fresh, spouting wounds in the earth and old black disused towers over her dried-up scars, rotting away between the grinding teeth of time.

During the stifling summer months, the town was swathed in clouds of acrid fumes. At night, one heard the whistles and wailing of the oil-tankers leaving for Persia and Turkestan.

They were guided on their way by the beam from a lighthouse which was called the Maiden's Tower and where a mad Khan had once kept his favourites. The tankers' keels glided over the roofs and minarets of a town on the bottom of the sea which the Caspian had swallowed and drowned many centuries ago.

All this was mixed up in Fedya's mind with the coming of the Great Change. Some of the other children prattled about an old man who sat on a throne high above the petrol towers amidst clouds of reeking oil-fumes to watch and punish little boys who stole apples in the bazaar. Fedya knew from his father that this was a superstition, invented by people called capitalists, who were the cause of the malaria, the eye-disease, the poverty and the evil smells. They had invented this nonsense to prevent the coming of the Great Change. And yet nothing could prevent its eventual advent; and when it came the sunken town would rise from the bottom of the Caspian, the mad Khan's beautiful wives would come dancing out of the lighthouse, and the smell of snowdrops would be everywhere in the room and the streets.

He never lost this belief. He learned that the change might only come gradually; that it would not fall from the sky, but had to be helped by man's endeavour, including his own; that to reach the ultimate goal, one might have to follow many detours and at times even lose it from sight. When Grisha was killed and Tamar died soon after, the idea of the change became tinged with the idea of revenge. But despite these modifications, the belief in the Great Change remained the guiding star of all his thoughts, his conscious and other actions; it was the root and the source, nourished from depths as great as those from which the earth threw up its fuming jets under the drill-towers.

Fedya was five when on a certain winter evening the lawyer with the pince-nez came in in such a rush that he almost fell over his feet, and flinging his hat on the mud floor instead of carefully hanging it on a nail, barked out in a hoarse, sobbing voice: "It has started! It has started! In Pe-ters-burg."

Fedya understood at once what it was that had started. He hopped to the window on one foot (for he had promised himself that when it started he would hop on one foot for a full day) to see whether the sky was already red. It was still grey, but soon extraordinary things began to happen in the room.

Grisha, who a moment before had been lying on the rug with his teeth chattering from malaria, had risen in his shirt and thrown his arm round the lawyer's neck, and they began to kiss each other, weeping like children, and another minute later they were hopping and dancing round the room like madmen. Then the bearded doctor came in, flinging the door wide open, and collided with Fedya's mother who was just slinking out of the door with an empty bottle in her hand and they too started kissing, which was the more incredible as his mother only talked to other men with her eyes downcast—if she talked at all, which happened rarely.

From then on everything got confused. The room filled with men who all talked at once and kept hitting with terrific blows each other's shoulders, and his mother came back with the bottle full, and then another one, and the tenor came in with a tureen full of caviar which tasted bitter and filthy, and Fedya was made to sit on the doctor's shoulders and encouraged to pull at his beard which he had always wanted to do, and the tenor went and came back with more bottles with corks that popped like gunshots and a boxful of *rachat locum* for Fedya. Then he was made to drink a glass from a popping bottle, and now the change began in earnest: the familiar room assumed a new, strange and beautiful aspect; all colours became bright and shiny; the sky outside the window had become immense, the moon and stars were incredibly bright; he felt a joy which soon became unbearable in its intensity, so that he had to hop and hop round the room on one foot, until the walls began to wobble and tilt, and the noise became a deafening thunder in his ears and his stomach threw up the former happiness in a terrible convulsion. After that he felt peaceful and very remote from the others, even from his mother who was nursing him to sleep, smiling at him from a very great distance, her oval face framed by her dark tresses, her smile sweetened by the little gap of a broken front tooth.

He woke up the next morning, feeling ill; and from that day until the journey to Moscow a few years later with Grandfather Arin, events remained confused and incomprehensible. The Change had started, but in another town, very far away, and it approached only slowly, as slowly perhaps as the shadow of the minaret behind the house travelled on long afternoons through the dust in the street—it might take a week, or even a year, until it arrived in Baku. So much he understood; but the events around him he was unable to understand, though Grisha, talking to him as if he were a grown-up, tried to explain. Only many years later did the chaos of those two years become sorted out in retrospect: the rapid succession of wars, governments, executions and foreign occupations. Like the walls of the room on the evening of his first drunkenness, peoples and armies south of the Kaukasian mountains danced and reeled in a deadly frenzy. There was first the Federal Republic of Transkaukasia, then a rising of the Tartars and the proclamation of an Independent Moslem Republic, then a fight of Russians and Armenians against the Moslems, then a short and ephemeral Revolutionary Government which was overthrown by the Central Caspian Dictatorship before it had time to bring about any great change; then a British occupation followed by a Turkish occupation, and in between another minor war with Armenia—each change of regime marked by the arrest and execution of the previous rulers who only yesterday had represented the Law and Government. Grisha became a victim of one of these overnight reversals of legality. He was arrested by the British occupation troops after the fall of the First Baku Soviet, shipped with a score of his comrades, including the bearded doctor and the lawyer with the pince-nez, across the Caspian, marched into the Karakum Desert and there shot and buried in the hot sand. Among the habitués of the room the opera singer alone escaped in a clever disguise; he became a high dignitary after the liberation of Baku by the Revolutionary Army, and was only shot much later, in the great purge of 1938.

Grisha was in hiding when they arrested him, but they brought him back to the room when they came to search it for weapons and gold. The soldiers who brought him were drunk; Fedya, then six, woke up when they came in, leading his father on a rope, like a goat; the rope was attached to his hands which were tied behind his back. He stood squarely in the middle of the room, smiling at Fedya much as usual, and trying to give the impression that he was holding his hands behind his back of his own will. But Fedya understood at once; he pulled his trousers over his shirt, put his boots on, stood in front of his mother to protect her, and held her hand to calm her. With his shaven head, round like a billiard ball, his freckled face and light, somewhat slanting eyes, Fedya looked an exact replica of his father. Grisha nodded approvingly; he had ceased to smile and his green eyes now looked fully into his son's green eyes, imparting to him a message which the boy was meant

never to forget and never did forget. It was a message of
hatred, cruelty and revenge; it was also a message of love, of
unshakable faith in the Great Change, and of a childlike belief
in the marvels and happiness which it would bring. The
soldiers ransacked the room, but there was little to ransack and
little to search; it only contained a few mats, rugs and a shelf
with frying pans and books on it. But the soldiers were drunk
and had got this idea about some hidden gold into their heads;
so they began to beat Grisha to make him tell them the hiding-
place. At the first fist-blow which landed on his face, Grisha
shook his head like a boxer who has been hit, and said quietly:
"Take me outside. Not in front of my son." They were the
only words he spoke during the whole scene, and his last ones
as far as Fedya was concerned. It seemed to have a certain
effect on the soldiers, who probably also had sons. They kicked
him in the shins and genitals, but without much conviction.
Grisha stood with his two feet planted on the floor and his eyes
planted in his son's, showing neither pain nor anger; he had
always treated Fedya as if he were grown-up and the message
of his eyes was addressed to a grown-up. One of the soldiers,
after swearing about the gold, hit him over the skull with his
riflebutt. Now Grisha collapsed; but he fell slowly and carefully, first on to his knees as his legs gave way, then, after a
last, hard look at the boy, his eyes closed and his body, relaxing with dignity, came to lie sideways on the floor. The
soldiers stood for a while undecided, then dragged him out of
the room by the rope. Grisha's head lolled on his shoulder; he
seemed peacefully asleep.

The next day Fedya's mother had a miscarriage. An old
Tartar woman in a black veil looked after her, while Fedya was
given shelter by some neighbours, who had six children and did
not mind taking in a seventh. The children all slept in a heap
on the mud-floor, Fedya next to a girl of twelve, who taught
him various love-plays which he found almost as pleasurable as
munching rachat locum. The second or third night he was
woken up and taken to his mother who was dying of an infection. She did not recognise him and she looked so changed
and ugly with her grey, sunken face and hollow temples, that
he was more shocked than pained. At the Tartar woman's
bidding he kissed her reluctantly on her wet forehead, then he
was taken back to the neighbours' room where his girl friend
clasped her arms round him in passion and pity; he fell asleep,
pressed against her body, warm and comforted. The next day

Tamar died; the pattern of her life had been a faithful rep-
etition of her mother's who had also been called Tamar and
had also died in puerperal fever, like countless other Tamars
before her.

Fedya's fate, too, was a rather average fate for a proletarian
child in those latitudes during the years of the Revolution and
Civil War. He was luckier though than the other waifs and
strays whom the Great Change spouted out by the million all
over that vast continent as the mud-volcanoes spouted their
bubbling refuse over the oilfields. He did not catch syphilis,
thieved only as an amateur, and had a girl-friend who loved
and mothered him. He was rescued a few months later by his
grandfather Arin, who had managed to sell the shop just before
Armenia attacked Georgia and the Georgians in Tiflis started
killing the Armenians in the bazaar. Arin had come to fetch
his grandson and take him away, far to the North; the Kaukasus had proved to be still too near to Urfa, and the memories
of Urfa had caught up with him again. The rancour, greed
and sheer stupidity of the unvanquished monkey had now
swallowed his second family; out of the profuse seed of his
loins Fedya alone survived; he decided to take him to the
fairyland which had first put the monkey to retreat. He had
only seen Fedya once before, then still an infant at his mother's
breast; and he was surprised, but not displeased to find that the
child had taken so completely after its father. There was not a
trace of his Armenian ancestors in him, nor of the Georgian
from his Grandfather Niko's side; Asia seemed to have re-
treated from his blood, as it had from the blood of Grisha's
forebears—except for a slight relic, in the slant of his eyes,
of some remote Tartar admixture.

Fedya took at once to the tall old man with the dignified
stoop, the mahorka smell and the sparkling, close-set eyes under the white scraggy brows. But for his big feet and callous
cobbler's hands, Arin would have looked like an aristocrat.
They set out on their long journey to the capital in a spirit of
high adventure; Fedya forgot even to say goodbye to his sleep-
mate. Like his grandfather and unlike his mother, he could
love with great passion, but could forget just as quickly and
completely; he had the precious gift of being able to cut his
losses almost automatically. Even the last scene with his father
he only remembered rarely; it was not a memory for every-
day use, and too weighty to remain floating on the surface of
his thoughts. It was enough to know that in those moments

when he had stood unflinchingly his father's gaze and let his
message get into him, he had accepted a covenant more bind-
ing than any vow of a religious order.

The journey took them several months. They travelled by
oxcarts, trains, on foot, and on soldiers' wagons, traversing
several fronts. They had no travel-papers; when asked their
purpose and destination, Arin gave invariably the same answer: "I am an old man from Urfa and this orphan is my
grandchild." Once or twice they were taken for spies and the
soldiers threatened Arin to shoot or hang him; but he pretended to be feebleminded, repeated "I am an old man from
Urfa and this orphan is my grandchild," until some officer or
Commissar, impressed by the old man's dignity and reluctant
to have the child on his hands, told them to beat it. But as a
rule the soldiers gave them a meal or at least some bread,
sometimes they were also offered a few kopecks which Arin
refused. Fedya was rarely frightened, and as they progressed
deeper into the territory held by the Armies of the Revolution,
he lost the last trace of apprehension and asked for food and
shelter as their due; he knew that he was now among his
father's friends. Once they were taken before a high-ranking
Commissar, who had the same quiet directness of speech and
simplicity of manner as the men who had come to the room
in Baku. He asked Arin a few questions but the old man only
repeated his stock-phrase; so the Commissar turned to Fedya
and said to him, as if they were old friends: "Tell your grandfather to stop this fooling." Fedya said without hesitation: "If
he hadn't been fooling we would both have been killed like
. . . so now he's got into the habit." "Killed like who?" asked
the Commissar. Feyda looked at him for a second, hesitated,
then he said with an angry sternness: "Like my father."
"Where was your father killed?" "In the Black Town in Baka."
"What was his name?" Fedya said it. The Commissar looked
at him curiously. "Mention the names of some of your father's
friends." Fedya named, always in the same stern, hard voice,
the lawyer, the doctor and the opera singer. "So you are really
Gregor Nikitin's son?" said the Commissar, looking at him
even more curiously. Feyda, who found this question superfluous, said nothing. "He is an orphan and I am an old man
from Urfa," said Arin, worried about the outcome of all this.
The Commissar stared hard at Fedya, who returned his gaze
until the Commissar began to smile at last. "Do you know that
your father was a great hero of the Revolution and that hi

name will be famous in history?" "No," said Fedya, "he was a foreman at the Nobel refinery in Baku."

They arrived in Moscow in the spring of 1920, when Fedya was eight.

5

WITCHES' SABBATH

WHEN Hydie was told that Julien Delattre had rung up and left his telephone number, she called him back at once. Last night she had felt no desire ever to see him or the other members of the triumvirate again. But nowadays she could not refuse an invitation, particularly from a new acquaintance. The lurking hope of the unexpected and the fear of missing the real thing just round the corner drove her on; so she rushed to parties and receptions as the incurable go from one quack doctor to another.

Julien said something vaguely apologetic about last night, then asked whether he could take her out for dinner and afterwards to a "very funny place." He spoke to her in English, as he had done the night before in the taxi, and again his careful pronunciation over the telephone reminded her vaguely of Sister Boutillot.

"What kind of a funny place?" she asked cautiously.

"Oh—a kind of witches' sabbath; very drôle indeed."

"I am rather fed up with naughty nightclubs."

"Nightclub? But my dear, I propose to take you to the night-session of the Rally for Peace and Progress."

She thought the "my dear" was somewhat premature, put it down to his being French, and accepted. They had a very good dinner in a restaurant which looked cheap and was expensive, frequented by corpulent, middle-aged bourgeois couples who looked poor and were rich. At the table next to theirs one of these couples was eating away with grim concentration. The man looked like a prosperous butcher in his Sunday-best, but he had a pearl in his necktie and gold cuff-links, so he was probably a minor industrialist or at least an *avocat*. He had his napkin tucked into his collar, and during three courses had not said a word to his wife. The wife was also in black; her improbably huge breasts were pressed up-

wards by the tight corset like two balloons; she could almost
rest her chin on them. The faces of both were flushed dark;
the woman occasionally dabbed her moist upper-lip with her
napkin, and the man uttered between courses a whistling sound
by sucking at the bits of food stuck between his teeth; otherwise they ate and drank in complete silence.

"Look at them," said Julien, his eyes twitching in a nervous
tic. "This is our bourgeoisie, the backbone of France, the true,
honest-to-God middle-middle class. Once they were called the
Third Estate, their ancestors stormed the Bastille, they gave
the world the Rights of Man and heralded in the age of
Liberalism. It's only a century and a half since all that happened, barely five generations; I would bet that some great-
grandfather of the character behind you beat the drum in the
Battle of Valmy. And now look at them—do they not remind
you of the unhappy companions of Odysseus who were turned
into pigs after eating a porridge of barley meal and yellow
honey on the Island of Aeaea?"

The man with the tucked-in napkin wiped the rest of the
gravy from his plate with a piece of bread, swilled it down
with a gulp of wine, wiped his lips with a napkin and resumed
the sucking of his hollow tooth, waiting for the salad. His wife
spoke the first words in half an hour. She said, "It is hot here."
The man gave no answer; he extracted, with thumb and index
finger, a fibre of meat which had been stuck between his teeth,
held it up to look at it, and stuck it on his napkin.

"We didn't do Greek at school," said Hydie. "What happened to Odysseus' shipmates?"

"Odysseus saved them by the use of a little magic, and after
rushing Circe with his sword. In other words he made a revolution to get his companions back into human shape. It was
perhaps the only revolution which ever succeeded in doing
that. But it is true that he had some help from the gods, so he
did not have to write odes to the Cheka. And he came through
it unscathed . . ."

Julien was, as always, sitting in profile to her with only the
good half of his face showing. Hydie would have liked to tell
him that it was silly of him to mind about the scar—which in
fact she hardly noticed any longer—but he seemed so tense
and bitter that her courage failed her. Instead she asked:

"What gave you the initial push—to start on your odyssey, I
mean?"

Julien emptied his glass and lit a cigarette. "The first time I had this experience that the people around me suddenly lost their human shape was at my grandmother's funeral. It was like a stroke of magic. A moment before it happened I was a normal boy of thirteen, sitting at the rear end of the long table at the funeral meal. The next moment all the uncles, aunts, cousins and in-laws had ceased to look as they always did and were turned into an assembly of strange beings with flushed faces, pigs' eyes, gurgling or squeaking voices. It did not last long, but the experience repeated itself later on various occasions . . ."

He paused, the cigarette stuck to his upper lip, and Hydie thought that Julien had probably never been "a normal boy of thirteen." He must have been chipped and damaged long before he acquired his limp and his scar. His tough, slangy way of talking was a pathetically transparent disguise for his vulnerability; he was one of those predestined to become a target for all slings and arrows, like herself. That was why she felt so much at home with Julien, and why she would never go to bed with Julien; it would be like incest. But Julien would of course think it was because of the limp and the scar . . .

With one eye closed, and the extinct cigarette between his lips aimed at her like the barrel of a gun, Julien continued:

"The point of the story is that this grandmother of mine died a grotesque death after a grotesque life and that everybody including myself knew it, yet pretended not to know it. My family comes from the Landes, that pious and tradition-bound country south of Bordeaux where more women poison their husbands with arsenic and get away with it than in any other part of the world. My grandmother was one of the richest and most avaricious women in that country. She owned acres of a famous vineyard, and a pottery. The workers in the pottery—men, women and children—slept in a crowded dormitory as was the custom in those days. That dormitory was equipped with an ingenious contraption of her own design. It consisted of tiers of wooden planks which served in lieu of pillows. These planks were connected by a system of ropes and pulleys with a cord that hung over my grandmother's bed. Every morning at 4:30 she pulled this cord which caused all the headprops in the dormitory to collapse. . . . You look incredulous. Read the chapter on child-labour in 'Das Kapital', of Engels' 'Condition of the Working Classes in England.' Of course they refer to conditions at the beginning of the nineteenth century. But France has always been lagging a few decades behind, and my grandmother, as I said, died at the age of ninety."

He lit a fresh cigarette and smiled at her with the good half of his face.

"My father was the youngest of her seven sons. At twenty-two, he became secretly engaged to my mother, but my grandmother opposed the marriage because we were a wine-growing family and my mother's a wheat-growing family, which is considered socially inferior in the Landes. For fourteen years the old woman succeeded in preventing the marriage by the threat of cutting my father off without a penny. My mother was thirty-three when she came into her own inheritance and thus romance could triumph over money. But to the day of her death my grandmother never spoke a word to her . . ."

Outside in the street, newsboys with shrill voices were calling out the special late edition of the evening paper. The man at the next table asked morosely for the bill.

"You haven't yet told me how your sweet old granny died," said Hydie.

"The roof of her house had to be mended," said Julien. "When the tiler sent in his bill, my grandmother thought that he had cheated her and insisted on climbing on a ladder to the roof to check the number of tiles he had replaced. When she reached the top of the ladder she fell off and broke her neck, to everybody's relief."

He paused.

"Admittedly she was an extreme case, and yet typical. If you were to probe into the past of the high-bosomed *bourgeoise* behind you, you would come upon a number of similar stories. I shall never forget those hot June days of 1940, when a hundred thousand families took to the roads before the German advance, and our honest farmers watched the stream of refugees pass by and offered them water at one franc the glass. . . . Greed, avarice and selfishness have turned half of this country into pigs, though the hypocrites pretend that they are still human. No wonder that the other half want to stick their knives into them to get at the bacon. Nor should you be surprised that the offspring of this respectable bourgeoisie writes odes to the Cheka. My generation turned to Marx as one swallows acid drops to fight one's nausea."

One of the newsboys had come in and was making the round of the table. Most of the placid diners bought a paper, threw a glance at the heavy, front-page headline, sighed and turned with redoubled application to their plates. The waiters, while serving them, glanced at the paper over the guests' shoulders, and their expressions became reserved, inscrutable. A hushed atmosphere descended on the restaurant, as in the presence of a corpse. The patronne behind the counter dabbed at her eyes and fiddled with the wireless in search of the news, but her husband told her sternly to shut up and swallowed a half-glass of vin ordinaire with an expression of profound disgust. Julien bought all the papers and scanned through them with half-closed eyes, cigarette stuck to his lip. "What does it say?" asked Hydie.

"Just another crisis," said Julien. "It seems that the Free Commonwealth is on the point of swallowing another rabbit. Your government has declared its particular sympathies for this particular rabbit, and that anyway it can't stand the smell of rabbit-stew any longer. . . . Why do you look so conventionally depressed? You too must have this secret longing that it should be over and done with. We all are affected by the nostalgia for the apocalypse . . ."

"The people at the other tables don't seem to have it," said Hydie.

"Oh, yes! Otherwise they would not be here placidly chewing at this moment. Don't underestimate the subtle cunning of the death-wish: Thanatos has just as many disguises as Eros. . . . And now it is time for our witches' sabbath."

They took a taxi and drove off towards the Velodrome, a great indoor stadium built for bicycle racing which now served mainly to accommodate political mass-meetings. As they approached the building, the aspect of the streets gradually changed. Fleets of police vans stood discreetly parked at strategic corners, small crowds were arguing in front of cafés, and a steady stream was still heading, despite the late hour, towards the Velodrome—while at other street-corners people were still dancing indefatigably to the sound of accordions or wireless loudspeakers, in honour of Bastille Day. Curiously enough, the dancers—mostly sales-girls partnered by shop assistants, with a sprinkling of older couples—bore an expression of grim determination, whereas in the other crowd walking toward the Rally, the faces looked fresh and eager.

The nearer the taxi approached their destination, the more the temperature in the streets seemed to rise. As they turned a corner they saw two people fighting on the kerb. One of them fell; some of the bystanders joined in and started kicking and trampling the fallen man. Hydie turned pale, and Julien shouted at the driver to stop; but the driver accelerated. Julien tried to open the door to jump out, but the driver, reaching back with one hand, held the doorhandle tight from outside and accelerated even more, hooting ruthlessly. They turned another corner and saw a group of policemen chatting near a public urinal. The driver pulled up near them. "There is a row on down there," he told them indifferently. "Where?" asked one of the policemen. "Round the corner, on the Boulevard." "Let them bash their heads in and mind your own business," said the policeman. The driver shrugged and jammed the gear in. Hydie tried to turn down the window to argue with the policemen, but Julien gripped her arm and put his hand across her mouth.

A hundred yards farther down the street he let go of her. "You coward," she said breathlessly. Her mouth was full of the sharp tobacco taste of his hand. He looked at her ironically:

"If you had started arguing with the cops, they would have taken you to the *Commissariat*, would have written down the dates of birth of all your four grandparents, and released you two or three hours later with polite apologies—all of which wouldn't have helped our friend in the gutter but would have made you miss the witches' sabbath."

He rubbed the lipstick mark from his palm after having sniffed at it, and Hydie was reminded of the blood trickling down Fedya's nose; in the last twenty-four hours she seemed to be fated to enter into the most unexpected physical contacts with men. She became uncomfortably conscious of Julien's bodily presence; but he had withdrawn into his corner of the cab, suddenly unattainable.

A little farther they found the street blocked by cars and several long queues of people slowly moving towards the Velodrome's entrance-gates. As Julien paid off the taxi, the driver said:

"If I were you, I would rather take the young lady to a cinema."

"My friend," said Julien, "you are old-fashioned. Nothing excites a woman more than displays of mass-passion."

"That's a point of view," said the driver. "One lives and learns."

They by-passed the queues and, Julien waving a couple of orange-coloured press-cards, pushed their way towards the main entrance. The façade of the building was protected by a chain of policemen, and behind them a score of men with sandwich-boards round their necks picketed the entrance. The pickets were walking slowly up and down, booed by the crowd on the other side of the police cordon. One of them was Boris; gaunt and grim, he stood leaning with his back against the wall and looking at the crowd with bored contempt. On the board round his chest one could see the garish picture of a kneeling man with his hands tied behind his back, and another man in uniform firing a revolver into the nape of his neck. Underneath was the inscription: "This is what they have done to my country—if you want yours to share the same fate, join this rally."

As they passed through the entrance, Julien waved to Boris who shouted at them to have good fun. This made the people who were thronging through the gate glance at them with hostility, and Hydie felt a faint shiver along her spine—it was not fear, but a sudden echo of the nameless horror of the days which had followed her expulsion from the convent. She grabbed Julien's arm and pressed her flank against his. He did not seem to notice it and steered her with some ruthlessness across the crowd. With the extinct cigarette butt stuck to his lips, he succeeded in bringing out more than ever the Montmartre-pimp aspect of his face—which, Hydie thought, given their surroundings, was just as well.

They climbed various flights of stairs and followed a labyrinth of corridors marked with arrows in different colours—then, passing through a padded door, suddenly found themselves high up on a gallery inside the dark, vast, amphitheatral hall. Around and underneath them a crowd of some fifty thousand people breathed and stirred, filling the enormous space with its heat, smell and pulsations. Several searchlights were concentrated on the platform; their beams traversed the hall in a criss-cross pattern high above the heads of the crowd as during a trapeze act in a circus-tent. As they edged their way towards their seats, Hydie's eyes became adapted to the semi-darkness and she was able to distinguish the forest of heads underneath them, craning forward like the kneeling victim on Boris' poster waiting for the bullet. But as her eyes turned to the brightly lit platform, the crowd dissolved again into shapeless, anonymous darkness.

A huge, handsome American Negro was talking on the platform in front of the microphone, denouncing the ignominies

inflicted on his race. Over his head, big flashing streamers
vaunted the boons of peace, disarmament and democracy, and
denounced the pests of imperialism, warmongering and the
aggressive provocations of the diabolical Rabbit State. On a
dais, behind the speaker's pulpit and under the streamers, sat
the members of the Committee, among them Fedya Nikitin in
his blue party suit. One could see, even at this distance, the
handsome prognathous shape of his face and the concavity in
his temples.

"Do you know him?" asked Hydie. The booming of the
Negro's voice, amplified by a score of loudspeakers, made
conversation in a low voice possible; it was not even necessary
to whisper. In fact a good part of the audience kept up a
half-voiced chatter which warmed the hall with its gentle,
humming vibration.

"The Negro? He is a film star with a guilt complex. All film
stars are becoming rabid revolutionaries; they sell syrup and
dream of prussic acid to redress the balance."

"I meant whether you know that man in the blue suit—the
third from the left on the platform."

"Nikitin? Oh, he is the Commonwealth's cultural something
or other."

"Your friend Boris said he is a spy," said Hydie, suddenly
remembering Boris' remarks at Monsieur Anatole's, which
curiously enough she had completely forgotten up to that
moment.

Julien shrugged. "In Boris' eyes everybody from over there
is a spy."

"Who are the others? And why do you call this a witches'
sabbath? It is all most respectable and civilised."

"That's the whole point. Most of the people here don't
know that they are bewitched. Take the first from the left on
the platform, the huge untidy man with the shaggy hair who
seems half asleep. That is Professor Edwards—Lord Edwards
—the physicist. He is also an amateur weight-lifting champion
and an eccentric; his friends call him Hercules the Atom-
Smasher. The English love their cranks and often mistake ec-
centricity for genius—but in his day Edwards was really quite
a good physicist. Only he cannot give up, even at fifty-five
playing the naughty little boy. He joined the Movement thirty
years ago, mainly because for an English aristocrat it was the
naughtiest thing he could think of. Then gradually the witch-
craft began to work on him . . ."

In fact, Lord Edwards in his young days had made an original contribution to Lemaître's theory of the expanding universe. But shortly afterwards the Central Committee of the Commonwealth decreed that the universe was not expanding, and that the whole theory was a fabrication of bourgeois scientists reflecting the imperialist drive for the conquest of new markets. The "hyenas of expansionist cosmology" were duly purged and Edwards, though he lived safely in England and had nothing to fear, published a book in which he proved that the universe was in peaceful equilibrium, without ever intending to expand. After the second world war, when the Commonwealth began to incorporate the neighbouring republics and to spread its frontiers towards East and West, the Central Committee decided that the universe was expanding after all, and that the theory of a static universe was a fabrication of bourgeois science, reflecting the stagnant decay of capitalist economy. After some twenty million factory workers and collective farmers had sent in resolutions calling for death to the "stagnationist vermin," Edwards published another book proving that the universe was indeed expanding, had always been expanding and would go on expanding *ad infinitum.*

At the present moment, Edwards seemed to be sound asleep. Julien touched Hydie's elbow:

"Look at the sweet innocence of his smile. If you told him that he is bewitched in the twentieth century . . ."

The Negro was on the point of finishing his speech. His two arms were raised above his head, with hands clasped; his voice vibrated with emotion. One could hear several women sobbing; somebody in the audience asked in a shrill voice: "How many?"

The Negro, unaccustomed to interruption, asked back naïvely: "How many what?"

The high-pitched voice shrilled across the vast hall:

"How many Negroes were lynched this year?"

The audience began to hiss half-heartedly, unable to decide whether the interrupter was friend or foe. The Negro star looked helplessly at the chairman. The chairman, a middle-aged French poet with the face of a ravaged cherub, rose and said:

"It is not numbers that matter, but the barbarous mentality which inspires these acts. Even if only a single one of our Negro brethren were killed in a year, it would be an indelible blot on our civilisation."

The audience burst into applause, but it was pierced by the same shrill voice as before:

"What about the two million Mordavians deported this year to the salt mines?"

He was a foe. A single roar rose from the audience, so unanimous and prolonged that it covered the heckler's screams, who had his face bashed in and was being thrown out of the door. Hercules woke from his slumbers and, seeing the scuffle, pushed the sleeve up his right arm and shook his fist at the foe with a comic grimace. The crowd's indignation changed into merriment; a wave of warm fraternal feeling swept through the hall. *"C'est un original, le camarade Anglais,"* a voice said near Hydie. The chairman turned to Edwards and said with a roguish smile: "We need your brains, Professor, not your fists. Our Peace Troopers are taking care of provocations—here and everywhere else. . . ." Lord Edwards rolled his sleeves down with a shrug of mock disappointment. There was renewed laughter and applause.

The Negro star was followed by the famous French philosopher, Professor Pontieux. He was tall and gawky and seemed unsure of himself. He placed the text of his speech before him on the lectern—it was a bulky sheaf of papers which the other speakers on the platform eyed with some apprehension—adjusted his glasses and began:

"Let me be perfectly frank with you. I am not a member of the Party . . ."

He paused, and to everybody's surprise the chairman began to clap, looking sternly at the audience. The audience joined in, somewhat half-heartedly. The Professor seemed moved. "Thank you," he said. "Your friendly homage is a proof to me of that broad-minded tolerance which is a specific feature of all progressive revolutionary movements in the course of history."

"Who on earth is this?" asked Hydie.

"He is a Professor of Philosophy. He can prove everything he believes, and he believes everything he can prove."

Pontieux had begun to expound the principles of neo-nihilism, a philosophy which he had launched in his famous work "Negation and Position," and which had been the fashionable craze after the second world war. There had been neo-nihilistic plays, neo-nihilistic night clubs and neo-nihilistic crimes— among them the famous case of Duval, a colour-blind upholsterer in Ménilmontant who had cut the throats of his wife and three children and had countered the question why he had committed the crime with the classic answer: "Why not?" This led to the splitting off of a radical wing of neo-nihilists who called themselves the "Whynot-ists" and founded a rival night club which, mainly thanks to a trio of attractive singers called the "Why-not-Sisters," captured the lion's share of the intellectually minded American tourists. Professor Pontieux was horrified by these developments; for he was a sincere moralist, a dialectician and a believer in the revolutionary mission of the Proletariat—all of which, as he did not tire of explaining in a stream of books and pamphlets, was the true essence of neo-nihilistic philosophy.

Blinking in the glare of the searchlights, Pontieux went on to define his attitude towards the universal crisis of values. He spoke haltingly, with obvious sincerity, his words punctuated by the jerky gestures of the timid when under the pressure of a strong emotion. The major part of what he said was couched in negative propositions. He was not, as he had already taken the liberty of pointing out, a member of the Party. As a humanist he was, needless to say, opposed to all restrictions of individual liberty. But this did not mean that the revolutionary process, which represented the dynamic will of the masses, should be thwarted by rigid legalistic concepts. He did not believe that the Commonwealth of Freedomloving People had solved all its problems and become an earthly paradise. But it was equally undeniable that it was an expression of History's groping progress towards a new form of society, whence it followed that those who opposed this progress were siding with the forces of reaction and preparing the way for conflict and war—the worst crime against humanity . . .

At this point Pontieux, who had lost his only son during the last war, was overcome by a slight trembling of his chin; he seemed to get lost in his text, turned a page, and declared, twice hitting the desk with his fist and upsetting the waterglass: "Man is only true to himself when he surpasses the limitations inherent in his nature."

He paused, the chairman clapped, and still clapping, walked to the lectern and set the water-glass right. There was a faint response from the audience, and Pontieux went on to explain that only in a planned society could man surpass his own limitations through the voluntary acceptance of the necessary curtailments of his freedom. As often as not, history realised its aims by the negation of its own negations. Thus in certain circumstances, democracy may manifest itself under the outward forms of a dictatorship, whereas in another situation dictatorship may appear under the guise of democracy. It must also be borne in mind that the rejection of nationalism did not imply the acceptance of cosmopolitanism. He declared himself in favour of world government, but against any restriction of national sovereignty. He condemned arbitrary arrests and imprisonment without trial, but recognised the right of the forces of progress to eliminate ruthlessly the exponents of reaction. He admitted being a descendant of the age of enlightenment, who held that religion was a dangerous drug for the people, and he praised the Freedomloving Commonwealth for its encouragement of religious observance for all races and creeds. He admitted being an ardent advocate of universal disarmament, but rejected any interference with the transformation of the countries of progress into powerful arsenals of peace. After some variations on this theme, he welcomed the victorious advance of the armies of peace in various parts of the world, thanked the Rally for the patient hearing they had given to his admittedly heretic remarks, and wished them good luck for their work in the interest of Peace, Freedom and Progress.

There was strong applause, and several members of the Committee shook hands with Pontieux, who hunched his shoulders modestly, explaining that what he had said was merely an application of the neo-nihilist methods.

The chairman now advanced to the lectern and said that before he called on the next speaker, he wished to make an important announcement. The glad tidings had just reached the Rally that all transport workers of the Paris area had gone on strike to demonstrate their solidarity with the Freedomloving Commonwealth, threatened by the provocations of the Rabbit State. He hoped, the chairman added, that in this momentous hour, members of the Rally would be prepared for the small sacrifice of walking home on foot because of the strike; and that they would all stay on to listen to the remaining speakers. He now had the pleasure of calling on Mademoiselle Tissier, member of the Executive Committee of the Progressive School Teachers' Federation and author of the three-volume classic "The Commonwealth of Freedomloving People," who had just returned from a short trip to that country.

There was stormy applause which, however, did not entirely cover the noise of people hurriedly scuffing for the doors. About one-third of the audience left under the disapproving murmur of the rest. Mademoiselle Tissier was a frail little woman with large youthful eyes in a wrinkled face; she could easily have passed, Hydie thought, as one of the sisters in the convent school. Her smile was gentle and disarming. As the audience kept hissing at those who left, she lifted her hand and said in a clear, ringing voice: "Be patient, comrades. Those who are leaving have probably a long way to go home."

"At last a sensible woman," said Hydie.

When the audience had settled down again, Mademoiselle Tissier began to speak. She spoke simply and modestly. This had been her fifth visit to the Freedomloving Commonwealth, she explained, unfortunately a rather short trip—and the first trip on which she had to go alone. . . . A hush fell upon the crowd, followed by a low sympathetic murmur. Everybody understood the allusion: on all her previous journeys, Mademoiselle Tissier had been accompanied by her colleague, Pierre Charbon, co-author of the great book and companion of her life, who had died a few months ago. He had been a gentle, scholarly man, almost as small and frail as Mademoiselle Tissier herself; they had been inseparable and their devotion to each other, together with the fact that they had refused on principle to marry and had lived in third sin for almost fifty years, had become part of the revolutionary folklore, a soothing contrast to the bloody memories of Danton, Blanqui and Charlotte Corday.

Yes, said Mademoiselle Tissier, it had been a shorter trip than planned, and she had no hesitation in explaining why. The people of the Freedomloving Commonwealth were fully conscious of the grave menace which threatened them. They knew that powerful and evil men abroad were conspiring to bring about the miseries of another war. They knew that spies and conspirators crossed their frontiers day after day, often disguised as friends of their cause; so it was only natural that they had developed a healthy distrust of all foreigners, regardless of the intentions which the latter professed. She had understood this at once on her arrival and had felt that just at this moment her visit was inopportune; only an enemy of the Commonwealth could have taken umbrage because his government was exercising the necessary precautions to protect the people. So, after a frank and comradely talk with the authorities and in full agreement with them, she had decided to cut the extensive journey she had originally planned to a short stay in the capital. Nevertheless she had had the opportunity of visiting the new tractor factory and several kindergartens and schools; and she could assure her listeners that never had she seen harder working men and nicer, better cared for children in any country under the sun. She could also assure them on her word—and here that young, disarming smile began to play in the corner of her lips—that notwithstanding certain newspaper reports, she had seen no people being carried off by sinister officers of the State Police, nor gangs of forced labourers clanging their chains in the streets and mournfully singing the Volga Boatmen's Song!

Mademoiselle Tissier waited smilingly until the laughter subsided, then went on telling her audience that notwithstanding her slight disappointment about the shortening of her visit, she had nevertheless gone through a thrilling adventure which she wouldn't have missed for anything on earth. Believe it or not, she had been arrested as a spy . . . ! She paused, gently chuckling at the recollection, and the audience roared with laughter. But really, she continued, it was true! It had happened this way. Being hopelessly absent-minded and muddle-headed, she had managed, on leaving for home, to get separated in the crowd at the railway station from her guide, translator and guardian angel, whom the Government in their kindness had put at her disposal. So there she found herself like a lost sheep alone at the railway station, pushed and buffeted about by the crowd, and what a crowd! People in the Freedomloving Commonwealth did not behave in railway stations like the staid French bourgeois—they all yelled and pushed and kicked at one another like happy children—it was a sign of the exuberant vitality of a healthy nation. So she had first lost her suitcase, next her hat, and before she knew what was happening to her, she was spotted as a foreigner and taken into custody by two huge, stern, spotlessly clean officers of the police. Of course she had tried to explain, but there was nobody to translate, and her passport did not impress them either. Frankly, Mademoiselle Tissier went on in a more serious voice, if she had the good luck to be a citizen of the Commonwealth, she would see no reason to trust a person showing a passport of this country. . . . There was loud applause at this, and Mademoiselle Tissier, reverting to her former tone of impish humour, told the audience how she had been taken to a police station, then to a second one, and finally to the huge, modern Central Prison Building where, despite her gentle protests, nobody took any notice of her for three days. Then at last she was taken to a clean, friendly, modern room with electric ventilation, where a very polite officer in a spotless uniform, who spoke excellent French, told her that she had better confess as the authorities knew everything about her and had a whole file of proofs that she was a spy!

Again the audience roared with laughter, and Mademoiselle Tissier went on to tell how she had tried to explain that there must be some confusion of identity, and how the nice officer got quite angry because of her muddle-headed way of explaining things, and how during three long interrogations, she got so rattled that she no longer knew whether she was a boy or a girl, and almost began to believe that she really was a spy!

And now, said Mademoiselle Tissier, came the point of her story, and the reason why she had thought it worth telling at all. That nice officer took his duty very seriously as was only natural in times like this, so he went on and on asking her questions until she actually went to sleep and had to be repeatedly woken up feeling very ashamed of herself. But in the end, as she kept denying that she was a spy, they led her back to her cell—by the way, a nice, hygienic, spotlessly clean cell which she had all to herself. And then what happened? Was she tortured, beaten, pressed into a chain-gang for having refused to confess? Well, she was sorry to disappoint the expectations of sensation-hungry journalists who might or might not be present in the audience—the audience booed and everybody turned his neck, suspecting the presence of a hostile intruder behind them—she was sorry, Mademoiselle Tissier repeated, that her story ended in an anti-climax, but the fact was that instead of being drawn and quartered in the "horrible torture chambers of the State Police" (here Mademoiselle Tissier actually drew the ironic inverted commas with her index finger in the air)—she was released the next day and, simply and without further ado, conducted to the railway station. It was just as simple as that.

And the moral of her thrilling adventure? First, that the people of the Free Commonwealth kept a good watch over their country and that all evil schemers who tried to smuggle in discontent and sabotage would be sure to get caught and to get a good rap on their fingers, no doubt about it! Secondly, the fact of having actually seen a Free Commonweath prison from inside had put Mademoiselle Tissier in a position to denounce from first hand experience all infamous allegations —and here her small voice actually shook with anger—about torture, deportations, and the rest. Thirdly and finally, here was direct proof that though people might occasionally get arrested by mistake, they had nothing to fear if they were innocent; all they had to do was to wait patiently until the truth came out. If on the other hand a person, high or low, confessed to his crimes, he did it because he was really guilty and ready to take his punishment. . . .

There was renewed applause, though somewhat hesitant and rather fainter than before.

Mademoiselle Tissier modestly resumed her seat next to Lord Edwards, who patted her back with such Herculean heartiness that it looked as if he would break her collar bone. The chairman now announced the next speaker: Leo Nikolayevich Leontiev, the celebrated Free Commonwealth author, winner of several Academy awards, owner of the decoration for Heroes of Culture, recently promoted to the honorary title Joy of the People and presented with a swimming pool by the nations.

Leontiev was a square, heavy man of rather military bearing with a low forehead, greying, bushy eyebrows and deep furrows in his face. As he marched to the lectern, accepting the cheers of the audience with a stern, unsmiling look, nobody could fail to realise that he was in the presence of a true Hero of Culture from a country where culture was treated in dead earnest, stripped of all decadent frivolity and escapist playfulness; where all ivory towers had been dynamited and razed to the ground like the strongholds of robber barons, and poets and novelists had become soldiers of culture— well disciplined, clean-minded, ready to turn the flame-throwers of their inspiration on any objective at the bugle's call.

Hero of Culture and Joy of the People Leo Nikolayevich Leontiev was at the present moment probably the most important commander on the literary front. His Orders of the Day appeared every Friday in heavy print on the front page of the journal "Freedom and Culture." His word decided who among the rank and file should be raised and who should be lowered, who should be pulped and who printed on Japan paper. He also presided at the periodical courts-martial at which those convicted of formalism, neo-Kantionism, titrot- skism, veritism and whatnotism were given their deserved punishment. No wonder that he was loved and respected not only by the writers of the Freedomloving Commonwealth, but also among those outside its frontiers who adhered to the Movement. These were from time to time court-martialled in absentia, but as the sentence could not be enforced, they were as a rule let off lightly after some symbolic act of contrition and penance.

Having announced Leontiev through the microphone, the chairman, Emile Navarin, did not leave the lectern but waited for the speaker and shook him warmly by the hand. At this moment, as if by a prearranged signal, the flash-bulbs of all the photographers went off. The French poet and the Commonwealth hero formed a very moving scene as they stood hand in hand on the platform—the former with his ravaged cherub's smile, the latter looking with grim distaste at Navarin's hand gripping his own and refusing to let go until the bulbs had flashed a second time. The pictures were sure to create a sensation because, as the initiated knew, Navarin was just passing through a rather difficult period. Only a few days ago, in last Friday's issue of "Freedom and Culture," Leontiev had mildly rebuked the French poet by calling him a decadent vermin who had wormed his way into the Movement by systematic double-dealing and deception. Now, however, once the photographs just taken were released, it would become obvious to everybody that the period of his disfavour was over; for even if Leontiev wanted to prohibit their publication, his order would carry no weight with the corrupt press of a country where cultural anarchy reigned.

At last Navarin yielded the rostrum to Leontiev, who took a typescript from his left breast pocket, placed it on the pulpit and was about to start when an orderly laid a note before him. He read it, slightly raised his bushy eyebrows, replaced the typescript by another one from his right-hand breast pocket, and started to read.

If Hydie, influenced by Julien's sarcastic comments, had regarded him up to now as a somewhat ridiculous figure, she changed her mind at once when Leontiev began to read out his paper. His deep, surprisingly soft voice, whose accent reminded her of Fedya's except that it was mellower and more modulated, had a curiously resonant and persuasive quality. At first she only listened to this voice; but when after a while she began to pay attention to what it said, she was even more pleasantly surprised. Leontiev's speech not only stood in amazing contrast to all that had gone before, but if one listened carefully, directly contradicted the previous speakers. There was not a word of abuse against the reactionary governments, no reference to vipers, warmongers and syphilitic flunkeys, not even the usual crack about the "Fearless Sufferers." The theme of the speech was the indestructible common cultural heritage of humanity, the royal road of man's progress towards the outer light and inner self-awareness, whose milestones were Moses and Christ, Spinoza and Galileo, Tolstoy and Sigmund Freud! As he gradually warmed to his audience, Leontiev's face relaxed, lost its martial appearance, and under the bushy eyebrows his glance lit up in a shortsighted, melancholy light.

Navarin had become very pale. He had demanded in his opening speech that the teaching of History in the schools should start with 1917 and that all that went before should be written off as rubbish; and though few people in the audience would remember this or detect any contradiction to Leontiev's line, he knew that, despite the stratagem with the photographers, he would have to spend many months eating his words and strewing ashes on his head. Lord Edwards nodded gravely, and as if by divine inspiration a set of differential equations began unrolling itself before his mind's eye which seemed to prove that after all the universe was stable and did not expand. The Negro looked blank. He had noticed no change of line, for nothing outside the problem of his penalised race was of any interest to him. Professor Pontieux looked slightly puzzled. He was mentally recapitulating his speech to check whether Leontiev's point of view could be fitted into it, and found to his satisfaction that no doubt it could—though he wished he had laid a little more stress on this particular aspect of the question. Only Mademoiselle Tissier seemed completely happy and at ease. She listened to the Hero of Culture with rapt attention: here was authoritative proof, if proof were needed, that the Commonwealth had always pursued a liberal, cosmopolitan, pacifist policy, undeterred by the calumnies of the reactionary mob.

Leontiev ended his speech with a strong condemnation of all aggressive tendencies, whether in the field of politics or culture. "What earthly purpose can it serve for a writer or politician to vilify his cultural heritage, the government and institutions of his own country? If he thinks thereby to further the cause of peace and progress, he is grievously and foolishly mistaken. He may think of himself as a revolutionary while in fact he is an outcast, a traitor to his country—and the Free Commonwealth does not like traitors, either at home or abroad. It resents interference in its own business and refuses to interfere in the business of others. This world of ours is large enough to house nations and social systems of all shades and colours. The task of the artist is to emphasise the common human heritage which unites them all." He ended by describing what he called a personal wish-dream, an International Pantheon of the heroes of culture, past and present, of poets, painters, philosophers and composers; and he proposed that the inscription greeting the visitors to this Pantheon should be:

"Recover hope, ye who enter here."

Leontiev was given a tremendous ovation. The chairman closed the meeting somewhat hastily; and after singing a revolutionary song, the crowd dispersed in very high spirits.

"That means," said Julien, as they walked back towards the Seine in the warm night, carried by the crowd which now moved in a peaceful and contented way, like a broad stream after the rain, "that means that the crisis is over. The Rabbit Republic has been temporarily reprieved, international tension will decrease, and we will all live in peace—at least for the next six months." He spoke with more than ordinary bitterness; even the cigarette dangled lifelessly from his lip.

"How do you know?" asked Hydie.

"Didn't you see the note passed to him, and how after reading it he produced another text from his pocket? He had prepared two versions, as they all do when a crisis is on, and the news that the crisis was over reached him just in time. So tomorrow the busses will run again and everybody will be relieved and happy like a dying patient between two attacks."

"I don't know why you are so bitter," said Hydie. "Whatever you say, this Leontiev was sincere. It was a simple and beautiful speech, and he meant every word of it."

They sat down on the crowded terrace of a café. The floor was littered with confetti and torn paper caps. A few people were still dancing in the street, half dead with fatigue. Their stubborn insistence on getting the last ounce of enjoyment out of Bastille Day was indeed remarkable.

"Of course he meant it," said Julien. "After all he is one of the old guard whose poems were sung by millions during the Revolution. Today he was in good form because for once the line happened to coincide with his convictions. But if that note hadn't arrived in time he would have delivered the other speech without batting an eye; and if the note had arrived in the middle of it he would have changed from one text to the other, again without batting an eye. He could only outlive his generation by becoming a prostitute; what you call his sincerity is the longing of the old whore for the lost days of her virginity."

Hydie wished she were sitting here with Fedya instead of Julien. Fedya was a savage, but oh, how refreshing after the gloom of the Ravens Nevermore. She remembered that tomorrow she would go with Fedya to the Opera, and she flushed with pleasure. This gave her a guilty conscience towards Julien, whose eyebrows had begun to twitch; more than before she felt the vulnerability behind his ironic and deprecatory manner.

"I only meant," she said, "that that longing of the old prostitute is a redeeming feature. As long as she has that, she is not lost—she is in her way even sincere, and you have no right to sneer at that."

"The trouble is you don't know what you are talking about," said Julien irritably; it was the first time that he had been discourteous to her. "You've never had any dealings with prostitutes, either real or political ones. That longing which so impresses you is the cheapest kind of sentimentality, which in no way prevents her from picking your pocket and giving you the clap—and in no way prevents the Hero of Culture from denouncing his colleagues and competitors to the State Police."

"But this has nothing to do with what I mean," said Hydie. "I only mean that you and your friends are probably right in hating them but hatred alone doesn't get you anywhere. This—sentimentality in Leontiev is something which you don't want to see, or if you see it you dismiss it with a puff of your cigarette. But I feel that it makes all the difference. That French poet in the chair was a phoney, but the others—the sweet, silly, old-maidish creature, and Hercules, and even the philosopher—they all have that longing which is genuine. I mean they have faith—however wrong they may be. Perhaps they believe in a mirage—but isn't it better to believe in a mirage than to believe in nothing?"

Julien looked at her coldly, almost with contempt:

"Definitely not. Mirages lead people astray. That's why there are so many skeletons in the desert. Read more history. Its caravan-routes are strewn with the skeletons of people who were thirsting for faith—and their faith made them drink salt water and eat the sand, believing it was the Lord's Supper."

"Oh, what's the use of arguing," said Hydie. "Let's go."

In the taxi she sat huddled in her corner and felt that familiar grip of emptiness and hollowness in her throat. She wanted to say: and what about those who did not even know that thirst? They were in no danger of following a mirage, they were condemned to plod in the desert all their lives without ever seeing a palm and a well—not even an imagined palm, not even an illusory well . . .

Julien and his friends had known the thirst. But they had been offered salt water to quench it—now they couldn't get rid of its bitter taste and only saw the poison in all God's rivers and lakes.

The taxi turned into the Boulevard St. Germain. It was deserted now; Bastille Day was over.

6

A SENTIMENTAL EDUCATION

THE Commissar whom they had met on the road to Moscow had given them a letter of introduction to the authorities in the capital; so, after a while they were given a room, and old Arin was made overseer in a shoemakers' co-operative, and Fedya was sent to school.

The room was in a large flat in the centre of the town, which had formerly belonged to a rich timber-merchant. When the revolution broke out, the merchant and his family had fled abroad and the flat had been parcelled out among people who had distinguished themselves in the service of the cause. There were now twelve families living in the seven rooms, for the larger rooms had been divided by sheets into two, or even three parts. Arin and Fedya had been lucky: they had a tiny former servant's room all to themselves. When they had first entered the room, Fedya had been speechless, and his hard grey eyes had filled with tears; he had never before seen such luxury. Instead of a stamped mudfloor it had parquet flooring; and from the ceiling hung an electric bulb with a paper shade. There was a brass bed, and also a table and a chair, which at night were moved into the corridor to make room for Fedya's mattress on the floor. It took some time until Fedya grasped the unbelievable fact that all this was theirs; then he understood that the Great Change had really come true.

For Arin too their new existence meant fulfilment of a life-long wish: he now had somebody who could read to him. Every night after their dinner of bread, tea and salted herring, old Arin sat down on the foot of the bed, smoking his ma-horka cigarettes, while Fedya sat at the table and read aloud to him. Fortunately, in those early years after the Great Change schoolboys had no home-work to do; it had been abolished, together with all other forms of slavery. The idea was that they should learn not by compulsion but by interest, and only what they wanted to learn; there were no punish-ments, no examinations, no marks and no fixed classes; the children were encouraged to form groups or brigades, and had to work out their own curriculum. After earnest discussions with Grandfather Arin, Fedya, then in his ninth year, decided to devote his school years to the study of the oppressed na-tions and classes. The first books which he read to Arin were works on the persecution of Armenians: Fridtjof Nansen and Pastor Lepsius. Fedya read the text and old Arin illustrated it with stories of what had happened at Urfa, and before; thus History and life became welded into one in Fedya's mind, never to be separated again. Other children learned History as a tale of abstract events in the abstract past; to Fedya, life was part of History, with old Arin, dead Grisha and himself as actors on its stage.

The two books by Nansen and Lepsius became Fedya's bible. About half of what he read remained obscure to him, but there were episodes which stuck forever in his mind. The Russian Tsar had wanted to grab Armenia, but without its stiff-necked people. So he had encouraged the Armenians to revolt against the Turks, while at the same time his Ambas-sador urged the Turks to kill the Armenians. It was all summed up in Prince Rostovsky's classic advice to Abdul Hamid: "Massacrer, Majesté, massacrer . . ."

Thus to Fedya the Tsar, the Sultan, the Pope and the British government became the diabolical members of a conspiracy which had burnt alive Arin's wife and six children. The effect of the books was the more overwhelming because their authors were moved not by hate but by pity. Their sorrowful indictment of the amorality of the great powers and the hypocrisy of the churches, together with the cold language of the documents they quoted, were proof to the child of the utter wickedness of mankind before the Change, and of the necessity to turn the world over as a plough turns over a field. He could not understand why humanity had for so long patiently tolerated a world whose kings were murderers, whose statesmen were liars and whose few rich aristocrats and merchants had made the rest of the people their victims and slaves. But Arin knew the answer: the people had suffered all this because they had been ignorant, illiterate and uncultured. It was Arin's and Fedya's privilege to live at the time of the Great Change when life started all afresh, as it had after the flood.

Life was indeed intoxicating for a boy in the early nineteeen twenties. After the war with Poland was ended, there was soon plenty of food for people who could pay for it. An event called the NEP, about which everybody talked but which neither Arin nor Fedya understood, had made this possible. The small shoemakers' co-operative in which Arin worked made and sold more shoes than ever. They now often had white bread for dinner, and sometimes a piece of sausage with the herring, or a big spoonful of pressed red caviar. Frequently they even had sugar with their tea—a yellow lump which you placed on your tongue; the gulps of hot tea passed over it, and were deliciously sweetened by the time you swallowed them. Fedya now had a pair of boots of real leather, and Arin a pair of steel-rimmed glasses. Once a week they went together to the cinema, to watch uncultured American cowboys shoot each other, or criminal gangs trying to kill a ravishing girl who like a cat had nine lives and who, in the text projected on the screen, had been transformed from a capitalist heiress into a revolutionary heroine. And about once a year, on tickets distributed in rotation by the Trade Unions, they went to the Opera or to the ballet in the Great Theatre. It was a life which only princes had led before the Change.

The school was no less exciting. Fedya could, if he wished, stay at home or loaf in the streets, but mostly he preferred the school. It was one of the best in the Capital, reserved for children whose parents were dignitaries of the Revolution or

had fallen in its service. To be the son of Grisha Nikitin, one
of the martyred Baku Commissars whose name had already
become legend, gave Fedya a position of a certain authority
from the start. At thirteen, he was the leader of a Brigade of
Pioneers which had set themselves the task of revolutionising
botanics by renaming all plants, as the French Revolution had
renamed the months of the calendar. The joint council of
pupils and teachers which ran the school enthusiastically approved of the plan, and asked the teacher of History to help
the Brigade to find appropriate names. Thus the oak became
"Pillar-tree of the Revolution," the weeping willow "Tree of
Liberal Decadence," flowers were called after revolutionary
heroes and all weeds were to be collectively known as "bourgeois parasite plants." After a few weeks however the attempt
had to be abandoned because there were more plants than
names they could think of. The Pioneer group accused the
teacher of History, who was a member of the pre-revolutionary intelligentsia, of sabotage; but before he could be tried,
the old man died of pneumonia, a victim of the difficulties on
the fuel distribution front.

Gradually, the remainder of the old teachers resigned, or
were dismissed, or simply did not dare to show up because
they had been beaten up by their pupils. They were replaced
by teachers of a new type: members of the Party, or of the
Komsomol, who had followed the Government's urgent call
for the formation of new educational cadres. They were sturdy
types, mostly of peasant or working class origin, who won
their pupils' respect because they were like children themselves, both in youth and mental outlook, by the freshness of
their eyes and their keenness on intellectual adventure. Their
professional qualifications consisted in a few months' training,
mostly in the form of evening courses. Their education was
only a little ahead of their pupils' and their spelling shaky,
often they good-humouredly allowed a boy of the ninth or
tenth form who had grown up under the old regime, to correct them and to complete the lesson. But all this did not matter; what mattered was that the whole school, children and
teachers, shared the consciousness of having embarked on an
enormous adventure. They lived in the first day of creation
when the heaven and the earth were being divided out of the
chaos; the world lay before them, to be known and conquered.
They were not weighed down, as other school-classes are, by
the depressing perspective of dreary, unending alleys of fact

which so many had trodden before them; for both the teachers and their charges regarded the knowledge accumulated by the past as so much rubbish, the relics of a sunken world. Its poetry was sentimental drivel, its history-books a pack of lies, its philosophy a means by which the old masters had tried to impress the ignorant people. Everything had to be started afresh by the generation after the flood. They were eager for knowledge, thirsting for culture—but it must be a new knowledge, a new culture, without roots in the past. Among the themes discussed in Fedya's class were: "How can we change the climate of our planet?" "When and how will science abolish death?" "Will schools still be necessary after the world revolution?" and "The social origin of the tyranny of parents." During his third year in school, Fedya could claim the authorship of several resolutions which his Brigade had adopted after heated debates: for the abolition of marriage; for the liberation of the Negro slaves in America; for compulsory inoculation; against the harmful theory that tooth-cleaning was a capitalist prejudice; and in favour of the theory that there are other planets inhabited by men.

At the approach of puberty, an inner unrest took hold of Fedya. The school no longer satisfied his intellectual curiosity; he felt an urge to burrow deeper into the mysteries of life, down to the atoms, "the little devils" as Arin called them, who guided the fate of the world. He read much and promiscuously—battered books printed in the old orthography on physics, astronomy, history, even poetry. Lacking the elementary foundations, he understood only in patches, and this shortcoming worried him. He was a respected member of the Pioneers; in a year or two he would be admitted to the Komsomol, and finally to the Party. A member of the Party must know everything, be able to fulfil his duties on any post where the Party put him, be a shining example of wisdom, character and will-power. But where was he to pick up these qualifications? A number of the older Pioneers were beset by similar doubts and worries. They formed a special Brigade "for the Conquest of Knowledge" and harassed the teachers with protests and requests. The teachers were helpless: the greater part of the old textbooks were banned and had not yet been replaced by new manuals; the schools were lacking in everything: classrooms, pencils, paper, slates, chalk, and most of all, qualified teachers. Why was this so? And why had the process of the Great Change apparently come to a standstill?

When Fedya had been ten, everybody had talked of the world
revolution in the making, which would bring everlasting peace,
happiness and abundance. Now, when he was almost fifteen, it
had still not materialised, and there was talk about the revolution being confined to this one country surrounded by blood-
thirsty foes, which would have to remain in a state of siege
for God knew how long. And even worse, at home too things
were not as they should be. There were rich and poor again;
though the rich were now called NEP-men and held in general contempt, the fact remained that they could eat and buy
whatever they wanted and that others could not do the same.

Then came a series of shocking revelations which explained
everything, dispelled all doubts and restored Fedya's faith. Not
that the foundations of this faith had ever been in question—
for it had grown as much a part of himself as his muscles and
bones, and without his being conscious of holding any particular faith, or that possible alternatives to it existed. It was
only that his faith had become slightly chipped, or blurred on
its fringes as it were, during these last dreary years when the
process of the Change had seemed to come to a standstill and
its final aim even to recede. However, after the expulsion from
the Party of the former Commissar of War, and the other
revelations which followed, the true causes of all difficulties
were revealed. The past was dead and buried, but out of its
grave grew evil plants to poison and strangle the future. The
foreign expeditionary forces had been defeated by the Armies
of the Revolution, but the imperialist governments were merely biding their time, ready to pounce again at the first sign of
weakness or disunity in the country of the future which they
hated like death, because it indeed heralded their death by
its mere existence. Against the International of the revolutionary workers they pitted their international of spies,
wreckers and agents in every possible disguise. These agents of
the counter-revolution, the forces of evil, lurked everywhere
around one. They had their main support in the pre-revolutionary intelligentsia, the men of the past, who had to be
tolerated and even given important posts because of their
specialised knowledge. No wonder all goods were short and
expensive when these organisers of industry had only the one
aim, as Engineer Ramsin had confessed in the great public
trial: to wreck the country's economy. Even some of the country's best-known leaders had succumbed to the tempter and
become agents of the counter-revolution. The Party had to

fight them all, to wage incessant battles on many fronts, visible and invisible. Every smiling, jovial face, a teacher's or one's best friend's, might be a mask behind which the tempter hid his true face. Not until the last among them was unmasked and liquidated, could the Great Change get into its real stride.

At a meeting of the Pioneers, a woman delegate from the Party had told the story of the martyr boy Pavel Morozov who had denounced his own parents for having hidden corn from the Government, and was subsequently killed by the backward villagers. Fedya thought how lucky he himself was that his parents had been fighters for the revolution; for to denounce them, or even old Arin, would have been an unpleasant duty. But then, if they had been counter-revolutionaries, they would have been quite different people: brutal, sly and treacherous, so that denouncing them would have been a real pleasure. He liked working out problems, and was pleased with himself for having found the solution of this one.

Fedya was just past fifteen when the uneasy lull of the NEP suddenly ended. The announcement of the First Five Year Plan came like the sudden roar of thunder which shook the country and whose echo reverberated throughout the world. The ship of the revolution had been becalmed; now it shot forward as if under a whip, with cracking masts and sails stretched to bursting. Fedya did not know at the time that for the rest of his life these sudden jolts and tosses would never cease; nor how many of his comrades would be swept overboard by the periodic assaults of the breakers. All he knew was that now the final stage of the Great Change had come into sight; within the next five years all the centuries wasted under reactionary rulers would be made good, and just around his twentieth birthday he would assist at the inauguration of the classless society of the Golden Age.

Discipline in school became stricter; each class, the teacher explained, was now to regard itself as a future shock-battalion in the battle for Utopia. Fedya's head buzzed with the figures of the Plan learned by rote: so many million tons of pig-iron after the first year, so many million kilowatt hours, so many million illiterates turned into cultured members of society. The sound of all these millions of riches, produced by the people for the people, was intoxicating. The kilowatt hours, the tons, bushels, gallons and kilometres became characters of a heroic saga. The setting for this battle of the giants was an enormous map which occupied a whole wall of the classroom. It was studded with little flags which indicated the main battlefields of the Plan. Far up north of the Arctic Circle, only to be reached by a ladder, pencil marks indicated the course of the future canal, the longest ever built by man. A red string, stretched between drawing pins several yards apart, showed the track of the future Turkestan-Siberian railway. A forest of flags in the Ural Mountains marked the sites of the future giant combines of steel; a red circle surrounded Dneprostroy, the mightiest power dam in the world; tiny motor cars and tractors cut out of paper indicated the factories where these shiny marvels were produced.

The boys and girls of the class were each fictitiously in charge of one or another branch of production, and had to report periodically on their progress. The best were chosen to look after the essential raw materials and key industries, the weaker ones after the consumer goods; the gentle little idiot of the class looked after the production of cuff links and collar studs, and developed a mania about them. When, on May Day parade, the director of the school told them in his speech that in other countries and at other times children stuck flags into maps to mark the battlefields not of industry and life, but of death and destruction, a wave of incredulity went through the audience. But when he went on to tell them that never before had a young generation lived at such a decisive turn of History and been made to participate in it with such full awareness, they all felt the truth of this in their brains and hearts.

This May Day celebration marked a peak in Fedya's life: it completed, without his knowing it, the henceforth unshakable foundations of his faith. In the future the structure of that faith was to undergo many changes—in fact there was a time when its façade was almost constantly being altered as if by the orders of a mad architect—but these were surface adjustments which did not affect the solid foundations. The first stone had been laid early by Grisha, who had implanted into the child's heart the mystic belief in the Great Change—the cataclysm which was to be followed by the Golden Age. The second had been laid just as inadvertently by old Arin when he told the boy about the secret of life, the little atoms which ruled supreme in the world. The director's speech completed the holy trinity of his creed. Henceforth he knew that happiness could be measured only in kilowatt hours, bushels and tons, for they were the only means of overcoming the age of darkness and the enemies of the people who fought with such tenacious cunning to perpetuate the evil past. These were the iron facts; everything else was backward superstition, heresy and diversion—like those annual prizes for literature and peace awarded by the same Nobel brothers who had owned the Baku refineries and invented dynamite.

In his last year in school romance entered Fedya's life in the slim, flaxen-haired shape of Nadeshda Filipovna, a comrade in the Komsomol. She was seventeen, a tempestuous girl both in body and mind, whose passion was to climb trees and read the poems of Mayakovsky while perilously balanced on a swaying branch. The daughter of a surgeon who belonged to the pre-revolutionary intelligentsia, her education had been superior to Fedya's, but this fact affected their relationship only in moments of irritation. Though she was by a few months the younger, and in spite of her violent temper and changing moods, there were moments when she displayed towards Fedya the same almost maternal affection as his childhood mistress, the little Tartar girl in Baku. On one of the rare occasions when Fedya discarded his cocky adolescent pose, he had asked her: "Why do you strike up with a fellow like me when you are so much more cultured?" And she had answered, rubbing her palm against the short bristles on his head: "Because you are clean and simple and hard like an effigy of 'Our Proletarian Youth' from a propaganda poster."

Their affair lasted only a year, until Nadeshda's father was arrested as a member of an oppositional conspiracy and enemy of the people. Fedya was rather fond of the girl and tried his best to help her in her predicament, within the limits which his political conscience and the demands of revolutionary vigilance permitted. She was well liked in the Komsomol, and even the comrades from the District Committee were apparently prepared to let her off lightly—for, viewed in retrospect, the years of Fedya's youth were a time of almost culpable tolerance and leniency; so the calamity which befell her was entirely due to her own stubbornness.

Fedya met her in the street a few minutes before she had to appear before the Control Commission and was surprised at the whiteness of her face, but explained it to himself as the after-effect of an abortion which she had been forced to undergo a few days before. Fedya felt both proud and a little guilty about this, though it had been she who had insisted on throwing all precautions to the wind. At any rate, she had made no fuss about it; but now, since this business about her father had started, she seemed quite off her head. Instead of a greeting, she said:

"My mother has divorced him, the bitch. Can you beat that?"

Fedya laughed good-naturedly: "Of course she has, since he turned out to be a counter-revolutionary."

She turned at him in such a fury, with nostrils drawn in and speaking between her teeth, that he was reminded of the hissing of an angry goose:

"You say that again and I will bash your damned freckled face in."

He laughed at her through slightly narrowed eyes: "This abortion business has upset you. But you must be calm before the Commission, that's very important." She walked along very fast, without speaking, and fell repeatedly out of step with Fedya. To humour her, Fedya kept readjusting his steps, though usually it was Nadeshda who did that, perhaps to make up for the fact that she was a little taller than he.

As they approached the building, Fedya said: "Now you must promise that you will behave reasonably." She did not even answer him, and entered the classroom where the meeting was to be held with an air of defiance which immediately antagonised everybody. The chairs were arranged in a semi-circle around the table where the comrades from the District Committee were to sit under the oil-prints of the two leaders, the past and the present one; but they had not yet arrived and the members of the Komsomol group had to wait for more than half an hour, chatting and nibbling sun-flower seeds. There were some twenty-five or thirty of them. As Nadeshda made her entry, the hum subsided and she was greeted by a few strained hellos; then they all resumed their chatter. Occasionally one of them stole a glance at Nadeshda, but on meeting her fierce stare looked away at once with a show of indifference. She walked straight to a chair at the end of the second row, which was separated from the others by four empty chairs. Fedya, following behind her, sat down on the chair next but one to hers. To take the chair directly next to hers, segregated from the rest of their comrades, would have looked like a demonstration or even the formation of a political faction; to leave her in complete isolation would have looked like a demonstration of the opposite kind; hence the correct solution was the next chair but one. They did not speak while waiting for the Commission. Nadeshda looked in front of her, white-faced, with a fierce and yet absent look; Fedya read the "Komsomolskaya Pravda."

At last the comrades from the District Committee arrived. There were three of them: a dark, squat little man with a humorous face and a gentle voice; a female factory worker with a kerchief round her head and a round, somewhat dumb face, who eyed Nadeshda with immediate hostility; and a dreary bureaucratic figure with glasses. The dark little man, whose name was Comrade Jesensky, said the necessary things about the duties of revolutionary vigilance and the importance of protecting the cadres against infiltration by socially unreliable elements; then the lengthy procedure of questioning Nadeshda about her activities, convictions, the social origin of her parents and grandparents took its course.

Her answers were short, precise and to the point; but they were uttered in a tone of defiance. It transpired that for two generations all Nadeshda's forebears had been of middle-class origin: her father's father had also been a doctor, even a specialist, with a house of his own in Petersburg; her mother's father had been a grain merchant, in other words a social parasite *par excellence*. She had only gained admission to the Komsomol thanks to the fact that her father had joined the Party several years before the Revolution and had fought as a Partisan commander in the Civil War. . . . "Was he already at that time a counter-revolutionary agent and spy?" asked the woman with the kerchief. Nadeshda looked at Comrade Jesensky, who acted as chairman, and asked: "Must I answer such idiotic questions?" "Yes," the chairman said gently. "And you are not to use abusive language against responsible comrades who are your superiors. If a man is found out to be a counter-revolutionary, it is not at all idiotic to suppose that he started to be one ten years ago." "You have no right to call him a counter-revolutionary," said Nadeshda, in a voice slightly shaky with suppressed hysterics. "A man is to be regarded as innocent until proved guilty by a court." "Where did you pick up this idea out of the liberal-bourgeois philosophy of law?" the chairman asked in a curious voice. Nadeshda hesitated, then she said uncertainly: "I read it somewhere in a book." The woman with the kerchief said: "No doubt in a book which belonged to your father?" There was a murmur in the audience. "No," said Nadeshda, and her voice began to tremble. "You are lying," said the woman. "Do you believe," the chairman asked gently, "that our comrades of the State Security Department would arrest a man without evidence of his guilt? Think before you answer," he added quickly, "for if you were to answer in the affirmative this would amount to accusing our comrades of the State Security Department of arresting innocents, that is of counter-revolutionary wrecking activities." Nadeshda bit her lip. "It could have been a mistake," she said at last. "The organs of the State Security Department act with the greatest caution and circumspection, which excludes the possibility of mistakes," said the chairman. "Do you deny this?" "No," said Nadeshda tonelessly. "You may sit down," said the chairman. "Who wants to testify about Comrade Nadeshda Filipovna?"

Several members of the cell came forward; their testimonies were rather contradictory and did not amount to much. A girl, generally known to have a crush on Fedya, said that she had always suspected Nadeshda of being a wolf in sheep's clothing; but when pressed by the chairman to mention the concrete facts which had given rise to her suspicions, she became confused and could not mention any. One boy testified in Nadeshda's favour that she had always been very keen in carrying out tasks allotted to her by the cell; but when the woman with the kerchief asked him whether this could not have been a calculated hypocritical attitude to mask her real intentions, he admitted that one could never know. Another boy said that she had always behaved in an arrogant manner which proved her bourgeois antecedents; but when somebody interrupted him with the remark that he resented having been jilted by Nadeshda, he blushed and his words were drowned by general laughter. Comrade Jesensky banged the table with his palm: "This is a serious matter," he said. "If nobody else has anything to say, I shall now call on Comrade Nikitin. Fedya Grigoryevich, you are held in high esteem by your comrades, and we all know that you were a friend of Nadeshda Filipovna. You will now give us a description of her character and her reliability as a social element."

Fedya rose in the midst of a hushed silence. He pushed back his black cloth cap and looked at Jesensky thoughtfully and without a trace of self-consciousness. "Well," he said, "I have thought about this matter. I have known her well for almost a year and never had any suspicion until the news came about her father." He stopped and seemed to think that he had said all there was to be said. The woman with the kerchief asked: "So your eyes did not open until you heard about her father? A nice vigilant comrade you are, I must say." Fedya scratched his head wonderingly: "Perhaps I was misled, but there seemed nothing much wrong with her." "Nothing much," said the woman, "except that her father is an enemy of the people, a protector of the kulaks, and that she knew all the time about his efforts to wreck the Party and the Government, and has succeeded in fooling you all by kicking her legs about and behaving in a brazenly flirtatious way." She looked round the audience and as her flat, matronly eyes caught one boy's gaze after another, the boys looked down at their boots; yet one could see that a light had begun to dawn inside each adolescent skull.

Comrade Jesensky turned to Fedya: "You have just said that you did not suspect her *until* her father was arrested. What did she say or do then to make her past behaviour appear in a new light to you?"

Fedya thought this over carefully before answering. Then he said: "Well—there were only little things, nothing very important. She was angry because her mother divorced him. This surprised me because her mother acted correctly seeing that he was found out to be what he is. Then here, during the meeting—she behaved as if she were among enemies. This made me think. It proves that she feels that she is not really one of us. . . ."

Comrade Jesensky cleared his throat. "Is that all?"

"Yes."

Comrade Jesensky's dark eyes wandered round the audience, and as they fastened on Fedya they regained some of their humorous expression.

"Well, it doesn't amount to much," he said. "Assuming she didn't know anything of her father's criminal activities, which according to the rules of political conspiracy is quite likely, his sudden unmasking must have been a painful surprise to her. How do you think you would have acted in her situation?"

Fedya rose again. He rubbed his head, trying to find the correct answer. "It couldn't happen to me," he said at last. "So I can't answer your question."

"Quite correct," said the woman in the kerchief. "Such things can only happen in families with a bourgeois kulak background. That's just the point we are discussing."

After some more inconclusive talk, the meeting was closed

and everybody left the room, except the comrades from the District Committee and Nadeshda herself, who was asked to stay behind and give a more detailed account of certain points in her evidence. The other members of the cell hung about for a while in the deserted corridors of the school, discussing her case. Their mood was moderately hostile to her, but the general consensus was that she would get away with a year's suspension from the Komsomol and with eating some humble pie, which even her friends admitted would do her no harm. But as the Committee's decision could not be expected before a week or so, they all soon left for their various evening occupations—a meeting of the School Hygiene Committee, or of the Teachers' Control Board; some set out on an hour's tram journey to a factory to give a talk about the Plan, or do cultural work at some assembly point for the liquidation of illiteracy. Fedya too was in a hurry, for he was supposed to give a lecture on dialectical materialism at a Culture-Base in the suburbs; but he thought it more polite to wait for Nadeshda and take her home first, thus sacrificing the time allotted for his dinner.

After about half an hour, Nadeshda came out at last, her eyes too bright, as if she were running a temperature. She looked as if she were displeased with him, and brushed past him with her nose in the air—like a princess in the cinema, he thought. He trotted patiently behind her, and in the street caught up with her. But though he repeatedly tried to adjust his steps to hers, she fell out again each time, as if on purpose. This, he thought, and her stubborn silence, was really carrying things too far; but one had to be patient with silly women, so he asked: "Well, how did it go?"

She stopped short in the middle of the street and literally hissed at him: "How dare you—dare you still talk to me?" "Why shouldn't I?" he asked in amazement. But there was no getting any sense out of her. "You dirty, filthy little swine, after what you said at the meeting, you . . ." And so she went on, hissing abuse at him, calling him a traitor, an informer and what not. He tried patiently to explain to her that he had only done his duty in telling the truth, and did she perhaps expect him to lie to the Party and thereby become a criminal only because they had had a physical relationship for their mutual convenience? At that Nadeshda slapped him in the face and ran off, almost getting pushed over by a tram. Fedya looked after her, very puzzled, turning his cap around on his skull;

then with a jerk he pulled it down over his eyes, deciding that that was that, not without a certain relief.

He never saw Nadeshda again; she did not turn up in school and it was said that she had been sent to work in a factory or a kolkhoz, somewhere in Central Asia. But about a week later Fedya received a message to ring up a certain number; and when he did so he was told by a friendly voice to report at a certain hour to a certain office and not to talk about this to anybody. Fedya knew that he was to see a comrade of the State Security Department and felt excited and thrilled. He also knew that it must be in connection with Nadeshda; and as he thought of her now, trying to sum her up in his mind so as to be able to give a lucid account of her to the comrade of the State Security Department, he had a curious experience. He remembered vividly the tone of her voice, and he remembered a habit she had of nibbling at his lips with her teeth which used to excite him tremendously, and he remembered the pleasant sensation of touching the smooth firm skin of her breasts and buttocks—but these were only bits of remembrances which did not add up to a whole. That is to say, he could remember parts and qualities of her, but not the complete Nadeshda as a living person: as a person her image had paled like an old photograph, it had developed cracks and had fallen to bits in his memory. Try as he might, he could not reassemble the bits; she was no longer real, and he wondered whether she had ever been.

After a little thinking, he discovered that this was not surprising at all. For he knew that what one called "a person" was after all merely an assembly of bits and qualities and odours and so on; apart from these bits and qualities, the person did not exist, was merely an illusion which vanished into nothingness. No wonder that he could no longer reassemble the fragments of that grammatical fiction which went by her name. There was still the memory on his lips, the ghost of a voice in his ear, a lingering sensation of kneading firm softnesses with his palms. But apart from these, Nadeshda did not exist and had never existed. Pleased with himself for having solved another puzzle, he put his cap on and set out for the State Security building—an imposing near-skyscraper which he had always admired from outside. It was said that unlike American skyscrapers which were badly built for quick profits, this one did not vibrate and sway: this was solid, unswayable reality, not fiction.

The man into whose office he was led, after a wait and a long walk along corridors and more corridors, rose behind his desk and shook Fedya's hand with earnest friendliness. At the first glance Fedya saw that Comrade Maximov belonged to that special race to which his father's friends had belonged: the doctor and the lawyer in Baku, the Commissar on the road, and Comrade Jesensky from the District Committee. He had the same manner of listening attentively, of treating an adolescent as an adult without condescension, of going straight to the heart of the matter and brushing aside everything irrelevant, like cobwebs, with a gesture of his hand. Though he was dressed in civilian clothes, he walked as if he were still wearing breeches and heavy knee-boots—all men did that who had fought in the Civil War and had met in mud-floored rooms before the Great Change; their legs seemed ill at ease in ordinary trousers, longing for the old Partisan days. And sure enough, the first words Comrade Maximov said, were: "I knew your father, Fedya Grigoryevich."

He had resumed his seat behind his desk; Fedya remained standing in front of it, politely waiting to be invited to sit. As Comrade Maximov said nothing more, waiting for him to speak, Fedya asked: "Where? In Baku?"

"Yes. I was Commissar of one of the oil-tankers which smuggled petrol to our troops across the Caspian Sea. You are too young to remember that."

"No. I remember. My father used to say: 'Tonight we are sending petrol for Ilyitch's lighter.'"

Ilyitch had been the popular name of the dead leader of the Revolution. Maximov smiled briefly at the ring of the once familiar phrase. "Petrol for Ilyitch's lighter," he repeated, as an aging bonvivant would hum the tune of a long-forgotten waltz. "How old were you then?" he asked, his face friendly and serious again.

"Six or seven."

"Right. Sit down. It is about your friend Nadeshda Filipovna. What do you know of her?"

"I have said everything at the meeting of the cell. And she is no longer my friend."

"No? Why? Do you think she is a counter-revolutionary?"

"That I don't know. But I have thought about it and discovered that she has always been a socially alien element from the class-conscious point of view."

"So you are sorry you ever got involved with her?"

Fedya considered this. "No," he said finally. "At that time I didn't know what I know today, so I couldn't have acted differently and can't be sorry about it."

"But you admit it was a mistake."

"Yes," said Fedya. His mind worked hard and a guarded, suspicious expression dulled his frank features. "No," he corrected himself. "As I didn't know it couldn't have been a mistake." His mind went on working, and suddenly his face lit up: "Yes. It was a mistake, *because* I didn't know."

"But you just said that in the same situation you would make the same mistake all over again."

"Yes, that is correct. I am guilty of having acted in a mistaken way, but as I was mistaken I could not have acted differently."

"If you are guilty, you ought to be punished."

"Yes."

"But as you could not have acted otherwise than you did you should be excused?"

"No."

"Why?"

"To be mistaken is no excuse."

"Can you be angry with a person because he makes a mistake?"

"No."

"But you would punish him?"

"Yes."

"Liquidate him if he becomes a menace to society?"

"Yes."

"For what?"

"For having become a menace to society by acting the way he had to act."

Comrade Maximov looked at him curiously and lit a cigarette.

"You haven't asked me yet what has happened to your Nadeshda."

"I know that I am not supposed to ask questions."

"You don't need to worry about her too much, you know . . ."

"I am not worrying."

Again Maximov gave him a curious look. Fedya returned his look with his untroubled youthful gaze through slightly shuttered eyes. At last Maximov said:

"Right. Let's get down to our business. The Plan imposes

sacrifices on the people. The backward sectors of the masses don't understand the purpose of these sacrifices. They only see that they get less to eat than a year ago. This situation is exploited by the enemy. The kulaks are hiding their crops and slaughtering their cattle. The opposition sides with the kulaks against the revolution. They are trying to undermine the Party; their children are assigned the task of undermining the Komsomol. We have proofs that Nadeshda was one of the leaders of this diversionist conspiracy. . . ."

He paused to wait for the effect of his disclosure; but strangely enough he did not look at Fedya. His eyes were fixed on an empty corner of the room, as if something of great interest were happening there, and his voice while he talked had been curiously flat. But Fedya was too thrilled to notice these oddities in Comrade Maximov's behaviour. He whistled softly, blushed at his own audacity and said: "So it is much more serious than I thought. That little bitch . . ."

And he thought of Prince Rostovsky's smiling face as he whispered into the Sultan's ear the words: "Massacrer, majesté, massacrer." However watchful you were, the enemy in his incredible cunning and perfidy went always one better. He thought of the girl's teeth nibbling at his lips in her fiendish way, and felt that his whole back along the spine was covered with goose-flesh. "Oh, the bitch," he repeated. Then, slowly and horribly, Grisha's image rose before his mind's eye as he had stood in the middle of the room while they kicked him in the belly, his eyes fastened on his own, pouring, pouring their liquid message into him.

At last Comrade Maximov tore his gaze away from the empty corner of his office and directed it at Fedya's hands, which were clenched tight, with their square nails dug into his palms.

"Now that you know the whole truth," Comrade Maximov said wearily, "you had better make a clean breast of it, in your own interest."

"But I have said everything I know," said Fedya with a moan of impotent fury.

"When did she first try to enlist you into the sabotage network?"

"But she didn't. That's the devil of it. She was so cunning, so sly, I didn't notice anything. Except . . ."

"Except?"

"She made remarks. At the time I thought them merely

stupid, but now . . ." His face lit up, began to beam: he had solved a puzzle.

"Go on," Comrade Maximov said, without enthusiasm. "What remarks?" He took a pencil and a pad.

"For instance, when the project of the underground railway was announced. We all were off our heads with excitement, but she laughed at us and said that there were underground railways in other countries too, so what's all the excitement about?"

"Did you believe her?"

"I told her she was lying, and she offered to show us photographs of an underground railway in Paris, or in London, I forget which."

"And did she show them to you?"

"Yes. From some encyclopædia."

"So in this case she wasn't lying after all?"

"But that isn't the point. She had no business to laugh at our railway and boost railways in Paris or London. Personally I didn't mind, for I know we were a backward country and the capitalists are ahead of us, but some of the others felt depressed—cheated, when they looked at these photographs of Paris. She had no business to go around showing photographs of Paris to undermine our morale, like . . ."

"Like what?"

"Oh—that has nothing to do with it."

"Say it."

"Oh—I just remembered, when I was a child in Baku there was a pond in the White Town, and Grisha—that was my father—made me a sailing boat from a piece of wood and the sleeve of his old shirt." He hesitated, then went on in a hard, cold voice: "Then, when I sailed it the first time in the pond, a boy came up dressed like a doll in a blue sailor's suit, and his governess carried a big model boat with three masts and a propeller and an engine in it, and the boy stuck out his tongue at me . . ."

Comrade Maximov got up and started pacing up and down the room. After a while he asked, as if forcing himself to do it:

"Was the incident about the underground railway the only one of its kind?"

"No. She often used to tease us that way. I remember one day somebody gave a talk about the victory achieved by the overfulfilment of the manganese production plan, and she said: 'I wish I could fulfil my tummy with manganese . . .'

And I remember once we went to a film together in which a revolutionary leader in a foreign country was tortured in a cellar by reactionary monks until the workers stormed the monastery and got him free. She giggled all the time and when the film was over she said it was the silliest film she had ever seen. . . ."

Comrade Maximov came to a halt and said in a casual tone:

"But you said in your evidence at the meeting that she had always been keen to carry out any job assigned to her?"

"That is true. She did everything, but she did it all in a way different from ours—like a game, for sport. . . ." He was searching for a word, and found it. "Frivolously. . . . She was never really in earnest. She displayed an attitude of frivolousness towards our task of socialist reconstruction."

Comrade Maximov resumed his place behind his desk. He looked weary, and Fedya had the feeling that Comrade Maximov was fed up with him, though he couldn't think why. Anyway, he didn't care much. His duty was to tell the truth, and he was doing that, whether Maximov liked it or not.

At last Maximov said:

"Listen well. I told you we had proofs against her. Now assuming I only said that to scare you, and that we have no proofs, only a suspicion. In this case her fate would depend on your testimony. Would you still stick then to what you have said?"

"Of course. Everything I said was true."

Comrade Maximov started playing with his pencil. His voice was grave:

"Would you still say that her attitude was calculated to undermine her comrades' morale?"

"Yes."

"Deliberately calculated?"

"I don't know. What's the difference? It comes to the same. It was her manner, her whole social background which made her act the way she did."

"In short, she is guilty of having played with a sailing boat, and is going to be punished for the boy who stuck his tongue out at you?"

Fedya wondered what Comrade Maximov was driving at with these curious questions. It almost looked as if he were trying to protect the saboteur girl. The enemy was everywhere, his agents managed to infiltrate themselves into the most important positions and unlikely places. Even the arch-traitor had once held some sort of job with the Army. But it was also possible that Comrade Maximov was merely putting him to a test. At any rate the question was so stupid that he thought it best to give no answer at all.

After a longish silence, Maximov said suddenly:

"All right." He spoke into the telephone and called for a stenographer. While waiting for her to appear, he said:

"Perhaps one day you will understand what you have done. But most likely you never will."

Though his tone was casual, Fedya knew that Comrade Maximov wanted to insult him. He sat in front of the desk, his lips tight, his eyes slightly narrowed. When the stenographer appeared, Comrade Maximov rapidly dictated to her a summary of Fedya's statement. It included the incidents about the underground railway and the manganese; it quoted textually Fedya's statement about Nadeshda Filipovna's frivolous attitude towards the task of socialist reconstruction, and concluded that her behaviour was objectively conducive to undermining her comrades' morale. Fedya listened carefully, in case some part of his statement had been omitted, but it was all there. If Maximov was a wrecker, he took good care to cover himself.

After Fedya had signed the statement and the secretary had left the room, Maximov asked coldly:

"What do you intend to do when you have finished school?"

"Go to the University."

"Have you ever thought of working for the Department of State Security?"

"No."

"Would you like to?"

"Yes."

"You seem to be eminently fitted for it. You may hear from us. Goodbye."

That was all. Maximov's last remark was probably the greatest compliment that Fedya could wish for, yet the tone in which it was made was again insulting—worse than that, contemptuous. But maybe that was also part of their testing technique.

Fedya was glad to get out into the fresh air. The devil take Comrade Maximov, he thought. An overcrowded tramway was just rattling by; he rammed his cap firmly to his skull, raced after it and managed to jump on the running board, alighting on the toe of a shabby elderly man with glasses. The man feebly muttered something to himself, and Fedya realised by the quality of his once resplendent overcoat that he belonged to the pre-revolutionary intelligentsia—that was why he didn't dare to curse aloud. Fedya smiled good-humouredly. The devil take them all, he thought: the man in the overcoat and Comrade Maximov and the rest of the old gang, whether they belonged to the Party or not. They were all of the past; what had they done to be so proud of themselves anyway? Conspired and thrown bombs and fought partisan actions— all romantic, outmoded stuff. They had not built a single factory, had no inkling of production and the Plan. Even his father's friends in Baku, the lawyer and the doctor, would by now have become old dodderers, tired winterflies crawling on the windowpanes of the future. . . . Fedya suddenly became very cheerful. He and his classmates would be just twenty when the Plan was completed and they would run the show— a show such as has never before been seen in history.

He pushed the cap back into his neck and started to whistle under the old fusspot's nose. What a lucky circumstance to be young and to live in these heroic times. And maybe Maximov's last remark was meant seriously and he, Fedya, would be sent abroad, among the savage finance barons in top hats and tails, a missionary of mankind's salvation. They would probably torture and kill him, as they had killed Grisha and Arin's people, but he was not afraid of that. The only thing in life he was afraid of was something which could never happen: to be cast out of the Movement like Nadeshda, into the outer darkness, where the damned writhed in the agony of their thirst, exiled forever in a dry and weary land, with no water in it.

7

CALF'S HEAD AND CHAMPAGNE

"I BELIEVED you would wear a silk evening dress and jewels," said Fedya with a disappointed look. He kicked the chair back as he sat down, but this time did not kiss her hand. Hydie had again been the first to arrive at the café. Fedya wore a black suit and his short-cropped hair was plastered down; but as the evening progressed, one hair after another stood up until they all bristled again. Hydie watched this progress with fascination, as she had once watched the shooting of popcorn being roasted.

"I didn't dress because we won't go to the Opera," she explained.

"But why? I have bought tickets, so we must go."

He looked so disconcerted, that she felt a wave of maternal tenderness. Hydie was in high spirits: "I want you to take me to dinner at a cheap place and to talk to me about yourself. That will be much more fun than listening to democratic music."

Fedya had that blank, guarded look which she knew already. Then a sudden glimmer came into his eyes:

"Ah—it is a sudden caprice of the spoilt American woman?"

Hydie burst out laughing. "Does putting labels on things make you feel happier?"

"But of course. It is always necessary to understand what causes an event. But now we must hurry."

"Why?"

"Because I must take you home in a taxi before I go to the Opera. It would not be polite to leave you in this café."

He rose, courteously waiting for her to get up in turn. Hydie bit her lip; she had turned pale. She hesitated for a second, was convinced that everybody in the café was watching her, got up and walked blindly out of the door. Fedya followed; they had to wait outside until a taxi came by. He had only had a moment's uncertainty while she got up from the table; it had been dispelled when in walking past him, her shoulder had brushed his—a contact unwarranted by the topography of the place. A taxi stopped; he opened the door for her, smiling. Hydie got in and told the driver in a flat voice: "To the Opera." Then she huddled into her corner, as far from him as possible, fighting her tears back and knowing that she had never hated anybody as she hated this man with his ridiculous clothes and manners; promising herself that at the Opera she would tell the driver to carry on and take her home; knowing that she wouldn't do it, and looking forward with horror to three acts of "Rigoletto" and to the rest of the evening.

At the Madeleine, the taxi had to wait in a traffic-jam. She stared at the Greek columns on the façade, illuminated by pink searchlights, and thought what an utterly hideous and cruel town Paris was, and of the desolate loneliness of the people in the stuffy flats behind the mean, sooty iron railings of the balconies. Suddenly, with a shock that made her jump, she felt Fedya's hard palm pressing down on the back of her hand, and heard him ask very gently:

"Do you really not want to go 'Rigoletto'?"

She shook her head, unable to speak.

"Then why did you not say this on Wednesday, when I invited you?"

She shrugged helplessly.

"You should have said it, then I would not have thought that it is only a caprice. But if you really do not like 'Rigoletto,' then we shall of course go to the cheap restaurant."

She wanted to throw her arms round his neck and kiss him, but wisely thought better of it and gave instead, in a somewhat shaky voice, the address of a little restaurant on the left bank to the driver. Then she got her compact out and steadied her nerves by occupational therapy with powder-puff and lipstick.

"It is a great pity you don't like 'Rigoletto,' " said Fedya. "It gives a good example of the corruption of the feudal class before the bourgeois revolution, and of the self-abasement which the feudalistic structure of society imposes on the victims. It has also some good music."

Hydie thought she would never find out when Fedya was talking seriously.

"I guess by good music you mean *la donna e mobile.*"

"What is that?" he asked.

"It's Italian. It means: 'women are volatile.' "

"Oh, the great aria. It is very beautiful, except for the words."

"What's wrong with the words? Oh, why are you such a pedant?" she asked hopelessly.

He shrugged, then said in his patient, explaining tone:

"All this talk about women being volatile and capricious and this and that is nonsense and very boring. When society is corrupt, morals become corrupt, instincts become corrupt, and corrupted artists make a living by refined works celebrating corruption, like the one who wrote this aria. Such artists are, as Leontiev has said in his last article, like maggots dancing a ballet on a corpse."

"And in your incorrupt society all women will be faithful."

"There are always exceptions. Some people have strong instincts which bring them into conflict with society and its institutions. But in general, when a woman has children and she likes her husband and she is sexually satisfied by him, she is not, as you say, 'volatile,' but feels very solid. Perhaps now and then she has a little wish to be a little volatile, but in a normal family in a normal society such little wishes are of little importance. But in your decadent society which has no faith and no convictions and no solidity, you take these little wishes terribly seriously because there is nothing else which you can take seriously."

"You know," said Hydie, "my granddad used to say just the same."

"Was he a member of the revolutionary movement?" Fedya asked with interest.

"No. He owned a castle and a famous pack of hounds in county Clare."

"He must have had very advanced ideas," said Fedya firmly. "But we shall not quarrel. I only wanted to say that my position with regard to the aria in 'Rigoletto' is, that when women behave in a crazy way it is because they live in a society which has no faith."

"I couldn't agree more," Hydie said grimly.

The restaurant on the Seine quai which Hydie had chosen looked indeed cheap. The checkered tablecloth was none too clean, the salt-cellar was chipped, and the spring of the leather bench gave way as they sat down. Fedya looked around him disappointedly:

"Why do you like such places?" he asked.

"Don't you think it's heaven?" She showed him the view through the somewhat grimy French window; their table stood in a little alcove, all by itself. "You can look at Notre Dame and you can watch the anglers on the bridge who never catch a fish but never give up. That's faith for you—even in a bourgeois society. . . ."

"But," he said impatiently, "there are many better restaurants on the river-bank which are clean and cultured. . . ." He looked at her, again with that guarded, distrustful expression which she so feared. It was worse than a glass cage—a stone wall, dividing two continents. Suddenly his eyes lit up and warmed his face again.

"Your father is very rich?"

"Not very—but fairly," she said meekly.

"Now I understand," said Fedya. "It is a very interesting phenomenon."

"What is an interesting phenomenon?" she asked, relieved that all was well again.

"The most interesting is that you yourself know nothing about the reason why you like places such as this. But you must have read Veblen?"

"Oh dear. I always pretended that I had. You had better tell me what he says about Paris bistros."

"Nothing about Paris bistros. But he explains the laws of the evolution of taste in the ruling classes. While a certain class, like the capitalist bourgeoisie, is still busy acquiring riches, its members compete in spending and wasting money to impress each other; so at that stage luxury is considered good taste. But when the class has become very rich, its members no longer need to prove their riches, and only those live in luxury who are not really very rich but wish to seem so, or who have acquired their riches only recently. So at that stage luxury is regarded as vulgar and Rockefeller leads the ascetic life and you have been taught to think it is cultured to like old, dirty restaurants because they are old and dirty."

Hydie laughed. "Most of the things you say are true, but only partly. Just as the drawing of a skeleton is only part of the truth about man. Bistros, for instance, are not only old and dirty—they also have atmosphere."

"Oh, yes, the atmosphere. The atmosphere of poorness, of the 'simple people' of the petite-bourgeoisie—you come from the grande bourgeoisie, so you can be Haroun al Rashid. You go to the bistros as tourists go to the Orient."

What hurt her most was that he spoke not aggressively, but with a gentle irony; bending down towards her, as it were, from the parapet of the impregnable fortress of his belief. And perhaps he was right? She could only look up to him enviously, shivering in the cold and insecurity of those who live outside the walls.

"Will you let me order the dinner?" she asked. "The food at least is good here, and I know their specialties."

He acquiesced good-humouredly, as one cedes to a child's whim. She ordered Bourguignon snails, an omelette, and calf's head in vinegar sauce. The proprietor, a fat, morose man, shook hands with them, visibly bestowing this honour for Hydie's sake.

"Now you feel very proud and democratic, eh," said Fedya, smiling, after the proprietor had left them.

"Oh, you do have a way of spoiling things. Why?"

"Because I dislike false sentiment."

"What is false about my liking the fat *patron?* You should see his wife. She is even fatter and her bosom is stacked up so high it is almost level with her shoulders."

"Would you invite them when you give a dinner party?"

"They wouldn't fit in, but that has nothing to do with it."

"Then you do not really like them."

She shrugged in exasperation. "You can always beat anybody at this sort of game."

"What game?"

"Oh—pinning one down, and so on."

"I do not understand. If you fight and you are pinned down you have lost."

"But I don't want to fight with you."

He gave her that naked, feline look which she remembered. "Then what do you want to do with me?"

"Heaven knows. Go to bed, I suppose, and have done with it."

At least she had the satisfaction of seeing him genuinely shocked. His eyes popped, and the freckles became visible on his cheeks—it was probably a way of blushing.

"Now I guess you will think me very 'uncultured'," she said viciously, but already on the defensive again, and ready to fall back into the docile pupil's part if given a chance. To her relief, she saw a sudden flash of understanding in his gaze; he had solved another puzzle, and all was well.

"Not uncultured, only a little—decadent," he said, in answer to her last remark. "It is the frivolity of the leisure class. You say these things as children use bad words of which they do not know the meaning."

She left it at that, and the snails arrived. She felt quite hollow inside, and consequently very hungry. She prayed in silence that he would not think the eating of snails decadent or uncultured, but he seemed to like them. They tasted deliciously of garlic and of little else.

"Do you like snails?" she asked cautiously, hoping to be on safe ground.

"They are very good. The French like them," he said politely.

"What kind of dishes do you really like?"

His face brightened. "Shashlik. And shushkabab. . . ." A little shamefacedly he added: "And afterwards rachat locum."

"So you come from the Kaukasus?"

"How do you know?"

"Everybody knows that shashlik is a Kaukasian dish."

"I was born in Baku. In Tchornaya Gorod—that means the Black Town." He seemed a little mellowed by the strong, full-bodied Rhone wine that came with the snails.

"Will you tell me something about your life?" she asked timidly.

"It is not interesting."

"But it does interest me. I have absolutely no idea what life is like on the other side."

"Our people work very hard and are happy constructing the future."

"Amen. Now tell me about yourself."

He tipped his glass down, pushed his plate away and looked at her, rubbing with a humorous expression the mop of stiff hair on his head, which by now had dried and stood up like a brush. Hydie suddenly discovered what was missing to complete his face: a soft peak-cap of black cloth which he could push back or pull over an ear, or over his eyes, according to mood.

"It is not very interesting," he repeated. "I had a grandfather who was a member of an oppressed minority nation, an Armenian. He belonged to the artisan class. Because he belonged to an oppressed minority, his family had been massacred and he was forced to flee. My father was a member of the revolutionary proletariat and was killed by the counter-revolution. My mother lived in ignorance and poverty like all oriental women, and died of disease. Then I went with my grandfather from Baku to Moscow during the Civil War, and there I was educated in school. Then I joined the Youth Movement and later the Party. When the rich peasants opposed the collectivisation to sabotage the Five Year Plan, I was mobilised by the Party and sent back to the Kaukasus to help with bringing in the harvest which was needed by the workers in the towns engaged in the work of industrialisation. When that was finished the Party sent me to the University, and when I had finished the University I was engaged in various activities on the cultural front. . . ."

He beamed at her, like an uncle who has just given a present to a child. Hydie played with her wineglass. "Now I know all about you," she said brightly.

"Yes."

"What did you study at the University?"

"History, literature, diamat, and culture in general."

"What is diamat?"

"Dialectical materialism. It is the science of history," he explained patiently.

"And this is your first assignment abroad?"

"I have been in other countries," he answered vaguely.

"Doing what?"

"On cultural missions, like this one. . . . Now it is your turn to tell everything."

"All right. I was born a member of the decadent ruling class; my family on my mother's side were bloodsucking Irish landowners, on my father's side mercenary soldiers from West Point. The decomposition of bourgeois society drove my mother to alcoholism, my father into the quixotic obsession that he must save Europe, and myself into a Catholic convent. . . . Now you too know all about me."

"Yes," said Fedya gently, "I do—not all, but much, although you think you were joking. You have drawn the skeleton, as you said—but he who knows the skeleton knows the animal."

"For one thing," said Hydie, "the skeleton always grins. You are clever and 'cultured' too, but yours is a sort of skeleton culture—all grinning teeth and jawbones."

"Why did you leave the convent?" Fedya asked, dismissing her remark with a smile.

"Oh—just the usual reasons. But I would rather not talk about it."

"Why not?"

"If you were to leave the Party, would you feel like discussing it over an omelette?"

Fedya smiled. "But that is different. One does not leave the Party. But your convent—you know that it was all superstition. . . ."

"If you were to discover that the Party too is superstition, wouldn't you leave it?"

He still smiled, but the smile was wearing thin. "You talk about things you do not understand. I asked: why did you leave the convent?"

His tone was so disagreeable, that Hydie decided on a last effort to save her self-respect. "I am eating my omelette," she said in a level voice, feeling her heart beating.

Fedya filled her glass and emptied his own. He looked at her steadily. "Why did you leave your convent?" he asked.

This was really getting fantastic, Hydie thought. But it did not help. Her heart was beating more perceptibly.

"Is this an interrogation?" she said, smiling bravely.

"You will not answer my question?"

"I would like to know who you imagine you are and what gives you the right to talk to me in this way."

"Good." He put knife and fork down, leaned with both elbows on the table and kept looking at her steadily. "You are not stupid, so you will understand this. We meet on a balcony. You provoke an incident. You take my notebook. You examine it. You ring me up. You propose to meet to give back the notebook. You make advances and accept an invitation to 'Rigoletto.' You decide not to go to 'Rigoletto' because you want to talk with me. You ask me questions about my life. Then I ask you a question about yours and you say that you want to eat your omlette. You are a very spoilt woman of the luxury class and you think I come of a country of uncultured savages so you can allow yourself to behave this way."

"My God," Hydie gasped, kneading her handkerchief. "I swear you've got it all wrong—please believe me. . . ."

"Now I see on your face that you understand you have behaved mistakenly, so you want to cry because you think then everything will be all right."

"But this is absolutely horrible. You've got everything wrong. I didn't want to draw you out and I am not spoilt and I don't despise you and I don't feel superior at all, on the contrary. That is just why I didn't want to talk about—well, how I lost faith. Because it gives you such a terrible advantage over me."

"Why?"

"But don't you see—you have something to believe in, and I—we—well we haven't."

He saw by the nervous little jerks of her arm that she was tearing at her handkerchief under the table, and her face had become ugly with excitement. He knew when that happened to a woman that she meant what she said.

"So you behave in this way with me because you are envious that I belong to the movement where I can be socially useful?"

"What's the use of talking about this sort of thing? Talk makes everything seem sentimental and ridiculous."

"That is so because you are haughty and spoilt. We, if we have committed mistakes, we denounce them in public, and then one is punished or forgiven, it depends on the crime. But you did not want to answer my question because you do not have the humbleness to confess your errors, because you have not really been purged of your harmful beliefs by denouncing them openly as lies and superstition."

"Oh God. Can't we stop?" For one moment his voice seemed to echo the last, nerve-racking talks with her Confessor as it droned on, battering with remorseless monotony against her spiritual pride and rebellion. Through the filter of that recollection, Fedya's voice seemed to come from a distant past:

"As you like. I am talking in your own interest. You complain because you can believe in nothing, but this is only because you have not the courage to tear out of your heart the superstition and the lie. . . . Now we can talk about the omelette, and then I shall take you home because it is late."

The *patron* brought them the calf's head, grunting at Hydie to eat it while it was hot, and looking at Fedya with gloomy distaste. She sat in silence, her face white and pinched, picking at the calf's head for the *patron's* sake. Suddenly, to her own surprise, she heard herself talking in an even, almost bored voice:

". . . During the war one wing of the school was transformed into a hospital. Some of us worked as auxiliary nurses. We had some plastic surgery cases—mostly pilots who had been shot down and burnt. Some of these boys of twenty had no noses and looked like obscene syphilitics. One had no lower jaw; one breathed through a rubber tube which came out of a hole in his throat. Some had to spend days with their arms or legs sewn to their chins, to make a graft take—curled up like overgrown embryos. Others had hands shrivelled up like birds' claws, others slept with open eyes like fish because they had no eyelids. One who had hardly any face left, only bandages like Wells' Invisible Man in the film, wrote on a slate before he died: 'To Hell with God. Yours sincerely.' I should have been horrified, but I found that I agreed with him, so I knew that I was lost. Perhaps I would have got over it nevertheless, but one day a girl in the school developed cerebral meningitis. She was only eight, but precocious, pretty and gay. She was very attached to me, so I insisted that I should be allowed to nurse her. . . . Cerebral meningitis, as you perhaps know, produces a headache which is considered the severest pain caused by any natural disease. This child, who had the silly name Toutou, lay for eighteen hours on her back before she went into the final coma, and during those eighteen hours she kept turning her head without respite, and uttered every thirty seconds a certain cry—a high-pitched bird-cry which is characteristic of cerebral meningitis. Just before she went into the coma she had a short moment of relief, and her eyes, which had already shown only their white, focused on me. I bent over her and said something silly about God's great love, and she whispered into my ear: 'Hydie, Hydie, I am afraid—because I think He's gone crazy and I am in His power.' Then, as I said, she went into the coma and died three days later. But this idea of a child of eight got a strong hold on me, for at that time I believed that nobody else before had hit on it. It seemed to explain a lot of things: the sheer malign stupidity of the Power which had put that child on the rack and wrenched those inhuman bird-cries from it; the surrealistic horrors of the plastic ward, and later on, the gas chambers and the death-trains with the chlorine. You see, I could not imagine the world without God just as I couldn't imagine myself as just tissue without heart and a mind, and maybe I can't even today. And as nothing could happen without His will, and as those things kept happening, the only explanation was that God suffered from some malignant form of insanity. . . .''

She stopped, pulled herself together and began to make up her face: "There you are. A complete confession. . . ."

Fedya watched her with curiosity:

"All this is very remarkable. A person of the cultured classes in the twentieth century living in a convent and making crazy theories about the madness of God. Were your parents religious?"

"Oh, no. Most horribly enlightened."

"Now you see. In the Middle Ages superstition was natural. But you were born during the first Five Year Plan, and you went back to the Middle Ages because the corruptness of your civilisation drove you back to the past. It is the same with many of your poets and writers and scientists. They capitulate and surrender to the Middle Ages because they cannot support to live in the Waste Land."

"Do you mean you have read Eliot?" Hydie exclaimed gratefully.

"But of course. I said I have been to the University."

"And he is taught there?"

"Some of his poems are shown to the students as examples of the phenomena which I have described."

"I see."

"And then what happened when you left the convent?"

"Oh, the usual thing. I married somebody who happened to be at hand, and then I divorced him. Then I got an obsession about breaking glass cages. And as you have studied Eliot you can guess the rest. . . ." She leaned back and, smiling into his eyes, recited slowly:

> *"If to be warmed, then I must freeze*
> *And quake in frigid purgatorial fires . . ."*

His face went blank: "This I do not undersatnd. It is too formalistic."

"Never mind. We know each other considerably better now. For instance I know by now most of the expressions on your face. The guarded, distrustful look with all shutters down. The bright flash when you have solved one of the puzzles which our decadent world puts before you. The relaxed debonair look when you push back the cap which you wore as an urchin. The sexy look—we won't go into that. And finally the gentle look which goes with the kind, pitying voice when you explain the laws of history to your ignorant and obedient servant. . . ." She ended with a little curtsey.

Fedya laughed—for the first time he laughed wholeheartedly and abundantly, pushing the invisible cap back and even giving the table a gentle thud. Hydie felt herself flush with pride, and despised herself for it.

"This was very witty, very brilliant," he said with naïve admiration. "I must remember it and tell my friends. How many looks are there altogether?"

"Five. I have counted them on my fingers."

He burst into laughter again. "Now we must drink a little champagne."

She tried to protest that champagne wouldn't go down well with the calf's head, but he insisted. The *patron* brought the bottle with an air of philosophical contempt, studiously avoiding Hydie's eye. As soon as he was gone, Fedya took the bottle from the ice bucket and opened it deftly with a pop like a pistol shot. "Now," he announced, "we must drink five glasses, one to each look."

"You don't mean that you want me to down five glasses running?"

"Oh yes. You must be—a sport. All Americans are sporting,

no? And I shall put on a different look for each glass. It will be very amusing."

He put on the guarded, one-way gaze, clinked his glass to hers and emptied it at one gulp. Hydie followed suit and he filled the glasses again. He went through the rest of the performance with great good humour and a sincere histrionic effort, in the form of exaggerated grimaces such as one puts on to amuse a child. The *patron*, disgusted, had left the bar and gone to the kitchen. Hydie, unwilling to risk another row, dutifully emptied her five glasses in the half-regretful, half-amused knowledge that by making her drunk, Fedya unwittingly defeated his own purpose. He could of course not know that her inhibitions worked in a direction opposite to the usual; that the moment she became intoxicated, the Catholic tolerance of the weakness of the flesh vanished and out came, from under the ill-fitting cloak of the libertine, the cloven hoof of the puritan.

"Now you must take me home," she said, her eyes slightly swimming, "otherwise I shall get quite drunk."

"Oh, no," Fedya said happily. "First we will have coffee and brandy, then we will go to listen to gramophone-music in my room. . . . The aria from 'Rigoletto,' " he added, smiling.

"I agree as far as the coffee and brandy," said Hydie. She saw that he did not believe her, and was filled with pity at the thought of having to disappoint him. At the same time she felt apprehensive at the prospect of another scene. Out of the colourful alcoholic haze around her, she drew a sudden inspiration. Sipping her coffee, her eyes modestly lowered towards the cup, she said melodramatically:

"You only desire my body, not my soul."

It had an effect beyond her expectations. Instead of denouncing the soul as a bourgeois invention, Fedya began to explain with fervour that her reproach was unjust and an insult to his deepest feelings. Ordering a second round of brandy he told her that, though it would be a lie to pretend that he had never embraced a woman before, he had never done so without being deeply in love with her, body and soul. Then he told her about his loneliness in Paris and the profound impression she had made on him at their very first meeting.

Hydie listened avidly and with great satisfaction; every word he said was honey and nectar to her. She thought that this must be what a hungry spinster felt in reading the love-letters she had written and posted to herself.

In the taxi she allowed him for one moment to draw her close and kiss her eyes. Even in that short moment before she pushed him back, she felt how perfectly their bodies fitted, the sympathetic understanding of their skin, the ease of their mutual response. Then the lock-gates of guilt opened and let loose the floods of revulsion. To avoid the ghastly struggle which could only end in his humiliation, she had to use the odious gambit of pretending to be indisposed. This too had its immediate effect. He let go of her at once and, not even trying to conceal his ill-tempered disappointment, told the driver to take them to her address. By the time they arrived he had sufficiently recovered his poise to kiss her hand in saying goodnight; but he did not mention another date.

When Hydie got home, the light was still shining in her father's room. He greeted her, turning round in his desk-chair, with the habitual phrase: "What have you been up to?" It did not mean that he was expecting her to give an account of her evening; it was merely a greeting, and at the same time, by implying that the worst she might have been "up to" would amount to some harmless mischief, it gave her absolution for whatever she had really been doing. Besides, if Hydie had been making love with a man, she would have gone straight to her room; thus each time she came to bid him goodnight was a precious gift to him.

"I went and had dinner with that Russian we met at Monsieur Anatole's."

"Nikitin? Did you have a good time?" His tone was level and neutral. She sat down on the couch, slipped out of her shoes and curled her feet underneath her. She knew that for some reason this made her father happy.

"We quarrelled, mostly. He is quite incredibly primitive, and at the same time has a kind of crude, trenchant intelligence which makes everything appear simple, and our cherished complexities as so much hot air."

"Yes, I noticed that when I had dealings with them."

"Are they all like that?"

"We-ell—you know about the man who thought all French waiters have red hair. But I got a feeling that over there all waiters really do have red hair. . . ."

Hydie did not want to pursue the subject. "Are you glad you have to make no more lists?" she asked.

He leaned back in his chair, smiling at her wearily.

"You said the other day that you were really frightened only during lulls. Now we've got another lull. They have already forgotten about the lists—everybody is a bit ashamed of having panicked, so nothing will be done until the next panic when it will probably be too late. We've got a few months, maybe a few years, and we'll fritter them away again. Sure, we've got all these missions working, and some money is being sent and some arms—but it's just quackery, not medicine."

Hydie wished she hadn't started him off. At the same time she was moved by the puzzled look on his pink brow—the Perplexed Liberal's expression which was so pathetic and endearing to her.

"The trouble is," he rambled on, "you can't save anybody who has no wish to be saved. Something has happened to Europe—God knows how it happened, but it's frightening and appalling. Do you think a whole continent can somehow lose the will to live? If that's so, then we have to clear out from here before we get contaminated by the death-bug."

"You don't mean that—and what's more, you know that you don't mean it," said Hydie brightly.

"Hell, of course I don't. But one can't go on fooling oneself all the time. And if one stops fooling oneself, it's even worse. Anyway, what has your generation to offer? As a rule the young have their programmes and patent-solutions and treat their elders as half-wits. Come to think of it, the most frightening thing is that your generation treats us with such respect. That's a very bad sign."

"Somebody has said that there are situations which admit of no solution. One can't swim in the hollow of the wave."

"Is that all you have to say? I wonder, I wonder . . ." He rubbed his smooth forehead. "Of course in the fourth century A.D. not even the wisest guy could have found a remedy for the galloping consumption of the Roman Empire. . . . You know, I think I am going to read Freud, to find out about this death-bug. History doesn't get you anywhere. It's full of analogies which cut both ways. . . . Hell, there must be some solution."

"As far as I am concerned," said Hydie, "the solution is a stiff highball, and then to bed."

8

THE FALLEN ANGELS

THE day after her dinner with Fedya in the little bistro, Hydie was, as she had foreseen, sorry for her victory. She knew that defeat would have been bliss—for once not the cold purgatorial fires but physical fulfilment. Her thoughts of Fedya were neither intellectually nor erotically articulate, but almost wholly epidermic; she thought of him with her skin. She had no wish to call him on the telephone, and only half a wish to be called by him; for she was convinced that what she felt could not fail to reach and touch him, was propagated through space like radiation; that a physical rapport existed between them, a kind of skin telepathy, which for the time being was enough and all that she desired.

In the afternoon, however, she had to go shopping. This distraction broke the contact and immediately produced a feeling of hollow emptiness. She had meant to go to a cocktail party but rang up Julien instead. Because Julien was an opponent and the total negation of Fedya, being with Julien meant to re-establish the broken current through its negative pole as it were.

He seemed pleased that she had rung and asked her to come to his flat as he had some friends in for drinks. But by the time Hydie got there, only one visitor was left, Professor Vardi. The flat was small, on the third floor of an old house in the St. Germain quarter. Julien's study looked into a narrow street with a shabby little hotel on the opposite side, whose rows of windows made one think of women undressing silhouetted on the curtains at night. The flat smelled pleasantly of the scholarly dust on the paper-bound books on the shelves; it had an atmosphere of stillness and peace which she had not expected. Even Professor Vardi, sitting in an armchair with a small glass of sweet vermouth in his hand, seemed more relaxed. He did not get up when Julien showed Hydie in, and in an odd way this seemed a compliment, a sign that she had been accepted.

"You are lucky to be late," said Julien, mixing her a cocktail out of doubtful looking ingredients. "You missed one of those boring and venomous discussions which one always swears will be the last one, and then starts all over again, like some particularly pointless vice."

"An argument with the demi-vierges," Vardi put in, by way of explanation.

"How fascinating," Hydie said politely. "Did you try to seduce them?"

"Ha—ha," said Vardi. His laughter consisted of two or three mirthless but polite bellows, stating amusement. "We call demi-vierges a certain category of intellectuals who flirt with revolution and violence, while trying to remain chaste liberals at the same time. They are an obscene lot and represent a sad perversion of the intellect."

"We, on the other hand," said Julien, with a flourish of his glass, "we who gave all that innocence can offer and never take back, we are the fallen angels."

He leant his back against the bookshelves with their rows of tattered, paper-covered books, which make French libraries look like cemeteries of literature.

"This afternoon," he continued, "there were three of them: a writer, a painter and a girl. This girl is married to the writer whom she loves but sleeps with the painter whom she detests, and commits suicide unsuccessfully every six months. This tangle has been their main preoccupation for the last five years because we French are a conservative nation and we like even our disorders to have a cachet of organised continuity. Their second main preoccupation is the Revolution, which will realise the Kingdom of Heaven on earth and solve their tangle and all other tangles. Vardi and I had no wish to start a discussion, but Vardi happened to mention a mutual friend of ours who had recently been executed over there, so the three of them jumped at us like furies: first he had not been executed, secondly he had been a traitor anyway, thirdly the Revolution has a right to kill even innocents for higher motives, and so on, the whole diddle-da-doum. Now you see all this would be just silly if it were not that this type of mental perverts wield, contrary to accepted belief, a considerable influence. . . ." He paused, put off by his own pompousness, and Vardi cut in:

"Let us be more specific. With regard to positive ideas, the improvement of artistic taste and so on, the intelligentsia has only a small, slow influence over the masses. But in a negative way, as a corroding, destructive agent, its influence is enormous, particularly in this country."

"And the devil of it is," continued Julien, "that this type of intellectual half-virgin is practically incurable. A man who has slept with a revolution knows what he is talking about. But they remain the eternal flirts, they never give themselves to an idea, they masturbate with it. And if you try to tell them what the object of their solitary day-dreams is really like, they smile indulgently, call you a bitter and disappointed person, or accuse you of persecution mania. . . ."

He paused, his eyes blinking from the smoke of an imaginary cigarette.

"Why do you mind that?" said Hydie. "When you decide to become a renegade you must be prepared for that sort of thing."

"May I point out," Vardi said, looking at Hydie with severe benevolence, "that the use of the word 'renegade' in this context is misleading. If we renounced the revolution it was because the revolution has renounced its ideal; our position is simply the negation of a negation."

He spoke with the angry precision of his rabbinical pathos, yet his manner was defensive, as if he were driven by a permanent urge to justify himself. Both he and Julien seemed to be badly shaken by their failure to convince those whom they knew to be unconvincible.

"Oh, shut up," Julien said irritably. "Miss Anderson is right. People don't mind if you betray humanity, but if you betray your club you are considered a renegade and they don't like a renegade whatever his motive. Has it never struck you that even atheists respect the Catholic convert, whereas everybody despises a priest turned atheist? Protest as much as you like—they will never forgive us for having renounced an error."

"Your masochism is incurable," said Vardi. "I haven't renounced an error, because it is not I who committed the error but the Party."

"My dear man, an apostate is an apostate, even if the Pope happens to sleep with his own sister."

"There was a man called Savonarola . . ."

"With whom you have certain affinities," said Julien. "He was burnt alive."

"And what does that prove?" said Vardi, turning for judgment to Hydie. "I ask you: what does that prove?"

Hydie had been drifting along the bookshelves looking at titles and listening to the argument. What Julien had said about defrocked priests had struck her as true; it explained why she felt so at home in this room, the peculiar bond which united her with Julien and even with Vardi, despite his priggish self-righteousness. She too was a fallen angel, a dispossessed of faith, one of the Ravens Nevermore. And she understood that not only would they never be forgiven for having renounced their error, but that they were also unable to forgive themselves.

"I think," she said in her bright party manner, replacing a book on the shelf, "I think the fact that Savonarola was burnt proves Julien's point."

"It's simple," said Julien. "The people disliked the corruption of the clergy, but they hated the apostate monk even more."

"Nonsense," said Vardi. "They burnt him because the masses were not ripe for his apostasy. What about Luther? And what about Henry VIII?"

"They were both foreigners to Rome," said Julien. "So they were not considered renegades but rebels, supported by a new national consciousness. Besides, Luther gave the Bible to the people. . . . What have we to offer, Vardi?"

"I regret," Vardi said caustically, "but I can't offer anything in the prophetic line. I am just a pedantic, flat-footed radical with a carefully formulated platform, opposed both to the anarchy of capitalism and the tyranny of the totalitarian State, opposed to all military blocs whether of the East or the West."

"And you sit in the no-man's land between the fronts, suspended between heaven and earth like Mohammed's coffin," said Julien.

". . . With a carefully worked-out platform," Vardi repeated, ignoring the interruption, "and a tentative programme which, if I may point out in all modesty, is gaining increasing support in certain sections of the thinking public. And what is more," he added, turning to Hydie, "Julien is one of the co-authors of that programme and when in a normal mood, an active member of our League."

"Yes," said Julien dreamily. "As you said, we are gaining rapid support. During the last year the number of our followers has increased by fifty per cent: from eight to twelve. . . ."

"Ha—ha," stated Vardi, rising to his feet. "Not a new joke, but always effective. Now I must go; I hope you will soon get over your attack of masochism. . . . He has those attacks from time to time," he explained to Hydie, "like bouts of malaria. Perhaps you can have a therapeutic influence on him."

"I should like to," said Hydie coldly, "but I must go too."

"Oh, don't," said Julien. "Can't you stay for another drink?"

"All right, but what will the Professor think?"

"The worst—ha, ha," said Vardi in a tone which gallantly implied that she was above vulgar suspicion. He shook hands with her in his ceremonious way, a little awkwardly.

"How do you like my friend?" asked Julien, when Vardi had gone.

"The first time I thought him rather horrible. Now I find him quite endearing."

"Don't underestimate Vardi," said Julien. "He's got one of those brains like Swiss wrist-watches which wind themselves up automatically. But believe it or not, he has got a complex about women taller than himself. It cramps his style; that's why he is so pompous when you are about."

Hydie sighed. "Other people's complexes are always a mystery to one." She thought of the burn-scar on Julien's face which he was still trying to keep out of her sight.

"Yes. For instance, I can't imagine for the life of me your complex about having left your Church. And yet it seems to affect you in the same way as our apostasy affects us."

"Have I told you about it?"

"No, but you made some hints, and the rest is not difficult to guess."

He was sitting on the window-sill of the little alcove, with his back against the iron railing. Twilight was descending into the narrow street; in one or two windows of the little hotel opposite the lights had gone on and vague shadows moved across the Venetian blinds. A woman in the street called: *"Marcel! Marcel! Tu as oublié ta bicyclette";* and the fact that Marcel had walked off forgetting that he had a bicycle seemed one of those poetic minor mysteries one meets in life which will never be solved. A vague idea drifted through Hydie's mind that one should pay more attention to this kind of mystery: perhaps they held out some clue. Carrying her glass, she sat down in the other corner of the window-sill, her elbow on the railing, and looked down into the street. The people walking unhurriedly towards their apéritifs in groups of two or three with the dawdling, shuffling gait of the left-bank Parisian had a soothing influence on her mood. She realised that for hours she had not thought of Fedya, and her heart contracted in the familiar spasm of pain-delight. Julien was talking again, on a different subject; she had missed the first few sentences:

". . . The reason why Europe is going to the dogs is of course that it has accepted the finality of personal death. By this act of abdication we have severed our relations with the infinite, isolated ourselves from the universe, or if you like, from God. This loss of cosmic consciousness which you find expressed everywhere—in the cerebral character of modern poetry, painting, architecture and so on—has led to the adoration of the new Baal: Society. I don't mean the worship of the Totalitarian State, or even of the State as such: the real evil is the deification of society itself. Sociology, social science, social therapy, social integration, social what-have-you. Since we have accepted death as final, society has been replacing the cosmos. Man has no longer any direct transactions with the universe, the stars, the meaning of life; all his cosmic transactions are monopolised and all his transcendental impulses absorbed by the fetish 'Society.' We do not talk any longer of homo sapiens, of man; we talk of 'the individual.' We do not aspire toward goodness and charity: we aspire toward 'social integration.' Anthropologists no longer study the habits of people: they 'work in the social field.' And so . . ."

"And so?"

He made a nervous grimace:

"I am boring you. I would much rather make love to you."

"The fact is you would much rather go on talking."

Julien laughed a little forcedly:

"Assuming for the moment that you are right—why?"

"Because I am such a good listener and because I am interested."

"All right," said Julien with a sigh of resignation. "What I mean is this. As religious convictions have been replaced by social idolatry while man's instinctive horror of apostasy remained the same, we are all bound to perish as victims of our secular loyalties."

"Is that not the same thing as perishing in a religious war?"

"No. In a religious war you had at least the consolation of going to heaven while your opponent went to hell. But that isn't really the point. The point is that the deification of society entails a cult of logistics and expediency. Now take expediency as the sole guide of action; multiply this factor by the effective range of modern technology, and let the product loose in a conflict of boundless secular loyalties; the inevitable result is mutual extinction. The only, the one and only hope of preventing this is the emergence of a new transcendental faith which would deflect people's energies from the 'social field' to the cosmic field—which would re-establish direct transactions between man and the universe and would act as a brake on the motors of expediency. In other words: the emergence of a new religion, of a cosmic loyalty with a doctrine acceptable to twentieth century man."

"Who is going to invent it?" asked Hydie.

"There is the rub. Religions are not invented; they materialise. It is a process like the condensation of a gas into liquid drops."

"And all we can do is to wait for it to happen?"

"Oh, one can always go on fiddling with programmes and platforms. But it comes to the same thing."

The street below them was humming with the life of the twilight hour, the blue hour of the Seine valley. On the open-air counter of the dairy shop, the display of manifold sorts of cheese began to get blurred into a pale still-life: *"Fromages Variés, 195–"* A bored policeman was contemplating the row of peacefully dead hares suspended from hooks in front of the poultry shop; his hands, crossed behind his back, were playing with his white baton. The same voice as before called out, invisible under a doorway: *"Marcel! Marcel! Tu as encore oublié ta bicyclette."* The mystery deepened, and so did the shadows of the evening. Round the corner of the Rue de l'Université the gas lights were already on.

"Why don't you write instead of working on platforms and arguing with demi-vierges?" asked Hydie.

"Because I can write no more," he said in an indifferent tone. "I told you so the first evening in the taxi, only then I was slightly drunk and dramatic." He got up from the window-sill and began to pace absent-mindedly through the room. Hydie had quite forgotten that he limped; just now, however, the limp was more than usually noticeable. He caught her watching him and at once the limp became less pronounced.

"That," he said with a grimace, "and the scar on my mug, are souvenirs of the battle of Teruel, anno domini 1937. Spain was the last act in that comedy of innocence—the climax and apotheosis of the great buffoonery which preceded the Fall. By the way, Vardi was in it too. That surprises you, doesn't it? He kept losing bits of his rifle and never quite knew in which direction the front was, but he stuck it out to the end. . . I was in the hospital when I read in the paper that the last Mohicans of the Revolution had all confessed to be spies, and were whimpering for a bullet into the back of their necks as a man in pain whimpers for morphia."

He paused, then said in a changed tone:

"But you were interested in my limp. You have probably noticed that it gets more or less pronounced according to one's emotional state, like nervous stammering. If—when I pull myself together I hardly limp at all. . . ." He looked at her with hopeless pleading underneath the fixed ironical smile; he had actually blushed, standing at a little distance in front of her, cigarette dangling from his lip.

"Other people's complexes are really a mystery," said Hydie in a dry voice. "You were talking about why you can't write."

"Oh—if you are really interested I can give you a whole catalogue of reasons. As far as poetry goes—that was finished the day I left the Party. Fallen angels don't write poems. There is lyric poetry, and sacred poetry, and a poetry of love and a poetry of rebellion; the poets of apostasy do not exist. It worried me for a while; then I accepted it as an empirical fact, and took to writing novels instead. The first one was quite a success—it was meant to be the beginning of a trilogy. Then came the war, the defeat, the Resistance and so on; and when all that was over, I knew I should never write the second volume, nor any other volume."

"But why?"

He remained standing a few feet distant from her, between the desk and the window. The soft, grey light made the better half of his face with the clean, high forehead dominate the other one; it almost effaced the scar and the bitter curve of the lips with the indispensable cigarette stump.

At last he said:

"Art is a contemplative business. It is also a ruthless business. One should either write ruthlessly what one believes to be the truth, or shut up. Now I happen to believe that Europe is doomed, a chapter in history which is drawing to its finish. This is so to speak my contemplative truth. Looking at the world with detachment, under the sign of eternity, I find it not even disturbing. But I also happen to believe in the ethical imperative of fighting evil, even if the fight is hopeless—you have only to think of what happened to the family of Boris. And on this plane my contemplative truth becomes defeatist propaganda and hence an immoral influence. You can't get out of the dilemma between contemplation and action. There were idyllic periods in history when the two went together. In times like ours, they are incompatible. And I am not an isolated case. European art is dying out, because it can't live without truth, and its truth has become arsenic. . . ."

He paused, and Hydie shook her head:

"What you say sounds quite logical—but it also sounds like finding excuses. . . ."

Julien ignored her interruption.

"There is another point about art: objectivity. Now assuming I were to try to put you and your friend Nikitin as characters into a novel . . ." His eyes blinked at her reflectively, like a portrait-photographer's watching a model. "It would be all right for perhaps twenty pages, then the whole thing would go to pieces because, whatever I did, the figure of Nikitin would turn sour under my pen. Do you understand?"

"No, I don't. And must we be personal?"

"We must. You asked why I can write no more, which is a question more personal than to ask a man why he is impotent. Besides, I didn't mean to say anything nasty about the real Nikitin; I was talking about him as a character in fiction. And the trouble with the fictional Nikitin is precisely that he is not fiction but reality."

"I still don't understand."

"Let me put it this way. Reality cannot be directly translated into fiction; it must be digested, assimilated, then sweated out in little drops. Everybody knows that if you want to write about a murderer, you must swallow the murderer and become one yourself—as the savages swallow a man's heart to acquire his courage; and you must sweat murder through all your pores. It is a kind of sympathetic magic; the writer must have the digestive system of a cannibal; his quality depends on it. But Nikitin is indigestible; Nikitin lies like a stone in my stomach; Nikitin makes the ink curdle in my pen . . ."

"But must you write about Nikitin?"

"What else is there to write about? If you sit in the condemned cell, the only person of real interest to you is the executioner. But my imagination refuses to be Nikitin. She— I mean my imagination—is greedy, voracious, amoral, a cannibal and a harlot; but when it comes to Nikitin, she baulks, turns suddenly priggish and chaste, becomes full of moral indignation and aesthetic revulsion. A single look from Nikitin's eyes makes her wish to retire to a nunnery or to preach a sermon—and when a writer becomes a preacher, he is finished."

"You mean you hate Fedya so much that you are unable to draw an objective picture of him?"

"Oh, is he called Fedya? I did not even know he had a Christian name. To me, he is merely a mass-produced pattern: the ancient Neanderthaler with a modern robot-brain. As I said, I didn't mean to be nasty about him presonally."

Hydie rose and, with her hands on the railing, looked down into the street, half turning her back on him. "You were not nasty," she said quietly, "merely envious. . . ." He wanted to interrupt her, but she shook her head. "I don't mean envious of him as a man. You are envious because he believes in something in which you have ceased to believe."

"That's fairly obvious, isn't it?" he said. "The question is whether you think that kind of belief enviable."

"That question," she said, "is beside the point. You are envious because you have lost one faith and cannot find another. I know that, because it is the same with me. Sometimes I feel like a snake which has shed its old skin but can't grow a new one. It makes one feel naked and vulnerable. But you walk about with a false skin . . ."

"My dear," he said, "who doesn't?"

"Fedya doesn't. Nor Monsieur Anatole. . . . And what I particularly dislike about you," she continued softly and deliberately, "is your attitude of arrogant heart-brokenness."

He smiled fixedly across the half-dark room, then said: "Touché."

"I don't care." Her voice became even more toneless, soft and deliberate. "What I want you to tell me is how the story between Fedya and me would end—if we were characters in your book."

He tried to see the expression in her eyes, but she was looking down into the street, showing him only her profile.

"Why do you want to know that?" he asked.

She kept looking down into the street, waiting for his answer.

"It can only end," he said, "according to one of two classic patterns—as you yourself know only too well, my dear. The first pattern is the Taming of the Shrew. The second is Samson and Delilah."

She gave no answer. He looked across the room at her bent

profile, now merely a silhouette. He added in a more hesitant tone:

"There is of course a third possibility: Judith and Holofernes . . ."

Though he had spoken haltingly, almost shyly, the idea for a moment had a strange quality of certainty. She turned and said lightly: "I think you are crazy. Now I must be going."

From the street, the woman's voice called: "Marcel! Marcel . . ."

"Who is that?" asked Hydie.

"Who?"

"The woman who called 'Marcel.' "

"Did she? I am deaf to street noises."

"About somebody having forgotten a bicycle?"

"I beg your pardon?"

He looked at her in bewilderment, as if he had woken up from sleep. The room was dark. She had an unusually strong impression of *déjà vu*. "Will you turn the light on?" she said.

"Of course. I am sorry." He switched the light on and said, blinking, as he opened the door for her:

"By the way, Boris has been taken to a hospital."

Since their meeting on Bastille Day, she had hardly thought of the embittered Pole. Now his gaunt figure stood with sudden vividness before her eyes, and she had a feeling that for some reason his fate affected hers in a personal way.

"Is it serious?"

"He is on the danger list. If you could perhaps drop in for a visit—that is if you are not too busy seeing Mr. Nikitin . . ."

There was no insolence in his voice, only a calm hostility which made her understand that he thought of Nikitin not in connection with her, but in relation to Boris. Ignoring his remark, she said:

"I would willingly, but I hardly know him—besides, I had a definite impression that he disliked me."

"Boris doesn't like anybody much. But a visit from a woman, with a few flowers. . . . I don't think he knows a single woman in Paris."

"All right, then, give me his address."

He wrote it down for her; it was the public ward of a State hospital for the destitute.

Out in the street Hydie hesitated between having dinner alone in a restaurant and ringing up some people. But she was not hungry, and she knew that once in a telephone box she would dial Fedya's number. She had refused Julien's invitation to dine with him under the pretext of being booked, and she knew that he was convinced that she was dining with Fedya. She stood forlorn and undecided on the pavement of the Boulevard St. Germain, until two American students tried to pick her up. She refused with such a Bostonian drawl that the students apologised and took to their heels. At that precise moment she seemed to hear the telephone ring at her home, in the flat in Passy. She hurriedly stopped a taxi and promised him double fare if he drove fast. As she fumbled with the latchkey of the flat, she heard the patient, intermittent buzz of the telephone; she could tell by its sound that it had been ringing for quite a while. It stopped in the split second between her reaching for the receiver and actually lifting it. She knew that she now had four or five hours of hopeless waiting before her; and probably twelve hours tomorrow, and the day after. She accepted it with the resignation of a person afflicted with a chronic disease waiting for the beginning of a new attack. For now at last she had the courage to admit to herself that she was in earnest.

Mechanically, she made the necessary preparations: she took some cold food from the icebox, carried it to her room, fetched a bottle of Scotch, a bottle of soda, a volume of poetry, a detective story, three gramophone records. Having laid out everything within reach, she undressed and went to bed without looking into the mirror. Now she was ready for the siege.

She knew by experience that the first phase of the attack was easier to endure in the warm darkness of the bed, her head under the blanket, curled up like a dog or an embryo. But even so it was fairly bad. After a few minutes she threw the blanket back and poured herself a drink.

By now the white plastic telephone receiver lying silently in its cradle had become the focus of the room; the radiations of its silence filled the whole space. She knew that it was as useless to try to keep her eyes away from it as it was useless to try to hypnotise it into giving sound. Matters must take their preordained course; nothing she did, or omitted to do, could alter it.

9

FATIGUE OF THE SYNAPSES

Leo Nikolayevich Leontiev had been struggling for three hours to write the eight hundred words of the cabled version of his speech destined for home consumption. To reach the deadline of the next Friday issue of "Freedom and Culture," the text of the cable had to be delivered by 8 p.m. at the latest to the office of the Commonwealth Government's official News Agency. It was now 6 p.m., and the Agency had already twice telephoned for the text. Leontiev had two hours left to write it, and to change for the reception which Monsieur Anatole was giving in his honour. He rose impatiently and crossed the soft carpet to the French window.

The hotel was one of the famed old buildings in a side street from the Rue de Rivoli, and the windows of his suite over-looked the Place Vendôme. The square looked even more solid and restful than usual at this late afternoon hour of a hot summer day. It had con-ti-nu-ity, as his old friend Monsieur Anatole would say. Leontiev tried to recall the sight of the slums of Belleville as an antidote, but did not succeed. The image that appeared before his mind's eye was that of the Palazzo Vecchio in Florence.

He went back to the graceful Regency desk and started once again on his labours. The trouble was that it was not enough to translate the text of the speech into the ritual terminology, the rigid, Byzantine, catechismal style required for home consumption. He had to produce an entirely different text with an almost opposite message which, however, did not show any direct, open contradiction to the original, and which, moreover, preserved some of his original phrases as connecting links. He started on this task for the sixth or seventh time; and again at the first phrase he got stuck at a preposition, crossed it out, replaced it, got involved with the syntax and had to erase the whole sentence. This had now been going on since three o'clock.

He knew the symptoms well. Professor Gruber had called them "fatigue of the synapses." The synapses were the junctions between brain cells, across which the nervous impulse had to pass. There were millions of them in the brain. Sometimes something went wrong at these junctions; the impulse could not get past and certain thoughts and actions were blocked. The cause of this, according to Gruber, was certain toxic substances produced by fatigue, which accumulated at the synapses and paralysed their action. These toxic chemicals, then, had the power to block thought, or certain kinds of thought. Other toxic substances, of course, had the opposite effect, as Gruber had patiently explained. They reduced the normal resistance at the junctions, so that channels of thought were thrown wide open which in a well-regulated brain remained prudently and mercifully closed. Liquor was a relatively harmless substance of this kind. But there were others, less harmless, capable of rearranging the whole heirarchy of brain junctions, so that channels normally open were closed, and those normally closed were opened. It was amusing, Gruber had explained, growing lyrical, what you could do with a man in that state. You could make him believe the weirdest things if you only hammered them in with sufficient intensity; you could make him believe that he was Cæsar or Brutus, a hero or a criminal—provided of course that he had some potential inclination, within the normally blocked channels of his mind, to become either of them. But then, who hadn't? Who of us hasn't killed his Mandarin?

"What's that?" Leontiev had asked absent-mindedly. And Gruber, who on that evening had been curiously excited and talkative, as if he himself were under the influence of a drug, had explained:

"It is a psychological test invented by some French wit. If you could become rich by pressing a button with the result of killing a Mandarin in China whom you had never seen, and without anybody ever knowing about it—would you do it or not . . .? Needless to say, every one of us has, on some occasion, killed a Mandarin in his thoughts . . ." Gruber had paused, then continued with a kind of suppressed enthusiasm in his voice:

"But now listen. The beauty of playing about with the synapses is that we have discovered methods whereby we can make a man believe that he has *really* killed his Mandarin and confess with earnest conviction that the victim had a gold crown in his left upper molar, that he met him at such-and-such a place, at such-and-such an hour, and killed him in such-and-such a way with the help of X, Y and Z, who were

his accomplices. . . . Damn it all, if we were allowed to publish our results, our colleagues at the American universities
would realise that we are ten years ahead of them."

Gruber had shut up abruptly and there was a silence during
which, as it so often happened at that time and in that country, the listener realised that the speaker had realised that he
had said something which should have remained unsaid. Their
thoughts echoed each other's, and each silent rebound reinforced their apprehension. They were about the same age,
both in their early fifties; but Leontiev with his sturdy build
and military countenance looked about ten years younger than
the Professor. The latter was completely bald, held his head
cocked to one side like a bird, fidgeted incessantly, and had
such a jerky way of moving about that Leontiev wouldn't have
been surprised if Gruber had suddenly jumped to the top of
the cupboard and continued the conversation with his feet
dangling from it—as in fact he had been in the habit of doing
in their student days.

The two men had been on friendly terms at the University,
then they had drifted apart and for the last twenty years Leontiev had completely lost sight of Gruber. But everybody else
had also lost sight of Gruber at that time; he seemed to have
vanished from circulation. The last paper he had published, on
the effects of two little-known exotic drugs, had created a
minor sensation in academic circles. Gruber and his associate,
another young psychiatrist, had studied the effects of the
drugs on themselves in a series of experiments over a period
of three months. It was rumoured that they had both become
addicts, and a few months after they published their paper,
Gruber's associate shot himself. Shortly afterwards Gruber
had been mobilised for some research job with the army.
There were more rumours, followed by some discouraging
hints from the proper quarters which had the required effect:
Gruber's name was no longer mentioned either in public or in
private, and was soon conveniently forgotten. It had cropped
up, quite unexpectedly, a few weeks before Leontiev's journey
to Paris when, at the end of some official banquet, he had
complained to an old friend about his growing inability to
work, and his apprehensions of a nervous breakdown. This
friend belonged to the inner circle of the ruling hierarchy,
but it was rumoured that he had fallen in disfavour: at the
last May Day parade he was not seen on the official stand,
his name had vanished from the newspapers and his demotion

seemed imminent. On that evening he had been fairly drunk and had grinned at Leontiev with sympathy: "So you are cracking up, eh?" he said. "Why don't you consult Gruber?"

Leontiev, who could not have survived thirty years of campaigning on the cultural front had he not acquired a perfect control of his reactions, nodded absently, but on second thoughts he thought it proper to express mild surprise. "Gruber?" he said. "Oh, yes. I didn't know that he was—available."

His friend grinned even more. "You did not know, eh? How are you going to write the chronicle of our times if you know nothing about Gruber?" Then he stopped grinning, conscious of somebody's gaze alighting on them. He added indifferently: "No, he is not available—only in exceptional cases. But I guess a Hero of Culture and Joy of the People qualifies as an exceptional case. I'll see what I can do. He will either come and see you tomorrow, or you had better forget that I mentioned him."

The next day Gruber, in an enormous limousine, had turned up at Leontiev's country house; had taken an appreciative look at the tennis court and swimming pool; had put his stethoscope in a perfunctory way to Leontiev's chest—all this in a manner as if they had only parted yesterday—and a little later on, over a bottle of Burgundy in Leontiev's study, had explained to him about "the fatigue of the synapses." Then, carried away by the subject, or by the unusual heavy Burgundy, or by the gap of twenty years since their last encounter, he had begun to talk about the chemical reconditioning of the mind, the means of injecting a sense of guilt into a man's veins with a sterilised needle, of grafting a criminal past into him as one grafts a bone-flap onto a fractured skull.

"The funny thing is," he had said with a sudden boyish giggle which stood in unpleasant contrast to his aging bald man's face, "that though we are not allowed to publish our results, they have in fact been the most publicised news in our time." Then another of those abrupt silences had descended between them in which each weighed the consequences of having read the other's thoughts. "Of course you understand that it was all a joke—a fantasy. I was pulling your leg," said Gruber.

"Of course," said Leontiev, smiling with his famous blue stare straight into the other's eyes. "You always used to pull our legs, even as a student. But what I wanted to ask . . .

Can you somehow unblock this—this fatigue of the synapses, in regard to my writing?"

"Hm," said the Professor. "It depends. Science is not magic. I cannot invent your Mandarin; that's your job. I must have something to build on—something real, even if it is only ten per cent of the goods to be delivered. That's what I have always tried to impress on these blockheads of ours."

"I don't follow you," said Leontiev.

"Don't you? I thought you knew the elements. . . . After all, you are a writer—a profession which is supposed to require some imagination." He became irritated, started fidgeting again on his chair. With his egg-shaped skull and frail, thin body, he gave Leontiev the impression of an oversized, aged embryo—except for some irritating detail which he could not define. Now suddenly he found out what it was: the bald Gruber's eyebrows were dyed black, and these dyed eyebrows had an extraordinary mobility.

"You must be a little more explicit," said Leontiev.

"Explicit?" the Professor giggled. "My poor friend, that is the last thing you should ask for, (a) as an artist, (b) in view of the particular circumstances of our age and time . . ." He frowned; then shrugged; then seemed to have made his mind up. "All right," he said. "If you really want me to help you. How is Zina?" he asked abruptly.

"She is fine. We have no children, you know."

"How old is she now?"

"Nearing fifty. Still pretty. At least *I* think so."

"Always devoted to each other like two turtle-doves?"

Leontiev smiled. "You are not married."

"Not in my line . . ."

There was a silence. Suddenly the Professor asked in a casual tone: "Why don't you clear out?"

At first Leontiev thought that he had not heard well; then he composed his features and put on the stern, bushy-eyebrow look which made people like the poet Navarin change their colour.

"I haven't understood you—at least I hope so," he said gravely.

"All right, all right, cut it out. As soon as I leave, you can rush to the telephone and denounce me. I shall then say that I have deliberately tried to provoke you. Maybe that's what I am doing, who knows? Anyway, you are one of the few who are allowed from time to time to go abroad to congresses and what not. But of course each time you have to leave Zina behind as a hostage. Hence the choice before you is: to sacrifice Zina or to go on sacrificing art, truth, integrity, et cetera. Personally I don't know what art, truth, integrity, et cetera, mean—not in my line. But I know that to some people they mean something—enough to make the synapses go haywire in conflicts of this kind. . . . Now, I have watched your reactions—I bet you imagine you have what people call 'an inscrutable face'—so I know that although you long to clear out, and write the one honest book of your life, you are too much of a moral coward to let Zina end her days north of the Arctic Circle for the sake of Honesty, Truth and so on. . . . Shut up," he screamed suddenly, as Leontiev tried to interrupt him, "shut up, and let me finish first. You wanted me to be explicit, didn't you? . . . Anyway, solution number one has to be eliminated because of your sentimental attachment to Zina. The other solution is more complicated. You have difficulties in writing; these difficulties will increase gradually; soon you will be entirely blocked. Nobody can go on raping his conscience indefinitely. I use 'conscience' as a shorthand expression though it isn't in my line; what I mean is a given pattern of conditioning. You can go against it for a while, even for years, but it requires more and more effort, and once the toxic fatigue-products begin to accumulate, you are done for. The only way out is to alter the pattern through reconditioning. I have done that successfully in a number of cases—but there the required effect was rather the opposite to that in your case. . . ." He giggled. "Unless you fancy the part of a Christian martyr—that I can do for you without difficulty. . . ."

"You are talking utter mad, criminal nonsense," said Leontiev with dignity. "Now I must beg you . . ."

"That's right. It was a perfect line. Just the correct words. Now listen. Why am I taking such an interest in you? Answer the question for yourself. I never liked you particularly, and since we last met you have become a pompous ass. But I never had a chance of trying my hand on a case like yours. And my work is beginning to bore me—always the same monotonous job. In your case the method and aim would be just the opposite. I feel a kind of creative itch; I have a feeling that I could not only remove your inhibitory blocks but make you write a real masterpiece within the strict limits of orthodoxy. That may sound a little fantastic to you, but after all the per-

formances of our self-styled Mandarin-killers were no less
fantastic. . . ."

"Assuming," said Leontiev, "that I gave the slightest cre-
dence to your mad and treasonable fantasies—which I do not
—let me ask for curiosity's sake how you would set about it?"

Gruber laughed and, reaching across the table, patted Leontiev's shoulder. "Perfect," he giggled. "You are the most perfect ham actor I have seen. . . . Now to the method. It is
fantastically simple. I can put it into one phrase." He paused,
then said with emphasis:

"I will make you believe in what you write."

There was a silence. Leontiev was on the point of saying
"how dare you" in a majestic voice; then he gave up. They
had now both gone too far. They had delivered themselves
into each other's hands; his tension snapped and suddenly he
didn't care any longer. Instead of "how dare you," he said
with a tired smile: "And how are you going to do that?"

"Ah," said Gruber. "There is a good boy. It is less difficult
than you imagine. All I need is, as I said before, something
real to build on. You remember old Archimedes: Give me one
firm spot on which to stand and I will move the earth. After
all there must be *something* in which you still believe. . . .
Let's see. You believe in the storming of Bastilles? Good. In
the Barricades of 1848? In the Commune of 1871? In the
Proclamation of 1917? Better and better. Now I see the pattern. You believe that basically all our premises were right,
and that at a certain point, by sheer accident of persons and
circumstances things began to go wrong. Well, if you believe
that you are not a difficult case. All you need is to be made to
see that everything that happened happened not by accident
but by necessity; and that consequently if our premises were
right, the outcome must be the will of History which, ex
hypothesi, is always right. It's perfectly simple, isn't it?"

"Perfectly."

"Only you don't believe a word of it. It will be my job to
persuade you."

"How? With syringes and pills?"

"Mostly by arguments. The arguments will be a little repeti-
tive and may involve a certain amount of bullying—that's part
of the reconditioning therapy. The bullying is designed to
abolish the main source of resistance—your notions of self-
respect and so on. The chemical paraphernalia serve merely
the purpose of making you more receptive to the arguments

by opening certain channels and blocking others. After a few weeks at the utmost, the whole layout of your brain will be altered as thoroughly as the map of Europe after the last war. You will believe everything you write, and you will write with conviction and gusto as befits a Hero of Culture . . ."

There was a pause. Leontiev said:

"You are right: it is perfectly simple. And perfectly disgusting."

"Of course. Nothing more disgusting than to watch a film-actress having her beauty treatment—the slapping of the grease-covered face, the lifting of the bosom, the curling of the locks in the electric machine. But the result is a dazzling sight, and the procedure only seems disgusting to those who entertain naïve illusions about the body. My proposal is disgusting to you because you have equally naïve illusions about the working of the mind."

"Maybe. But I won't do it."

"I thought so. Bad luck for me, worse for you. I miss an experiment, you miss a unique chance to become the first synthetic writer in history. But I never had any luck in persuading patients to submit to voluntary treatment—not even members of the 'Fearless Sufferers.' Maybe I shall have to have you locked up for our mutual benefit, and that of the reading public."

"I would not be surprised if you did," said Leontiev.

"We are both past the age where anything surprises us. Nevertheless I am surprised at something I have discovered about you. You are, as I said, a pompous ass, a ham and a ruthless scoundrel. But for all that you have a curious kind of innocence. . . . One night during the great famine, in a town infested by hordes of waifs and strays, I stepped on a child sleeping rolled up in a doorway. It was a girl of eight or nine; she woke up, rubbed her eyes, made me a proposal in words which would make a corporal blush, and then continued in the same sleepy voice: 'All right, uncle, if you don't want to, you could at least tell me a fairy story. . . .' You have this same naïveté of a corrupt child."

They had talked on for a little while, then Gruber had left. Leontiev could still see him waving goodbye, his bald head stuck out of the window of the big black limousine, agitating his dyed eyebrows like a clown.

Leontiev tore the paper up with resignation, went back to

the window and looked down at the restful square, his fists
jammed into the pockets of his dressing-gown. It was a blue
flannel dressing-gown which Zina had given him on the tenth
anniversary of their marriage, nearly twenty years ago. He
had worn it ever since at work, and it had become such a habit
that by now he felt himself quite unable to write in any other
attire. A classic example of conditioning, Gruber would say.
Also, for the last twenty years whenever Zina had come into
his study and seen him standing at the window—with his fists
jammed into the pockets of the dressing-gown, his legs apart
and his shoulders squared, he gave the impression of a Cos-
sack hetman gazing out into the steppe—she would invariably
say, in her soft Ukrainian singsong: "Don't strain the pockets
so, Lyovochka, it makes them bulge." At first this had made
him furious; then it had become an essential ritual of his
working day—another conditioned reflex, in Gruber's terms.
The "study" had at first been a corner of their kitchen-bed-
sittingroom, partitioned off by a sheet; then a tiny, former
maid's room in a shared communal flat; finally a huge library
in their country house, complete with Bokhara carpets and
goldfish bowls. But the dressing-gown had remained the same,
and Zina's soft inflection had remained the same, and for all
he knew the soft curves of her body too—for she was a
Ukrainian peasant girl, passionate but modest, who in the
thirty years of their marriage had never shown herself to him
in the nude. He knew her body like a blind man, only by
touch; its gentle curves, and the languid rhythm of her movements in the dark had always appeared to him like an echo of
the lilting singsong of her voice. Just now he would have given
anything to hear her open the door behind him and say, with
a resigned, absent-minded sigh: Don't strain the pockets, Lyovochka . . . He was sure it would do the trick and enable
him to finish the revised version of his speech.

It was almost seven; he had only an hour left. If he pretended to be sick he would have to notify the Cultural Attaché, and they would at once send the Embassy doctor. A
man could fake any emotion or belief, but not a cold, not even
an indigestion or a serious headache. Which went to prove the
correctness of a philosophy which took only the body seriously and had destroyed the very notion of a hypothetical mind.
Though, if Gruber was to be believed, the mind could nevertheless directly affect the body by producing the famous
fatigue of the synapses. At present he felt as if a whole drug-

store of poison were working at them—the accumulated toxins of thirty years. Yet to pretend sickness would inevitably arouse suspicion—they had a sixth sense for that kind of thing. He could of course get away with it, but it would be entered as an item on the debit side of the book and one could never know for certain what one's balance-sheet looked like: how much credit one had left, where the overdraft began; it was a peculiarity of the system that once one had over-drawn, one was never given a chance to redress the balance. Besides, if he reported sick, he could not go to Monsieur Ana-tole's reception. And the prospect of visiting Monsieur Ana-tole again had been the one bright spot in this whole trip. He felt an almost physical longing to see people move about at a party without squinting over their shoulders at invisible shadows; to hear them chattering frivolously, irreverently, ir-responsibly—not for the record, not in the desperate hope of improving the unknown balance-sheet, but for the sole pur-pose of exercising their wits and vocal chords. He himself of course could take no part in all that; he would have to pose, as always, for his own statue, looking at them from under bushy eyebrows, the martial image of a Hero of Culture. But he would nevertheless hear them talk and see them move about, gossip, laugh and munch sandwiches at their ease. The last time he was allowed abroad had been five years ago; the next time would probably never be. He needed an evening like that, just one evening like that, more than he needed any-thing in life. But he could only go to Monsieur Anatole's if he finished the cable. Well then, he was going to finish it, even if all the synapses burst under the strain. Let them burst . . .

His clenched fists were straining against the lining of the pockets. He turned round to go back to the desk. Suddenly he felt something give way under the tense downward pressure of his right fist. The strain had been too much for the dressing-gown; the seam of the right pocket had burst open. In twenty years this had never happened before. He looked at the loose, torn pocket in alarm verging on panic, and at the same mo-ment he heard the telephone ring. He covered the pocket with his hand, like a wound, and lifted the receiver. The deferential voice of the hall porter announced that there was a messenger downstairs who insisted on seeing him personally about a cable. "Tell him to wait," said Leontiev. "The cable will be ready in half an hour." "Yes, sir," said the porter, "what cable, sir? He says he has got a cable on him and that he has been told to deliver it personally."

For a second Leontiev's mind did not connect. Then he told the porter to send the messenger up; then hesitated. "Yes, sir. Anything else, sir?" asked the porter. "Yes," said Leontiev. "I want a needle and some thread." "Something to repair, sir? I'll send the valet at once." "I don't want your valet," said Leontiev. "I want a needle and thread." He hung up; the idea of having a valet tinker with Zina's dressing-gown was insupportable. He examined the torn pocket and found that not only had the seam burst but that there was also a rent in the fabric. This gave his premonition of an impending catastrophe the seal of certainty. When he heard the messenger's knock at the door, he knew already the nature of the catastrophe; or at least it seemed to him afterwards that he had known. At any rate, he could remember no feeling of surprise when he read the short message stating that his wife had died that morning "from internal hæmorrhage following a motor car accident." The message had arrived on the ticker-tape of the Commonwealth News Agency half an hour ago. The head of the Agency had sent it along accompanied by a covering note, which read:

"Deep regrets. Under the circumstances we don't want to trouble you about the speech and shall edit the cabled version ourselves unless you have already finished it, in which case please hand over to the messenger."

The messenger, a pale youth with a thin, alert face, was eyeing Leontiev with curiosity. He was a boy from a working class suburb and a member of the Party, who had never before seen a Hero of Culture, nor such a luxurious hotel apartment; he felt that the combination of the two was vaguely disturbing. On the other hand, the old, worn dressing-gown and the fact that its pocket was even torn, impressed the boy favourably. He had a secret vice which he was unable to part with though he knew that it did not go with a revolutionary conscience: he collected autographs. Worse, the autographs in his collection were mainly those of boxers, bicycle champions and film stars, all of whom he knew to be parasites of a putrid society, whose sole function was to divert the attention of the masses from their economic plight and the revolutionary struggle. Now at last he was offered a chance to improve his collection by the signature of a confirmed Hero of Culture.

The great man was standing with his back to him, looking out of the window; he had apparently forgotten the boy's presence. There was something forbidding about the way he held his back and shoulders; but after all, the boy told himself, they were comrades in arms, members of the same movement. He cleared his throat:

"Monsieur," he called; his voice came out curiously thin in the silent room. Leontiev turned round. He stared at the boy, and for a moment the boy thought that Leontiev was perhaps blind. He once more cleared his throat and steadied his voice. "Please will you sign this for me, Monsieur?" he asked, holding out his cheap autograph album. Leontiev looked at him absent-mindedly, his fists in his pockets; suddenly he became conscious of the rent in the gown, quickly pulled his right hand out of the pocket and seemed to wake up.

"Yes," he said. "I will sign the receipt."

He took the album, looked sternly at the blank page, then a curious flash occurred in his eyes—it was, the boy thought, as if the current had been short-circuited behind his eyeballs.

"Wait," Leontiev said. "I wish to write a message to the head of the Agency." He took three quick steps to the desk and began to write in the album; he seemed to be electrified. The boy gaped, but did not dare to protest. He watched Leontiev write his message and it struck him that while the Hero's face was grim and his jaws pressed together so that the muscles stood out in knots on both sides, there was at the same time an odd smile at the corners of his mouth. Leontiev wrote:

"I cannot authorise any altered version of my speech. It has to be transmitted according to the original text. I shall make you responsible for any deviation from it."

He signed and gave the album to the boy. The whole man seemed to be changed. There was a flicker in his eyes. "Here," he said, handing money to the boy, "this is to buy yourself . . ." He stopped, and looked at the boy with a kind of absent-minded curiosity. "What do boys of your age buy themselves in this country?"

The boy hesitated. At the sight of the unusually large tip,

he had quickly weighed the alternatives between taking his girl to the pictures or to a dance hall. Now he desperately searched his mind for a more class-conscious investment. "It depends . . ." he said cautiously, his mind working. He was saved from further mental effort by a knock at the door and the entry of a valet in a striped waistcoat, just as valets were dressed in the movies. The boy took his chance and with a mumbled phrase of thanks, sidled out of the door.

"You asked for a needle and thread, sir," said the valet, offering these objects on a small silver tray with a look of unconcealed contempt. Leontiev had quite forgotten his request; now that he remembered it, it seemed to him that a considerable time had elapsed since he had made it. "Why did it take so long?" he asked sternly. "Now it is no longer necessary." "Very good, sir," said the valet, turning on his heel. "Wait," said Leontiev, and took his dressing-gown off. "You may keep this. It is made of very good material." The valet held the dressing-gown between two fingers, his little finger stretched out to indicate his disgust. "Very good, sir. I shall give it to a charitable organisation." "Yes," said Leontiev absently. "And bring me some brandy." "That's the room-service, sir," said the valet, giving the waiter's bell-button a vicious push as he went out. The valet was a member of the National Rally, who hated all foreigners, and particularly those from the Commonwealth.

As the door closed behind him, the telephone began to ring again. Leontiev lifted the receiver; it was Nikitin calling from the Embassy. He had just heard the news and wished to express the Ambassador's and his own sympathies. He went on to say that though everybody sympathised with Leontiev's bereavement, he had been instructed to ask Leontiev not to cancel his appearance at Monsieur Anatole's reception, as cultural propaganda was at the present moment more important than ever. "Of course I shall go," said Leontiev absently, and hung up.

There was another knock at the door and an old waiter with sidewhiskers came in, asking what Leontiev wanted. Leontiev said he didn't want anything. The waiter respectfully insisted that Leontiev had rung the bell. Leontiev suddenly became angry and began to curse the waiter in his native language, telling him to go to the devil and leave him alone. The waiter looked at him uncomprehendingly then, with a show of dignified distress, made for the door. "Wait," Leontiev called after him in French. "I wanted some brandy." "Very good, sir," said the waiter. He was a member of the Royalist Rally, and found his opinion confirmed that the Commonwealth was populated by savages.

The telephone rang again. It was a secretary of the personnel department of the Embassy who called to say that accommodation for Leontiev's return journey had been reserved for the next day; the plane would leave at 8 a.m. "It is no longer necessary," said Leontiev in the same voice in which he had refused the needle and thread. The secretary sounded startled; Leontiev hung up.

There was another knock at the door; the old waiter came in carrying a large glass of brandy on a tray. Leontiev downed it in one gulp, asked for another, and began to dress for Monsieur Anatole's reception.

He was ready now, and decided to walk instead of taking a taxi. He looked at his watch—a heavy gold watch, personal gift of the Marshal of Peace for Leontiev's fiftieth birthday. Only half an hour had passed since he had torn the pocket of his dressing-gown and events had started rolling in quick, smooth succession. Now that the brandy and a cold shower had cleared his mind, the events of that half hour appeared in retrospect like a film played with its sound-track switched off. The missing sound-track was his own numbed thoughts while he had talked to the messenger and written his note and answered the telephone and dealt with the valet and the waiter. He had done all this without a single conscious thought, functioning like an automaton whose responses to any stimulus are built into the mechanism. Only at the moment of contact with the cold water under the shower had the sound-track been suddenly switched on again. He knew then that his wife was dead and that he was alone to carry the burden of his freedom.

He glanced into the mirror and saw with wonder that nothing in his appearance had changed. He spread a street map on the table—the Cultural Attaché had provided him with one at his request, for Leontiev disliked asking people for information and being at the mercy of cab drivers. He saw that he only had a ten minutes' walk to Monsieur Anatole's. He knew that for the next few hours he was still physically safe; that it would be more prudent not to return to the hotel, but that he must leave his things as if he intended to return. He did

not care about their loss, except for the six new shirts which
he had bought yesterday; they were of a quality unobtainable
at home. This reminded him for the first time of his library,
his country-house, his swimming pool. He knew that without
Zina the house would be a sepulchre; still, it was not easy to
accept the loss of the fruits of thirty years of labour. Fifty-five
was a difficult age for a man to start his life again, alone. Yet
he felt braced by the prospect. It would be a bitter but a clean
struggle.

He threw a last glance at the room, changed his mind,
wrapped one of his new shirts, a razor and a toothbrush into
a small parcel, using the paper in which the shirts had arrived.
It was an inconspicuous parcel; it looked like a present. Avoiding the lift, he made his way downward over the soft carpeted
stairs. The porter and the bell-boys bowed respectfully as he
walked across the hall; he wondered which of them was employed to keep a check on him. He also thought that they were
eyeing him with more than usual curiosity, but that was probably only his imagination.

As he walked down the Rue de Rivoli, the blue dusk of the
summer evening had just begun to soften the contours of
houses and trees. His feet were light, as if the magic of the
Paris pavement were counteracting the force of gravity. He
had only been to Paris once before, twenty years ago, also at
a Peace Rally—it had been in the days of the Popular Front.
This time he had almost succeeded in obtaining permission for
Zina to accompany him—but only almost. She had borne the
disappointment bravely, although her main wish in life had
been to go once abroad, only once; her chance had never
come. But he had talked to her about Paris as one talks about
a painting to the blind; and they had talked about the eternally
promised trip together as convicts under a life sentence talk
about the day of amnesty. He had shown her photographs of
Notre Dame and the quais; told her about the Montmartre
cabarets, of the bals musette in the Rue de Lappe, of onion
soup at daybreak in the Halles; and as he now crossed the
Place de Carrousel with its fairyland view of two miles of
gaslights blinking in the soft blue dusk, he kept up a silent
running commentary to Zina, and heard her little cries of
naïve delight. Then, as he stood on the bridge, with the parcel
dangling from his finger, and looked at the coloured lights
dancing on the river, he stopped his comments and became
emphatically silent; and he heard her say with her soft Ukrain-

ian lilt: But Lyovochka, it can't be that it has really come true. He felt a faint pain in his right index finger: the string of the spinning parcel must have tightened round it and cut the circulation some time ago; the tip of his finger looked blue and swollen.

He said soundlessly but distinctly: Zina, you must leave me alone because I still have some work to do. He saw her nod with resignation, and her image slowly faded away. Then he resumed his walk across the bridge.

10

A SOIRÉE AT MONSIEUR ANATOLE'S

GREAT elation reigned at Monsieur Anatole's. Once again the pessimists, the morbid heralds of the apocalypse, had been proved wrong. They had said that war was unavoidable, but war had been avoided. They had said that the Commonwealth wanted to swallow the Rabbit State, and lo, that small Republic was still alive at the price of some insignificant concessions. Her Prime Minister, an arch-reactionary individual who, it appeared, was at the root of the whole trouble, had been induced to resign; the Diet had been dissolved and new elections were to be called in the near future. Meanwhile, as a token of its goodwill and peaceful intentions, the interim Government of the Republic had agreed to the Commonwealth Government's request that both parties should raze their defensive fortifications along the frontier. The sweet reasonableness of this arrangement gave the lie to all those who, blinded by hatred and persecution mania, had accused the Commonwealth of aggressive intentions. Not only was the danger of immediate war avoided, but there were also rumours of an impending Conference of the Big Two, a Conference to end all Conferences, which would arrive at a lasting, general, final settlement. Once again reason had triumphed and panic been defeated; no wonder that great elation reigned at Monsieur Anatole's.

Monsieur Anatole himself sat in his habitual armchair in front of the fireplace, his crutches within easy reach, like sceptres of the realm of shadows where his imagination dwelt to an increasing extent and whither he was soon to pass for good. They had been specially made for him of ash, ebony and pigskin; it was known that his testament contained a clause providing that the crutches should be buried with him to make life in hell more civilised. To the left of the armchair stood, as usual, Mademoiselle Agnès in the faded pearl-grey silk dress which she had worn at all receptions as far back as anyone could remember; to his right, the guest of honour, Hero of Culture Leo Nikolayevich Leontiev. Today's was a reception in the grand style, so the doors to the dining-room and to the second reception-room, called the Blue Salon, had been thrown open, and a gargantuan cold buffet installed in the former.

As the guests filed past Monsieur Anatole's strategic position in twos and threes, to be presented to the guest of honour and take their punishment from Monsieur Anatole's bitter-glib tongue, Leontiev had the impression of watching an elaborate ballet. This impression grew more intense with every glass of champagne he downed at ten-minute intervals. He kept telling himself that the clothes these people wore, their florid gestures and amiable grimaces were natural to them and to their time; nevertheless he was unable to shake off the weird feeling that the whole reception was a kind of stage performance where the actors tried to represent their own period and personalities as convincingly as their modest gifts permitted.

Two men came in the entrance door, one with a huge and robust frame covered by the becoming white habit of a famed monastic order, the other a man in evening dress who looked like an actor. As they approached Monsieur Anatole's chair, the friar affectionately took the other man's arm. A few steps behind them trailed a tall girl of remarkable beauty and with a remarkably vacant expression, her lower lip pushed out in a pout, defying the world in general and for no particular reason.

"My dear Leo Nikolayevich," said Monsieur Anatole, "allow me to introduce Father Millet and Monsieur Jean Dupremont, our leading pornographist and a recent convert to the Holy Church. As for this young lady," he continued, gripping the girl's cool, slim fingers as a monkey clutches at a banana, "she is supposed to be Father Millet's niece. . . ."

Father Millet gave out his famous lion's roar of a laugh. "But she *is* my nice," he protested without much conviction. "Is it not so, my child?"

"It is time you invented a new joke," said Father Millet's niece, and, liberating her hand with a little jerk from Monsieur Anatole's claw, she left them and walked through the door to the Blue Salon.

Jean Dupremont turned to Leontiev. "The Father and I have been discussing that sect, the Fearless Sufferers," he said. "It is of course most interesting and most puzzling. May I ask in all humbleness what you think of them—or is that question too indiscreet?" He was at first sight a very good-looking man of the Latin-American type, tall and dark with a tiny fringe moustache; but as Leontiev watched him, weighing his answer, he saw that one of Dupremont's eyes was somehow set the wrong way. It was either a glass eye or merely a peculiar kind of squint which gave his face a touch of indefinable seaminess; and his dank, limp handshake reinforced this impression. The Father had a big florid face and blue eyes which looked in turn innocent and shrewd. They were both waiting for Leontiev's answer with curiosity.

It was the first time that a direct question had been addressed to Leontiev since his arrival at the reception. And for the first time in a quarter-century he felt free to say exactly what he thought. But he also knew that once he had said it he would have taken the decisive step into a weird and alien world with all bridges burnt behind him. He noticed with annoyance that his heart was beating wildly like a débutante's. The silence became heavy; Monsieur Anatole turned his head and was on the point of making some remark when Leontiev at last found his voice. It sounded, as usual, laconic and seemingly offhand, yet charged with authority. He said that he admired the courage of that small sect but knew little about them, as the censorship of his country suppressed any information relating to the Fearless Sufferers.

The faces of his listeners looked startled. Only now did it occur to Leontiev that they had no inkling of the events of the last two hours; in their eyes he was still the official dignitary and Hero of Culture of the Free Commonwealth. The Father's big, round eyes had become shrewd; they reflected the effort to work out the meaning of this apparently new orientation. Breaking the silence, Monsieur Anatole said rather lamely:

"Tien, tiens—so you are in sympathy with those heretics. . . ."

Leontiev gave his interviewers his bushy-eyebrow look and said slowly, savouring each of the unaccustomed words as he pronounced them:

"No true revolutionary should deny his sympathy to a minority which fights its persecutors in sincere faith."

Monsieur Anatole looked at him in genuine alarm. The Father cleared his throat; though his voice was voluble as usual, he was visibly feeling his way:

"If I understand rightly, these people practise flaggelantism and self-mutilation; in short they are a sect—if I may borrow an expression from modern science—of perverse masochists?"

"You understood wrongly," said Leontiev. "They act on a quite sound and correct theory. They have discovered that the main reason why men endure tyranny is fear. From this they conclude that if they could liberate themselves from fear, tyranny would collapse and freedom follow. The objects of fear are physical and mental suffering. These are inflicted by torture, exhausting labour, physical discomfort, separation from one's family and friends, retaliatory punishment of one's wife, parent or child, and so on. . . ."

Leontiev paused and saw that the circle around him had grown. Among his listeners he noticed with grim satisfaction the poet Navarin, Lord Edwards and Professor Pontieux. Monsieur Anatole was waving his crutches in great excitement at various people to make them join the audience. As Leontiev continued, he fell occasionally and without noticing it into the catechising style of speech to which he was accustomed.

"If, therefore, the threat of torture, of separation from one's family, of retaliation against those whom one loves, and so on, are the principal methods of inflicting fear, how can people achieve immunity against fear? Obviously this is only possible if they become immune against the various forms of suffering which give rise to it. . . . Who has no fear of suffering a loss? He who has lost everything. Who has no fear of torture? He who has become accustomed to bodily pain and conquered his fear of it. If you have a wife whom you love, how can you shake off the yoke of fear while you tremble at the thought that she will come to harm through your actions? You must leave her and fear will lose its grip over you. That is the reason why Jesus denied his mother at Cana, when he said to her: 'Woman what have I to do with thee?' . . ."

While Leontiev talked, the poet Navarin had discreetly slid out of the circle around him. Smiling his cherubic smile, he had gone in search of some reliable comrade to witness Leontiev's self-immolatory statements. Dupremont too had momentarily left the circle and hurried to the buffet to be the first with the sensational news of Leontiev's sudden madness and defection. There was now a whole crowd round Leontiev pressing against Monsieur Anatole's chair, who held them at bay by vicious little stabs with his crutches.

"Ah," cried Professor Pontieux in excitement. "But this is almost neo-nihilistic philosophy. Are we to understand that its tenets have at last penetrated the frontiers of the Commonwealth?"

Leontiev stared at him absent-mindedly. "What is he talking about?" he asked Monsieur Anatole.

"I don't know," said Monsieur Anatole with glee. "It has something to do with nightclubs, and some piquant technique of intellectual masturbation with a special appeal to mental adolescents of all age groups."

"Ah, but let me explain," cried Pontieux, spluttering with eagerness. He was, however, hissed down by the audience and pushed aside by the robust Father. "My dear Hero," the Father began, pronouncing the title with the equanimity of a man of the world saying My dear General or Count, "my dear Hero, your sympathies with what seems to me a very pernicious sect surprise me indeed. Immunity from fear seems to me equivalent to a license for anarchy, and more dangerous to mankind than the invention of nuclear fission."

"Hear, hear," growled Hercules the Atom-Splitter from the last row, where his shaggy mane could be seen overtowering the crowd. There was an assenting murmur, and some contradiction.

"Do you mean," said Dupremont, who had rejoined the crowd in the company of Father Millet's sulky niece, holding a damp hand protectingly over her bare shoulder, "do you really mean that it is possible to lose the fear of torture through training by self-inflicted pain? That would be most interesting."

"I don't know," said Leontiev. His momentary elation had gone; he felt only bored and disgusted with himself and his listeners. But they were waiting for him to go on, so he said:

"One should realise that fear of both mental and physical suffering is mostly irrational. Pain is an experience like any other, and it has its physiological limits. When these limits are attained, the organism loses consciousness of itself. From this follows that there is no insupportable pain. Political terror is exercised not through the fear of real suffering, but the fear of the unknown. . . ." His eyes sought out Father Millet, and he continued as if talking to him alone: "You wanted to know about that sect, so I have told you what I know about their theory. These people are trying by various means to conquer their own fear of the unknown, and thereby to make themselves invulnerable to the threats of their oppressors. They believe that if their example found sufficient followers, this would lead to a bloodless collapse of the reign of fear."

His listeners, who for a moment had only followed the argument and forgotten that at the same time they were witness of a sensational act of apostasy, now again became conscious of it and stared flabbergasted at Leontiev's square, soldierly figure and impassive face. Then a husky female voice said scornfully:

"It's simply a counter-revolutionary re-hash of Gandhism. Are you trying to pull our legs, or what?"

The voice came from a woman with vivacious features and a resolute air, who was Professor Pontieux's wife and represented the extreme pro-Commonwealth wing of the neo-nihilistic movement. As she spoke, Father Millet's niece disengaged herself from Dupremont's arm and squeezed her way to Madame Pontieux's side, whose turn it now was to lay a firm, protective hand on her shoulder.

"No," said Leontiev. "It is a more radical movement than Gandhi's. Ahimsa was entirely passive. This sect is waging an active fight against fear."

"What is their religious persuasion?" asked Father Millet.

"I don't know," said Leontiev.

"What is their political programme?" asked somebody else.

"I don't know."

"How many of them are there?"

"I don't know."

"If you ask me," grunted Lord Edwards, "they are just a bunch of rotters." Disgusted, he edged his way out and made for the buffet, muttering to himself. Several others followed his example, and the crowd began to break up into pairs and small groups to discuss the possible reasons for Leontiev's incomprehensible and fantastic pronouncements. Among those who still lingered on in front of Leontiev were Madame Pontieux and Father Millet's niece who was leaning her head languidly against the older woman's shoulder. On her other side stood the poet Navarin, smiling unwaveringly. He whispered to Madame Pontieux who nodded assent, and asked in her husky, resolute voice:

"Comrade Leontiev, I would like to ask you a straight question. Have you gone to Capua?"

There was a sudden and complete silence in the room. Even Monsieur Anatole, with his black silken skull-cap and white goatee, looked as a consumptive lemur would presumably look if capable of the expression of embarrassment. Leontiev thought that if all these eyes focused on him contained magnifying lenses, his black suit would have gone up in smoke. He squared his shoulders, looking more martial than ever, and said in a clipped, soldierly voice:

"To Capua—no. To Canossa—perhaps."

There was another second of dead silence, then as if at a sign from the conductor's baton, all the little groups came back to life and eloquence, and the whole room buzzed like a beehive. Monsieur Anatole, agitating his crutches, chased the last remnants of the group round Leontiev away.

"Enough, enough," he cried. "Leo Nikolayevich is my guest and should be left in peace."

Father Millet was the last to leave them. As he turned, he said to Leontiev: "All this is very regrettable. I had a presentiment that we were on the point of understanding each other—you cannot imagine how I was looking forward to this meeting. And just at that moment you had to fall into this—most singular heresy. . . ." He gave an abbreviated version of the lion's laugh and took the arm of the faithful Dupremont, who was patting his tidy fringe moustache while his eyes followed dolefully Father Millet's niece as she vanished on a nondescript young man's arm into the Blue Salon.

"Ha!" said Monsieur Anatole when at last he, Leontiev and Mademoiselle Agnès remained alone at the fireplace. "Did you understand the meaning of Father Millet's remark?"

"No," said Leontiev, bowing stiffly to Mademoiselle Agnès, who was filling his glass. "I understood very little of what these various people meant."

"I will explain everything to you," Monsieur Anatole said with relish. "First, Father Millet was dismayed because you . . ." He again seemed embarrassed, a most unusual thing with him, then continued: "He was disconcerted by what you said because there appears to be a Concordat in the offing. If Rome and Byzantium become reconciled, neither of them will have any use for heretics. And who can doubt my friend, that it would be in the logic of things that sooner or later they should become reconciled? Each party would have its little afterthoughts of course, but that would hardly matter. . . . Do you know, my friend, how surprisingly small the difference is between the effects of utmost cunning and sheer stupidity?"

Leontiev lit a cigarette and slowly emptied his glass. He felt entangled in a web of great confusion, but at the same time lightheaded, unconcernedly floating through chaos.

"What a splendid soirée," tittered Monsieur Anatole. "I am exceedingly grateful to you, dear friend. You have, with a magnificent gesture, thrown a stone into this stagnant pond in which we all live, croaking and hopping like frogs. You can see that the ripples have already reached the buffet; tomorrow they will spread over the whole of Paris, of France, of Europe. Then they will break on the cliffs of our Eastern shores and come rushing back at you with a vengeance. . . . But today is still yours, so for a few minutes I will divert you with my gossip and then release you to the pursuit of more virile pleasures; for I suppose that, coming from that different world of yours, the scenery here must be strange and confusing to you. Imagine then that you are Dante and I am Virgil; I adore that role. Of course I can show you neither Purgatory nor Hell—they have been closed down by order of the Préfecture; so I can only take you through the sewers to our little pond where the damned and the doomed frolic about happily while waiting for your brigade of engineers to arrive with drainpipes and bulldozers. . . . Ah, there is Father Millet's niece again. She has made my wilting senses tingle all evening. At my age and condition it affects one like pins and needles. What a ravishing little imbecile—did you notice how she pouts and sulks all the time? It is an attitude with our jeunesse. And what a genius of expression in that slender body! Her lips pout, her breasts pout, even her enchanting little buttocks sulk at you. As I said, it is an attitude with this whole generation. They despise us of course, they hold in contempt our feebleness, cupidity and most of all our threadbare ideals and lamentable illusions, but they have nothing to offer instead; they just sulk. The boys of that age are even worse; they have such a knowing air, nothing can shock them, nothing enthrall them, they talk to girls like born souteneurs, read books without cutting them, regard all convictions and philosophies as moonshine, and for all that are unable to tell the difference between Burgundy and Claret or between Shakespeare and Bernstein. Ah, my friend, it should not be permitted to be under twenty-five."

Leontiev smiled.

"I am boring you," said Monsieur Anatole. "Tell me when I bore you and I will give you permission to follow the sulky curves of Father Millet's niece."

"I have just thought of an interesting hypothesis," said Leontiev. "It is in the dialectic of nature that different generations dislike each other. In normal times the manifestations of this phenomenon are harmless. But in times of revolution it is different. At such times, the biological strife between generations may appear in the disguise of a political struggle. It may for instance happen that a cunning old wolf gangs up with the young males of the pack and incites them to devour all the other wolves of his own generation."

"Ah, but!" said Monsieur Anatole. It was his favorite opening gambit in any discussion, even if he did not know yet what would come after the "but." ". . . Ah, but in the end the old wolf's cunning would be in vain, for the young wolves would devour him too."

"That is not certain," said Leontiev. For a quarter century he could never permit himself to discuss these matters; now he felt that every cell in his brain was savouring the oxygen in the air; it was as if an exhilarating March wind were blowing through the synapses. "That is not at all certain," he repeated, "because, having accepted his leadership so far, the young males would be tied to him by the bonds of their blood-guilt. After having killed their fathers he would become father to all of them, and they would worship and obey him blindly to atone for their guilt."

"Ah but," began Monsieur Anatole; then he interrupted himself impatiently: "Perhaps, perhaps. You may be quite right—but did you not want to hear about Father Millet and his niece?" He resented Leontiev talking about subjects where he could not quite follow; besides, there was a danger of his monologue degenerating into a dialogue. This had to be prevented; taking Leontiev's silence for consent, he launched gleefully into his explanations.

"To come back to Father Millet's niece," he said, pointing at the girl at the other side of the room with his crutch, "the point of the story is that she really *is* his niece, though to please Father Millet everybody pretends to believe that she is his mistress or natural daughter or both. This flatters Father Millet no end, although he leads an impeccably chaste and virtuous life, devoted to saving lost souls in the world of the

arts and letters, and leading them back to the bosom of the
Church. Now you may ask why does a man of such diligence
and virtue cultivate the pose of a libertine abbé of the eighteenth century? Is it perhaps that he has read too much of
Rabelais, or of those would-be drôle pot-boilers of Balzac?
No, my friend, the reasons for this perversion of the mind are
deeper. The cardinal virtues have become so outmoded among
us French, and corruption so much taken for granted as the
natural order of things, that even a man in holy orders has to
hide his virtue like a vice and pretend to be a sinner lest he
be taken for a sucker; and not only to the world, but—this is
the point which I wish to make clear—even to himself, to
preserve his self-esteem. I would not be surprised if, having
encouraged the joke so often, the Father would by now be
convinced that the girl is really the child of his imaginary
sin. . . ."

Leontiev smiled; his imagination drew a vivid picture of
what would happen to Father Millet if he were to fall into the
hands of Gruber and his men. A little re-attuning of the synapses, a few pills and discussions, and he would reveal to the
astonished world that he was Rasputin himself.

"As for the niece," Monsieur Anatole continued relentlessly,
"that enchanting little half-wit is at present the centre and object of one of those mysterious crazes which from time to
time befall the world of the arts and letters. She is portrayed,
under the thinnest of disguises and with the greatest wealth
of intimate detail, in a number of neo-nihilistic novels and
plays, and no author or critic of either sex can enjoy public
esteem without being known or at least rumoured to have had
an affair with her. And this though everybody agrees that she is
as hopeless in bed as she is inane in conversation, and altogether the most sulky and disagreeable little bitch on the whole
Left Bank. How does your dialectics explain this mystery, my
friend?"

Leontiev's heroic blue eyes began to twinkle: "Nature
adores a certain kind of void," he said.

Monsieur Anatole tittered. "Not bad," he said. "It is a
miracle that after thirty years in a hebetating and besotting
milieu you have kept that sparkle alive. But to finish my story:
would you believe that nobody knows even her name? She is
only known as 'Father Millet's niece.' Our age has a morbid
raving for the Absolute, and Father Millet's niece fulfils the

function of the absolute and adorable void. She is the sulky
Astarte of the neo-nihilists, who

> "*Advance to attack and climb to assault*
> *Like a choir of young worms at a corpse in the vault—*

as our arch-symbolist poet sang a hundred years ago. However, to change the metaphor and illuminate the mystery of
this modern Astarte-cult from a different angle, I can imagine
a fable written by La Fontaine, called 'The Dogs and the
Lamp-Post.' It would tell how the dogs in a village all lived
happily until a new lamp-post was erected on the market place
and one of the dogs absent-mindedly paid homage to it in
passing. From that day, driven by that well-known and mysterious urge of the canine community, all dogs felt compelled
to pay their homage to that one lamp-post and nowhere else.
This is how such cults start. . . . And now watch out, my
friend, for I see our Saint George has arrived. You had better
brace yourself for the impact. . . ."

Leontiev, following with his eyes the direction of Monsieur
Anatole's crutch, saw a dark, slim man charging into the room
with every limb of his body in dynamic movement. His face
kept twitching in remarkable contortions, his arms and legs
moved forward gawkily like those of an adolescent but at the
same time with utmost energy, his head was thrust forward
as if he were preparing to ram it into an enemy's belly. The
people who were standing about in little groups gave way as
he advanced and engaged in hushed comments behind his
back; even Father Millet's niece glanced at him sideways in an
awestricken way.

"It is Georges de St. Hilaire, the novelist-knight errant,"
whispered Monsieur Anatole. "We call him Saint George because he is always engaged in spearing some dragon, Fascist
or Communist or whatever other monster happens to be at
hand. He fought in the ranks of the Abyssinian tribesmen and
of the Stern Gang in Jerusalem, and last year set out in a
monoplane to blow up the Kremlin but ran out of petrol on
the way. But he is a very esoteric and highbrow knight errant;
compared to him, Lawrence of Arabia was a flat-footed philis-
tine. When he talks to you, you will understand only one
phrase in ten, which need not disturb you as you won't have a
chance to put a word in anyway; but those ten per cent are
worth listening to."

Roving with his long arms and furiously grimacing, St. Hilaire arrived at their corner, having already started to talk while he was still a few yards away.

"Salute," he greeted Monsieur Anatole, "inquiries after your health being obviously out of place one has to judge your case by precedents like that of the Irish Methusalem though it should be remembered that he is of the non-carnivorous kind which invalidates the parallel and also of a non-amorous disposition which poses the question whether your insistence on remaining with us is from the hedonistic point of view worth your while—good. Now as for our problem," he pursued, turning to Leontiev and tugging at a button on the Hero's suit, "the chances of re-acclimatisation are of course only partly a function of physiological age, just as the comments 'too late' or 'already' are not determined by a function of time but by various factors to be analysed—good. As the increasing frequency of similar acts of apostasy and mental harakiri stands in inverse ratio to their effectiveness, the question of utilitarian purpose should obviously be eliminated, and what remains is the value of the gesture as such; for we should not forget that in the gesture alone, regardless of purpose, can the dignity of man find its ultimate fulfilment. Good—we both know that this re-discovery of the dignity of the gesture—the great, and possibly mad, but not of the silly gesture—is only apparently a shift from the pragmatic to the aesthetic scale of values; for as far as man's cosmic destiny is concerned the two scales cannot be separated. I don't need to remind you that Kepler's search for the planetary laws was more an aesthetic than a pragmatic pursuit—which permits us to regard the insistence of planets on moving in elliptical orbits in such a manner that the squares of their periods remain proportionate to the cube of their main distance from the sun, as a particularly elegant gesture of God. You will agree then, that once we come to power it may not be necessary to castrate Pontieux knowing his testicles to be filled with sawdust; after all the dignitaries of the second Ming dynasty found it quite satisfactory to block the traitor's anal orifice with grade three cement while feeding him every two hours some chop suey with soya beans and rice from a green jade bowl. Good—as we both know the essential thing is to conquer the future as if it were the past. After all it is man's destiny to live always on the other shore; the details we shall discuss later."

And he left them with a rather disarming smile at Leontiev,

which broke through the savage contortions of his face like a
ray of light through a sky torn by chaotic clouds.

"What did I tell you," tittered Monsieur Anatole. "Of course
he hates Pontieux and the neo-nihilists because he is probably
the only true neo-nihilist alive; those who call themselves by
that name all have sawdust in their testicles as he said."

"He tore a button off my jacket," Leontiev said wistfully,
and he wondered whether Zina would find a fitting one in her
rich collection of buttons which she kept in an old chocolate
box. Then he remembered that Zina was dead, and for a moment he thought that the parquet flooring was giving way under him like a trap-door on the stage. He downed another
glass of champagne, and his iron determination to enjoy this
reception at any price gained the upper hand.

"It was a sign that he liked you," said Monsieur Anatole.
"He always takes something from the flats of people whom
he likes; it is a mania with him. Once he took a cube of ice
when I was shaking a cocktail and carried it home in his
trouser pocket, and once he dismantled the handle on the
lavatory door of the President of the Academy, which is why
he was never elected."

At the other end of the room St. Hilaire could now be seen
holding forth with the intensity of a jet engine to a young
American. The American was the type of University graduate
in whom shyness is matched with a modest self-assurance, the
latter being the result of his having accepted his own shyness
as a natural disability, like myopia. He even seemed to succeed in putting in a word now and then. While they talked,
Dupremont the pornographer kept prowling round them, trying to listen to what St. Hilaire was saying and to incorporate
himself into the group; but though St. Hilaire appeared to be
completely absorbed in his own eloquence, he remembered to
keep his back turned on Dupremont each time the latter shifted
his position; so that the group kept slowly swinging to and fro
like a pendulum, until at last Dupremont gave up and prowled
back to the buffet. Monsieur Anatole, who had watched these
manœuvres with relish, explained:

"Of all the frogs in our little pond Dupremont is probably
the queerest. His first novel, *Voyage autour de mon bidet*, was
a tremendous hit; the critics called him a new Zola, Dante,
Balzac, all in one. Needless to say, my friend, I relish pornography, but I hold that its perusal should be restricted to men
of my age and condition who have no other solace; youth

should devote to Priapus a maximum of action and a minimum of thought. Naturally Dupremont had to build up some kind of philosophy round his *bidet,* the sort of thing which the reader skips but which calms his conscience and allows him to indulge in the illusion that he is engaged in the pursuit of culture. But what will you, it was just these philosophical trappings to which the critics took exception: they said they were embarrassing claptrap which made them blush. After each new book they admonished him to stick to the point, that is to the *bidet,* but that is just what he refused to do; and so in each new book there were less orgies and more dialogue about Life, Death and Immortality, until his publishers became seriously alarmed. You see how even a successful pornographer can succumb to this morbid longing of our age, the nostalgia for the Absolute. Fortunately at that time he met Father Millet and underwent a religious conversion which for all I know was quite genuine. Of course he wanted at once to give up pornography and write religious tracts, but it was explained to him that there existed plenty of people to do that whereas he, Dupremont, had a public which otherwise could not be reached by the message of salvation; so he should go on writing in his usual manner, avoiding the method of frontal attack and endeavouring to take the enemy by the flank as it were—which is an unusually apt metaphor, you must admit. Now everybody is happy; Dupremont, like a martyr, turns out more luscious orgies than ever for the sole purpose of making the sinner repent in the last chapter, which the reader leaves uncut; and he has come to regard his *bidet* as a vessel of salvation—just as the Jacobins regarded the guillotine as a sacred tool preparing the Golden Age of mankind. *Moralité:* have you ever reflected, my friend, upon the fate of those who, in the words of the cruel parable, were called but not chosen? I will tell you what happens to them: they set out in search of the Kingdom of Heaven and land in a brothel, convinced that they have almost arrived. . . . And now you must leave me and refresh yourself at the buffet and cause a few more ripples in the pond. I am tired."

His face seemed suddenly to shrink, as often happened after one of his sustained monologues. Mademoiselle Agnès, who had never left his side and never said a word nor showed any interest in the goings on around her, stepped silently forward and helped him out of his chair. Supported by his crutches, and with his daughter's arm around his slender waist, Monsieur

Anatole without a word of farewell quickly and morosely hobbled out of the room.

Leontiev felt suddenly abandoned. Though he was the guest of honour, or probably because of it, nobody seemed to dare to approach him; a lonely and martial figure, he remained standing in front of the fireplace next to the empty armchair. After a few minutes of this he decided that the position was becoming untenable and had to be abandoned. But he told himself that it was too early to leave; that he had not yet enjoyed himself sufficiently at this unique and memorable evening; and besides he had nowhere to go. Slowly, with his shoulders squared, his blue eyes looking straight ahead of him, he began to move across the room toward the open dining-room door. He had drunk uncounted glasses of champagne on an empty stomach but did not feel their effect and did not know that his steps described a slightly wavy curve, nor that everybody else in the room was noticing it. He had almost reached the door of the dining-room when he saw the round, freckled face of the Cultural Attaché, Nikitin, as he came in through the entrance door. Nikitin looked round the room with his quick, winning smile, pretending not to notice Leontiev; so he knew already. The poet Navarin hurried to welcome him. They shook hands warmly and began to talk in a low voice, both careful to avoid looking in Leontiev's direction. Leontiev knew the technique; he had often enough behaved in the same way towards colleagues who had fallen from grace. His body even more rigid and erect, he continued his progress towards the dining-room, only once stumbling over the corner of the thick carpet, but regaining his balance with dignity.

While the waiter at the buffet put cold chicken, ham and various salads on his plate, Leontiev suddenly discovered that he was very hungry. As he moved with his plate towards a corner of the dining-room, he bumped into Lord Edwards. The latter was also carrying a plate heaped with an unlikely quantity of meats, and with the mien of a wild animal making for his lair with his prey, was looking for a quiet corner in which to devour it. Hercules grunted something which may have been an apology or an insult, but to Leontiev's surprise trotted after him to an empty recess near a bay-window. They both began to eat, Leontiev pretending to ignore Edwards' presence, while Edwards seemed repeatedly on the point of saying something; but each effort ended in an inarticulate grunt. Suddenly, holding a half-gnawed drumstick under

Leontiev's nose, he uttered a series of guttural noises, then said:

"Do you mean, er, that you have really gone and done it?"

His voice sounded curiously uncertain like a deep-voiced adolescent's who, prompted by lascivious curiosity, is unable to refrain from asking a highly indecent question. Leontiev raised his glance from his plate, but Hercules was looking studiously the other way with a guilty expression round his shaggy eyebrows.

"Yes, I have left," said Leontiev evenly.

"Hmm," said Hercules. And unexpectedly, in a grumbling manner as if he were reproving one of his students at the University, he declared:

"You should be ashamed of yourself—at your age."

It sounded so incongruous that Leontiev had to smile.

"What has age to do with it?" he said, amused.

"A lot, Comrade, a lot," snorted Edwards. "At our age— I take it we are both on the wrong side of fifty—one does not change allegiance. It is indecent—positively indecent," he grunted; and as if to erase the last trace of doubt, he repeated with satisfaction: "positively indecent."

Leontiev found nothing to say. He had once read a book called "Alice in Wonderland," and since that time knew that it was no use trying to argue logically with an Englishman.

"And what are you going to do now—eh? Join the chorus of the jackals? A fat lot of good that'll do you."

Though his words were offensive, the tone of his voice was not. Leontiev detected in it the same hesitation, the same curiosity which had prompted Edwards' first question, and which he had also noticed in the attitude of some other guests at the reception. At the same time he was conscious of the minor sensation which the fact that Hercules was talking to him had created in the dining-room. He felt relieved at not having to stand eating alone in his corner, at this temporary break in his isolation. Then he saw Navarin coming into the room, and he remembered how, only a few days ago, he had despised that individual for sucking up to him in front of the photographers. He answered drily:

"I am not interested in whether it will do me good or not."

"Rot," said Edwards. "The devil a monk wou'd be." He gnawed at his drumstick in silence, then bit off half of the bone, crunched it between his teeth and swallowed it. "There. Can you do that?" he asked with profound satisfaction.

"During the famine at the time of the Civil War," said Leontiev, "we used to grind the bones and made a porridge of them."

Edwards went suddenly red in the face. "You do rub it in, don't you?" he snorted. He threw the remainder of the bone disgustedly into an ashtray and stared in front of him moodily. After a while he said abruptly:

"Anyway, what else is there?"

"That is what I shall try to find out," said Leontiev.

"Ha! I can predict the result of the experiment. You will crawl back on your knees, begging to do a five years' stretch in a camp and be quits."

Leontiev smiled. "One does not return from a camp," he said.

Hercules muttered something, then said accusingly: "You see you have already joined the jackals."

Leontiev gave no answer.

Edwards crunched a wing of chicken between his teeth but changed his mind, relinquished the bone and put it into the ashtray.

"Anyway," he said, "why just now and not five or ten or fifteen years ago?"

"I had obligations towards my wife," said Leontiev. "Now she is dead." And before Edwards could say anything, he continued:

"But over you they have no power. Then why . . . ?"

Edwards went red again. He wagged a finger in front of Leontiev's face and grunted:

"I call that a most impertinent question. Positively imperti nent. . . ." He put his empty plate on the floor, pushed it away with his boot, put his hands into his baggy pockets and began with nervous impatience to rock himself on his heels. Looking away from Leontiev he said after a while:

"I told you there is nothing else. You will soon find that out yourself. Besides—once you've invested all your capital in a firm, you don't withdraw it—not at our age, not after thirt years. It is indecent I tell you; positively indecent. . . ."

He stared with distaste at the people crowding at the buffe or standing round in little groups, most of whom had by now become rather flushed and vivacious. The steady hum of con versation in the three reception-rooms had by degrees de veloped into an insistent buzz and was still mounting in

crescendo, with an occasional high-pitched laughter or exclamation going up here and there like miniature fireworks.

"Lovely little bitch," Hercules grunted suddenly, referring
to Father Millet's niece, who could be seen coming in from
the Blue Salon with her slow, slinking gait, looking for nobody in particular. Professor Pontieux was trailing after her,
carrying an empty plate and a glass, and cautiously wending
his way with hunched shoulders towards the buffet. Edwards
hailed him in a booming voice which carried across the room
and made people start:

"Hi, Professor . . ."

Pontieux changed direction and started working his way
towards them, still balancing his plate and glass. Father Millet's niece also changed direction and for no particular reason
came after him, looking as if she were walking in her sleep.

"Well, Professor," growled Edwards, speaking to Pontieux
but looking at the niece. "What do you say? He's gone and
done it."

"So I hear, so I hear," Pontieux began eagerly, with a short-
sighted nervous smile at Leontiev.

"It's a disgrace," interrupted Edwards. "There will be a
scandal and it will do no end of harm."

"No doubt," said Pontieux. "On the other hand . . ."

"Why do you think," interrupted Edwards again, talking
this time directly to the niece, in the weighty manner of questioning a candidate in an examination, "why do you think
people commit such stupidities?"

Father Millet's niece seemed to awaken from a dream in
which an infinitely boring young man had tried to make love
to her. Her eyelashes went slowly up like a curtain heavy to
lift, and her slim bare shoulders rose languidly in a slow-
motion shrug.

"Why not?" she said with sweet lassitude.

"Why not what?" Madame Pontieux burst in. She had spied
the group from the Blue Salon where she had been talking to
the young American graduate and had hurried to join battle,
lest her husband take up a too philosophical attitude towards
Leontiev instead of acting in the determined manner which
the situation required. The young American, whose name was
Albert P. Jenkins, jr., had followed her carrying his highball
glass. The precarious balance between his timidity and self-
confidence seemed to have tilted, though only slightly, in
favour of the latter. He gave Father Millet's niece, whose

shoulder-strap had somehow slipped to the wrong place, one sidelong glance of awe and wonder; then, as nobody seemed to volunteer an answer to Madame Pontieux's question, he took his courage in both hands and, moving up to Leontiev, said aloud: "Let me congratulate you, sir, on your very courageous action."

For the moment everybody was speechless. Pontieux's nervous smile expressed humanistic tolerance; the shaggy mane of Hercules seemed to bristle; Jenkins jr. was rather sheepishly pumping Leontiev's hand, while Leontiev, for the first time in hours, found his bushy-eyebrow-look again and accepted the homage with a slight, dignified bow. Everybody in the dining-room was now staring at them. Madame Pontieux, regaining her breath, exploded at last.

"This is perfect," she said in her deep voice and laid her arm round the shoulder of Father Millet's niece, as if to protect her against some vile emanation from Leontiev. "Perfect," she repeated. "He has left his football team just an hour ago and already he is offered a place with the other. Don't forget," she continued in a slow, insulting voice, addressing herself directly to Leontiev, "to learn to like chewing gum and to spit at a Negro when you see one. Otherwise you can't become a Hero of Culture in New York."

"Now, now, Mathilda," said Pontieux soothingly, contorting his gaunt body in a pantomime of appeasement like a snake charmer. Leontiev's first impulse had been to turn his back and walk out on the group in the dignified fashion of the Commonwealth delegates at international conferences when a vote went against their wishes; then he decided that he had to stick it out.

"It is strange," he said, studying Madame Pontieux's classic if wilting features, "I have often heard our radio talk like that, but that was for home consumption—for the backward masses as we say."

"Wait, Mathilda," said Pontieux, genuinely distressed. "You see," he explained eagerly to Leontiev, "already Hegel has pointed out the contradiction between the principle that if one is convinced of the rightness of an action one should carry it out regardless of consequences—and that other, equally valid principle that the probable consequences of an action should be our sole measure in assessing its desirability. Considered from this point of view you have of course done great harm to the progressive cause and strengthened the reactionaries . . ."

Hercules seized the opportunity he had been waiting for. Bending from his towering height over Father Millet's niece, he grunted with a shaggy twinkle in his eye, like a bear sniffing for honey at a beehive: "Shall we go and have a glass of champagne at the bar—what?"

Father Millet's niece raised her lashes with an effort, glanced slowly and briefly at the young American who was absorbed in listening to the argument, then wriggled herself free from Madame Pontieux's arm. "Why not?" she said sulkily and, with a little pull at her shoulder-strap which restored the correct, pointed profile of her bust, began to move towards the bar—like a slender tugboat towing a huge ocean steamer. Madame Pontieux was talking again to Leontiev, but she had switched her attack from the personal to a more general plane which had no obvious connection with the argument:

"You think you have come to a free country, and you don't seem to realise that you have come to a country under foreign occupation, in the process of being transformed into a colony," she said with a kind of slow-burning passion. "You cannot enter a café or a restaurant without finding it full of Americans who behave as if the place belonged to them. They tip the waiters fantastic sums, so they get all the attention and French customers are treated like dirt. Soon we shall have reached a state of affairs when no self-respecting French person will go to a public place—we shall have to stay at home behind locked doors as in a besieged city. . . ."

The young American, standing beside Leontiev, was absorbed in the occupation of wiping his horn-rimmed spectacles.

"According to a field research survey of Chicago University," he said to Madame Pontieux, on a tone of polite apology, "eighty-two per cent of the American population hold pleasure to be inseparable from noise. Of the remaining eighteen per cent, who abstain from noise, two-thirds suffer from psychoneuroses. The American people have not yet learned to enjoy themselves on muted strings. According to the last social anthropology bulletin of Harvard, it takes three and a half generations in families with continuous prosperity to learn that art."

"This is very remarkable," said Professor Pontieux. "I think these statistical methods are a great help to the mutual understanding between people. Besides, one should not forget my dear, that we need dollar tourists. . . ."

"Tourists . . . !" Madame Pontieux burst in. "Tourists are a necessary nuisance. I am not talking of tourists, but of their military missions and propaganda offices and what nots—the colonial administration which has become our real Government and reduced us to the state of natives. Are *you* a tourist?" she turned on Albert P. Jenkins, jr. "I bet you are not. I bet you are attached to some military headquarters and imagine you are here to save us from the blood-thirsty savages of Asia."

The young man, having finished polishing his glasses, put them on, found them still unsatisfactory, and resumed the task of rubbing them with his handkerchief. "As a matter of fact," he said, becoming embarrassed again, "I have come over on an assignment connected with the project of unifying and transforming categories A and B of American war cemeteries in France. A are those of the first World War, B those of the second," he interpolated by way of explanation. "The idea is to transform these sites into Places of Repose of the Californian type—you know, with a continuous musical programme from concealed loudspeakers, coloured waterworks, cypresses and that kind of thing. But it is feared that maybe it would hurt the susceptibilities of the local population to see dead foreigners cared for in this preferential manner. So I have been assigned to make a field investigation by sample polls among the rural agglomerations adjoining these sites to see whether these apprehensions are justified. Also some people in Washington think it may be expedient to make provisions for an eventual category C, so as to save the trouble and expense of starting the job all over again the next time. . . ."

"The next time!" exclaimed Madame Pontieux. "Did you hear that, citizen Leontiev? The next time . . ." There was now more despair in her voice than passion. "What do you know about the last time, young man, and about the one before that? When you have been invaded and bombed and occupied? Oh, certainly, some of your friends lost their lives in Normandy and Flanders instead of losing it in an automobile accident after too much drink. But don't tell me they did it out of love for our blue eyes. What did they know of France? The brothels and the Folies Bergères and the Eiffel Tower. Don't let us be sentimental—they came to fight partly because they love to fight, 'pour le sport' as you say, and partly because

Wall Street could not afford to lose Europe as an export market. . . ."

"Now, Mathilda," Pontieux said in an imploring voice, "this question should not be discussed in an emotional manner. After all . . ."

But Madame Pontieux paid no attention to him. She seemed to have forgotten even Leontiev's presence, and was addressing herself only to Jenkins junior.

"Do you think anybody in Europe wants another liberation à l'américaine ! ? . ." Young Jenkins suddenly felt like a grocer's boy who has cheated on the bill, faced with the wrath of a Parisian housewife. ". . . Do you think," Madame Pontieux continued, "we have forgotten your air raids which brought more destruction upon us than the army of the invader? And your drunken soldiers raping our girls and paying them with cigarettes and swaggering as the saviours of France? My dear young man, you don't have to go around gallup-polling to see that the people of France have only one wish, to be left alone. . . ."

The young American fingered nervously his spectacles. "Yes, of course, Madam," he said respectfully. "The only question is whether you would be left alone if we didn't . . ."

"Well, don't," interrupted Madame Pontieux who had become slightly hoarse. "You can fight your war somewhere else —that is all we ask."

The young American turned to Leontiev. "Do you think it possible, sir, that Europe could remain a no-man's land?"

"No, that is not possible," said Leontiev. "Nature abhors the void."

"I am surprised at your moderation, citizen Leontiev," Madame Pontieux said sarcastically. "I thought you would tell us that without this young man's protection the Commonwealth army would at once march to the Atlantic shore."

"It would," said Leontiev. "I believed that everybody knew that."

It looked as if Madame Pontieux would flare up again. But she merely gave an impatient shrug and said with great conviction: "I don't believe it. Whatever you and your like say, I refuse to believe it. But if choose one must I would a hundred times rather dance to the sound of a Balalaika than of a juke box."

"But I don't admit," Pontieux protested eagerly. "I don't admit the fatalistic view of the inevitability of the choice. I

protest, and shall go on protesting to the end against the imposition of what Hegel calls the 'false dilemma.' I refuse . . ."
He was shivering with inner emotion like a gaunt, pathetic marionette.

"All right, Pontieux, calm down," Madame Pontieux said in her husky voice, which sounded suddenly weary. "Pontieux lost his son by his first wife in the war," she explained. "If it comes to that, I lost two brothers. That shows you why no French family is very keen on another Liberation. . . . There are too many gaps, and we keep filling them up with foreign material—Poles in the north, Italians in the south. Soon there will be more patches than original fabric left. . . ." She talked listlessly, and kept sending covert glances at Father Millet's niece who had settled at the bar, displaying an attitude of passive non-resistance to Lord Edwards' bearish advances. Perhaps she was affected by the niece's desertion, or just by some feeling of the general hopelessness of things, for she continued in a changed, impatient voice:

"Anyway this is all claptrap; Europe is a small peninsula of Asia—and your America is an island somewhere in the ocean. What's the good of going against geography? You will always be too late to save us. All you can do is to prepare our liberation by some new gadgets which will raze to the ground whatever has remained. . . . Besides, once one has been raped one might resent being rescued without having asked for it. Anyway, who are you to restore our virtue? We know your pious sugar-daddies who read the Bible to you while they run their hands up under your skirt. . . ."

"But, Mathilda," Pontieux interrupted in growing agitation, "this is not the point. Notwithstanding that . . ."

"The point is," Mathilda Pontieux said, losing her patience and speaking with the savage frankness of despair, "the point is that if you know you are going to be raped you might as well make the best of it and convince yourself that your ravisher is the man of your dreams; and if he happens to smell of garlic, that garlic is your favourite smell. What else have they invented their dialectics for?"

"I don't follow you, Madam," said the American, having another go at cleaning his glasses.

"Never mind young man, you go on with your field researches and snooping-polls. Maybe they'll show you the facts of life. We Europeans don't need so much statistics to learn them; they have been rammed down our throat too often. And anyway," she ended abruptly, getting bored with them all, "you are a Negro-baiting, half-civilised nation ruled by bankers and gangs, whereas your opponents have abolished capitalism and have at least some ideas in their heads, So there . . ."

She turned on her heel and, taking a small mirror from her handbag, snapped it shut with an air of finality. Then she walked to an empty corner of the bar, scrutinised her face without deriving any pleasure from it, patted her hair which she wore done up in a classic bun, and asked the waiter for a glass of Vichy water.

Neither she nor the three men whom she had left in the recess of the bay-window had noticed the change of atmosphere in the room—the curious hush that had descended first on the Blue Salon, then spread from group to group in the dining-room itself. Presently a few people left the buffet for the main reception-room where somebody could be heard holding forth in a grave voice. Others followed their example, and soon the dining-room became empty except for Pontieux, the young American on the War Cemeteries project, and Leontiev. Pontieux had involved young Jenkins into a new argument, and Leontiev, who had long ago given up listening to them, gazed sternly into the empty room. His mind was pleasantly blank, or nearly so—for from time to time he was worried in a vague manner by the thought that he had nowhere to sleep. But it was a distant, almost impersonal worry, for the waiter kept making his rounds with more glasses of champagne on a tray. Everything seemed wrapped in a soothing, dreamy haze, so that he was not even surprised when he saw Navarin, the poet, enter the empty room in great agitation and, on perceiving Leontiev, hurriedly walk straight up to him. His cherubic smile had vanished entirely, his face was pale and contorted.

"Leontiev," he said in a strange, strangled voice. "Leontiev, don't you know it yet? The Father of the People is dead."

The weather had been abnormal for some time.

At first the weather reports contained merely the usual state-ments about "the hottest 11th September since 1885," "the worst Atlantic gale in twenty-seven years" and the like, based on data which were assembled by bearded men in Meteorologi-cal offices who were probably called "Meteorological Regis-trars" or "Assistant Weather Statisticians," and whose one ambition in life was to be able to announce "the 15th July with the heaviest snowfall on record"; though there was pre-sumably also an oppositional faction among them who were passionately searching for a "15th July nearest to the statistical average" and for "the most normal summer since 1848." It must also be assumed, given the mentality of pre-Pubertarian man, that the two factions who called themselves respectively the "Apocalyptists" and the "Normalists" hated each other with as much idealism and venom as any two rival political parties, philosophical schools, government departments or lit-erary cliques.

However, this time the Apocalyptists were scoring an un-interrupted series of victories, and visibly getting the upper hand. The "hottest 11th September since 1885" was soon fol-lowed by "the hottest of any September day since 1852," and this by "the hottest September on record." By that time the daily weather report had gradually migrated from its tradi-tional place at the bottom of the first column on the last page to the top of the front page. The bearded Assistant Weather Registrars were having the time of their lives and beginning to dream of the Legion of Honour or the C.B.E.; for just like the lucky gambler at the roulette table or the winner of a lot-tery, they felt that in some obscure way this sensational weath-er was all their own doing.

Few other people, however, seemed to share in their feeling of elation. The heat and the drought (caused by the smallest amount of rainfall in any September since 1866) killed the late crops, burnt some of the most renowned English lawns and laid a number of hydro-electric stations dry. This led to

*the usual dreary consequences: municipal warnings to save
water and electricity, followed by reductions in the industrial
power supply, and so on. The European public, which during
the last few years had developed a violent allergy to all kinds
of rationing, saving and public-spirited exhortations, became
increasingly irritable and weather-conscious. Swarms of heli-
copters and aeroplanes were mobilised to make rain by sprinkling silver nitrate and dry ice on the mean little cirrocumulus
clouds high up in the troposphere, but all they achieved were
short local thunderstorms and a number of casualties among
the rain-makers themselves, who got caught in the small but
violent atmospheric sneezes which their chemical snuff produced. The newspapers published their stock pieces about sun
spots, eleven-year cycles and magnetic disturbances, while ignorant rumour spun yarns about the mysterious after-effects
of the latest X-bomb trials and radioactive clouds. These rumours were fed by the exciting controversy between the American and the Commonwealth Press about the recent X-bomb
explosion in the Ural Mountains.*

*It had been an unusually gigantic bang, whose tremors had
been recorded by seismographs over half the earth, and which
had been wrapped in an equally enormous and dense cloud of
official silence on the part of the Commonwealth. A full week
had passed before a short, laconic statement by the Commonwealth News Agency mentioned in an almost deprecatory
manner that the biggest-ever X-bomb had been exploded in a
routine trial with "satisfactory results." But no sooner had this
statement been made public, than the U. S. State Department
released a series of photographs to the Press. These photographs had been taken by one Captain Bogarenko of the Commonwealth Air Force who had been sent on a high altitude
reconnaissance mission over the trial area and, on seeing what
there was to be seen, had suffered such a shock that he decided
on the spur of the moment to "go to Capua." He had headed
southward, refuelled twice in Oral and Tashkent, and reached
Persia, where he had contacted the U. S. Legation.*

*The photographs showed no particular horrors. The high
altitude panoramic view displayed a rather lovely valley surrounded by rugged mountain peaks, and a medium-sized crater
in the centre of the valley. Round the crater there could be
seen faint, concentric rings as in bird's-eye views of volcanoes,
which obviously marked the area of devastation. Under the
magnifying glass, however, there appeared in the devastated*

areas tiny specks of a regular shape, and it was the sight of these which had aroused Captain Bogarenko's curiosity and induced him to circle lower and lower, in defiance of his explicit instructions and of the dangers of radioactivity. The remaining photographs, taken from medium and low altitudes, revealed the startling fact which was responsible for Bogarenko's flight abroad. The site where the trial bomb had been exploded was the approximate centre of a large, modern, thickly populated industrial town. Judged by the number and size of its buildings, this town must have housed at a conservative estimate at least five hundred thousand people.

Though only a few of the buildings had remained standing, it was easy to see that they were recently erected ferro-concrete structures: large regular cubes and long, brick-shaped buildings equipped with power-plants, transformator installations and high-tension wires; in other words these buildings had obviously been factories and laboratories. The whole town had a strictly geometrical, semi-circular lay-out which showed that it had been planned and built for some definite purpose.

Captain Bogarenko, who was a nice and energetic but not a very bright man, had come, while he circled over the dead town, to the conclusion that it had been built, populated and equipped with all modern conveniences for the express purpose of being destroyed as an experiment. Though he considered this procedure unnecessarily wasteful and cruel, it was no concern of his, and he would probably have passed over it with a shrug, as he had often done before when faced with similarly puzzling decisions of his Government; in fact this kind of energetic shrug which involved the whole upper part of the body was Captain Bogarenko's most expressive gesture. However, as he lowered his plane to almost roof-top level, he saw here and there a few human shapes emerge from the rubble and crawl among the charred corpses. They had probably been attracted by the roar of the plane and tried to signal for help, but somehow their gestures and the way they moved did not seem right, for every single one of the dozen or so of these shapes crawled on all fours, obviously unable to rise to its feet. Whether they were insane, blind, in great pain, or all of these together, it was impossible to determine; at any rate they gave Bogarenko the creeps and made him turn the nose of his plane towards Persia, with "the balance of his mind temporarily disturbed" as English coroners are fond of saying when pronouncing a verdict of suicide. Only when it was too late, and he had already delivered the photographs and his somewhat incoherent report, did the truth dawn on him.

The truth was of course that the town had not been destroyed on purpose, but had blown up by accident. It had in fact, as the photographs unmistakably showed, not been a real town but an enormous assembly plant for X-bombs and probably other experimental weapons, purposely built in one of the most inaccessible areas of the Ural range. Its existence had for some time been known to the competent American authorities, but this knowledge had been kept secret by them. It was quite inconceivable that the Commonwealth Government should have deliberately destroyed its latest and biggest effort of safeguarding Peace through Strength. Some of the capriciously unstable tritium nuclei must have got out of hand; or maybe some of the physicists on the spot had decided that the most reasonable course for them to take was to blow themselves up, plant and all. However that may be, it had certainly been, to use the language of the weather statisticians, "the biggest bang in recorded history," and a severe setback to the Commonwealth.

For a full week after publication of the photographs, there was again complete silence from the Commonwealth. Then another bomb exploded, this time a metaphorical one: a diplomatic bombshell. It came in the form of an official Commonwealth communiqué, addressed to the world at large. It stated that the Commonwealth Government's "Commission of Inquiry into the recent explosion in the territory of the autonomous Republic of Kasakstan" had produced irrefutable evidence to the effect that this explosion had been caused by a high-powered nuclear bomb of American type, which had been dropped from an aircraft belonging to the armed forces of a "hostile power." This unprecedented act of criminal aggression had caused the "death of tens of thousands of men, women and children" who had been engaged in a peaceful large-scale irrigation project to transform the barren mountain area into fertile vineyards and cotton plantations. The Government of the Commonwealth of Freedomloving People reserved the right to take all necessary steps of self-protection and retaliation against the hostile power responsible for this cowardly crime of undeclared warfare. As a precautionary measure it had ordered a partial mobilisation of its armed *forces and closed the frontier of its territory to all traffic, telegraphic and telephonic communication.*

On the same day the Commonwealth Press carried a short notice in small type to the effect that the Director of the Commonwealth News Agency, which had issued the original communiqué about the "successful trial," had been arrested for having published "misleading information referring to the causes of the explosion," and had confessed his crime.

Naturally the Commonwealth Government's new disclosure had caused widespread indignation, panic and disorder in both hemispheres. The general strikes in France and Italy were accompanied by huge peace demonstrations which clashed with the police, smashed the windows of several U.S.A. consulates and burned several consignments of American orange juice in the ports. The French extreme Left asked that the President of U.S.A. should be immediately tried as a war criminal. The Conservative papers suggested that Europe should be declared neutral territory, and that it would be a good idea for the American President to meet the new Father of the People to discuss world peace. A progressive pacifist organisation launched an appeal for funds to send relief to the devastated town as a gesture of international good-will. This appeal found an exceptional echo; money and gifts poured in from every country of the globe, like sacrificial offerings to placate the gods and deflect their wrath. And as charitable gifts are always accompanied by sympathy and goodwill, the Commonwealth had never stood higher in the public's favour for many years past; even her most fanatic enemies had to admit that her leaders had, on this occasion at least, shown a remarkable restraint by not going immediately to war.

The United States Government of course cut a deplorable figure in all this general excitement. The more they kept repeating "We haven't done it," the more suspect they became in the eyes even of their sympathisers. Matters were made worse by the indiscretion of a certain publicity-loving Senator, the head of some appropriation committee or other, who, in the course of a television interview, declared with great solemnity: "I know as a fact that our conscience is clean in this matter. It must have been done by somebody else." This seemed to knock the bottom out of the official theory that the explosion had been caused by an accident, which by that time nobody believed anyway. "In a planned socialist industry no accidents are possible," the new Father of the People declared in a massive four-hour speech, two full hours of which were devoted to a bitingly ironic discussion of the main events of History in the light of the State Department's "accident theory": "No doubt from now onward all children in the so-called schools of the so-called United States will be taught that Brutus killed Cæsar by accident (laughter), that the Emperor Nero put fire to Rome by accident (laughter), that Titus destroyed Jerusalem by accident (laughter), that the Turks took Constantinople by accident (laughter)," and so on. By the time he arrived at Napoleon's burning of Moscow by accident, and being destroyed by the Russian armies by accident, with another hour of examples to go, everybody in the audience was hoarse, faint and weeping with laughter. From then onward no progressive-minded person could mention the accident-theory without blushing; the very word "accident" had become an international joke.

This, incidentally, had been the new Father of the People's first public speech, and it had struck a sensationally novel tone: the public was delighted to discover that the somewhat monotonous and didactic style of his predecessor was to be replaced by the delicate humour of what came to be known as "Socialist Sarcasm in the Service of Peace." Almost immediately Socialist Sarcasm became the approved style of Commonwealth public life, letters and art. The whole Commonwealth Press published portraits of Serafim Panferovitch Polyushkin, a stakhanovite of sarcasm who had committed five hundred and forty-seven sarcasms in a single hour; a number of editors, painters and novelists were dismissed from their posts and delivered to public contempt for "insufficient attention paid to the struggle on the Socialist Sarcasm front." But all this merriment did not alter the fact that war might break out from one moment to another. The people listened to the flood of Socialist Sarcasms with chattering teeth.

Somewhat belatedly, the State Department advanced the proposal that an international Commission of Experts should investigate the causes of the disaster, and submit its findings to the world. To everybody's relief, the Commonwealth Government accepted the suggestion at once. The Security Council, which had not met for several years, was resurrected in haste to decide the procedure to be followed. The debates, however, dragged on, for the two principal parties were unable to agree on the exact wording of the resolution. The resolution submitted by the U.S.A. proposed "that all avail-

*able information and full co-operation should be given and
extended by the organs of the Commonwealth Government
to the Commission in order to facilitate its investigations on
the spot"; whereas the Commonwealth resolution proposed
"that all available information and full co-operation should
be given and extended by the organs of the Commonwealth
Government to the Commission in order to facilitate its investigations."* The Commonwealth resolution was the first to
be put to the vote; but although the difference between the
two texts consisted merely in three words, the U.S.A. and
its client states voted against the resolution, whereupon the
delegates of the Commonwealth indignantly walked out. Thus
once again the U.S.A. Government stood branded before progressive world opinion as the saboteurs of peace and international understanding.

Just at the moment when the tension had become well-nigh
unbearable, the Commonwealth Government issued a new
communiqué which caused enormous surprise and a world-
wide sigh of relief. It stated that the Commission of the Commonwealth Government Experts had terminated their inquiries into the recent explosion in the territory of the autonomous
Republic of Kasakstan and had confirmed its earlier findings
according to which "this explosion had been caused by a high-
powered nuclear bomb of American type dropped by an aircraft belonging to the armed forces of a hostile power." The
Commission, however, had found additional and irrefutable
evidence which enabled it to identify the hostile power in
question; it was the Rabbit Republic. The main evidence was
the discovery, arrest and subsequent confession of the pilot
himself who had committed by order of his Government
this criminal and cowardly act. Losing control of his craft
subsequent to the dropping of the bomb, he had bailed out
over a deserted range of the Urals, and after wandering about
in the mountains for several days, had been discovered by a
Commonwealth Security Patrol, still carrying in his wallet
the written order for the dropping of the bomb, together with
a detailed map of the location. On his arrest the pilot had
declared: "I admit that I have committed a crime against
humanity by order of my criminal superiors, and want to clear
my conscience by a full confession exposing the devilish
machinations of my Government against the Commonwealth
of Freedomloving People." His public trial would take place
within the next few days.

As already mentioned, the surge of relief was enormous all over the world. It completely drowned the feeble squeak of protest from the Government of the Rabbit Republic, which was promptly overthrown and replaced by members of the Unified Party for Peace and Progress. When the new Government asked the Commonwealth army for help and protection against the enemy within, a request which was generously granted before it was even made, the U.S.A. and her client states were only too glad to confine themselves to the handing in of their routine protest-notes on printed forms and to leave it at that.

These printed protest-forms which had lately come into diplomatic usage, and which simplified to a considerable extent the work of the various chancelleries, were modelled on the accident report forms of motor car insurance companies. The somewhat stilted formulae used on these occasions were all set out on the forms in beautiful italic type, and only the date, the nature and place of the alleged violation of the treaty, law or legitimate interest in question, had to be filled in by hand. The protest forms were of five categories: "F" (friendly), "C" (cool), "S" (sharp), "G" (grave), "G²" (very grave), and "G.S.²" (grave and very sharp). As a rule, diplomatic controversies consisted in the successive exchange of these protest-forms running through part or whole of the gamut, from "F" to "G.S.²"; and by the time a G² or G. S.² was handed in, the measure against which the original protest was directed had of course become a generally accepted fait accompli. The cumbersome coded instructions which in earlier days governments used to send to their ambassadors abroad were now reduced to laconic messages based on the language of a popular card game, the most usual of which was "raise him by two."

Thus once more the clouds had passed, but again only metaphorically. The real cloud in question—that curious spiral-shaped cloud which Captain Bogarenko's photographs had shown hovering like a coiled serpent over the dead town— kept haunting the public mind. Was it going to dissolve, or expand, or drift away; and if so in what direction? In spite of all the reassuring statements by experts, who ridiculed the notion that a radio-active cloud which had been observed more than a month ago in the distant Urals should exert any influence on the climate in Western Europe, the superstitious

*public mind continued to suspect some mysterious connection
between the super-bang and the abnormal weather.*

At last, on October 2nd, the hottest autumn spell in the
history of weather recording came to an end. Rain fell abundantly, the temperature cooled down to normal, the Assistant
Weather Statisticians of the normalist faction began to creep
out of their dens and to prove that, by taking the last winter
equinox as a starting-point, the total amount of rainfall and
the mean temperature in the shade, computed over the whole
period, came closer to the ideal average than in any other
year since 1903. Unfortunately, within a fortnight from the
first rainfall, a hitherto unknown form of influenza epidemic
began to spread new disquietude among the public with its
already frayed nerves. The average course of the disease was
a mild three-day attack with the usual symptoms of a common cold, though accompanied by higher temperatures. This
was followed by a period of apparent recovery, lasting from
ten to fifteen days, during which the patient displayed symptoms of a pleasurable over-excitation as if under the influence
of an intoxicating agent. The third and final phase was char-
acterised by vomiting, violent headaches, and disturbances of
vision of the neuralgic type: the patient's visual field appeared
as if cut in half either horizontally or vertically and, while
in one half vision remained normal, in the other half it was
distorted, blurred, or completely blacked-out. These symptoms again lasted from ten to fifteen days and were followed
by, as far as anybody could say, complete recovery. The mor-
tality rate was low, and in the few cases in which death
occurred, it was due either to secondary complications or to
constitutional weakness.

Unfortunately, one of the first people who fell ill with this
new type of 'flu was Captain Bogarenko who, as an American
video commentator put it, "had swallowed more radish soup
than any other living person on earth."[1] This led to a new
wave of superstitious rumours, so stubborn and widespread
that the new epidemics came to be known as "Bogarenko's
disease"—regardless of the unanimous opinion of the whole

[1] "Radish soup" was a popular slang word of the period, of somewhat
obscure origin, but probably originating in England and modelled on "pea
soup"—the Cockney word referring to the thick, yellow texture of the London
fog. Before they had their first real taste of it, people in Europe had no very
clear ideas about diffuse, atmospheric radioactivity; they imagined it variously
as seated in a cloud, mist, or dense fog. Hence the expression "radium soup"
which soon became transformed into the more homely "radish soup."

medical profession, according to which radioactive infection could never produce these symptoms. Incidentally, the virus of "Bogarenko's disease" was soon afterwards isolated by Kronenberg and Dietl of Johns Hopkins: it turned out to be a virus which had been driven crazy by the unending spate of new antibiotics and by the effort to keep abreast with them by developing new and better drug-resisting strains. Thus the unfoundedness of the public's apprehensions was once more demonstrated beyond doubt.

Nevertheless, the public remained nervous and apprehensive; and its apprehensions grew when, at the beginning of November, the thoughtful British Government decided to provide every holder of a National Registration Card with a pocket Geiger-counter and an anti-radiation umbrella, free of charge. This purely precautionary measure, the Home Secretary explained in the first of a series of broadcast talks, was designed to get the public into the habit of thinking in terms of modern weapons, and to give them a feeling of safety and self-assurance. "You all remember," he concluded his speech, "what a hellish nuisance it was to carry our gasmasks during the whole of the last war although the occasion to use them never came. I hope that these new gadgets will prove just as superfluous, and I am sure you will keep them nevertheless handy and in good repair, if for no other reason than that they cost a lot of money, and this money comes ultimately from the taxpayers, that is your own pockets."

This speech caused a number of indignant protests from bishops and clergymen because of the unprecedented use of the word "hellish" in a broadcast talk. "Where will we be," wrote the Archbishop of Canterbury, "if Members of the Cabinet give the nation the example of using bad language?" The matter was raised in the House of Commons at question-time, when several young Labour members tried to defend the speech on the grounds that expressions like "Hell, Go to Hell, What the Hell," etc., had become so firmly incorporated into American parlance and hence into fictional literature, that they could hardly be considered any longer as bad or offensive language. "But this country is not America," answered several voices from the floor. In the end both the House Secretary and the British Broadcasting Corporation had to apologise; so everybody was satisfied and the whole matter was soon forgotten.

But not so in France, where some enterprising private firms opened a line in Geiger-counters and anti-radiation umbrellas, and made a roaring trade in them. Unlike the solid and clumsy British G-counters which looked like grandfather's watch complete with utility chain, and made everybody's pockets bulge, the French variety was disguised as fountain pens for men, and as lipsticks or compacts for women. One firm even produced them in the shape of ankle bangles which were supposed to start jangling like castanets when radio-activity was about. As for the umbrellas and parasols, there was no limit to fantasy in their shape, colour and design; and as the action of these umbrellas depended on a built-in electric circuit which was supposed to absorb or deflect radiation, it was only logical to use the current to feed at the same time a tiny camouflaged radio-receiver.

The boulevards had never been more enchanting than on these late, sunny November days when crowds of promenaders walked under their gay, open parasols, everyone surrounded by a faint aura of music from the Radio Diffusion Nationale—*like a procession of figures on a musical clock. It hardly seemed to matter that the delicate G-counters kept going haywire all the time, and indicating deadly doses of radiation whenever the vacuum cleaner or the refrigerator was turned on. The umbrellas, on the other hand, had a tendency to charge the people who carried them with static, which sometimes discharged itself in crackling sparks at a handshake, kiss or other bodily contact. This was of course a heaven-sent gift to the cartoonists and the song-writers;* "My Radioactive Baby" *became the popular hit of the season.*

Soon, however, the usual strident voices from the Left were raised in protest. These professional spoil-sports and fun-killers, who would never let people quietly enjoy themselves, pointed out that "the masses" were unable to afford these expensive gadgets and were therefore left without protection, while survival had become a luxury reserved for the privileged bourgeoisie. At the same time, however, they claimed that the gadgets sold to the gullible public were completely ineffectual, which somewhat spoiled the argument; for if they were really useless, then obviously rich and poor were in the same boat, and democratic justice was re-established. Then came the famous "Scandale des Parapluies"—*the disclosure that one of the main shareholders in the Company which produced the umbrellas (Société Anonyme pour la Fabrication des Parapluies Anti-Radio-actives," abbreviation: "SAPAR") was the*

Radical Socialist Minister for War. The Government was forced to resign, there were more strikes and demonstrations; finally the new Government gave a solemn promise that Geiger-counters and anti-radiation umbrellas of the most reliable make would be distributed free of charge to every citizen as soon as supplies were available in sufficient quantities. But now both the independent and the dependent Left raised a new hue and cry: they charged that the Government's statement was the clearest proof of its policy of war and aggression in the service of the bankers of Wall Street. Whereas the moderate Left merely deplored the Government's squandering the nation's resources in this unproductive way instead of concentrating all efforts on raising the standard of living, the extreme wing exhorted the masses "to refuse to accept the sinister gadgets of the imperialist warmongers and thereby to become accomplices of their aggressive designs." The whole controversy, however, remained largely theoretical, as the first consignments of Government-supplied counters and unmbrellas had already been cornered by the black market and smuggled into Belgium, where they were sold at a handsome profit.

Thus the golden autumn days passed by like a procession of pilgrims, occasionally frightened by marauding tribesmen, sometimes anxious, sometimes gay, exhilarated by adventure, and increasingly tired by their journey into the unknown. As the days passed they became shorter, and there was a curious air of finality about this shrinking of the span, by a few minutes each day, between the rising and the setting of the sun, and the steady lengthening of the night. Of course, after the winter solstice the process would be reversed; but who could nowadays be certain even of that? The hottest September in human memory had been followed by the strangest epidemic ever known; now there were all kinds of curious disturbances in radio-reception, and jagged stars or lightning bolts appeared across the television screens. In the end all these mysteries turned out to be quite unconnected, except in the superstitious public's mind, with the coiled spiral cloud in the Urals. Nature herself seemed to wage a war of nerves on her latest prodigal offspring, as if to discourage his incestuous poking in her sacred nuclear womb.

PART TWO

1

THE RETURN OF THE PRODIGAL SON

"In short," said Vardi, "I have been offered the chair for modern history at the University of Viennograd, and I am going home. I came to say goodbye."

Julien was so stunned and horrified that the cigarette stump fell from his lip.

"They have given me solid guarantees," Vardi calmly continued. "The past is written off. I have a letter signed by our new Ambassador guaranteeing my safety, which I can deposit with a lawyer here. They no longer have any interest in paying off old scores. They want qualified people to help in the work of reconstruction."

"Are you completely mad?" Julien repeated, looking in desperation at Vardi who stood in front of him, short, calm and composed.

"Won't you offer me a seat?" Vardi said at last, smiling. Julien gave no answer; he began pacing up and down his study, dragging his leg.

"I am waiting for your explanations," he said, while Vardi settled down in the armchair.

"What about a drink?" Vardi asked with the same composed smile.

Julien pushed a bottle and a glass before him. It was a bottle of sweet vermouth, the only drink Vardi liked. "I am waiting," Julien repeated, leaning against the bookshelf and looking down at Vardi.

"Why are you so dramatic?" said Vardi. "It's a long story. Relax."

"Are you trying to pull my leg?" asked Julien.

"No."

"Do you mean to tell me that you believe in their guarantees and assurances?"

"More or less. Things have changed since the death of the old man."

For the third time Julien asked:

"Have you gone completely mad?"

Vardi sipped at his drink and put it down. "Look," he said.

"I can give you a shorter and a longer version of it. The shorter one is that I have been a Red emigré for eight years while the Whites were in power at home, and a White emigré for ten years since the Reds have come to power. That makes eighteen years of sterile hatred and impotent hopes. I was a promising man of thirty when I left, and now I am nearly fifty. So I thought it was time to get my dialectics right."

"I am still listening," said Julien.

"I thought you were going to remind me of the Arctic camps, the State Police, and so on. You can save your breath. All that is included in the equation."

"I am listening to your equation."

"It is a simple one. The future versus the past. The twenty-first century against the nineteenth."

"You have written three books to prove that the future is not theirs, and that they are not on the side of the future."

"I have also given dozens of lectures on the subject. Self-deception is a powerful motor. It can keep a man going all his life. But once the motor stops, it is dead."

Julien gave no answer. Vardi continued:

"You may of course ask how I know that I am not the victim of a new self-deception of the opposite kind. But I have gone into that carefully. Self-deception is always accompanied by wishful thinking. Wishful thinking means hope. Since I have stopped fooling myself, my mood is not one of hope but of resignation. Hence it cannot be based on self-deception."

Julien took two steps towards Vardi and shook him by the shoulder. "Wake up, man," he said. "Shake it off. If we were living a few centuries earlier, I would say that an incubus has got possession of you."

Vardi calmly pushed Julien's hand off his shoulder. "On the contrary," he said, "I have at last got rid of the incubus which has been leading me a dance all these years. Anyway, what are you so surprised about? Just remember our last discussion when you were showing off your pessimism in front of that American girl. You should be the last one to be surprised."

"For God's sake," said Julien. "You have got everything confused."

"There has never been less confusion in my head—and my memory, as you know, works with considerable precision. You accused me on that occasion, and on many others, of sitting in the no-man's land between the fronts. I now admit that you were right, and am going to take up a more realistic position.

You should be rather proud of having helped at least one person to clarify his ideas. One person is perhaps not much, but then you have not been having a large public lately."

This time Julien found no immediate answer. He remembered, like an echo, Hydie's words: "What I dislike most about you is your attitude of arrogant heart-brokenness." He limped over to the alcove and sat down, his chin propped on his fists. In his high-necked polo sweater he looked like an exhausted cyclist after a race which he has lost.

"Well," said Vardi. "Now it is I who am listening."

The nervous tic reappeared round Julien's eyes, but almost at once he became aware of it and checked it. He was sitting with the scarred half of his face turned to Vardi. He said slowly:

"You can accuse me of giving free vent to my pessimism without regard to its demoralising effect on others. On this point I plead guilty. But surely you can't make me responsible for your wanting to commit suicide by going back to the other side?"

"Why all these metaphors?" said Vardi. "I have a concrete mind. I have been deceiving myself in the belief that a consistently neutral attitude is possible. This delusion has come to an end, and you have helped to destroy it. As I am nearly fifty and faced with the inevitability of opting for one side or the other, I have opted for that side which the logic of History indicates."

"For God's sake. What oracle has revealed to you the logic of History?"

"I take that to be a rhetorical question. You know that I have never departed from that solid dialectical foundation which alone enables one to see order in apparent chaos. That has always been the essential difference between you and me."

Julien had at last sufficiently recovered from his shock to notice that Vardi was talking more pompously than was his habit when they were alone. He had crossed his short legs and was sipping vermouth with a somewhat forced smile, as if he were giving a stage demonstration of superior calm and sang-froid. Gradually Julien began to realise that there was no hope of making Vardi change his mind. But it was essential to continue the argument, at least to gain time.

"Yes," he said slowly. "I have always regarded you as a modern version of a mediæval scholastic. . . ."

"May I point out," interrupted Vardi, "that this is the

second time you refer me back to the Middle Ages. First I was
possessed by an incubus; now I suppose you are going to draw
a parallel between the scholastic exegesis of Aristotle and
social analysis based on Marx."

"Yes," said Julien. "The truly dreadful thing is that we understand each other so well. Thus you will probably admit
that the parallel is not a superficial one. The trinity Hegel-
Marx-Lenin has surprising affinities with the trinity Plato-
Aristotle-Alexander. Marx did to Hegel more or less what
Aristotle did to Plato; he accepted in essence the master's
system and turned it upside down. And Marx is to Lenin as
Aristotle to Alexander the Great. During more than four
centuries Aristotle was referred to by the scholastics simply as
'the Philosopher,' the last word of wisdom for all time to come;
and Marx is treated by you and your like much in the same
way. The resulting sterility, rigidity and venomous dogmatism
is in both cases the same."

"It just goes to show what a dilettante you are," said Vardi,
and his smile became less forced as he warmed to the subject.
"From the ninth century roughly to the end of the fourteenth,
Aristotelian exegesis did indeed remain the most fruitful starting point of philosophical orientation, and for the time being
Hegelian dialectics still remain the only satisfactory approach
to the philosophy of History. If you call me a scholastic, I accept it as a compliment; if I am as sterile as Abelard, as rigid
as Occam, and as venomous as Thomas Aquinas, I shall congratulate myself."

"You haven't by any chance forgotten that the leading
scholastics gave their blessing to the crusades, the heresy-hunts
and so on?"

"Of course I haven't forgotten. They were the necessarily
painful spasms out of which the Renaissance was born. Apply
that to the present conditions in the East, and you will see why
I am no longer afraid of accepting the logic of History."

"You know," said Julien wearily, "all these arguments cut
both ways—if not three ways. I could for instance challenge
the necessity of those dark and bloody detours, and you would
answer that all that happens is inevitable and cannot happen
otherwise, and thereby defend any beastliness and stupid
cruelty as a function of 'the logic of History.' "

"Quite correct. The basic difference between us is that I am
a historical determinist, whereas you have ceased to be one
and have swallowed the whole mystic balderdash about free

choice, ethical absolutes and so on. The difference in axioms leads of necessity to the difference in our conclusions."

"And so?"

"And so we no longer have any common language."

Julien resumed his limping wanderings through the room. He was at the end of his wits and looked for a new opening to prevent Vardi from leaving. But apparently Vardi was in no hurry; he helped himself to another glass of vermouth, which was rather exceptional with him, and resumed the discussion:

"The unfairness of your method of arguing, my dear Julien, should become obvious by the fact alone that it was you who dragged the incubi and mediæval scholasticism into the discussion; and when I answered on the same terms, you remarked airily that such arguments cut both ways. If they cut both ways why did you bring them in? Because you don't want to face the concrete realities. Forget Aristotle and look at the facts. Within a few decades from now the world will have been unified. Even the woolliest liberals admit that. The whole planet is today in a situation comparable to that of the three hundred odd German principalities in the middle of the nineteenth century, before Bismarck unified the Reich. We don't think Bismarck was an attractive figure, but he had History on his side. The Iron Chancellor, the Man of Steel—the tools of destiny are rarely lovable characters, but after a century or two, who cares about their methods? The victims are forgotten, but the achievement remains."

"And you are fed up with the part of the victim?" Julien asked quietly.

"Precisely. I appreciate the absence of sarcasm in your question. I am also prepared to admit that there are situations in which History may justify one's being on the losing side. I would rather have been one of the last-ditchers at Thermopylae or in the Paris Commune than a soldier of Xerxes or General Gallifet. . . ."

"Why?" interrupted Julien. "Were not the Persians, and Gallifet's firing squads also instruments of the will of History?"

"No," Vardi said imperturbably. "They were merely episodic characters. One has to distinguish between the ripple and the tide. The Athenian democracy, the French Revolution, the Revolution of 1917, are phases of one continuous tidal movement. The Paris Commune, though precocious and abortive, was part of the great tidal surge. In such it is dialectically correct to be on the losing side. But only in such cases. There is no intrinsic value in being on the losing side. There is no value or significance in the quixotic gesture. History draws a clear distinction between martyrs and fools. The Communards in the Père Lachaise were martyrs. The Swiss Guard in the Tuileries who died defending Marie Antoinette were fools. . . . The rest follows by logical deduction. What ideal would I be defending if I remained on the losing side with you?"

"For one thing," said Julien, "the legal right and the physical possibility to talk as frankly as we are talking to each other at the present moment."

"I don't underestimate that," said Vardi. "I have used that argument myself for the last twenty years. I warmed myself with it when I was freezing in my filthy hotel room, and I ruminated it when I had nothing to eat. And I have been wondering all the time why it was steadily losing its effectiveness. Until I discovered that this sacred right to talk becomes pretty meaningless if nobody has anything to say worth listening to. And why has nobody anything to say? I mean, anything to answer the only question which matters, the question how to survive. Because, my dear Julien, there is no answer to it. Because, as we both know, the survival of Europe has become a mathematical impossibility."

"People used to say that about England in 1940."

"The people who said that were right. England was mathematically lost. She survived, temporarily, because the other side committed a howling blunder. But only temporarily. She came out of the war more weakened than her defeated enemies. Postponement of the execution does not invalidate the verdict. A short adverse ripple does not alter the course of the tide. Europe cannot count on a miraculous blunder similar in magnitude to the German Army's turning East in 1941. And however much the leaders of the Free Commonwealth may blunder, their superiority is so crushing from every point of view that the fall of Europe can only be a question of time."

Vardi gave himself another glass of vermouth. He had spoken with some vehemence. He was obviously determined to convince both Julien and himself that their cause was hopelessly defeated. To justify his position he had to squash every glimmering spark of hope with the acid logic of his despair. Julien knew that it was no use arguing with him, for Vardi would have a ready answer to every argument. If he were to speak of certain defections in the Commonwealth camp, Vardi would minimise their importance and accuse him of wishful thinking. If he brought in the United States, Vardi would say that America could not defend Europe any more than the Allies could defend Poland in 1939; it could only fight its duel with Asia over Europe's dead body. And at any rate, in Vardi's system the U.S.A. represented the past, a post script to the Liberalism of the nineteenth century, whereas the Commonwealth represented the revolutionary future. Moreover, a regime which had History on its side must of necessity be ruthless and cruel; the agony of a million wretches was a mere ripple on the surge of the tide. And if Julien were to ask how a drowning man could distinguish between the ripple and the tide while the bitter foam was choking his lungs, Vardi would explain that Julien's woolly humanitarianism was an expression of his belonging to a doomed class, and thus additional proof of the correctness of Vardi's diagnosis. . . . Oh, they knew each other's answers in advance, like two chess-players who have played the same opening variation over and over again; and Julien had to agree with Vardi that the right to argue became pretty meaningless when it led into such barrenness and sterility. Here they were, two intelligent men of good will, whatever that might mean, and they were turning round and round like animals in a trap. Had something gone wrong with their brains so that they had become like those operated rats which can only turn in one direction? Or was it because the trap in which they found themselves had really no exit . . . ?

Vardi sat in his armchair with crossed legs, holding himself very stiff and erect. His sharp-lensed glasses gleamed in the afternoon sun; on his thin lips the sweet vermouth had left an oily film which looked incongruous and repulsive.

"To change the subject," he said to Julien. "Assuming that I were going back out of sheer opportunism, because after eighteen years I have at last got fed up with wasting my time fighting windmills, because I am nearly fifty, and homesick, and can only talk and write properly in my own language; because I want to live in my own country and do a constructive job instead of arguing with you and gradually going off my head like Boris—even on this cynical assumption, would you blame me; and if you did, in the name of what principle or values?" He cleared his throat, and his glasses gleamed at Julien with a sarcastic and at the same time hungry look.

"I would not call this assumption cynical," said Julien.

"It would be cynical," Vardi said sharply, "if I were not convinced that the future is on their side. You missed my point."

"All right, have it your own way."

"My point is that you can't call it opportunism if one itches to help to push the cart of History towards the future. He who helps to push it is in the right, he who tries to hold it up is in the wrong. There is no other way of moral judgment."

"We have been through all that before," said Julien.

They fell silent. In the little hotel on the opposite side of the street a woman was humming the old tune of *Parlez-moi d'Amour:*

> *"Talk of love to me,*
> *Tell me tender things . . ."*

Vardi cleared his throat. He said, speaking through narrowed lips:

"What I want you to say is that you don't blame me."

Julien, sitting on the window-sill, shrugged, and relit his cigarette stump:

"Who can blame a man determined to commit suicide?"

"Ah. So you still think it is suicide. Then how can you talk about opportunism?"

"I didn't talk about opportunism. You did."

"I was merely voicing your thoughts."

"Those were not my thoughts. My thoughts were that you are possessed of some crazy, logical, suicidal madness."

"If you don't think it is opportunism, then you have no right to blame me," Vardi repeated stubbornly.

Julien couldn't bear to look at Vardi any longer. A drop of the sticky vermouth had trickled down from the corner of his mouth to his chin; it looked somehow both obscene and frightening, but Vardi took no notice of it. He sat with his short legs crossed, with both hands on the arms of the chair, stiff and tense like a patient at the dentist's who is determined not to show how frightened he is. Julien looked away from him and said:

"They will make you confess that you went back with a bottleful of germs to spread the bubonic plague."

Vardi smiled mirthlessly:

"Typhoid would sound better. Anyway, you won't believe it."

"Do you know how they execute people over there?"

"Everybody knows that," said Vardi. "They shoot them i

the back of the neck." He turned his head to Julien and said with the same mirthless smile:

"If you are trying to frighten me you are really more stupid than I thought."

"There is a little detail," said Julien. "They stand the man with his face to the wall, tell him to open his mouth, and put a rubber ball into it."

"What for?" asked Vardi, keeping up his smile.

"It is quite ingenious. The ball is pierced by the bullet, but it holds the mess back. This saves the trouble of whitewashing the wall each time."

"Well, what's your objection to that?" Vardi's glasses again caught the sun which transformed them momentarily into two round, white shields before his eyes.

"What do you think your chances are that they will honour their promises of safety?"

"I should say about one in two," said Vardi. "In view of the circumstances I call that a reasonable risk."

"I should say one in ten," said Julien. "Or less."

"That's where you are wrong," said Vardi. "Things have changed since the death of the old man. I have got fairly precise information."

"You mean you have swallowed the bait."

"You know me well enough to realise that I am not exactly a new-born babe."

"Who passed you that dope? Our friend Nikitin?"

"The days of our friend Nikitin are numbered," said Vardi.

"That's news to me." Julien couldn't help looking startled.

"There is more news to come. . . ." For the first time since he had entered the room, Vardi looked a little embarrassed:

"You must understand, Julien, that our relations have undergone a functional change. As long as we talk in general terms it is all right; but where concrete political events are concerned, we are no longer quite on the same side."

"I see," said Julien.

"You don't have to look so sarcastic, for you understand perfectly well that this has nothing to do with you personally. Anyway, I had two long and frank talks with our Ambassador; and I have made some other contacts. You would be surprised how much the atmosphere has changed. We lost touch with them a long time ago, Julien. One always has a distorted picture of the other side. They are neither as stupid, nor as cynical as we both thought."

His voice would have sounded pleading had it been capable of such an expression. Julien said:

"How lucky that I am a native of this country. Otherwise I might be tempted to follow you. It sounds like a perfect idyll."

"An idyll—no," said Vardi, ignoring the sarcasm. "But one feels, as soon as one crosses the lines, in a different world. One feels the gigantic constructive effort, the earnest sense of dedication and self-confidence, and an absolute unquestioning faith that the future is theirs. . . ."

"Why don't you say 'ours'?" said Julien.

Vardi smiled. "I thought it might hurt you and sound unnecessarily—provocative. But seriously, Julien," he continued urgently, "you would be surprised what a different world it is. We have both forgotten what it was like twenty years ago. We have become embittered and venomous like old maids. . . . Once the initial tension was over, everything became suddenly changed for me. It is difficult to describe—like feeling all of a sudden young again . . ."

Across the street the woman was now singing full blast:

> "Parlez-moi d'amour
> Dites-moi des choses tendres . . ."

To judge by the voice she must have been an elderly, wispy-haired charwoman, probably engaged in sweeping the dust and the cigarette stumps from the threadbare carpet down under the cupboard, where they could not be seen, only smelled.

"Did you cry in each other's arms—you and your Ambassador?" said Julien.

"Not exactly. Most of the first interview—over an hour—consisted in an exhaustive discussion of my books. He had read them all and made some astonishingly acute critical remarks. They were entirely unorthodox, and as frank as discussions between you and me used to be. He belongs to our generation—Spain, five years solitary, Resistance, and so on. He has apparently even been mixed up with the Bucharinite block, but he got away with a few years' suspension. In short, he might have been one of us—only he never lost faith in the final outcome and stuck it out, through fire and mud. . . ."

He seemed at last to notice the small trickle of vermouth which had dried just under the corner of his lips, and licked it off with the tip of his tongue. His tongue had a rough, whitish surface which was probably due to indigestion. Julien got up, feeling an urgent need for a brandy.

"May I remind you," he said, "of one of your favourite tenets: it is not we who renounced the Movement, it is the Movement which has renounced its ideal."

Vardi made a brisk deprecatory gesture. "That was correct as far as appearances went, but our analysis did not penetrate deeply enough the reality behind the appearances. And you must also remember that I always said that my own position relative to the original programme has remained unchanged; that it was the negation of a negation. Now the two negations have cancelled out, and the balance has been re-established."

He paused, and after a while continued:

"Then I met another man—a certain Smyrnov, who was indirectly connected with Nikitin and his outfit. He was just as frank, and what a type! In eighteen years of exile I haven't met a single person like our Ambassador and this Smyrnov; and over there there are thousands of them. When I told him I didn't like characters like Nikitin, and that the Nikitins were the cancer in the tissue of the Revolution, he laughed and said that I have seemed to have slept through the events of the last months, that Fedya Nikitin and all the other Nikitins were finished and done with; then he added a few unprintable remarks about the Father of the People in his grave. . . ."

"And that impressed you?"

"You must admit that a few months ago this would have been unthinkable."

"And he convinced you that since No. 1 is dead, the Golden Age has begun?"

"No. But he made me understand that there is a chance to make the end of No. 1 the end of the era of the Nikitins. A chance, you understand, not more; but don't you think it is worth taking some risks? It was No. 1 who created the Nikitins; there is no reason why they should not vanish with him."

"On your theory of inevitability, it is the Revolution which created both No. 1 and the Nikitins."

"Wrong again. The theory of inevitability only applies to long-term developments—to the movements of the tide, not of the ripples. The era of No. 1 was a ripple, an episode and not more. That is the essential fact which you don't want to see. And the reason why you don't want to see it is that you prefer to persist in your morbid pessimism, which suits your masochistic temperament and your longing for the apocalypse."

"I shall believe every word you say the moment there is a general amnesty, a revival of Habeas Corpus, abolition of censorship and so on."

"That is precisely where people like Smyrnov and our Ambassador and myself come in. I told you there is a chance, not more; but it will be wasted if there are no people willing to take the risk. When No. 1 pegged out, two hundred and fifty million people sighed with relief; and two hundred and fifty million sighs cause a considerable stir in the atmosphere. Our task is, if I may vary an old saying, to beat the corpse while it's hot."

"You seem to be developing a particular sense of humour," said Julien.

"I was actually quoting Smyrnov."

"Does it not strike you as rather curious that these people are in such a hurry to take you into their confidence when their projects seem to be of a highly conspiratorial nature?"

"I told you the opportunity must not be allowed to slip. They knew my record, and they knew that I had never gone over to the other side. They knew that I was in opposition to the regime, but belonged to their own camp. I am not the only one who has been approached. . . . In fact, the idea is to re-unite the whole opposition, to undo the crimes of No. 1 and the Nikitins—in short to go back to where we started in 1917. . . ."

Vardi paused and reached for his glass. Only his breathing betrayed his suppressed excitement. He drank, and said with an air of finality, getting up from his chair:

"Perhaps now you have gained a better understanding of my reasons. I was not supposed to tell you about all this. That is why at first I was hedging and talking in generalisations. But I know I can trust you. We have known each other for years and I don't want you to get the wrong idea of me as we part. . . ." He hesitated, then repeated for the third time his stubborn request:

"I want you to say that you don't blame me."

His voice, though dry and pedantic, sounded hungry, and his eyes in the ugly, intelligent, aging face had an equally hungry gleam. Julien felt that it was almost impossible, and certainly inhuman, to refuse to satisfy this hunger. He narrowed his eyes, let the cigarette nonchalantly dangle from his lip and said as airily as he could:

"You can't blackmail me into saying that. You haven't got a chance and you know it. There is no resurrection for fallen angels. It is not I who suffer from the morbid urge of self-immolation, but you."

Vardi turned on his heel; for a moment his features were convulsed like a person's who has been hit in the face, but only for a moment. He marched towards the door on his short legs; Julien slid down from the window and limped after him. At the entrance door he caught him by his elbow, but Vardi wrenched himself free and started walking down the stairs. Julien remained standing on the landing. Half a story lower down, on the opposite landing where the stairs changed direction, Vardi had to turn, but he did not look up. Julien leaned over the railing, and as Vardi was now directly underneath him, continuing his descent with the precise steps of under-sized soldiers, Julien noticed for the first time a bald patch like a tonsure on the crown of Vardi's head.

2

LOVE IN THE AFTERNOON

"Wait," cried Hydie, "wait! You are tearing my blouse to pieces."

It was a rather pretty blouse with a high, embroidered collar, and Fedya was tugging at it with the impatience of an adolescent. She tore herself free from him, fled to the corner of the room where the wash-basin stood, and, smiling at Fedya, pulled the blouse over her head; then with the un-selfconscious movements of a mannequin undressing, stepped out of her skirt. Fedya, with a crestfallen look, watched her slip into the bed. "What is the matter?" she called, snuggling under the blanket. "Aren't you going to take your things off?"

He felt cheated, shocked and embarrassed. This was only the second time they were together, and she had undressed shamelessly in front of him as if they had been married for years—and that at five o'clock in the afternoon. The first time she had followed him willingly enough to the hostel, but once here she had seemed to change her mind, perhaps because of the rather cheerless and squalid look of the room, and had put up a gallant resistance, so that he had been obliged to take her virtually by force. And that, he felt with deep conviction, though he would have refused to put it into words, that was as things should be. Her matter-of-fact behaviour today not only deprived him of an essential part of his enjoyment, for to conquer the female's resistance, even if it is only coquetry and make-believe, was after all the male's natural role; it also lacked decorum and culturedness. One lived and learned; now he had an American mistress of the highest social background, who undressed and got into a man's bed as one prepares for a game of tennis.

But however that might be, Hydie's face on the pillow and her bare shoulders uncovered by the blanket looked extremely desirable; and fortunately she had still kept her brassière and slip, and resisted having them taken off with the light on. To tear them away with gentle savagery restored Fedya's happiness, made them both breathless and raised their blood temperature. Hydie had only time to whisper that he should take his horrible suit off, but he did not get further than flinging his jacket away, wondering with half his mind what there was horrible about it while she swept the bedside lamp onto the floor, where it broke with a crash exploding into darkness; then each of them raced along separately their united path into self-oblivion, panting as it carried them more and more steeply uphill, until they were lifted as if by the vortex of a hurricane, over the last, vertiginous culmination of the track, up to the peak. There the hurricane abated and the world became serene and calm again. For a short while they were still permitted to float through the rarefied air, and experience that utter stillness of body and mind which is the mountaineer's reward. Then the feeling of high altitude began to diminish, gradually the clouds which had hidden the earth dissolved; they were back in the valley, and the dingy hotel room, though still mercifully shrouded in darkness, began to take shape again with the wash-basin as its focus and centre. Some soft, crumbling object was touching Hydie's front, then creeping in a zigzag across her face. It was Fedya holding out a cigarette and groping with it in the darkness for her lips. She half parted them, and the cigarette found its way to her mouth. She kept her eyes closed while he struck a match and lighted her cigarette and his own. He blew the match out and said: "You look very beautiful." She felt pleased, and in a fleeting caress touched his hair and his chest through the open shirt. Then she lay back, sighing with contentment, to smoke her cigarette.

She had never had a lover so primitive and inconsiderate, and though he never waited for or helped her ascent, he was the first who had made her reach complete fulfilment. The young English art critic whom she had married three months after leaving the convent had made love like a bird: a peck, a flutter, and it was over. Fedya's manner was the opposite: he made her feel as if she had been run over by an express train. In between these two she had entered into partnerships of the body with three or four others—one with whom she had fallen in love, one whom she had desired, one who had a reputation for erotic virtuosity, and one with whom she happened to get drunk. This last venture had ended in disaster and humiliation; the others had been partly harassing, partly exciting and near-satisfactory but never entirely so—not even with the virtuoso, though he had exerted himself in a most praiseworthy manner to live up to his reputation. The glass cage had never entirely melted around her, and each time she had been left trembling in the frigid purgatorial fires—glowing and scorched, but never consummated. The nearer she knew herself to that elusive, ultimate fulfilment, for which her flesh longed as she had once longed for a sign of being chosen—so tantalisingly within reach, approaching, receding, mocking her frenzy—the more bitterly disappointed she felt; and in the end she would each time break into tears from nervous exhaustion. It was a miracle that citizen Nikitin should have succeeded where all others failed.

She inhaled the smoke of Fedya's cigarette and heard him splashing with great vigour at the wash-basin. No, one could not say that he was either a tactful or a skilful lover. Why then had he alone succeeded in lifting her over the invisible barrier of guilt which had always prevented her ultimate surrender? And, even stranger, why had she known from the beginning that he would succeed? Was Fedya the only one who knew some "Open sesame" to which she unconsciously responded? A shiver ran down her spine, for she suddenly remembered the only other person of whom she had known by instinct that he could make her respond in the same way, though she had never consciously thought of him as a man: it was her confessor in the convent school. But what did these two men have in common? Nothing—except their faith which was their irresistible appeal and magic armour, which made surrender to

them an act of humility and devotion, free of guilt; which
enabled them to lift her up, limp and willing, into their safe
and fertile world where all doubts were dispelled. Theirs was
a world where one could never go astray and lose oneself,
where good and evil were clearly defined and marked on all
crossroads, like signposts pointing North and South. The won-
derful thing about Fedya was that he knew the answers where
others questioned; that he was sure of himself where Julien
was ashamed even of the limp acquired in honourable battle;
that he stood firmly on the solid foundations of his creed where
others hobbled and crawled in the mire. That was the magic
wand which dissolved the frustrating guilt in her flesh and
made it surrender willingly and with joy—surrender to what
Julien had once called "her almost obscene craving for faith."

She heard Fedya's creaking steps on the floorboards then,
without warning, the top light went on. She blinked, and saw
him standing near the door, in his black mourning suit and
mourning tie, his yellow hair plastered down with water,
laughing at her and looking with admiration at her half-
covered body. "Will you not get up?" he asked. "It is time for
the apéritifs."

While Hydie dressed behind the paper screen near the
washstand, her head bobbing up and down as if she were engaged in Swedish gymnastics, Fedya sat on the bed, smoking,
and considered the situation. Two months had passed since the
death of No. 1, and the tension had begun to ease a little.
The rumours that all personnel abroad would be called home
had abated. Life in the Embassy and relations in the Service
were much as they had been before. Only the Ambassador had
been recalled, and five or six other people—some of them
fairly high up in the hierarchy, others in quite unimportant
positions. They had not been heard of since, and as tact and
good manners required, their names were never mentioned.
Among them was Fedya's former neighbour in the hostel,
Smyrnov, whose disappearance Fedya had greeted with some
relief. Obviously the people who were recalled had been mixed
up in politics, so they had only themselves to blame. It was remarkable though, that only one of them had gone to Capua;
the rest obeyed the order to go home. Like so many others,
they had probably overestimated the relaxation of discipline
which the death of No. 1 would cause. Fedya himself had
never entertained any illusions on this point. He had been re

lieved, like everybody else, at the old man having pegged out at last, and had enjoyed the humour of the decree which ordered every member of the diplomatic missions to wear mourning for a full year. No doubt the old man had become insupportable long ago—capricious, vengeful, full of crotchets and twists. It had, of course, been necessary to build him up into a kind of idol for the backward masses who were not yet sufficiently cultured to be led toward their own happiness without a leader whom they could worship. If one had not given them portraits of No. 1 to hang on every wall in every room in the country, they would have hung up the old ikons again, and there you were. Their need of somebody or something to worship was a heritage of the dark past; it would take another two or three generations to cure them of it. Besides, a people's democracy surrounded by enemies within and without must inevitably take the form of a centralised pyramid, and a pyramid must have a top. Hence the Father of the People was a necessary institution, and the people abroad who ridiculed the outward forms of this cult had no smattering of the dialectics of history. They were like savages in an opera house who want to shoot the villain on the stage because they don't understand that everything on the stage is make-believe, and that this make-believe nevertheless serves a higher purpose, and is taken seriously by the cultured people in the audience. On one occasion he had tried to explain this to Hydie, only by hints and allusions of course, and in spite of her deformed mentality, a product of her social background and education, she seemed to have at least understood that matters were not quite as simple, and he, Fedya, not quite such a simpleton as her people thought. But all this had no bearing on the fact that No. 1 had been a rather depressing kind of idol, and that it was undeniably a relief to have got rid of him.

The fools abroad had hoped that once the top went the whole pyramid would collapse. That only proved once again that they had no inkling of the science of history and were unable to distinguish between a reactionary tyranny and a revolutionary dictatorship. When a reactionary tyrant died, the whole regime went to pieces like an organism whose head has been cut off. But a revolutionary dictatorship was rather like that fabulous animal which, if you cut its head off, grew a new one at once. Even the Church did not die with the Pope though, while he was alive, people kissed his slippers—and the Church had once been the embodiment of the ideology of the

Roman proletariat, and had only gradually degenerated into an instrument of reaction.

Nevertheless, the last few weeks had been rather trying. Particularly during the first fortnight, before the name of No. 1's successor had been officially announced, it had been necessary to move warily and to watch one's step with extreme care. There had been, for instance, that last conversation with Smyrnov, when Smyrnov had come to Fedya's room under some pretext and, after a few indifferent remarks, had asked casually: "Do you know by chance when Marius lived?"

"Marius? What Marius?" said Fedya.

"The democratic Tribune in Rome who fought a civil war against the dictator Sulla."

"Oh, that one," said Fedya. "Why, are you writing an article on history?"

Smyrnov, instead of an answer, had offered him a cigarette, and both had produced their lighters—which reminded Fedya of Smyrnov's remarks on his buying a French lighter the day Hydie had stolen his diary. But that was now an old story and Fedya, always pleased to oblige, racked his brains to remember something about Marius the Tribune. The only date in Roman history he knew was 73-71 B.C., the years of the Spartacus revolt.

"Wait," he said, "when did the proletarian revolution under Spartacus start? 73 B.C.—if I remember rightly. Now all I know about Marius the Tribune is that he was some time before or after Spartacus, and without great importance owing to his bourgeois liberal ideology."

Fedya had been quite pleased with himself for this answer, but Smyrnov had only smiled, hardly perceptibly under his black moustache: "Marius," he said, "was the man who destroyed the Roman Empire."

Fedya did not know what Smyrnov was driving at, but he thought he smelled a rat somewhere, and wished he had refused to be drawn into this conversation. "How did he do that?" he asked indifferently.

"He replaced the old Army based on compulsory military service among the Roman citizens by a mercenary army," said Smyrnov.

"Well, well, the devil take him," said Fedya noncommittally.

"Within one generation from that change," said Smyrnov, "the power had shifted from the Senate to the Army. It was the Army who put the various Cæsars into power and held them at their mercy."

Now Fedya knew what Smyrnov was up to. He was pro-Party, anti-Army, and wanted to test Fedya's position. Fedya had no fixed opinion on this subject—which was the only real issue in the question of the succession; he was not a politician but a member of the Service, who did his duty. But if the succession could not after all be settled smoothly, and if it came to that kind of cold, covert showdown behind the scenes by which such conflicts were settled, then even a too emphatic attitude of neutrality could later on be held against one. He said carefully:

"I know too little about the history of Roman class struggles. Fortunately in our case no such dangers can arise because the Army and the Party are both instruments of the People, though of course now one and now the other has to take the lead, according to the concrete requirements of the situation."

The answer had been correct in itself, yet precisely because of its correct neutrality it had been an implicit rejection of Smyrnov's overture; so that if the silent struggle behind the scenes was to end with the triumph of the Party over the Army, as Smyrnov wished, then Smyrnov could accuse him, and rightly so, of the crime of "objectivism" and "double-tongued hypocrisy." Thus, by rejecting Smyrnov's advances Fedya had, up to a point, thrown in his lot with the Army. He had done it almost unconsciously, by instinct, for he felt that certain features in the structure and function of the Party were out of date, that the death of No. 1 would lead to a general overhauling of the machinery, and that the bureaucratic hierarchy would come out of it considerably weakened —it had become too much imbued with the less pleasant emanations of the No. 1's personality. The masses expected some relaxation in the rigours of the regime as a kind of funeral gift as it were; on this point both he and Smyrnov would doubtless agree. But Smyrnov had apparently set his hope on an internal rejuvenation of the Party—there had been some cautious hints and rumors in that direction, and even speculations in the foreign press about a limited amnesty for the opposition. Fedya on the other hand was convinced, again more by instinct than by calculation, that the Party could not afford any such conciliatory gesture and slackening of the discipline without letting loose some fatal mechanism which would lead to its destruction. Nevertheless, some gesture had to be made to meet the great expectations which the old man's death had raised in the masses; and as the objective situation did not permit any real loosening of the reins, the only logical solution was to shift some of the responsibility for unpopular measures, together with some of the burden of executive power, on to the Army. This would inevitably lead to a certain displacement of the centre of gravity. The Party and the Army were the only socially conscious structures in the country which replaced, as it were, the functions of social classes in other countries; and, as in the class struggles of the older type, the weakening of one structure must inevitably lead to a strengthening of the other.

After a few more indifferent remarks, Smyrnov had gone back to his own room—and that was the last Fedya had seen of him. History had cast its dice and they had both announced their stakes—Smyrnov because he was a meddler, Fedya, because he had been forced into the gamble. As it happened, Fedya had won and Smyrnov lost. Had the dice fallen differently, Fedya would have been the loser and would have borne the consequences without demurring; and if accused of having planned and plotted a military dictatorship, would have recognised his guilt according to the rules of the game. Only in a decaying and doomed civilisation did people imagine that they could eat their cake and have it; and that was precisely why they were doomed. They lived in a Capua of political licence and liberal self-indulgence; their parliaments were brothels where each man could choose among a dozen factions according to taste; their press a hotbed of a hundred heresies and discords. But at the end of the soft season in Capua stood the destruction of Carthage.

"I am ready," said Hydie, stepping out from behind the screen, fresh as a flower which has just been watered. "Ah," said Fedya approvingly; he had quite forgotten her presence.

The bar where they usually took their apéritifs was still nearly empty. It was run by three good-looking young barmen called respectively Albert, André and Alphonse, who loved each other dearly and slightly queerly, and looked so much alike that only the habitués could tell which was which. However, the three young men accepted willingly being called by each other's names, which they had thrown into a common alliterative pool, as it were. They were pooling their money too, because they were planning, as soon as they had collected enough of it, to open a café, with a petrol pump next to it, in a small town in Provence. They were conscientious in the mixing of drinks though they themselves only drank tomato juice and an occasional glass of champagne; they were extremely well-behaved, nice young men who made everybody feel at home.

The bar had mild, diffused lighting, comfortable leather armchairs, and an aquarium full of strange, coloured, goggling fish which had a calming effect on people's nerves. It had been frequented by the neo-nihilists until the day when a friend of Father Millet's niece had poured a double martini into the aquarium, making the fish first drunk then die. He had been sued for damages by the proprietor, a mysterious gentleman whom nobody had ever seen, and who was rumoured to be a commercial attaché to one of the South American legations. The trial had created an enormous sensation, for the culprit, a pupil of Professor Pontieux, had based his defence entirely on the tenets of neo-nihilistic philosophy. His lawyer had read long passages from the master's "Negation and Position" to show that the "why-notist" attitude in general served a high moral purpose and social function, and that in the particular case in question, the fish had probably attained a degree of happiness before dying which in the normal course of events would forever have been withheld from them. The defendant's action, he claimed, had enabled them to become free in the profoundest sense of the word, and thereby to surpass the limitations of their ichthyological condition. The judge, however, had awarded the proprietor full damages, which amounted to a considerable sum, as the fish had been imported from tropical waters. The neo-nihilists were outraged; they launched a public subscription to collect the fine, and denounced the judge as a collaborator, a Fascist, an enemy of the revolutionary Proletariat and of the Freedomloving Commonwealth. They also imposed a boycott on the bar, much to the relief of the three nice barmen and of the more staid clientele.

Fedya still drank his pernods undiluted, but he never got drunk. Hydie listened in happy contentment to the soft jazz music which came from a tiny wireless receiver behind the bar, and which agreed so well with the soft lighting and the soft gliding movements of the fish behind the glass wall of the aquarium. Fedya was humming the tune from the radio; he liked this bar which, he had once explained to her, had a truly cultured though slightly decadent atmosphere; he could sit still, or humming to himself, for half an hour on end with an air of perfect contentment.

"What are you thinking about?" asked Hydie.

"I think of nothing. It is like being on a holiday."

She waited for him to return the question; it was childish, yet she would have been pleased to hear him ask "And what do *you* think about?" Fedya, however, wasn't interested. He lifted his finger to a hardly noticeable degree, and as if attracted by some magic power, Albert or Alphonse at once approached their table smilingly, to fill up their glasses.

"It still works," said Hydie.

"What?" Fedya asked innocently, though he knew perfectly well. In fact since their first drink at Weber's, he had made a point of exercising his gift with growing refinement.

Hydie remembered their first meeting on Bastille Day. She asked, smiling a little wistfully:

"What marks have I now got after my name in your notebook?"

"I don't know what you mean," said Fedya, and his face closed. She at once regretted having asked the question; but now she had no choice but to go on:

"Of course you do. Those lists in your notebook."

"Ah, that," Fedya said offhandedly. "I do it no longer. It was a stupid game to amuse myself."

Hydie had the impulse to put her hand quickly into his pocket and grab the notebook to see whether he was lying. She checked herself just in time, knowing that this harmless joke would infuriate him. This made her reflect how little real intimacy existed between them. Never before had a man physically satisfied her, and she had thought that would make all the difference. But though the glass cage melted each time they made love, only a little while later it was there again.

"And what are *you* thinking about?" asked Fedya, smiling at her in a friendly way. But the question came too late; and she felt it meant not what it should have meant, but was somehow connected with the notebook.

"I am thinking," she answered, "that I sometimes feel lonely in your company."

"Ah?" said Fedya with genuine amazement. "But one cannot always talk. And one cannot always—make love." He never liked to refer to love-making in a matter-of-fact way.

To talk of bed must be an act of seduction; it had to be done in an appropriate voice and with an insinuating smile.

"It isn't that," said Hydie.

"Then what is it?" he asked, visibly bored.

"Oh, never mind."

A party of three people came in through the glass door, and Hydie's face fell: they were Julien, a dark-haired woman with a sharp, ugly, intense face, and another man. They noticed Hydie and Fedya in the order they came in. The woman's look grazed Hydie indifferently; then, as she recognized Fedya, she gave a start and kept staring at him with an expression of frank, undisguised horror. Julien, if he was startled, did not betray it; he nodded amiably to Hydie, the eternal cigarette dangling from his lip. The third man, who had come last, looked blank. The woman said something half aloud to Julien who shrugged, then nodded smiling assent. She turned on her heel and walked out. Julien held the door for her, then for the bewildered other man, and went out last, controlling his limp. He hadn't looked at Hydie again.

Alphonse, the barman, said something to his colleague André. They whispered for a while, then went back to their job polishing the bar and manipulating their bottles. At last Hydie found the courage to glance at Fedya. He looked unconcerned, just as before the incident, humming the tune from the radio; only his eyes had slightly narrowed.

"Do you know these people?"

"Who?"

She hated his habit of always pretending at first not to understand what she was talking about.

"The people who just came in," she said impatiently.

"Ah—I have perhaps seen the woman and the crippled man somewhere before."

"He is not a cripple. He was wounded in the Spanish War."

"Yes? Perhaps you know them better than I."

"Listen," said Hydie. "Don't talk that way to me. I was in bed with you an hour ago. I can't bear it."

"But what have I said?" Fedya asked with surprise and concern. "Please don't be hysterical."

"Those people walked out because they saw you."

"I also thought so," Fedya said comfortably. "Perhaps they don't like me or my country. Maybe they are your friends, but they are bad people. The woman has run away from her own country because she did not like the new regime there which took the land from the feudal landlords and gave it to the hungry peasants. If she did not like it, let her go and live somewhere else, but then she has no right to make speeches and write articles asking the whole world to go to war and kill each other so that she can get back her estate and make the peasants starve and remain illiterate as before. And the cripple —the man who limps—maybe he was in Spain, but he is a very cynical, decadent man with a bad conscience. If he did not have a bad conscience, why should he have run away from me like the others?"

Hydie bit her lip. She knew she must control herself, otherwise there would be a scene and afterwards she would either have to humiliate herself or lose him; and she could not afford to lose him. She said as evenly as she could manage: "He did not run away. He walked out because he hates the sight of you."

Fedya noticed her agitation. He smiled reassuringly and said very gently, as one speaks to a child, laying his hand on hers:

"If you go to a public locality and there is a woman sitting there to whom you are hostile, you do not walk out. You sit down at another table and you pretend you do not see her. You only walk out if you have a bad conscience. Or if you feel that all your hatred is in vain because the other person does not care and is only laughing at your hostility. Is that not so?"

Hydie found nothing to answer, though she knew that her silence was a betrayal of Julien and Vardi and Boris and herself. She could not even bring herself to withdraw her hand from Fedya's hold. The surface where their skins touched was the only warm source of life in the barren waste inside her. She rubbed her knuckles against his palm, and the sensuous pleasure which this gave her brought up a wave of such profound disgust at herself that she feared she was going to be sick, and for a second the perennial nightmare of an accidental pregnancy made her forget everything else. Her hand lay still while her mind went through the dreary routine of computing numbers and dates as if it had been momentarily transformed into a jangling cash-register machine. The mechanism clicked, the ticket with the date fell out; she was still safe. She gave a little sigh of relief, and withdrew her hand.

"I want a drink," she said.

Fedya too was relieved; these ever-recurring scenes bored

him no end. "But it must be the last one, otherwise you will not have enough time to change for the Opera."

Almost imperceptibly he wagged his broad index finger, without lifting his hand from the table. One of the barmen left at once his bottles and, pleasantly smiling, came forward to change their drinks.

3

DECLINE OF A HERO

In his small hotel room, half-way up the hill of Montmartre, Leo Nikolayevich Leontiev sat in front of a new polished desk, bought the previous day in a department store. He had considered this acquisition for about a fortnight; each day as he passed the department store he had stared with hungry eyes at the shining modern office desk with its smooth surface and handy drawers on both sides. He knew that under his present circumstances it was folly to buy the desk; but each day he became more convinced that the reason why he couldn't work was that the table in his hotel room disgusted and depressed him. It was covered with circular stains from the glasses with liquor or toothpaste which former occupants of the room had stood on it, and it would not keep still on its wobbly legs however carefully Leontiev wedged folded strips of paper underneath them. He had tried to obtain a better table from the morose couple who owned and ran the hotel and bullied the tenants from their glass-panelled concierge box, but was told that if he wanted more luxurious furniture he was free to go somewhere else. He had repeated to himself that he could no longer afford to be fussy, and had tried to force himself to work sitting at the rickety table, sometimes during eight full hours a day; but he was unable to concentrate. Finally he had come to the conclusion that it was foolish not to buy the desk which was an essential investment, if without it he could not get on with his book, was wasting his time and eating up the small capital which the publishers had advanced on it. If he lived very cautiously, particularly with regard to drinks, it would probably last three or four months, and he could not obtain more until he delivered the manuscript, or at least a

substantial part of it. So yesterday he had at last made up his
mind and bought the desk.

It had been delivered this morning by the department store's
furniture van, and its arrival had caused a considerable stir in
the hotel. Monsieur Marcel, the owner-concierge, had declared that it was not permissible for guests to bring their own
furniture, and that there was no space for Leontiev's old table
in any of the other rooms; and he had repeated that if Leontiev did not like the place, he only had to say so and go somewhere else. Fortunately the removal men from the store had
declared that they could not waste their time listening to arguments, that their orders were to deliver the desk to the buyer and that, if the landlord objected to this, they would dump
the article in the passage in front of the concierge box, for
such was the custom in disputed cases. Leontiev's dignity was
saved by the circumstance that the quarrel now was between
Monsieur Marcel and the removal men, so that he could stand
by passively, his stern gaze fixed on the shining desk. In the
end Madame Marcel, a sluttish female who wore carpet slippers even on her shopping expeditions, emerged from her
windowless, garlic-odoured kitchen, and after giving the removal men a bit of her mind, whispered something to her husband which Leontiev made out to refer to the fact that the
desk would represent a security against any future defection
in his paying the rent. So after some face-saving remarks,
Monsieur Marcel finally gave in and with a jerk of his head
directed the removal men to proceed up the staircase and into
Leontiev's room on the second floor. There a further difficulty
arose owing to the smallness of the room, which made it impossible to get the desk in without getting the old table out.
The removal men, however, who seemed to sympathise with
Leontiev, solved the problem by carrying on their own initiative the old table down the stairs and depositing it in front of
the concierge box, whereupon they departed with broad grins.
The remarkable thing was that they had refused to accept a
tip. The younger of the two had asked Leontiev what he needed
the desk for, and on learning that it was to serve for the writing of a book, both had nodded with respect and understanding, and the older one had said with an encouraging wink:
"That's right. Give it to them, Comrade."

It was this remark which prevented Leontiev from concentrating as he sat in front of the new desk, with a sheaf of
creamy paper laid out neatly on its smooth top. The removal

men, on seeing how helpless he was against the proprietor's bullying, had automatically included him in their fraternity, and had drawn the obvious conclusion that a writer who lived in a hole like this could only be engaged in the promoting of the social revolution. Had they discovered what kind of book he was writing, their grins would have vanished and their fraternal solidarity turned into contempt; they would have treated him like a leper and in all probability the desk would never have got into his room. And the point was that he could not blame them; nay, that with all his instincts and feeling he was forced to take the removal men's side against his own.

Leontiev suddenly remembered a phrase which that curious character whom they called 'Saint George,' had uttered at Monsieur Anatole's memorable party: he had referred to Leontiev's escape as an act of mental hara-kiri.

And yet during the first few days everything had looked so hopeful. When at the end of Monsieur Anatole's party the news had broken of No. 1's death, Leontiev had at once seen his chance to rescue his new shirts and the rest of his luggage from the hotel. He knew that in the midst of the turmoil created by the old man's death, the Special Service people would be too busy to bother about him. So he had gone back to his comfortable suite and spent the night there. He had even considered the possibility of such changes in the regime as would enable him to go back after all; at any rate he could wait a few days before he made his final decision.

The decision, however, was taken out of his hands, for the news of his defection had spread quickly from Monsieur Anatole's party, and the next morning several newspapers had carried headlines like, "Hero of Culture Goes Capua," "Commonwealth Star-Author Denounces Oppression, Sides with Mystic Sect," and the like. These headlines had of course been smaller than one could normally expect, for the death of No. 1 had occupied most of the available space; but nevertheless a whole string of reporters had called in the morning at Leontiev's hotel, and by the afternoon two American publishers had cabled advantageous offers for a book to be called, "I Was a Hero of Culture"—curiously enough they had both hit on the same title.

Once his defection had become public, the thought of his returning had of course to be ruled out. Whatever changes occurred in the regime, there was one thing which they would never forgive him: to have expressed his sympathy for the Fearless Sufferers.

Leontiev slid his fingers tenderly along the polished surface of the desk. In its exact centre lay the sheaf of soft, creamy paper; at the head of the top page the title in neat, printed letters:

I WAS A HERO OF CULTURE
BY
LEO NIKOLAYEVICH LEONTIEV

That was as far as he had got. Some fifty pages which he had written with an immense effort during the previous three weeks he had thrown away. He knew they were no good: stiff, spiteful, apologetic, sensational. He had to start afresh.

But where . . . ? Logically the story should start forty years ago, when his first poem was published in the illegal "Iskra." Or even earlier, with his childhood and social background. But the agent who represented his publishers in Paris, an intelligent and energetic young man, had argued that according to sound journalistic principles, the book should start with a dramatic and topical chapter, explaining the circumstances and reasons for his break, the terror and intimidation to which artists in the Commonwealth were subjected—all this illustrated by ample anecdotical material, and contrasted with the complete freedom which their opposite numbers enjoyed in the democratically enlightened West. This part, written in the crisp and colourful style which the American public appreciated, should constitute the bulk of the book; the author's past, and the earlier years of the Revolution, which were matters of more restricted interest, should only be brought in where absolutely necessary for the understanding of present conditions, and could probably be condensed into one short autobiographical chapter. Of course, the young man had added as he noticed Leontiev's bushy stare of disapproval, of course Leontiev was free to write his book exactly as he liked; he had merely ventured his advice because the public's taste was different in every country—and prompted by his sincere wish that the book should meet with the greatest possible material and moral success. Needless to say, the chances of any book for both material success and political effect were vastly increased if it was written with an eye on the possibilities of screen dramatisation, of serial publication in the big magazines, of broadcasting, and particularly of television. . . .

"Whether you and I like it or not," the intelligent young man had continued, "it is a fact that in the course of the last five years or so, no book has been a paying proposition unless it lent itself to exploitation on one of the sidelines which I mentioned."

Leontiev had let the young man talk, for his mind was made up to write this book exactly as he wanted to write it. It was to be, as Gruber had cynically said, "the one honest book of his life."

How often he had dreamed, during these last ten, twenty years, of the voluptuous sensation it would be to write the truth, the whole truth and nothing but the truth; to reinstate words and phrases in their original meaning, to rescue them from slavery and prostitution and restore to them their lost virginity! He had written whole chapters of the book in his head, chapters of scorching indignation which had the majestic yet devastating flow of liquid volcanic rock; chapters of heartbroken lament as if written by the waters of Babylon; passages of melancholy wisdom, and others radiating his unshaken faith in the ultimate victory of justice and progress. Alas, they had never been put to paper, not a single word of them. To do so at the time would not only have meant taking foolish risks, it would also have increased the strain on the synapses beyond any endurable limit. So long as the book remained in the realm of day-dreams it had still been possible for Leontiev to go on functioning as a Hero of Culture, just as one can commit mental adultery and yet continue to fulfil one's conjugal duties; but he knew that once he started actually putting down his dream-chapters on paper, he would no longer be able to turn out his annual patriotic drama—the recurrent gala-event of the theatrical season for the last ten years—nor even to write a single line for "Freedom and Culture." Besides, he had always been convinced that, given the opportunity to escape, he would only have to open the sluices and all the material, pent up for years behind the synaptic lock-gates, would pour out like a torrent.

And now, instead of that liberating stream, all he could squeeze out of himself were these mean, prickling, acid drops of sweat.

Again he ran the tip of his fingers over the sheaf of paper. The touch of its smooth surface gave him a sensuous pleasure and at the same time seemed to rouse some unpleasant memory which for days had been lurking just on the threshold of his mind. The blank, creamy expanse of the paper seemed to deride him, it had a tempting and at the same time paralysing effect; and this mixed sensation of desire and impotence was uncannily familiar. . . . Suddenly he remembered; or rather his fingertips remembered having once caressed, with the same helpless greed, another smooth, creamy surface—the skin of the first woman he had seen in the nude. She had been a prostitute, there were no other opportunities for a student in those days; a splendid specimen with large spongy breasts, generous haunches and the somewhat coarse but by no means repellent features of a hefty country wench. She had always been standing on the same corner, under the same gaslight, as he walked home from school, and for a whole year she had been the inspiration of his erotic reveries. Soon these had become an obsession; his daydreams of her were of extraordinary vividness and intensity; in their careful planning and minuteness of detail they were in fact not unlike the imaginary chapters of the unwritten book.

It had taken him several months to assemble the funds and the courage to approach her; but when the great moment had at last come, and she had undressed and lay waiting on the bed—a bewilderingly strange figure displaying details of the body which he had previously only seen on statues—he had been just as helpless and paralysed. Sitting on the edge of the bed, with those huge, smooth, creamy surfaces before his eyes, he had timidly run the tip of his fingers over her flank and felt the same sensuous pleasure mixed with shameful inability as now. She had just lain there, waiting, with raised, majestic thighs and hands folded behind her head, ready to allow the long daydream to materialise; until at last her smile had turned to derision and every single curve of her body had seemed to mock him. But on that occasion he did not have to rack his brain for an explanation. Stretching herself lazily on the bed, the wench had made a comic grimace, wrinkling her nose and sticking her tongue out at him; then she had said contemptuously:

"There—one can see what a vicious little boy you are. I bet you are always thinking of it and doing it when you are alone; that's why you can't do it now. Vicious and corrupted—that is what you are. Now go away, go home and do it again, all by yourself. That's what you are good at. . . ." She had made an obscene gesture with her hand and watched him groping for his clothes, his head burning and the tears ready in his eyes.

"That's right—just start crying and sniffling. You are all alike, you vicious cry-babies—it is the town which does it to you, and the teachers in the school. . . ." She seemed to find a venomous pleasure in humiliating him by venting her peasant philosophy. "They hold you on a tight rein, they keep you in cages and frighten the life out of you with their don't do this and that, until you can't act the honest natural way any longer. No, you have to lock yourselves into the lavatory and do it to yourselves where nobody can see you. That's what you are good at," she concluded, repeating her gesture, "but not at this," and she slapped her hand into her bushy lap. For a moment she looked like a statue of the goddess of truth which Leontiev had seen in a museum.

He got up and paced up and down in the tiny room, missing his dressing-gown. He could not understand what was happening to him. He vaguely sensed the connection between that memory and his present feeling of impotence in front of the new desk and the paper laid out on it, offering itself to him with its blank, provocative, mocking stare. He even derived a certain satisfaction from the strange trick his memory had played on him, from the beautifully symbolic ways in which his mind worked. But though he saw the symbol he could not interpret it. How could the only too understandable confusion of an inexperienced boy be compared to this humiliation of the mature, experienced writer? The parallel just did not seem to work out. There was nevertheless a rather reassuring side to it: for though the memory was embarrassing, it referred merely to a passing episode. On the next opportunity, under less crude circumstances, he had not been found wanting; and from then onward, thank God, he had never again met with trouble of this particular kind. Perhaps his present predicament would pass in the same way, all by itself? In that case the best policy would be not to force the issue, and to give those synapses a well-deserved rest. . . .

Nonsense, he told himself. One had to pull oneself together, clench one's teeth and concentrate. After all, if one had always been able to work on command under the most repugnant and degrading pressure, it would be grotesque and paradoxical if one should not be able to work under conditions of complete freedom. Others, dozens of Leontiev's colleagues, had become paralysed by fear or disgust, had collapsed or made fatal mistakes and gone down the drain; while he had stood the race and taken all the hurdles—practically the only one in his whole generation. It would be too absurd to give way just now.

Leontiev took two aspirins and again sat down at his desk. The paper stared at him exactly as before. He wondered whether he had a hangover, but could detect no obvious symptoms. He never touched drink before his dinner at 8 p.m. But even so . . .

A fortnight before, when Leontiev had still been in vogue, a young American couple, both of whom worked for some newspaper or magazine, had taken him to a place called "The Kronstadt." It was a kind of nightclub, but it had a bar to it where one could sit for hours on a high stool, sipping a brandy-soda or two at a reasonably cheap price, and watch people dance to a small gypsy orchestra or listen to the artistes, most of whom sang Polish, Ukrainian, Czech or Hungarian folksongs. Both the artistes and the habitués came mostly from those countries—people who had "gone to Capua"; others whose job it was to spy on them; still others without a political past who had simply escaped when their countries were liberated by the Commonwealth. Recently there had been quite an influx of émigrés from the Rabbit State.

But there were no grand dukes, taxi-driving generals, or princesses at the Kronstadt, the doorman was not an ex-officer of the Guards, and the barmaid not a former ballerina of the St. Petersburg Opera. The legendary days of that kind of champagne-cum-caviar joint belonged to the past between the two wars. The Kronstadt's driftwood had been washed up by a later and different tide. Instead of grand dukes and ballerinas, it consisted mostly of lawyers, journalists, ex-Under Secretaries of Ministries of Agriculture, and Members of Parliament of the Liberal, Democratic and Socialist Parties. There were also a few fallen angels from the Movement itself, and in addition the usual curiosities: an Esperantist from Bucharest and a philatelist from Kovno, whose hobbies were proscripted because of the cosmopolitan tendencies and foreign contacts which they involved; a Jungian psychoanalyst, a geneticist of the Mendelian school, a painter of formalist inclinations and a philosopher who had fallen into neo-Kantian banditism. They were a dingy lot; the best the Kronstadt could offer in the way of social glamour was a Baltic Baroness at reduced prices;

and even she had once been a member of the Radical Small-Holders' Party in her country.

The Kronstadt looked like a long, padded tunnel which was divided into two halves by a plush curtain. In the front half towards the entrance stood the polished mahogany bar and a few small tables; the rear half of the tunnel, on the other side of the plush curtain, was two steps lower, and the tables stood along the wall, leaving a narrow strip along the centre for the dancing and the floorshow. At the back end of the tunnel there was a door with "TOILET" written on it in luminous letters so that it could be read when the lights were turned low; the lettering was of the kind which appears in aeroplanes at the moment of the take-off advising the passengers to fasten their safety belts. In theory the curtain should have always remained closed, shutting off the padded inner sanctuary from the noisier bar; but Monsieur Pierre, the proprietor, often left it open to let the habitués at the bar listen to their favourite artistes or watch the dancing. Pierre, who looked like an aging *souteneur* from the Pigalle quarter, which indeed he had been, practised a kind of Robin Hood democracy; he fleeced the suckers mercilessly and poisoned them with doctored champagne, but if he took a liking to one of the down-at-heel habitués he let him sit at the bar for hours on end with a single extra-large brandy-soda in front of him, and on rare occasions even gave him credit for a week or so.

The evening Leontiev had visited the Kronstadt for the first time he had been recognised by several of the habitués who had seen his picture in the newspapers. The artistes had sung his favourite songs, the Baltic baroness, the formalist painter, the Under Secretary of State at the Ministry of Agriculture, and several others had joined their table, and Pierre had offered a magnum of champagne on the house. The American couple who were Leontiev's hosts enjoyed themselves hugely and soon got drunk. They were both youngish and very radical, former sympathisers with the Movement, and deeply moved when Pierre explained that he had called his establishment the "Kronstadt" in memory of the revolt of the Baltic sailors in 1920, whose ruthless suppression had marked the turning point in the history of the young revolutionary state, and the beginning of its degeneration into a police regime. They were even more deeply moved when the painter, the philatelist, and one of the journalists told their stories of persecution and escape. The American couple suffered from guilt-complexes for having for so long supported the tyrannic regime; they exchanged meaning looks while the stories were told, and the young man repeatedly remarked in an aside to his wife: "There but for the grace of God go I." As more bottles appeared, and more of the habitués joined them, the couple became the more convinced that the two of them were chiefly responsible for all this misery and disaster; to atone for their past they treated everybody to drinks and the evening soon got enjoyably out of hand. In the end the young American disappeared with the chief victim of his criminal past, the Baltic baroness, after having confessed to her that he had been an agent of a secret Commonwealth spy-ring—a dramatic improvisation in which he was henceforth firmly to believe himself—leaving half of his traveller's cheques with Pierre, who had some trouble in dissuading him from leaving also his overcoat, hat and tie behind for one of the victims of tyranny and oppression.

Leontiev found himself left with the American woman on his hands, a situation which he found both stimulating and embarrassing. He was in a serene mood but far from drunk, partly because he had a strong head, and partly because he had drunk some olive oil before going out—an old habit to avoid the traps and pitfalls which lurked beneath the effusive hilarity of official Commonwealth banquets. He offered to take the woman home to her hotel, and was faintly puzzled when she asked him up to her room for another drink. For a second he thought it might be some trap, but the young lady, misunderstanding his hesitation, assured him airily and with a valiant effort to focus her eyes, that her husband certainly wouldn't get home before morning, and that they both granted each other complete freedom in these matters. As soon as they got to the room, she made love to Leontiev in a swift, efficient and hygienic manner, and fell promptly asleep. Not before he had got back to his own hotel after a refreshing walk on foot, did it occur to Leontiev that he did not even know the name of the hospitable couple of young radicals; but he decided to keep them always a grateful memory.

A few days later, Leontiev, feeling lonely and depressed, had returned to the Kronstadt and spent a pleasant evening chatting with the baroness and the painter over a bottle of champagne. Pierre greeted him as an old, honoured acquaintance and invited him to come again the following Friday for a "quiet little celebration" on the occasion of the marriage of one of the artistes. The celebration had lasted through the night, and Leontiev, yielding to the pressure of the other guests, had recited two of his poems from the early days of the Revolution, followed by a forgotten song of the partisans which he sang in his strong, manly baritone voice. From that night on he was considered a habitué, privileged to consume brandy-sodas instead of champagne, according to his mood. At first he had rationed his visits to two, then to three a week; but during the last few days he had visited the Kronstadt every single night, though on some occasions merely for a short half-hour, to relax at the bar over a brandy or two. He never got drunk, never lost distance, and was treated by everybody in a friendly and warm, but respectful manner. Gradually he had come to look forward to the hour of his visit to the Kronstadt as the one bright spot of the day, and the only reward for his stubborn and sterile labours.

The attraction which the place exerted on him was not nostalgia for the past, nor the drinks, nor the Baroness, but the curious fact that after the first few sips of champagne or brandy at the bar, at a safe distance from his desk, the book no longer seemed to present any problems, and that he could again write whole pages of it in his head. It had even occurred to him to write them down at the bar as they came floating through his mind, but somehow this plan never materialised. It would have been an act of exhibitionism to write in public; besides he felt that if he were to try it, the flow of words in his head would dry up at once. It would spoil his only pleasurable, relaxed hour of the day . . .

Leontiev went to the window, and looked out over the maze of gabled roofs in the pale morning sun. Why was it so difficult to write "the one honest book of one's life"? What was the nature of that invisible barrier between his mind and the sheaf of lined paper? It was as if a curse had been laid on him, an evil charm which made the words that sounded true in his head turn into lies as soon as his pen touched the paper. Even more uncanny was the fact that although he had been determined to stick to his original plan—that is, to start the book with his childhood, the ecstasies of the early days of the Revolution, and to write exactly as he felt, with supreme disregard for his publisher's advice and the public's taste— he nevertheless started each time with the story of his escape, as the intelligent young agent had told him to do.

"I Was a Hero of Culture," by Leo Nikolayevich Leontiev. . . . He set his jaw, planted himself firmly on the hard chair before his desk, wrote "Chapter One: My Escape," and covered five pages with his angular, martial handwriting without lifting his head, falling automatically into the "crisp, colourful and dramatic style" which the agent had recommended. This, of course, he told himself regretfully, was not his own style. But the style in which he had written during the last twenty years had not been his own either. At some point during that long, dreary journey, he must have lost his identity; but it was impossible to determine the exact moment when this had happened. It had been rather like the process of losing, one by one, one's handkerchiefs in the laundry.

He re-read the five pages and tore them up. He felt an emptiness in his head so horrible and threatening that he was seized with panic and decided to go to the Kronstadt an hour earlier than usual. He clutched at this idea with the relief of a drowning man discovering a floating safety-belt. There, at the polished bar, after the first brandy and soda, that unbearable feeling of hollowness would give way, and the vast emptiness would be filled by a pleasant inner glow. The relief was as predictable and certain as the law that nature abhors the void.

His panic was gone now. Only the fatigue at the synapses remained; and some hazy image of the statue of Truth made flesh, lying on a couch with her raised, majestic thighs, her arms derisively folded under her head.

4

THE SHADOW OF NEANDERTHAL

"I HAVE convened this gathering of what gossip columnists would call 'some representative members of our intelligentsia,'" said Julien to the guests assembled in his study, "because it would after all be too unpardonably stupid, and a betrayal of our reputation, if we accepted to go down like sheep driven to the slaughter-house. I propose we do at least some bleating, though I confess that I am rather sceptical about the results. However, if the pessimism of the philosopher is a valid attitude, the duty of the active humanist to go on hoping against hope is no less valid. The reproach of morbid despair, of wallowing in the mire of doom, which is so often levelled against us, seems to me provoked by an insufficiently clear division between the two parallel planes in our minds: the plane of detached contemplation in the sign of infinity, and the plane of action in the name of certain ethical imperatives. We have to accept the perpetual contradiction between these two. If we admit that defeatism and despair, even if logically justified, are morally wrong, and that active resistance is a moral necessity even if it seems logically absurd, we may find a new approach to a humanist dialectic . . ."

Father Millet, who sat in an armchair near the window, gave out a faint sound of pain as if someone had trodden on his toe. "That word, that word," he groaned. "Can't we do without it?"

"I can find nothing wrong with that word," interposed Professor Pontieux. "After all . . ."

"Pax vobis," said Father Millet. "I withdraw my objection."

Julien, leaning with his back against the bookshelf, looked round the faces of his seven guests, trying to fight down his aversion. After all, every age is guided by such lights as happen to be available. And from the close quarters of contemporaneity, the stars of other ages must have looked equally clouded and dim. Father Millet with all his rather likeable weaknesses, or perhaps because of them, was still the greatest influence among intellectuals with a religious leaning; his recent essay on Jung, which had put the seal, as it were, on the holy alliance between Psychiatry and the Church, had created a considerable stir; there had even been some jokes cracked about the impending canonisation of Dr. Sigmund Freud. As for Professor Pontieux, he remained the favourite philosopher of the younger generation, who liked his writings because of his incisive clarity of style and complete ambiguity of content; neo-nihilism was the philosopher's stone which permitted them to prove everything they wanted to believe, and to believe everything they could prove. However, since the beginning of the Bogarenko affair Pontieux had resigned from the Rally for Peace and Progress and signed a manifesto asking for funds for the refugees from the Rabbit Republic; for which he had been duly branded by the Commonwealth press as a syphilitic spider—the 'bloodthirsty hyenas' having gone out of fashion since the advent of Socialist Sarcasm.

Then there was Dupremont, the novelist, who had recently published a new best-seller, his biggest success yet. He was one of the few who were still able to go on writing at a time when most writers were drying up and the panorama of literature and the arts resembled more and more a parched dust bowl. He was probably the most naïve among them all, and it was this innocence which enabled him to carry on where others gave up. His last novel had a particularly original twist to it: the hero, a young priest, remained chaste to the end, in the teeth of a long series of luscious temptations described with an incomparable wealth of detail. These temptations provided the juice for the moral uplift of the story: the reader, by force of his identification with the hero, could let his imagination wallow, while at the same time he was filled with a lofty sense of virtue.

The other guests were Leontiev, who was expected to provide some guidance on the possibilities of a cultural resistance movement, and Boris, who had just come out of hospital looking more gaunt and cadaverous than ever; Julien had invited him mainly in the hope of shaking him a little out of his increasing apathy. There were two more men present—one the editor of the most read Paris daily paper, the other belonging to the vague but no less influential category of Men of Letters, whose name appeared on all committees, functions and juries connected with high-spirited causes. St. Hilaire had also been invited, but seemed to be late as usual.

It certainly wasn't an inspiring company. But, Julien repeated to himself, the members of the erstwhile Jacobin Club or of Lenin's émigré crowd, packed into a small, smoke-filled study, would probably not have looked very impressive either.

"I suggest," he said aloud, "that each of us in turn should talk for a few minutes about his own perspective for war and occupation. I know that this sounds rather school-boyish and naïve, but the fact that you have accepted my invitation proves that you too feel this urge to exchange our ideas—or absence of ideas if you like."

That he had no cigarette between his lips showed that Julien was not his usual self. It might have been due to the news of the opening of the great Viennograd espionage trial against "Professor Vardi and accomplices"; or to the imminence of catastrophe which everybody felt in his bones. His cynical aloofness seemed to have collapsed, temporarily at least; he had been almost pathetically keen on this meeting which, by the very heterogeneity of its composition, appeared amateurish and doomed to sterility. Some of his guests were the more embarrassed as they hardly knew him. During the last few years his literary reputation had been in decline; he never went to literary parties or first nights, and the few essays he had published at lengthening intervals had been permeated by such acid, yet lucid, hopelessness that they only made people uncomfortable. Finally the critics had reached a kind of tacit agreement about him, as often happens to writers who have for a while been the object of violent controversy; they had labelled him a "prophet of doom," and it was generally assumed that his defeatism was in some subtle psychological manner connected with the crippling wound he had received in the Spanish War—his limp and scarred face had probably affected his masculine vanity and thus given rise to his general pessimism of outlook. It was also rumoured that he had recently come under the influence of Father Millet and was on the road to religious conversion, which so many of his ex-revolutionary colleagues had taken before him. However that might be, his voice on the telephone had sounded so pathetically urgent that his guests could not very well refuse this curious invitation—if for no other reason than to provide themselves with an alibi before their own consciences. It now transpired that this desperate search for an alibi had also been Julien's main motive for calling the meeting.

The fact that on Julien's own admission nothing serious was expected to come out of it made everybody feel more at ease. The editor of the influential paper gave expression to the general feeling when he said, in the manner of addressing a board meeting:

"By all means let us talk. I must confess that when our friend, Monsieur Delattre, was good enough to invite me, I was at first slightly bewildered and could not guess the exact purpose of this meeting. But I think I have now got the idea: the very fact that we all represent such different walks of life and political opinions may provide a new approach to the problems confronting us. I agree that one should always try to by-pass the sterile controversies between existing political parties, to explore new avenues of thought, and to arrive at original solutions. But is a solution possible? And is it not under certain circumstances preferable to adopt an elastic and understanding attitude towards new developments on History's chessboard, particularly if they present themselves in the form of fatal inevitability, than to invite more suffering and retaliation by a rigid refusal to co-operate and by acts of irresponsible provocation? That is what I would like to ask as a preliminary question as it were. . . ." Monsieur Touraine subsided.

He was a fleshy, eminently prosperous-looking man with gold cufflinks and a pearl in his heavy but discreet necktie. He had, as everybody knew, thanks to the indiscretion of a gossip columnist, recently acquired a house near Casablanca in Morocco and a private aeroplane to get him and his family there when the emergency started. This was probably the reason for his calm and detached attitude.

His short speech was followed by silence. Father Millet, relaxed in a wicker chair which Julien had borrowed from the concierge, gave a scornful poof. The remainder of the guests sat around wooden-faced, with a somewhat resentful air. Reluctantly, Julien had to start again:

"It has always puzzled me," he said, "why it is so difficult in a gathering of more than four people to make the speeches uttered clinch with reality. All those here present know that we are living the last days of Pompeii—but unlike the Pompeians we are forewarned. Though we cannot foresee the exact shape and moment of the outbreak, we know by and large what will happen. The moment the conflict starts we shall have civil war. After a few days we shall be occupied, either openly, or under some convenient disguise and pretext, and incorporated into the Commonwealth of Freedomloving People. . . ."

There were some indignant murmurs. Julien, turning towards them the scarred half of his face, continued in a deliberately offhand manner:

"We shall, as I said, be occupied. Forgive me for mentioning naked facts, though this is considered in bad taste among intellectuals. But as it happens you all know that the armies of the French Republic have neither the technical capacity nor the will to fight. . . ."

"Ça alors!" interposed M. Touraine. "You are going a bit far, are you not?" He looked round for support, but except for the Man of Letters, who also made some indignant noises, he only saw wooden, expressionless faces and dull stares.

". . . nor the will to fight," Julien repeated. "Not to mention such over-obvious facts as the disparity in the number of divisions, and the strategical impossibility for the Americans to hold any line in Europe this side of the Pyrenees . . ."

"I disagree with that," Dupremont interrupted in growing agitation. "I don't know what you are driving at. I protest . . ."

"In God's name, let him finish," boomed Father Millet. He puffed, and in the general silence added with a sigh: "Be honest, gentlemen. Delattre is only repeating what we all know by heart."

"A few days after we have been occupied," Julien continued, "the great hygienic operation will start. The entire French nation, its political and cultural institutions, its libraries, traditions, customs and ideas will be put into that huge steam-laundering machine like a heap of dirty linen. Most of it will disintegrate in the process. Only the coarsest fabrics will survive. Even they will come out mangled, shrunk, starched, sterilized, unrecognisable. After this operation the world as we know it will have ceased to exist."

M. Touraine cleared his throat. "May one ask," he said looking at his watch, "for what purpose we are supposed to listen to this sermon of doom?"

Julien regretted having invited him. But he had hoped that the presence of a man so influential in public affairs would give the gathering an atmosphere a little less futile, less purely an affair of "the intellectuals." He summoned his resources of patience and said:

"Because, for all we know, even such small informal meetings as this will be impossible in the future. People who have lived under that regime—inside the great sterilising machine— told me that they would have given half their lives for the privilege of talking, for a single hour, as freely as we still can do it in this room. . . ." He looked at Leontiev; but Leontiev was gazing sternly out of the window. "In a week, or a month, or three months, we too shall have lost this privilege. And then each of you here in this room will feel that you would willingly make any sacrifice for an opportunity like the present, to discuss with others possible courses of action. But then the opportunity will no longer present itself. . . ."

His guests shifted uncomfortably. Dupremont started to say something, but thought better of it. At last it was Professor Pontieux who spoke:

He could understand, he said, Delattre's anxieties in the face of a critical world situation, but thought nevertheless that they were exaggerated. Even if one granted, for argument's sake, certain possibilities mentioned by Delattre, it did not follow that one had to accept the unmitigatedly black picture of the consequences which he had painted. At any rate, Delattre himself had said that it was impossible to foresee the concrete circumstances under which those possibilities might come true—though he by no means believed that their coming true was inevitable; and as the course of any action was necessarily determined by the concrete circumstances, it was difficult to say how, in ignorance of those circumstances, decisions could be reached or even fruitfully discussed at the present moment. He agreed however that it would be wrong to wait fatalistically for the catastrophe, and that the utmost watchfulness was required to defend peace, democracy and the interests of all oppressed nations and classes. . . .

He put a strong emphasis on his last words and ended abruptly, to let the full significance of the phrasing sink in. Indeed the way he had put the "oppressed nations" before the "classes" could only be interpreted as an oblique reference to the conditions prevailing in Eastern European countries. In his own way, Professor Pontieux had gone as far as he was capable of going to meet the challenge of the hour. Nobody however seemed to appreciate this, except M. Touraine, who with unexpected enthusiasm cried, "hear, hear," and at the same time rose from his chair. With another glance at his watch—which was equipped with a Geiger-counter in place of the second-hand—he approached Julien:

"I believe," he said with a conciliatory smile, "that Professor Pontieux has summed up the situation with great lucidity, and that nothing much can be added at the present stage. You will excuse me, gentlemen . . ."

Julien saw him politely to the door. Out in the corridor, M. Touraine seemed slightly embarrassed. "To be perfectly frank, mon cher," he exclaimed half apologetically, "when you rang me, I had been under the mistaken impression that the meeting was called to discuss some new publishing venture—a literary magazine or the like. If you have any plans in that direction, don't hesitate to call on me. Meanwhile, if I may venture to give you some friendly advice, don't give way to morbid pessimism. The cult of doom is a very deplorable symptom of our times." Gripping his elegant anti-radiation umbrella firmly under his arm, he waved to Julien and descended the creaking stairs with careful and disapproving steps.

As Julien closed the entrance door, the Man of Letters, who had not said a word during the discussion, was preparing to leave too. He was a short, elderly, carefully dressed man who wore old-fashioned spats. "I regret," he said drily. "I must have misunderstood the purpose of this meeting. Should a committee issue from it, I must ask you not to include my name

. . ." He hesitated, and while collecting his hat and gloves, added a little uncertainly: ". . . Or at least, not at this stage. It remains to be seen who else is on it. Perhaps you will be good enough to send me in due course the list of sponsors, honorary members and so on. . . ."

When Julien returned to the study, the atmosphere had considerably eased. Pontieux and Dupremont had started on a discussion, and Father Millet was talking to Leontiev. Only Boris, seated on the window-sill, kept staring into the street in complete apathy. Since he had entered the room an hour ago he had not shifted his position once.

Father Millet levelled his shrewd gaze at Julien. "Why on earth did you invite those types to a gathering of this sort?" he asked.

Julien shrugged: "I have never liked them, so I thought I should invite them. Penance for spiritual pride—to speak your language . . ." He limped back to his favourite place in the corner of the room, and rubbed his back against the bookshelves: "I don't know whether anybody understands why I called this idiotic meeting. Trying to appease my conscience, I suppose. In the previous wars the intellectuals failed so abjectly and miserably. I always thought that, as far as our particular brand is concerned, the sins of omission are the worst—to use your language again."

For a moment Father Millet watched Julien rubbing his spine against the bookshelf, like an animal in pain. He said half aloud:

"Is it not that you are getting ripe for adopting our language in good and earnest?" He immediately capped this with a short burst of Rabelaisian laughter, but his eyes remained shrewd.

Julien shrugged:

"I would swallow the immaculate conception and the rest of your dogmas like a dish of oysters, if you only knew the answer to the steam-laundering machine. But, bless your innocent heart, you know it no more than Touraine . . ."

Julien had been to school with Father Millet and the memory of erstwhile intimacy still lingered between them. Father Millet was on the point of answering him when Boris jumped off the windowsill like a statue coming suddenly alive. His gaunt figure rigid and stretched to its full length, he raised an arm with an accusing gesture at Pontieux. The room became suddenly silent.

"Why don't you get rid of that man too?" Boris asked in a shrill voice. "He is a traitor."

Julien limped quickly over to Boris to calm him. Pontieux rose abruptly, gasping for words. The other three men in the room were silent. "You mustn't mind, Professor," Julien said quickly. "My friend is very excitable—experiences among the Freedomloving People, and so on. . . ."

Pontieux was still speechless; his head was trembling a little. Father Millet and Dupremont spoke to him soothingly. But the gentle burr of their voices was pierced by Boris, speaking on an even shriller note than before:

"He is a traitor," he repeated; then, turning directly on Pontieux, he said, suddenly much calmer: "You are a traitor though you don't know it. Get out of here."

There was a new outburst of soothing voices; even Leontiev seemed to awake from his daydreams, watching the two men with curiosity. Pontieux had at last found his breath. "How dare you, Monsieur," he repeated several times, and each time with a little more dignity. It looked as if at any moment he might produce his card and challenge his opponent to a duel in the Bois de Boulogne. This possibility had, in fact, just crossed his mind with its full train of probable consequences; the tremendous publicity which it would bring to the neo-nihilist movement; the subtle essay in which a revival of the ancient chivalrous custom would be defended, with certain qualifications, as a symbol of the historically inevitable emergence of an individualistic antithesis to the collectivist trend in society. He was just beginning to warm to the subject when he remembered that he had no visiting card; and without a card, or at least a glove to throw in his opponent's face, the gesture would lack inner conviction.

"I am afraid that unless your friend apologises, one of us has to leave this meeting," he said to Julien, his head again slightly trembling. But instead of asking Boris to leave, as Pontieux had expected, Julien, adding insult to injury, said quietly: "I will explain to you while I see you out."

For a moment there was again silence in the room and, with all eyes fixed on him, Pontieux once more lost his breath. Then, in a voice which was meant to express dignified restraint but came out like that of a petulant schoolboy, he said to Julien:

"Thank you, I can find my way out alone."

His exit was rather pathetic. Julien hobbled after him, and

while Pontieux was collecting his things, said with a wry smile:

"My meeting doesn't seem to be much of a success." Pontieux expected an apology, but Julien merely opened the door with a half-hearted shrug.

"Allow me to tell you," said Pontieux, "that I find your conduct unpardonable." He was still obviously waiting for an explanation, pathetically standing in the open door. Julien had to make an effort:

"Of course," he said wearily, "since Boris was the offending party, it was he whom I should have asked to leave. But as I told you, he has suffered certain experiences . . ."

"That does not excuse his behaviour. Nor yours either," said Pontieux, still standing in the open door, his head trembling.

"It does in this case," said Julien, and his voice hardened a little.

"Does it also excuse his calling me a traitor?" Pontieux exclaimed in the peeved voice of an undergraduate who has never grown up.

"He said you were a traitor without knowing it. . . ." Julien left it at that. But despite his silence, and the expressive gesture of his hand holding the door open, Pontieux still could not get himself to go.

"And what principle or value have I, pray, betrayed?" he asked in the same peeved voice.

"Oh, Jesus, man," said Julien. "I am neither your judge nor your confessor."

"But this—this is unheard of," said Pontieux. He seemed on the verge of bursting into tears. Julien knew that if he were to call him back, Pontieux would come eagerly, regardless of any abuse. He too was looking for an alibi before his conscience, ere the trumpets of the day of judgment called him to account. But if he were allowed to return to the room, he would continue in the same vein and the same voice where he had left off. It occurred to Julien that Pontieux might be suffering from some peculiar, but wide-spread, form of insanity.

"You had better go, Professor," he said softly, and closed the door in his face.

When Julien returned to the study, he found Dupremont

and Father Millet in subdued conversation, and Boris impatiently stalking up and down.

"Ah, here you are at last," cried Boris. "Now that you have got rid of that traitor, we can get down to business."

"Go ahead," said Julien wearily. It looked as if Boris were also going insane, in a different way. The other three in the room eyed him curiously.

"It must by now be clear to everybody," Boris began without interrupting his march up and down the room, "that we have all along been fooled into believing that He was an ordinary man, whereas now we have at last discovered the obvious truth that He is the Antichrist. How we could have been so blind for such a long time I do not know. Of course we were deliberately made to believe that the enemy's was a country or party like any other. But we should have discovered long ago that no country or party has ever done such things as the enemy does. . . . Yes, yes . . ." he impatiently waved aside some imaginary interruption, and smiled down at Father Millet, stopping in front of him. "Yes, your inquisitors did some nasty things some time ago. But that was child's play compared to this. Or, perhaps a rehearsal . . ."

He seemed struck by this idea, and pleased with it: "Yes, it must have been a rehearsal," he continued triumphantly, resuming his wanderings. "But this time it is not a rehearsal, and He has started the real show. The women and children are carried off into the wilderness and are left to die. The men are carried into the polar night, and after a short time are turned into beasts. Others are submitted to torture or have drugs injected into their veins to make them bear witness for Him. Sons are taught to denounce their fathers, soldiers to betray their country, idealists to serve Him with heroic self-sacrifice. We all thought that it was only a kind of mass-madness, but now it has become evident that it is magic. Even words are turned into the opposite of what they mean; they are made to stand on their heads like devils at the black mass.

"Of course we have known all this for a long time; but we did not know the reason. Now that we know the reason, we also know the remedy. The remedy is, of course, that He must be killed by being crucified upside down. There are many technical difficulties: passports, costly train tickets, the overpowering of the bodyguard, and so on. And we haven't much time left. But once we have agreed on the method, the difficulties will be overcome. . . ." He smiled his bony smile at

Julien, and added with a certain old-world courtesy: "I am sorry I have talked so long about such an obvious matter. But none of you gentlemen seemed inclined to make a beginning."

In the silence which followed, Julien said quietly:

"Whom are you talking about, Boris?"

Boris seemed surprised at the superfluous question. "The Antichrist, of course," he said a little impatiently.

"Yes, but under what human guise?"

"The pock-marked one with the assassin's eyes, of course."

"Do you realize, Boris, that he died three months ago?"

Boris smiled indulgently. "Of course. It was foolish of me to forget that they gave out that story. But I never thought that you would be taken in by it. Naturally they had to invent that story to protect him."

His nervous elation seemed suddenly gone. He looked at his three listeners with suspicion.

"I see that you are no better than others. You don't want to see the facts. I must have misunderstood the purpose of this meeting. One must do everything by oneself . . ." He hesitated for a moment, hovering in the middle of the room, a lone prisoner of the silence around him.

"Have a drink, Boris," said Julien, pretending that nothing had happened.

Boris stared at him blindly for a second, then seemed to wake up. He shook his head. "No—I must go," he said. "None of you understand—what is really happening. You think I am mad; I have noticed that in your glances. If it makes you more comfortable, you can go on believing it. But I tell you, millions are dying from dysentery. They are left in the fields, like bundles of rags, lying in their excrement . . ."

He opened the door, and with an oddly stiff gait walked out into the corridor. Father Millet looked at Julien questioningly. Julien shrugged:

"There is nothing to be done," he said. "It comes and goes. The doctor says he isn't dangerous and that there are hundreds of similar cases walking in the streets. If I were to see him home he would only become suspicious and it would make matters worse." He hobbled after Boris into the corridor to see him out.

Boris was waiting for him on the landing. "Have I gone off the rail again?" he asked guiltily, with a cramped, bony smile.

"A little. You must pull yourself together, Boris," said Julien

"I know. If you tell them too much they think you are mad."

"Don't start that again."

"They have arrested that fool, Vardi," said Boris, still smiling.

"Yes. His trial started a few days ago. Don't you read the newspapers?"

"He was crazy," said Boris, hovering on the landing undecidedly.

"Won't you come back?" said Julien. "We could all have a drink."

Boris shook his head. "No. I have work to do." He was still hesitating when Dupremont joined them outside. "I am afraid I must go too," he said, collecting his black homburg hat and looking at them with uneven eyes. He patted his trimmed moustache uncertainly. "It was a very instructive gathering," he said.

"Now you too are going to tell me that you misunderstood the purpose of it," said Julien.

"No," said Dupremont. "I believe I understand quite well. Only you see . . ."

He looked at them nervously. But for that slight and vaguely suspect irregularity of his eyes, he would have been a very good-looking man. It had never occurred to Julien that Dupremont, for all his cocktail-party manners and his aura of a writer of mystic-erotic bestsellers, was a very shy person.

"You see," Dupremont repeated hesitatingly, "for what you had in mind it is either already too late—or too early yet . . ." He fingered the narrow fringe over his lip and turned to Boris:

"Perhaps I can give you a lift—I have a car outside. . . ." He said it apologetically, and seemed genuinely embarrassed by the fact that he had a car. To Julien's surprise, Boris, who had never met Dupremont before, accepted at once with a courteous little bow. They walked down the stairs together.

Now there were only Leontiev and Father Millet left in the study.

"Your meeting seems to be turning out like the story of the ten little Indians," said Father Millet when Julien joined them again, having collected a bottle of brandy and some glasses from his kitchen. "Ah—I could do with a drink."

Leontiev too looked relieved at the sight of the glasses.

During the last half-hour he had been counting the time which still separated him from the moment when he would enter the bar of the Krontadt. He had said nothing during the discussion because he had nothing to say. And yet he felt that this oddly pointless gathering had taught him something, explained something which had puzzled him ever since he had "gone to Capua." This new insight, though negative in character, was important. It was the end of his illusions about the powers of resistance of Capua. It provided, in some obscure way, the final clue to a series of puzzles which had started with his brief encounter with the young couple of American radicals and the swift hygienic act in which it had culminated. He had at last come face to face with the great void which, like a carefully hidden secret, was at the core of everything. It was a naked and bitter kind of void—not the easy-going *nichevo* of olden days, but the laconic *pues nada,* the ultimate *nihil.*

"You have not said much tonight, Monsieur Leontiev," said Father Millet.

Leontiev looked at him coldly, remembering their first argument at Monsieur Anatole's party. "There was not much occasion for discussion," he said.

"No," said Father Millet. "But now we are alone; and I have always thought that three is the best company—provided of course that none of the three belongs to the other sex. . . ." He gave a short burst of Rabelaisian laughter; Father Millet had the rare gift of laughing heartily alone without expecting others to join in. "Our friend Julien looks so dejected that I shall in his stead ask the question which he wanted to discuss with us, and which you alone have the experience to answer—to wit, whether you believe in the possibility of organized intellectual resistance under the regime which you know so well? I am referring to spiritual, not to political resistance—for this, if I am not mistaken, is the question which Julien had in mind."

Leontiev had a suspicion that Father Millet was mocking him. His question amounted to asking a deserter whether he thought that his routed army had a chance of winning. These people talked, but they knew nothing. They talked of tyranny and oppression—but what did they know of such creeping terrors as the fatigue of the synapses? He stared into Father Millet's florid face and said with indifference:

"I don't know what you mean by 'organised intellectual resistance.'"

"The question is simply whether you believe that there is any alternative to waiting passively for the end," said Julien.

"Few people wait passively for the end," said Leontiev. He smiled a little: "You will see that the majority of your friends will display a great activity in professing their loyalty and denouncing each other. A few will perhaps make a gesture of protest and vanish. A few others will perhaps try to conspire, as you suggest, and will also vanish. The classic methods of conspiracy have become impracticable and out of date."

"That sounds as if you believed in some new method?"

Leontiev shrugged politely and rose:

"There are some people . . . that sect . . . who are trying something else. But I don't believe many in your country would follow their example. It is perhaps too late." He moved towards the door; it was time for the Kronstadt.

". . . Or too early?" suggested Julien.

Leontiev looked at him indifferently. "Perhaps too early," he agreed with a shrug. "If you prefer to believe that."

Julien had hardly closed the door behind Leontiev when there was an impatient ring and St. Hilaire burst in. His face twitching in cheerful contortions, he shook hands with Julien and Father Millet and, refusing to sit down, came at once to the point:

"Salute, friends," he greeted them, "whose number seems to have shrunk through discord and cowardly defection, both perfectly predictable, which explains the deliberate lateness of one's arrival and the further fact of the waiting taxi downstairs, its clock ticking away in an inexorable and obviously symbolic manner. In short, you have come to no conclusions whatsoever."

"None," said Julien. "The more's the reason for sending your inexorable taxi away and enlightening us."

"Your two suggestions, though uttered in the same breath, stand in an obviously faulty logical relation," St. Hilaire retorted sharply, "which betrays the fallacies of so-called common-sense. The simplest experiment should convince you that it is economically more expedient to keep one taxi waiting for the required five minutes, than to pay the initial charge of a second hired vehicle, not to mention the doubling of the obnoxious tip—good. It is equally obvious that the kind of enlightenment you request can only be conveyed in a brief flash, or not at all. Elaboration is the death of art, and our immediate problem is the art of dying which, though apparently of a political, is in fact of an aesthetic nature."

He was talking less obscurely than usual, and there was a great urgency in his voice and in the strange contortions of his face. To Father Millet's surprise Julien, who had been listening to St. Hilaire more attentively than to anybody else before, now said hesitantly:

"I am beginning to come around to your point of view."

"Excellent," said St. Hilaire, "though not surprising in view of our sharing certain axiomatic beliefs. Needless to say, among those who share them differences of opinion can always be resolved into differences of language and grammar; and that in times of crisis these disappear to the extent that the semantic Babel is replaced by the lingua franca of tragedy. For after all, destiny's challenge to man is always couched in simple and direct phrases, and requires an answer in equally elementary terms of subject and predicate without relative clauses. The noun in the language of destiny is always an affirmative symbol, and the verb always a gesture of protest. That's all—the details we shall discuss later."

St. Hilaire made for the door. On the landing he turned once more to Julien, his face momentarily in repose:

"Rest assured that the proper message will reach you at the proper time . . ." His arms swinging with the gauche, lusty movements of an adolescent, and taking two or three steps at a time, he hurried down the stairs and vanished from Julien's sight.

Father Millet was still smiling indulgently when Julien returned to the study. "It beats me," he said, "how you or anybody else can take him seriously."

Julien poured himself a drink and sat down on the window-sill. He felt exhausted and suffered from that feeling of unreality which nowadays befell him more and more often. Across the street several windows in the little hotel were lit up. Shadows moved behind the curtain, as every night, adding to the narrow street's atmosphere of peace and intimacy. A gramophone played the popular hit, *"My Radioactive Baby."* In this street even the threat of the apocalypse was reduced to cosy familiarity: when the four black horses appeared in the skies, the people of the *quartier* would rush to the bookmakers to place bets on them.

Remembering Father Millet's question, Julien said:

"He is the one person who deserves to be taken seriously."

Father Millet laughed good-humouredly and rose. "It was a most stimulating little gathering," he said, "most stimulating. I hope we will continue our unfinished conversation some other day."

"I haven't heard *your* answer yet," said Julien.

"Always the old one, dear boy, always the same, old answer, the same symbol and gesture, to quote your friend." His last burst of reassuring laughter still echoed through the study after he had gone.

Julien returned to his seat on the window-sill. The street was alive with the shuffling steps of the evening crowd walking towards their dinners. A newsboy ran through the street calling out the latest headlines from the great Viennograd trial; apparently Professor Vardi and accomplices had all confessed and been sentenced to hang. Julien sipped his brandy with a dull feeling of relief. The meeting had turned out more or less as expected: he had done what he could, and procured an alibi before his conscience. The mere shadow of impending events had been enough to destroy what cohesion there was left in the tissue of a crumbling civilisation. At least for the time being Dupremont had been right: it was either too late or too early—or both.

BRIDGE MEN AND TORRENT MEN

LEONTIEV woke up about noon with a medium-bad hangover.

Since he had accepted the job at the Kronstadt, this happened about three times a week. His heart pounded, quietened down for a while, then began to pound again; he was afraid. It was a diffused, floating kind of anxiety which would fasten on the first object that came to his mind: one day it was the fear that he might incur Pierre's displeasure and lose his job; at another time, that the publishers might start a lawsuit because he had not delivered the book at the agreed date, and obviously never would; or that the Service people might kidnap and deliver him into the power of Gruber and his men.

One half of his mind knew all these fears were unfounded: he was one of the main attractions of the Kronstadt; the publisher seemed, if anything, rather relieved that the book did not materialise, and the Service had long ago lost interest in him. But none of these arguments had any power over his anxiety, which was something purely physical, a function of the rhythm of his heart-beat and of the pressure in his head. This pressure was the worst; it could only be compared to the pain caused by wearing boots one size too small—but in this case the boot was his skull and the squeezed toes his brain. It was so unbearable that he wished for the pressure to increase beyond measure, to smash the grey mass to pulp and have finished with it.

Each time he woke up like this he swore that it would never happen again, and each time he drank beyond a certain point he had to go on and it happened once more. He had asked the baroness to stop him when she saw that he had had his measure, but once or twice when she had tried it he had dismissed her interference with a single glance of polite but stern rebuke. He never gave any outward sign of drunkenness; his countenance remained martial and dignified; but inwardly he experienced an infinite well-being which abolished the future and the past, and made the present moment the sole reality, aglow with life and meaning. This actually was the reason why, once launched, he not only did not care about the horrors of next morning's awakening, but was quite incapable of believing in them, though experience had taught him that they would inescapably recur. It was not weak-mindedness which made him go on regardless of the price to be paid, but the fact that payment was situated in the future, and that in those moments the future had no reality—it had literally ceased to exist as if a whole department of his mind had been amputated with a knife. Once or twice, when he had felt himself just agreeably under way, he had tried to remember the physical symptoms of waking up with a hangover. But he had been unable to do so, unable to recall the fear, the pounding of guilt in the chest, the torture of the contracted skull—just as at the present moment he was unable to recapture any echo of the carefree happiness which a few hours ago he had experienced in the padded tunnel of the Kronstadt. Obviously there existed physical barriers to imagination which broke the continuity of experience and made it impossible to remember what it felt like to be hungry

when one was replete, to be replete when one was hungry.
The evermore of desire and the nevermore of satiety; the
glow of the intoxicated present, and the torments of past and
future were located in different universes of experience which
did not communicate through memory or anticipation. Each
had its own logic and values, as different from the other as
the language of a chartered accountant from the language of
the dream.

The strangest thing about this particular torture was that
Leontiev knew perfectly well how to end it. He only had to
dip his head into cold water, swallow a small glass of brandy
and a tablet of benzedrine with his breakfast, and in half an
hour he would be feeling normal again. The remedy was
within reach, but to apply it he would have to get up, and
his acute state of anxiety prevented him from doing so; for
the only protection against its terrors, short of crawling back
into the womb, was to hide in the stuffy bed with its grey,
crumpled sheet and stained cover. There was sweat on his
temples, even the bushy eyebrows were dank; and unlike his
hair which showed only a few threads of grey, the stubble
on his cheeks and curls on his chest were white.

Leontiev forced himself back into sleep. But instead of
relief, it brought him a peculiarly tormenting and familiar
dream which kept recurring since he had finally abandoned
his book. It was a dream about Zina's death. According to
the official announcement she had died in a motor-car accident; but in the dream Zina committed suicide by jumping,
with a lazy, leisurely movement, out of the window of a high
building. He did not actually see her fall, he only saw her
climb out of the window, moving backward, so that her face
remained turned to the room in which he was standing and
watching her, his hands in his pockets of his dressing-gown.
He made no move to stop her, nor did she expect him to do
so; it looked rather as if, crawling backward on her hands
and knees across the window-ledge, she were acting on a
tacit agreement. Her round, Ukrainian peasant's face was
smiling with a somewhat mysterious expression. Then abruptly
the face and the crouching figure vanished as it began its
invisible fall through a hundred feet of air towards the pavement, and only the empty frame of the window remained.

Leontiev woke with a jerk, the dark cross of the window
still printed on the inner side of his eyelids, like the image
which appears after staring into a dazzling light. It seemed to

him that he had expected this dream, and that he had stayed in bed seeking not protection but penance. Now he could get up. He stumbled to the wash-stand, and felt with immense relief the cold water run over his scalp and down his neck.

An hour later Leontiev, his normal self again, entered the little restaurant in which he took his lunch every day. It stood in a narrow street leading up to the top of the hill of Montmartre, and was frequented mainly by taxi-drivers, municipal workmen engaged on an apparently never-ending job of pipe-laying in the next street, and two elderly clerks who worked in a nearby income tax office. The tables were covered with chequered paper, except Leontiev's and the two clerks, who, in recognition of their rank in life, were awarded real table-cloths. They also each had a napkin in a ring, kept in a cupboard and changed once a week. Leontiev's napkin ring was marked in ink, "Monsieur Leo"—the name under which he was known and respected in the restaurant.

At Leontiev entered the place, the clerks were just finishing their meal, and the pipe-layers were having their little glasses of marc, preparing to leave. Denise, the proprietor's daughter, came forward at once to greet him and to spread the cotton cloth on his table. "You are late today, Monsieur Leo," she said, laying out his napkin and cover with bustling efficiency. "We thought you might not come at all, but I kept you nevertheless a nice pork chop."

She was a buxom, friendly-looking girl who was engaged to the charcutier on the corner, which accounted for the excellence of the restaurant's pork chops, pig trotters and salted ribs.

"And what are you going to have as a first dish?" Denise inquired in the special chanting voice of the Paris waitress—a manner which combined the solicitousness of a baby's nurse with the precision of a telephone operator.

Leontiev studied the menu which was chalked on a slate over the bar, and after hesitating for a moment between fillet of herring in oil and anchovies in vinegar sauce, decided in favour of the latter dish.

"A plate of anchovies, and half a litre of red for Monsieur Leo," Denise yelled to the kitchen in a tone of great approval, as if Leontiev had just made a particularly bright and original suggestion. "I will fetch your wine at once," she added, bustling off.

"Hi, Denise, what about my change?" called one of the pipe-layers.

"Can't you see that I am busy fetching Monsieur Leo his wine?" said Denise indignantly.

The two elderly clerks walked out with a polite nod to Leontiev, which Leontiev returned with measured courtesy. He had never talked to the two men, but he appreciated this little ceremony, and found a mild satisfaction in the attentions paid to him by Denise and her parents. Presently Denise's father came out of the kitchen, wearing a white chef's bonnet, and shook hands with Leontiev.

"You are very late today," he said, then added with a wink: "Always poring over those strategical maps, aren't you, Monsieur Leo?" For the proprietor had somehow got it into his head that Leontiev was a retired colonel or something of that sort, and that his hobby was studying the maps of the last war. Leontiev nodded non-committally, and the *patron* moved on to the pipe-layers' table, and shook hands with each of them in turn. Then he went to the bar, poured with a mechanical gesture half a glass of red wine down his throat, and walked back with a contented look to the kitchen.

Leontiev ate slowly through his meal, reading the morning paper. When he had finished, it was already three o'clock, and he had not yet decided what to do with his afternoon. The possibilities to be considered were going to a cinema, taking a leisurely stroll down the Champs-Elysées, or visiting a museum. He paid his bill, put his napkin into the ring, watched it being placed in the cupboard, and walked out into the street, accompanied by the effusive farewells of Denise as if it were a parting forever.

He walked down the steep incline, interrupted in the middle by a flight of steps, of the street named after the Chevalier de la Barre, who had lived under the fifteenth Louis, had refused to uncover in front of a religious procession and had duly been punished by having his head cut off. As an act of protest and defiance, the free Commune of Montmartre had erected a statue of him plumb in the middle of the terrace in front of the Church of Sacré Coeur, and in addition had given his name to one of the little streets which led up to the hallowed place. Leontiev softly chuckled to himself each time he descended the flight of steps. A few weeks ago, when he had stumbled on the Chevalier's story in a guidebook, the idea had occurred to him that he might start his own book by telling this anecdote as a kind of symbolic motivation for his flight to Capua. But even while he was sketching out this chapter in his head, he had found that the symbol had grown somewhat stale and no longer added up to much; and that the Chevalier's statue stood in front of the church merely because it had been forgotten there, as an idyllic scandal of the past. Once more Leontiev felt the figure of Truth mocking him with her raised thighs and ironic stare. The Chevalier had been dead for the last two hundred years; if Leontiev were ever to write the one honest book of his life, it would have to start with the admission that the attractions of Capua were all of the past; and that his own flight was not an act of challenge and defiance, but a wild goose chase for a vanished world. That, however, was not the book that people expected of him.

But at least this realisation left him free and without responsibility. After so many years he was able to face the mocking stare of the wench without averting his eyes, and to return her grimace with a resigned smile. He had ceased to care whether the goddess of Truth stuck out her tongue at him; for he was a tired man who no longer desired her.

Smiling to himself, Leontiev decided against the museum and in favour of a short walk in the pleasant wintry afternoon, followed by a thriller picture in the local cinema. Then it would be time for his late-afternoon nap, before his work at the Kronstadt began.

With firm, measured steps, discreetly swinging his silver-handled walking-stick—another inscribed present from the late Father of the People—Leontiev walked down the Boulevard de Rochechouart, where the annual street fair with its lottery wheels, roundabouts and hoop-la stalls was in full swing. On a sudden impulse he entered a shooting gallery and brought down five ping pong balls balanced on a fountain jet. The proprietor of the gallery was impressed and offered Leontiev three free shots on the house. Leontiev smiled politely and brought down two more ping-pong balls, enjoying the "ah's" of the crowd.

The dressing-room of the Kronstadt was a small cubbyhole, containing a dressing-table and a built-in cupboard in which the artistes kept their costumes. It could only hold two people at a time, but this was sufficient for the purpose, as the artistes' numbers were spaced out to give the clientele time for dancing. Leontiev's first appearance usually took place between 10 and 11 p.m.; the second after 1 a.m. But the Kronstadt kept no rigid schedule, and Pierre adjusted the programme to the number and mood of the guests.

Today's was one of the quiet evenings. Apart from the habitués at the bar there were few guests: a noisy party of five American tourists composed of three men and two girls, and a quiet pair of American residents, who had chosen the table farthest removed from that of their visiting compatriots. Pierre disliked this kind of arrangement; it made the room look too empty. Usually the artistes had their dinner, which was provided by the house, together at a long table; but on quiet nights like today's Pierre broke them up into several parties, to fill the room. Accordingly, Leontiev was dining in *tête-à-tête* with the Baltic baroness, which he rather enjoyed; it gave him a feeling of privacy and decorum, for before the floor show started none of the other guests could know that he was an employee of the establishment.

The dinner was excellent as usual; Pierre might have a dubious past and drive a hard bargain when it came to the artistes' wages, but he was generous to them in matters of food and drink. It was early, just after nine o'clock; Leontiev had almost a full hour before him until he had to dress for his number. He and the baroness never talked much, but they got on well and found each other's company relaxing. Once or twice, when they had been detained till a late hour and she had felt too tired to take a taxi home to the Left Bank, she had slept with Leontiev who lived much nearer to the Kronstadt, but neither of them attached much importance to this. The baroness was a tall, well-preserved blonde, with a portly bust and a direct and resolute manner. The only thing which Leontiev sometimes resented was her outspoken way of expressing herself:

"The one good thing about this coming war," she was saying, "is that I know I shall never become an old whore. This certainty makes one feel young again."

"You are in the prime of life, Baroness," said Leontiev, putting his glass down with a measured gesture. He always gave her her title, a habit which she found ridiculous and agreeable.

She laughed aloud, in her somewhat deep-throated manner. "Look at those two in the corner if you want to know what the prime of life is," she said, indicating the pair of

Americans who sat so tightly squeezed together that they only seemed to occupy the space of a single seat. "They could travel on one ticket in the Metro," she added with a sigh.

Pierre, who had been talking to the other American party, approached their table. His smile seemed to be cut in two halves by a heavy scar which ran across one entire cheek. The Baroness had once remarked that some people have scars which command respect because one knows at a glance that they were acquired in the service of King and Country, while others have scars similar in appearance, yet one guesses immediately their disreputable origin. Pierre's scar was of the latter type.

"Those Americans at No. 2 came specially to hear you," he said to Leontiev.

Leontiev nodded politely, feigning indifference, but he was pleased.

"Nobody comes specially to hear *me*," said the Baroness.

"There is more to you than a voice," said Pierre gallantly, patting the black silk dress on her shoulder. "Those Americans are one girl short, and have respectfully inquired whether they might invite you and Monsieur Leontiev to their table."

"I wish they wouldn't," said the Baroness.

"I told them you will both be pleased to join them after your *numéros*," said Pierre. "They have just ordered their third bottle."

Smiling, he moved past the table of the quiet pair, discreetly squinting into their ice-bucket to see how much of the champagne was left. They still had about half a bottle to go, and Pierre decided they were not yet sufficiently drunk to have the bottle whisked away and replaced by a new one. Georges, the head waiter, hovered nearby, waiting for the quiet signal from Pierre which would tell him which course of action to take. Pierre discreetly wagged his finger as he passed, and Georges rushed to the couple's table to fill up their glasses, correctly replacing afterwards the bottle in its bucket.

"He is priceless," said the Baroness, who had watched the proceedings. "Lord, what a den!"

"He has always been correct in his dealings with me," said Leontiev in a tone of slight censure, for he abhorred any manifestations of disloyalty.

"You are priceless too," said the Baroness. "In fact you are a phenomenon. I sometimes wonder whether you are really human or just a bunch of conditioned reflexes."

This was the kind of remark which Leontiev definitely disliked. He finished his coffee and brandy in silence, then said:

"It is almost time for you to change, Baroness."

The Baroness' number always came first. She sang Estonian ballades in a Lithuanian peasant costume accompanied on the piano by a former Under-Secretary of the Fisheries Department. She had a full, resonant contralto voice which saturated the padded room to the last fold of its plush curtains. Her manner was dramatic, and her gestures violent; when she raised her well-shaped, fleshy hand to her face in a passionate gesture of despair, the guests never quite knew whether they were moved or embarrassed. The Baroness, for her part, did not care; she was giving them their money's worth, and whether they liked it was their concern. There was only one thing she would not tolerate: a party of drunks or ill-mannered people continuing their chatter during her act. On such occasions she became angry and let her voice out in a furious blast, until everybody in the tunnel fell into awe-stricken silence. As soon as this result was achieved, she would switch into a quiet, low-voiced recitative which, in the hushed room, was very effective and brought her more applause than she would receive on evenings when the audience was polite and attentive. She called this her "taming act" or *andante furioso*, and rather enjoyed it. Habitués of the place knew that if they wanted to get the best value out of the Baroness they only had to encourage their female companions to chatter or giggle during her turn.

Tonight, however, there was no need for the taming act; the American tourist party, though faintly drunk, had seen her at Leontiev's table, and accordingly listened to her in respectful silence. They even gave her a mild ovation when she had finished.

While the Baroness was changing back into her evening dress, two more parties arrived and things began to liven up. Georges, the head waiter, surveying the scene with his correct and impassive air, caught Leontiev's eye, and without a word or a sign brought him his usual brandy and soda. Leontiev knew that he had to go slow on it, for before his turn came Georges would not glance again in his direction. On the other hand, if it came to the worst, he could always order a brandy and pay for it himself. This reassuring knowledge was usually enough to make his one free after-dinner drink last until his first appearance. After that he was either invited to a table or bought himself one or two drinks; then, before his second appearance after midnight, Georges would again glance in his direction and send him another double on the house.

For some unknown reason, Leontiev felt slightly disturbed tonight; while dining alone with the Baroness he had drunk more wine than usual, and under normal circumstances he should by now have begun to feel the carefree, mellow glow of a present detached from future and past. But neither the wine nor the brandy seemed to take effect. This irritated him, and he was bored by the prospect of having to join, in a little while, the noisy American table. One of the two girls at that table was already coquetteering with Leontiev in an exaggerated and ostentatious manner; but he knew that she was of the type who considered this kind of display as part of the ritual of visiting a nightclub. She was small and blonde and looked pretty enough in her make-up, but she had rather a pug face and eyebrows without natural colour. When he would be sitting next to her, she would press her knee against Leontiev's and talk animatedly to somebody else; and the men at the table would, even though drunk, be bored with her and grateful to Leontiev for keeping her occupied. The other girl was dark and slender and much more attractive, but she paid no attention to Leontiev, and when he joined them would politely ignore him.

During these few weeks at the Kronstadt, Leontiev had learned more about women than during the preceeding fifty years of his life. But he was no longer of the age when this wisdom profited him much. His eyes met by chance the slender, attractive one's; he thought he could detect an amused, knowing gleam in them, and he suddenly had to think of the white curls on his chest glistening with a damp shine in his steamy bed in the morning. He drained his glass, which was to have lasted until his act, and sternly ordered another double at his own expense.

It was now the turn of Señorita Lollita, a tall, bony brunette who did a Spanish dance act with castanets. The girl's real name was Louise, and she was the daughter of a Paris concierge whose story everybody in the Kronstadt knew. Louise had been turned out of school at fifteen, for the twofold reason of being pregnant and distributing anarcho-syndicalist pamphlets. The cause of both of these afflictions was a Spanish refugee called Rubio, whose acquaintance she had made one Sunday afternoon at a Syndicalist meeting into which she had

drifted because it was raining outside, and where Rubio had
been the main speaker. After he was sent to prison, for Louise
had been under the age of consent, and after she had given
birth to a stillborn baby, Rubio's Syndicalist friends had got
her a job in a factory, and in the evenings she took dancing
lessons, which was what she had always wanted to do. Since
Rubio had served his term—an unusually short term, for
Louise had calmly told the court that if there was any question
of seduction it was she who had done the seducing—they lived
together in Rubio's room. He was now writing pamphlets and
articles for Syndicalist papers, and cooking lunch while Louise
slept; and she was helping him with the pamphlets in the afternoon, and cooking his dinner before she went off to the
Kronstadt. This was her first night-club contract; she had obtained it through an Anarchist friend of Rubio's, who knew a
Trotzkyite poet, who knew the formalist painter who worked
for Pierre.

Leontiev always felt slightly ill at ease with Señorita Lollita.
At first she had treated him with a shy reverence, because the
Syndicalists were anti-Commonwealth and she had consequently regarded him as a martyr. Lately, however, she seemed
to avoid his company—though she never failed to greet him
with the quick, jerky, awkward nod of her head which was a
characteristic gesture with her. Her movements were equally
angular and gawky like an eager, overgrown adolescent's; only
when she danced did her long, bony, rigid limbs suddenly un-
freeze, as if under the effect of the hot Andalusian sun which
had probably shone on one of her forebears. As soon as she
had finished she became stiff again, nodded to her audience,
and hurried back to the dressing-room, never consenting to
give an encore. In this contrast, more than in her dancing itself,
lay probably the secret of her success which, for a debuante,
was considerable.

Leontiev watched her act with approval. The second double
had at last done the trick; he felt peaceful and relaxed, with a
warm glow inside him like a sunset on a summer evening in the
steppes. He even began to take a certain interest in possible
developments with the pug-faced blonde. The only one among
the men at her table with whom she did not flirt, and who
therefore must be her husband, was the furthest gone of them
all; and Leontiev knew with what amazing simplicity American tourist couples managed to lose each other in the street, at
the height of a riotous evening. And, after all, why shouldn't

he take what was offered to him, while the going was good? Who was to repay him for his wasted years, who to thank him for missing an opportunity? One only lived once, and the only way to live a full life was to live in the present. The past and the future, even if they existed, were no more than water flowing past under a bridge. You could spend your life standing on the bridge and live in the illusion that you were moving towards the future, whereas in fact only the water was moving under you, future into past. Or, you could jump into the water and float with it, through eddies and torrents, always moving, yet always in the present. Those who stood on the bridge, watching, and saw only the future and the past, those were the bridge men; the others, who moved in the eternal, liquid present, were the torrent men. Had he, Leontiev, not been a bridge man long enough, and was it not time to become a torrent man? And if Zina had indeed committed suicide, what difference did that make?

Pierre stood at his table, smiling the polite and deferential smile which he put on when he talked to Leontiev under the glances of guests who had specially come to hear the Hero of Culture. So it was time to go to the dressing-room and change. Señorita Lollita had finished long ago, and the Baroness had joined the table of the Americans without Leontiev noticing it; he could not even remember seeing her come back from the dressing-room. Such little gaps in his memory had become a frequent occurrence since that afternoon in the hotel when he had torn his dressing-gown and the boy from the News Agency had brought him the telegram; and just as on that occasion, he now had the feeling that he was watching a motion picture whose sound-track had been switched off. During the last few weeks, these silent gaps tended to become more frequent and longer, sometimes extending over several hours of an evening; then suddenly the sound-track would be switched on again, and he would find himself wandering homewards through unknown streets in the early dawn, or waking up next to a sleeping woman in an hotel room, wondering where he had picked her up and how they had got there.

Leontiev emptied his glass, and walked with slow measured steps to the dressing-room. It smelled of the Baroness' perfume, of the Kaukasian tap-heel dancer's Turkish cigarettes, and of the not unpleasant perspiration of Señorita Lollita's young, bony limbs. He took off his suit and shoes, put them away in the cupboard, as neatly as Denise would put away his napkin ring in the little restaurant, and with a mixture of nostalgic pleasure and unavowed shame, began slowly to dress for his act. There was nothing fancy about the pieces of clothing he put on; they were solid, slightly worn garments—the unofficial uniform of the Old Guard, the men who had carried the Revolution to its triumph. A pair of breeches of undefined colour, knee-boots of coarse leather, an equally colourless tunic with a high neck—that was all. Leontiev had dressed in this manner for almost ten years, until the climate and fashions of the Revolution had changed. . . . He brushed his hair up, giving it an ever so slightly ruffled aspect, then lit a cigarette and waited, already transferred into another scenery and time—putting on the costume always and infallibly produced this effect on him.

There was a knock, and Pierre's face, with the smile cut into halves by the scar, appeared. "Ready?" he asked. Leontiev nodded; on these occasions he could almost believe that even Pierre's scar was of revolutionary origin. Pierre's head withdrew; a moment later his voice could be heard from the dance floor, asking the ladies and gentlemen for the privilege of presenting the Hero of Culture and Joy of the People in a recital of poems and songs from the early days of the Revolution. Pierre's voice rose in a crescendo, from solemnity to the pitch of a circus barker:

"Ladies and gentlemen—Hero of Culture, Bearer of the Order of the Revolution, Leo Nikolayevich Leontiev   . ." There was loud applause, drowned by a deafening flourish from the orchestra, and Leontiev stepped out through the door into the padded tunnel. He gave the audience a short, formal nod, then said without further preliminaries:

"I am going to recite to you the translation of a passage from Alexander Block's poem 'The Twelve.'"

The lights were turned down to a faint red shimmer, and as Leontiev began to speak the words in a deep, surprisingly soft voice, the orchestra played in pianissimo the March of Budonny's Cavalry which had stirred millions during the Civil War. The effect on the guests of the music, the light, of Leontiev's voice, and of the champagne they had consumed was very strong in itself; combined with the words of the poem, that wild, vulgar, obscene and mystic credo of the Revolution which somebody had called a symphony made out of dirt, it became well-nigh irresistible. The pug-faced blonde had started to cry, and the tears trickling down her face, caught in the red glow of the tunnel, looked like drops of blood. The quiet pair huddled in their corner with their heads bent together, temple to temple. As always during Leontiev's act, the curtain to the bar was left open for the benefit of the outer habitués who listened, perched on their high stools, immobile and silent to the words which they knew by heart.

After the extract from "The Twelve," Leontiev usually recited one or two poems of his own. But on evenings when he did not feel in form, he spoke some Mayakovsky instead. Tonight he could hear some soft, irreverent whisperings from one of the tables, and he felt a definitely hostile influence coming from it. It was No. 7, a small table to his left, which had been occupied by some new arrivals during his absence in the dressing-room. In the faint, red glimmer he could only see that they were a man and a girl; though it was impossible to make out their features, the shape of the man's skull seemed disturbingly familiar. All this Leontiev perceived only dimly and fleetingly, while he concentrated on the closing lines of "The Twelve".

He spoke the last words in a restrained and very quiet voice, which was the more effective as the background music had stopped and the silence was complete. Then the lights were fully turned on, and the applause burst out. Leontiev gave his short, measured bow; and while he waited with an impassive air for the applause to subside, he glanced from the corner of his eye at table No. 7, and recognized the Cultural Attaché, Fyodor Grigorevich Nikitin, in the company of a dark, attractive girl. Their eyes met only for a fraction of a second; but during that instant, while Nikitin's glance, with its impudent smile through narrowed eyelids, held his own, Leontiev understood that it held some secret knowledge concerning his own person, and in almost the same flash he guessed what the secret was. In fact, it seemed to him that he had known all the time—how else could that recurrent dream be explained? The somewhat mysterious smile on Zina's face, as she crawled backward out of the window on her hands and knees, was curiously similar to Nikitin's smile a moment ago. Those two were in league, they shared a secret. And the secret was, of course, that Zina had deliberately sacrificed herself to make it possible for Leontiev to get away and write the great immortal work, the one honest book of his life. Nikitin's smile a moment ago had said: Is this what she did it for . . . ?

At last the applause subsided. Leontiev cleared his throat to make his usual announcement:

"Three short poems by Vladimir Mayakovsky . . ."

But he could not make his announcement, for just as he was starting to speak, he noticed with a curious fascination that Nikitin had lifted a single finger of his hand resting on the table, and that Georges, the head waiter, after an apologetic glance at Leontiev, was moving across the empty floor toward table No. 7. There was a disapproving murmur from the audience and the girl at Nikitin's table was biting her lip in embarrassment. Nikitin, however, was not embarrassed in the least; lowering his voice just as far as politeness required, he asked for a bottle of champagne. Georges was bending over the table, and explaining in a stage whisper which could be heard across the whole, silent tunnel, that during Monsieur Leontiev's recital no drinks were served. Nikitin, with the same unembarrassed air and his frank, winning smile, said quietly:

"But we want the champagne now, I shall make amends to your artiste." And he again lifted a finger of his hand, this time aimed at Leontiev.

Leontiev had the familiar experience that the sound-track in his head was being switched off; he felt the warm, pleasant, inward glow; he no longer stood on the bridge but was flowing with the current. He saw, as in a dream, Pierre, who stood at the opposite end of the tunnel, make a sign to Georges, and Georges swiftly uncork a bottle which had appeared as if by magic. At the same time he watched with fascination Nikitin's raised finger bend and form a crook; and as it was beckoning to him, Leontiev felt himself getting into motion towards table No. 7, his high knee-boots creaking on the dance-floor. He saw Nikitin pulling out a thousand franc note from his wallet and offering it to him with his frank, engaging smile; and he understood that the only honest thing for him to do was to take the note with a curt, polite nod of thanks—for only by this act of complete humility and self-abasement could he atone for Zina's futile sacrifice, and be quits with her. He was just on the point of turning on his heels and walking away from the table, when he remembered that justice and honesty required a second action independent from the first; so he picked up the glass of champagne in front of him and with a brisk, offhand gesture threw its contents into Nikitin's face. Still moving along the silent track of his inner certitude, he turned and walked back with firm steps to the spot from where he had to recite, three yards from table No. 7. He heard, without taking any notice, the murmur in the tunnel and the dance band strike hurriedly a tune, and saw with equal indifference Pierre rush to table No. 7. The dark, striking-looking girl who was Nikitin's companion had risen, but Nikitin was gently forcing her back to the seat and, after smiling as if at an excellent joke, he could be heard explaining half to her and half to Pierre, that it didn't matter in the least as nobody could take serious offense at the act of a drunken bum. But all this did not concern Leontiev any longer.

He waited for a moment to see whether the dance music would stop so that he could at last make his announcement. But as the music went on and people took to the floor to dance, Leontiev turned on his heel and went back to the dressing-room. He changed, put his breeches, books and tunic carefully into the locker, next to Señorita Lollita's costume; then with firm, soldierly steps crossed the dance-floor, the bar and walked home.

When, on the next morning, he was woken up by two police-men and asked to follow them to the Commissariat, he was not surprised, and rather relieved. Freedom had proved too heavy a burden; with a last, nervous flicker of curiosity he awaited his extradition and the meeting with Gruber and his men. It seemed to him that he had always known it would end in this way; and that Gruber must have known it too.

6

THE DOG AND THE BELL

HYDIE had insisted that they celebrate New Year's Eve alone in Fedya's new bachelor flat. Though Fedya took an almost childish pride in the little flat, he would have preferred to dine out in a gay and noisy restaurant, but for once her wish had prevailed. She had arrived early and excited, laden with parcels of delicatessen and drinks, and had locked herself into the kitchenette with an apron fastened to her evening dress. Fedya sat down, resigned, in the sitting-room and turned the radio on.

Their affair was now about four months old and he won-dered without worrying what it was leading up to. He had his superiors' blessing; though nothing concrete could be expected to come of it, one could never tell. Anyway, the fact that he was allowed to carry on with an American colonel's daughter was a sign of their confidence, of their knowing that Fedya could be trusted never to "go to Capua." He smiled, humming out in his pleasant baritone voice the tune of the Toreador's March which came from the portable radio set—a white, ebony and chromium affair with luminous dials. He picked up the evening paper, and began to read an astrologer's prophecy of events to come in the New Year.

"The critical period," it said, "will be the end of August, when Mars enters into the second house. There will be an unusual fall of meteors, a period of abnormal weather, and a grave epidemic of a new variety. Whether war will break out will depend on the race between the powers of evil and the powers of salvation—the latter represented by the new religious sect which has arisen from a wild mountainous region in the East . . ."

Fedya laughed aloud and let the newspaper drop on the floor. "What's the matter?" cried Hydie from the kitchen.

"I invite you to have a drink with me," said Fedya. "You can cook later."

"I won't be a minute."

Fedya resumed the Toreador's March, stamping the rhythm out with his foot. His shoe left an imprint on the blue, fitted carpet which was still in the stage of moulding; he brushed over it lovingly with his fingers. The prospect of spending a whole evening alone in the flat with his mistress filled him with moderate boredom. He decided to get the love-making over immediately after dinner, and then go out to some place. He had never seen how the French bourgeoisie celebrated New Year's Eve, and next year it would probably be too late for that. This thought touched him for a moment with an unaccountable sadness.

"Here we are. Now for the drink," said Hydie, discarding her apron in the kitchen door and stepping over it. She looked rather beautiful in her black evening dress, but her face had grown thin, with deep shadows under her eyes, and her bright manner had something artificial about it, like the radiance of a neon-tube.

"You have trodden on that apron," said Fedya.

"Never mind, you can send it to the laundry with your things. I have brought three with me."

She saw that he regarded this as reckless squandering and

that it made him angry. Her eyebrows twitched once or twice —a nervous tic, rather like Julien's, which she had acquired recently and which made her face appear for seconds pathetically defenceless. With a gesture which had become a habit, she rubbed Fedya's mop of hair with her palms. "I have been invited for a drink," she said.

"What shall it be?" said Fedya.

"I will get it."

She brought a bottle of champagne from the ice-box and Fedya opened it with a loud pop. This always put him into a better humour.

"Now for the New Year's toast," she said brightly.

He thought of the ritual toasts one drank at home in strict hierarchical order, but none of them seemed appropriate. He suddenly remembered how, in 1938, they had all toasted somebody whose name, as he learned the next morning, was not to be mentioned any more, and how he had afterwards suffered from diarrhœa for a whole week. This was one of those little jokes which nobody here could understand, and the memory gave him a sudden pang of homesickness. "I don't know any New Year toasts," he said.

"I don't either," said Hydie. "But I know one for Christmas." She lifted her glass and said in her clear, soft voice:

> *"Peace on earth, and mercy mild,*
> *God and sinners reconciled . . ."*

She drained her glass, and poured herself a new one. Fedya smiled:

"Still the convent, yes?"

Hydie sat down in an armchair at some distance from Fedya. It was an armchair of the flowery French kind. "What have you been reading?" she asked.

He smiled. "The newspaper has a prophecy by a soothsayer. They say this newspaper is read by a million people. Every day they read it they get more stupid, and every day the proprietor of the newspaper gets more rich. Then he makes a speech at a banquet and says we must defend the freedom of the Press. You have teachers to educate the children, but you let these gangsters take charge of the uneducated masses who are just like children. What do you say?"

"You are right as usual, Professor." Her happiest moments were when she felt able to agree with him.

He shook his head, smiling:

"Why always this mocking tone. Is it necessary?"

"No. It's just one of those silly mannerisms. But you must be patient with my re-education, and you have to take into account my deformed mentality due to my social background."

He did not know whether she was mocking or in earnest; neither did she. After a moment's silence she asked:

"Anyway, what did the soothsayer say?"

"There will be meteors, and a plague, and a new religion coming out of the mountains. . . ." The bit about the war he did not mention; by a silent accord they avoided as far as possible talking about the impending war. "I suppose," he added, "that by the new religion he means the sect of madmen in the Carpathians."

"I have heard about the Fearless Sufferers," said Hydie. She was on the point of saying more, but stopped in time. Fedya noticed it.

"Perhaps you will join them?"

"Not for the moment, thanks. Who would look after our dinner?"

She rose and went back to the kitchenette. Fedya was bored, so he decided to help and followed her. In the tiny kitchenette they kept bumping into each other, and as they were both bending over the cupboard to get the plates out, her hair brushed against his face. He felt by the rhythm of her breathing that she longed to be picked up and carried to the couch, leaving the dinner to burn. His own desire sharpened; but he was hungry, and he knew that it was wiser to keep her on tenterhooks. He patted her on the back: "Now everything is ready and we can eat," he said contentedly.

She had brought two bottles of vintage claret, and after the champagne it went quickly to their heads. Fedya assumed the relaxed, debonair expression which Hydie called look No. 4; soon, she knew, No. 5, the sexy look, would make its appearance. "How was that toast?" he asked.

"The one for Christmas? I am glad you like it." And, leaning across the table, she repeated softly: "Peace on earth and mercy mild—Flesh and Spirit reconciled . . ."

"But these were not the words. It said, 'God and sinners reconciled.'"

"Of course. How very silly of me. . . ." She bit her lip and fell silent. Fedya always felt uneasy when that distant look appeared in her eyes, so he got to his feet and clicked his heels in mock solemnity. "I drink another toast," he said. "To the Fearless Sufferers. You see, I am becoming a counter-revolutionary to please you."

"Heaven knows what I am becoming to please *you*," she said wonderingly.

"But you are not becoming anything," he said gaily. "You cannot change. You are too hard for that—and also too soft. . . ."

"You are becoming quite lyrical," said Hydie.

"Yes—you are a mystery. A great mystery," Fedya cried enthusiastically. He was a little drunk and he knew that it flattered women to be called a mystery.

"I will solve the mystery for you," said Hydie. "I have a woman's body, a man's brains, the aspirations of a saint and the instincts of a harlot. Does that satisfy you?"

"Ah," said Fedya laughing. "How very banal."

"You are becoming sophisticated," said Hydie. "Well, I can tell you more. When I was nineteen I was sent to a psycho-analyst. My parents wanted a boy, but I was born a girl; the analyst said this was important. He also said that I had got a crush on my daddy and that this is why I fell in love with Jesus Christ. Then I went to another analyst who said I have got a masculine protest and also a low self-reliance, that's why I am such a chameleon, always acting the part which others expect me to. Then I got married to a very polite young man who made love like a bird, and he explained to me that I was frigid out of sheer selfishness because I lacked the generosity to let myself go. Then I met you and let myself really go, and you explain to me that I am a typical product of a doomed civilization. So you can see that I am not a mystery but a well-defined pattern; only, what does it all add up to?"

Fedya laughed; then he said in his gentle, pedagogical voice:

"At first you never wanted to talk about yourself, and now you do it all the time. You say you are no mystery but you really believe you are a very great mystery and you believe all people are great mysteries. You say 'what does it all add up to.' I will tell you it adds up to something very simple. There is no mystery, only reflexes, as in this radio machine." He patted tenderly the white ebony casing. "You turn a knob, there is a reaction. You hit it, there is damage; you repair it, it is all right again. It talks, it screams, it makes music—all very useful and amusing; but there is no mystery . . ."

Hydie yawned demonstratively. "You talk exactly like granddad," she said.

"The one who had a castle in Ireland?" asked Fedya, amused. "Who said that women should have a home and children and forget about their craziness? He was a very sensible and progressive man."

"No, my other granddad. He was a president of a railway company. In between buying up other companies, he spent his spare time reading pamphlets about 'the survival of the fittest' and 'man, a machine.' You talk just like him; what a bore!" She cleaned the plates away and brought the ice-cream with another bottle of champagne. "Anyway," she said, "this is New Year's Eve, and I intend to get tight."

Fedya opened the bottle, and after filling up their glasses he said with a mischievous smile:

"So you maintain there is a mystery, and not only reflexes?"

"Oh, shut up, darling," said Hydie. "Must you go on lecturing?"

"Yes. I wish to tell you about the dogs of Professor Pavlov."

Hydie felt her head swimming. She felt so mixed-up lately that she did not even know whether she was happy or miserable. To find out, she mixed some of the claret into the champagne, drank it and lay down on the couch, wishing that Fedya would come to her and blot everything out with his hard, crushing body. But he was still talking about Professor Pavlov and his dogs, looking at her with a curious smile through half-closed eyes—a new expression not so far contained in the catalogue.

"So, you see," he was saying, "after a while when the bell rings the dog drops his spittle although there is no meat. . . ." He walked slowly over to the couch. "And that explains what we are: conditions and reflexes, and the rest is stupid superstition." He was now standing at the couch, bending over her, and her heart was pumping away violently. "Oh, rot," she said breathlessly, waiting to be taken.

"So you don't believe it," he said, bending closer, with the same curious smile. He slowly stretched out his arm and his hand gripped her with firm pressure under the left armpit, his thumb pressing against her nipple. It was a grip more than a caress which she knew only too well; he always did precisely this at the precise moment of her physical climax. "Now . . ." he said. She felt her eyeballs turn upward, the familiar, blissful convulsion, then peace. Fedya relaxed his grip, walked back to the table and sat down, emptying his glass. "What do you think now of Professor Pavlov?" he said politely.

She gave no answer. Her mind was in a mist which she was very careful not to dispel; her body limp and relaxed. Without thinking she knew that she had suffered a humiliation past anything that a drunken customer might inflict on a prostitute, and that she would hate him for the rest of her life as she had never hated before. But as yet she felt no anger, only the blissful peace of her body reclining on the couch. Fedya, slightly embarrassed, poured himself another drink and asked her whether she wanted one. She slowly shook her head without opening her eyes. He turned the radio on, fiddled with the dials, found a station which was broadcasting a rumba. At the first sickly sweet bars of the saxophone she felt her stomach turn, rushed to the toilet and locked herself in. She was violently sick, washed and gargled, and after rubbing her neck with a cold sponge, felt a little better. She made up her face and went back to the room.

"Are you better?" Fedya asked solicitously, putting his arm round her. It was obvious that he thought it was time to stop fooling and to make love in good and earnest. She calmly shook his arm off and sat down in the armchair next to the radio:

"Where did you learn that trick?" she asked quietly, turning the radio off.

Fedya laughed, but he was getting impatient; the experiment had excited him. "It is a simple application of Pavlov," he said, smiling at her.

She asked in a level voice: "That grip plays the part of the bell which is rung each time before the dog is fed?"

"Yes—but now we will do better than the bell alone," he said, approaching.

"Wait. I thought that sort of thing did not work on humans?"

"Oh, yes. One can also condition the pupil-reflex, even without hypnotism. You ring a bell—the pupil dilates. You hit a gong—the pupil becomes small. It is very simple."

"What else can you do with a man?"

"Oh, many things. . . . Now will you come? Then afterwards we can perhaps go to a café?"

"Where did you learn about these tricks?"

"From a colleague who is interested . . ." His tone and

expression changed suddenly. "Why are you asking so many questions?"

She said in the same even voice: "You have just performed an interesting experiment on me, so of course I am interested."

It began to dawn on him that for some silly feminine reason she might be offended.

"But it was only a joke," he said. "To prove to you that Professor Pavlov was right, and that all that talk about mysteries of the soul is superstition . . ."

She lifted her pale, drawn face to him, but remained silent. Resigned, he drew up another armchair and sat down, facing her.

"What is the matter?" he asked gently.

"I don't think we can go on any longer, Fedya," she said.

There was another silence. "All right, if you wish it so," he said casually. "But what has happened?"

"It's no good going into it all over again." She knew this was the moment to rise and leave for good; but she made no move.

"If you wish that our liaison be terminated, I agree," said Fedya coldly. "But I require that you give an explanation."

Hydie felt hollow and worn out, trying to summon the energy to get up.

"Why must you have everything explained?" she asked wearily.

"Because . . ." He himself wondered why it mattered so much to him that she should explain the reason for the break, and found no answer. He became irritated. "Because it is uncultured to terminate a liaison with a stupid quarrel and no explanation."

"All right. I don't like to be experimented with." At last she found the force to get up.

"So it was because of this joke?" He felt suddenly relieved, and again did not understand for what reason.

"Let us call it that. Goodbye."

She had picked up her handbag and was already half-way to the door. He had expected a great farewell scene with tears, ending either in reconciliation or a dramatic exit. Her unceremonious manner left him for a moment speechless. He wanted to jump up and bar her way, but was too hurt and indignant. In the fraction of the second while she reached for the door, his heart froze in a sudden panic and several possibilities flashed through his mind. He could still grab her and drag her to the couch; he knew she would fight like a devil, but the moment he broke her physical resistance and took possession of her, she would give in and respond more passionately than ever. It was perhaps this certainty of the ultimate victory which made him renounce the attempt. He felt rather fed-up with her unrestrained physical passion; all his life he had preferred women who either pretended to be cold and to yield only to force, or who took a motherly attitude in his embraces, like the little Tartar girl in Baku. . . . Now she had actually opened the door and was halfway through it, without even turning her head. Fedya watched her, then, when she was almost on the other side of the door, he said in a strangled voice:

"You have forgotten your aprons and other things."

She shrugged, again without turning, and was gone. This shrug of her straight, slim shoulders was the last image he retained of her. He heard her stop in the corridor while she was putting her coat on, then the sound of the door closing behind her. She had not even banged it, as any woman of a normal, virile civilisation would have done in her place. . . . Fedya suddenly laughed aloud, imagining the devil of a scene which a girl of his own country would have thrown. They called this good manners, just like knowing which wine to order in a restaurant; in truth it was sheer hypocrisy and effete decadence.

Fedya lit a cigarette and stretched his arms with a feeling of sudden relief. It was only half-past eleven; in a few minutes he would go out into a gay café, and maybe pick up a girl with whom he did not have to argue all the time. He turned the radio on at full blast and went to the bathroom. There he adjusted his new tie before the mirror and began vigorously to brush his short mop of hair, smiling at himself with good-humoured irony.

When Hydie got out into the street she took a deep breath. The street was quiet, covered with a thin layer of fresh snow; more was still coming down in large, lazy flakes. She held her hand out to catch a few of them, then on a sudden impulse bent down, scooped up a handful of snow and rubbed her face with it. A thin, icy trickle ran down her neck and along her spine; it tickled pleasantly and made her feel clean again. Somewhere in the street she heard the closing of a door; it occurred to her that Fedya might follow her into the street to persuade her to go back. She hastened her step, then broke

into a run. Breathlessly she arrived at the corner of the boulevard, had the good luck to find a lone taxi on the stand, and
got into it. Now she felt safe to turn her head; but the little
side-street from which she had come was empty.

7

CONCERNING THE ANTICHRIST

ACCORDING to Julien, Boris was slightly better as far as his
physical condition was concerned. The doctors had tried
some of the new antibiotics on him without noticeable effect;
then, in the late autumn, when the climate of the Seine Valley has a notoriously bad effect on people suffering from afflictions of the chest, a sudden amelioration had set in. It may
have been due to a delayed action of the drugs, or to some
cause of a quite different order, as Julien vaguely hinted.

"When did you last see him?" asked Julien. It was New
Year's Day, and he and Hydie were walking along the quais
towards the hotel where Boris lived.

"Not for several months," said Hydie. Nor had she seen
Julien for several weeks. She had just run into him by chance
whilst she was looking at the bookstands on the Quai Voltaire.
Julien had suggested that they should go and pay a New Year's
visit to Boris. They had bought some flowers and delicatessen,
and now they were on their way to the Ile St. Louis, breathing
with relish the clear, frosty air.

"I went to see him once or twice in hospital," she continued.
"It must have been in September, I guess. How time is running . . . But he was so gruff and morose that I thought I
was getting on his nerves and stopped going to see him. . . ."

She was surprised how much at ease she felt with Julien
again. Perhaps it was because they had met by chance; if they
had made a date, she would have felt nervous. They walked
briskly, and Hydie noticed to her surprise that it was easier to
keep in step with Julien, in spite of his limp, than with Fedya.

"Boris told me about the row he had with you," said Julien.
Hydie was embarrassed. "I know it was my fault. But why
on earth did he tell you about it?"

On her last visit, she had tried to offer Boris a loan for a
cure in the Swiss mountains. Boris had been offended, and the

more she had tried to make him see sense, the more unpleasant he had become; finally she had left with a feeling of humiliation, knowing that she had bungled the whole matter and that he loathed the sight of her.

"The reason why he told me about it will probably surprise you," said Julien.

"Don't tell me he has gone and fallen in love with me," said Hydie.

"No, Boris isn't the kind to fall in love with anybody. . . . He only told me about it a short time ago, when this sudden amelioration set in which so much surprised the doctors. He told me about your offer and added this comment: 'If anybody were to offer me the money now, I would accept it at once.'"

Hydie looked at him in surprise, waiting for an explanation. Julien hesitated for a moment, then continued:

"To tell you the truth, he even asked me whether I was still seeing you. The implication was obvious."

"Why didn't you ring me?" asked Hydie.

Julien looked at her with a faint smile. "I didn't feel like it. I tried to rake up the money from other sources."

"And did you succeed?"

"No. Each month there are about ten thousand people who still manage to make their escape from the East, and the sources of charity are drying up. Fortunately only one in ten succeeds. The others are captured or shot by the frontier guards, and are spared the disillusionment awaiting them."

They had both slowed down their pace; now Hydie stepped out again.

"I have broken with Fedya," she announced quietly.

She did not look at him, but knew that the familiar tic had appeared on his face. She had to control her own, so strong was its contagious effect.

After a few steps he said in a slightly ironical tone: "Good news. When?"

"Last night."

He whistled softly to himself, and stopped to light a cigarette. "Must you smoke in this lovely air?" she asked, leaning against the stone balustrade of the quay and watching him. He was standing in front of her, fumbling with his matches. "It is a special brand," he said, "it goes out after three puffs and tastes better and better each time you relight it. But it tastes best when you suck it cold—like a pipe."

"How horrible," said Hydie, laughing, and suddenly her eyes filled with tears.

"What's the matter?" he asked.

"Nothing. I suddenly had a feeling of being back from a long journey."

They started walking again. "So what about Boris?" said Hydie. "I am so clumsy that if I broach the subject again there will again be a row."

"Don't broach it. Wait until I have talked to him alone, and if you are really willing to fork out the cash, I'll let you know."

Hydie nodded eagerly. It occurred to her that a cure in Switzerland might be quite expensive. She had little money of her own so she would have to make her father pay up; but she was confident that she could manage it.

"What do you think made Boris suddenly become reasonable?" she asked.

He blinked; the cigarette had gone out. "Reasonable?" he said. "You will find Boris changed. But I wouldn't call it a change towards reasonableness."

"What do you mean? To accept a loan to get oneself cured seems to me very reasonable."

They had arrived at the Pont de la Tournelle and were walking towards the Island which, with its row of frost-covered plane trees and its quiet front of eighteenth-century façades, seemed gently to float eastward on the immobile Seine.

"I don't think there is a chance of Boris getting cured," said Julien. "And I don't think he believes there is." He was accelerating his pace, as if to cut the conversation short.

"But then why . . ." said Hydie, bewildered.

"You will see for yourself. I warned you that you will find him rather changed."

He was obviously unwilling to enlarge on the matter, and Hydie got even more confused.

"But I thought he was so much better?"

Julien gave no answer. They had arrived at the little hotel where Boris lived. It was an old, very narrow building of three storys, and only just large enough for two close-set windows on each story. It was hemmed in between two massive houses, which seemed to grudge it even the little space it occupied and try to squeeze it out, for the façade of the hotel with its peeling stucco was bending over the street at an angle. Some paternal municipal authority had propped it up by means of two poles wedged under the second floor windows, so that the whole little hotel seemed to lean on crutches, rather like Monsieur Anatole. But it commanded a lovely view over the river, and one of the plane trees which lined the quay touched with its branches a window hung with washing. It was called Hôtel du Beauregard, and its signboard promised rooms by the day or by the month, with gas, electricity and running water. Despite its narrow façade it had an imposing carriage entrance of studded oak gates, in which a smaller door opened. Opposite to the entrance, on the side of the Seine, was a public urinal—one of those circular, wrought-iron affairs with a roof like a parasol, which hid its customers only up to the shoulder, exposing to public view the rapt, contemplative look on their faces as they attended to their manly business.

The passage on the other side of the gateway was almost dark. From the concierge's box a dark female shape emerged to inquire after the intruders' purpose. Julien gave Boris' name, and they were directed to the third floor. They climbed the creaking, narrow stairs, past the water-closets with milk-glass doors ingeniously placed on the landings half-way between two storys; each of them seemed constantly in action, for water was gurgling and rushing everywhere in the lead pipes along the walls, as if they were surrounded by a waterfall. They arrived at room No. 9, which was where Boris lived, but there was no answer to Julien's knocking. "Never mind," said Julien. "I'm sure he's in." He opened the door, went in first, then turned his head. "Watch out," he said, for the corridor was almost dark, "there is one step down into the room."

The curtains in the room were drawn, and at first sight there seemed to be nobody in it. Opposite the step leading down from the door stood the big brass bed; it was unmade, and occupied most of the space of the room. Behind it was the little paper-partitioned cubicle with the washstand and the *bidet;* on the other side the wardrobe with its half-blind mirror, standing lopsided, as it had lost one of its legs. As Hydie's eyes became accustomed to the semi-darkness, she recognised with a shock that Boris was standing barefooted and immobile in a dark flannel dressing-gown against the curtain. He did not answer Julien's greeting and did not move.

"Hallo—there are visitors," repeated Julien, and switched the light on. Boris still did not move and looked at them without blinking. "So you have seen me?" he said at last in a curiously hurt and disappointed voice. He looked even more haggard and cadaverous than when Hydie had seen him the last time; his face had now completely caved in except for the nose which had become longer and sharply pointed.

"Look—I have brought a guest," said Julien. "And there is caviare and a bottle of vodka in the parcel."

Boris turned his eyes to her. They also seemed to have changed: they appeared more close-set than before, almost squinting.

"And you, Madame?" he said to Hydie. "Did you, too, see me when you came in?"

Hydie managed to produce a laugh which sounded almost natural. "It was so dark I actually thought at first the room was empty."

"Ah—so you didn't see me?" said Boris on a note of triumph.

"Well, no—not at the first moment."

"Anyway, what does it matter?" said Julien in a deliberately rude voice.

"What it matters? It matters—but you wouldn't understand," said Boris absently. Still without moving, he began to wriggle his toes, watching them with great concentration.

"For God's sake let's get some air in," said Julien. He ripped the curtains open, and Boris had to move to make place for him. The broad daylight hit the room like a blow. Boris gave a resigned sigh and became suddenly animated. "It is extremely kind of you to come to visit me," he said to Hydie, bowing formally in his tattered dressing-gown. "Please sit down." He made a vague hospitable gesture with his arm which embraced the unmade bed and the only chair in the room, which was a rocking-chair with a frayed cane back.

"Go and get dressed, then we will see to the vodka," said Julien, sitting down on the bed. Boris seemed undecided. He hovered around Hydie, motioning her towards the rocking-chair, apparently eager to ask her some question, but doubtful whether this would be expedient. At last he made up his mind. "I will be back presently. Please make yourself at home," and he went hurriedly behind the partition. There was a vigorous splashing of water, accompanied by the hearty noises which men make when they dip their heads into a washbasin. Julien seemed to ignore Boris' peculiar behaviour; he was busy getting the bed into shape by putting the soiled, lace-cornered cotton cover over it, then he opened the parcel and arranged with its contents a kind of picnic on the bed.

"Throw my shirt over here, will you?" called Boris from

behind the partition. His voice now sounded clear and fresh, though it was followed by a slight cough. A minute later he emerged fully dressed, his sparse hair plastered down. He glanced at the caviare, the smoked salmon and ham displayed on the bed, and a greedy, pathetic look came into his eyes. "You shouldn't have done that," he said uncertainly, his gaze shifting from Julien to Hydie and returning to the bed as a needle returns to the magnetic pole.

"Shut up and let's get at the caviare," said Julien.

Hydie pulled her rocking-chair closer and, the two men sitting on the bed, they began to share out the snacks. Hydie tried only to pretend to eat, but Boris was pressing her with a great show of hospitality, and she had to give in for fear of offending him. After the first glass of vodka Boris became animated.

"I remember you now," he said to Hydie. "My memory has lately been playing tricks on me, but now I remember. We went to a party together—there were fireworks, and a Russian from the Service. . . . Later you came to see me in the hospital, and then you vanished. . . ." The expression of his eyes changed. "How did you do it?" he asked in a tone of secret understanding.

"Do what? Vanish?" asked Hydie, with an uneasy laugh.

"Never mind if you don't want to talk about it," said Boris. "I hope that I myself will shortly be able to. . . ." He checked himself and looked at them suspiciously. "I haven't said a word," he said menacingly. "Do you understand? Not a word, I warn you."

Julien put his glass down—they were all drinking out of Boris' toothpaste-stained glass—with a deliberate clang. "What is all this nonsense?" he said. "Pull yourself together, you idiot. You have been day-dreaming. It is time you snapped out of it."

Boris looked at him vacantly, then his eyes focused. "What have you been saying?" he asked in confusion. "Don't yell at me. What's the matter?"

"The matter is . . ." Julien hesitated for a fraction of a second, then took a plunge. "What's this new idea of playing the invisible man? You have spun yourself a yarn, and now it has become a web and you are getting yourself entangled in it."

Boris looked doubtful. "You shouldn't talk about these

things when . . ." he said, indicating Hydie from the corner of his eyes.

"She's all right, I guarantee for her," said Julien. "She is the girl who offered you money for going to Switzerland, don't you remember?" he added urgently.

An expression of sudden happiness came into Boris' face. "So you want to help me?" he said to Hydie, taking her hand. "Now I understand. But when you first offered me the money you were so conspiratorial—you pretended to believe it was really for a cure, so I felt insulted. . . . But now I understand, you were all the time in the know, you only pretended because you were over-cautious. . . . In fact," he added thoughtfully, "you were perhaps right. But there is always a danger in being over-conspiratorial; that leads often to ridiculous misunderstandings—sometimes even to tragedies. The difficulty is always to find the right balance between the necessity of caution and the necessity of taking the risk, of uncovering one's cards at the right moment. . . . Anyway, the main thing is, now that we have straightened this out, to get down to the job. . . ."

He had sprung to his feet and began pacing up and down the three steps between the bed and the window. Hydie looked at Julien; he motioned to her not to interrupt.

"You see," said Boris, stopping in front of her, "at the time when you offered to finance this action, the plan was only in its initial stage and the whole thing seemed mad, or rather childish. I started with the obvious idea: pretending to be a journalist to obtain an interview with him, and the like. But he hasn't granted an audience to a foreigner for the last two years, and even if by some extraordinary cunning you succeeded, there remained the question of the technical means. The routine is that on being admitted to the building, you have to deposit not only your revolver, but every metallic object in your pockets, cigarette cases, lighters, and so on. Even ambassadors have to submit to the procedure. Then, as you are led along those long flights of corridors, you traverse, without noticing it, an invisible thread of ultra-violet rays—the kind of contraption used in automatic traffic control to change the lights after a certain number of cars has crossed the beam. So anything you tried to hide in your pockets would be detected at once. After all, it is only logical; without these extraordinary precautions he would not be alive today, and the whole problem would not exist. . . ." He resumed his pacing, then stopped again.

"You see, the whole problem can be explained in a nutshell. He is the best-hated man alive, and the best-hated man who ever lived. At least ten million peaceful people who wouldn't kill a dog, would be prepared to kill him with a clean conscience and at the sacrifice of their lives. Moreover, all his favourites and near-associates know that one day their turn will come, so they too are interested in his death as a simple measure of self-protection. In the face of this extraordinary pressure of hatred concentrated on a single target of vulnerable flesh, he had to resort to equally extraordinary measures of precaution. After all, the target is only a few inches wide and between five and six feet long; to simplify matters you can reduce the central vulnerable surface to half a square yard. . . ."

Absentmindedly, his glance alighted on the snacks spread on the bed; he picked up a sandwich, nibbled the pink salmon off its top and threw the remaining bread with a careless gesture into a corner of the room, like a cigarette butt. "There are no ashtrays in this hotel," he said irritably. "One lives like a pig. Where have we got to?" He stared at Hydie, trying to concentrate, then found the thread and snapped his fingers with satisfaction.

"As I said, the whole problem is reduced to the question how to get at that vulnerable surface of half a square yard. You understand of course," he said doubtfully, "that when I talk of 'surface' I only mean the immanent aspect with a name, a moustache, and so on. But if we concentrate on the transcendent aspect, which is that of the Antichrist, we don't get anywhere, we only lose our time in sterile talk, and meanwhile he will kill you, and Julien, and all decent people. Not that it matters; but the point is to try to kill him first; if you ask me why, I'll tell you it is a point of honour. Don't you agree?"

"Go on," said Julien. "We are listening."

"I am afraid I didn't make myself quite clear. I didn't mean that it is a point of honour for me because I am a reserve officer and because of Maria and so on. What I mean is that it is a point of honour for humanity at large to kill him, because the Antichrist is a challenge and a test for the will to survive. Now I have expressed it clearly, haven't I?"

"Yes," said Julien. "But you just said that to discuss the

transcendent aspect is a waste of time. So let's get back to the practical problem."

"Quite right, quite right," said Boris. His features assumed an expression which, given a different face, would have been a benevolent smile. "We must get back to the immanent aspect. Now, how far have we got with that . . . ?" He again lost the thread, and his eyes became disturbed.

"Half a square yard of all too solid flesh," said Julien.

Boris nodded gratefully. "Correct. You are really a help. And you too," he turned to Hydie, and his glance became suspicious. "Have you brought the money with you? It is in your bag, is it?"

"That will be all right," said Julien. "But for Christ's sake get back to the point. You said you wanted to pretend to be a journalist, but that is out."

Boris nodded. "That was the initial plan. It is out, as you say, for the reasons which we have already discussed. . . ." He resumed pacing up and down the creaking board between the bed and the window: "Out because (a) no journalist admitted to the presence, (b) because of the impossibility of carrying weapons or any metallic object in your pocket." He counted off the two points on his fingers, and for a while kept the two fingers raised, as if he had forgotten to fold them again.

"Now, you see, if you analyse the matter, you will find that these two reasons are *independent* of each other. If you are admitted to the presence, you still can't carry a weapon. If you can cheat about the weapon, you are still not admitted. It is very important, in fact, it is essential, to see that the two points are independent of each other. It took me a long time to discover this, and meanwhile of course my thoughts turned in a vicious circle, like a mill."

He gave emphasis to this point by turning a finger round his head, and seemed to have to make an effort to stop the finger from turning.

"For example, I thought if I can't take a revolver, I could wear a ring with a little syringe in it; some of our comrades used to have them. . . ." He smiled at Hydie. "Do you know how we got the idea? From a book on the Borgias. We had a little Jewish silversmith from Krakow with us in the woods; he had studied books on Renaissance jewellery, and he made us those rings. You never know when a hobby may come in useful. . . ." The memory seemed to cheer him up, and he reached for the bottle of vodka, but put it back at once on the bedside table. "Better not," he said. "Doctor's orders. Where were we?"

"Independence of the problem of admission from the problem of the technical means," said Julien. "The latter illustrated by the example of the Borgia rings."

"Quite right," said Boris. "Now, do you know what the hitch about the ring is? You will never guess," he said to Hydie, preparing his effect. "The hitch is that even when he grants an audience *he never shakes hands*. Moreover, he sits behind a big desk, at a distance of several yards from the visitor. Several foreign ambassadors have remarked on this point in their memoirs. So, you see, the gambit of the rings must have occurred to him too. And quite naturally so, as he has studied the methods of the Borgias."

He frowned and resumed his pacing. "I thought of other tricks, and I am afraid I was led astray to invent quite fantastic contraptions. Every single one had a hitch, and I won't bore you with descriptions. But oh, the sweetness of the imagined moment when he slowly slumps down behind his big desk, and in the dull, clouding pig's eyes understanding appears at last—the understanding that he has been outwitted after all. And there is a great rushing in his ears which swells to thunder—and he knows it is the echo of the great sigh of relief of all good men all over the earth."

His voice had become soft, and for a moment his expression was nearer than at any previous time to a genuine smile.

"But, you see," he continued briskly, "day-dreaming is dangerous; one has to remain practical. Do you know that feeling," he asked Hydie, with a certain hesitation, "when you close your eyes and you see a heavy wheel turning—a very big, heavy wheel of wrought-iron which turns on a smooth, oily bearing? Somebody has set it in motion, and now the massive wheel continues to turn under its own momentum. Now!" he said, closing his eyes. "Try it. Just try to stop it with closed eyes. . . ."

Hydie looked at Julien; he was sitting on the bed, smoking, and watching Boris with an air of studied indifference. She closed her eyes, imagining the heavy wrought-iron wheel well launched on its rapid rotation, and tried to stop it. "It is impossible," she said.

Boris was standing in front of her, his eyes closed; he looked as if he were suffering from a violent migraine. "All right," said Julien, "you have convinced us. Now stop it—don't keep your eyes shut."

Boris seemed to tear his eyelids apart with an intense effort. "There you see," he said to them, "you can't do it. But one isn't allowed to give up and open one's eyes until one has succeeded in stopping the wheel. It is one of the exercises." He closed his eyes again, and his face contracted in the spasm of his effort. "You have to learn to slow it down—slow it down —like that—and then gradually—it will—stop. . . . Stop!" he panted through clenched teeth.

"Now," he said triumphantly, opening his eyes, "this time I did stop it. But I don't always succeed—not yet."

"What sort of exercise is it?" asked Julien.

"It is part of the training," said Boris. "But you shouldn't ask these questions, as I haven't explained yet. How far have I got? . . ." Julien was on the point of giving the cue, but Boris forestalled him. "I know," he said briskly. "I am not quite as absentminded as you seem to think, though I admit the exercises are a strain. . . . We got to the point where I explained that none of the obvious means are possible, nor any cunning gadgets, and besides, and *independently* from this, I wouldn't be able to get near him anyway. So, you see, when at last it occurred to me to fit these two independent halves of the problem together, I discovered that I have been moving in a vicious circle; and that circle is expressed by the wheel. This is why the wheel had to be stopped. Do you get me?" He seemed very anxious to make himself understood. Julien nodded.

"This point is essential," continued Boris, "because otherwise you could not understand how I came to make the discovery. You see, once you know the premises, it is very simple——" His face broke into a smile. "All discoveries are simple once you have made them. And now I will explain it to you. As, by his nature, he is both immanent and transcendent, *he cannot be destroyed on one plane alone*. In other words, I can only kill him in his immanent aspect—the pock marks, the moustache and so on—by making a detour through the other kingdom. But the other kingdom is of course immaterial and invisible. So, to finish the job, I have to pass through and come out of the invisible kingdom—so much is clear without doubt. . . . The rest is purely a matter of technique. There is of course the whole literature to be studied. Nobody in his senses can doubt the evidence that there were men who had the faculty of becoming invisible at will. Furthermore, you can't get around the fact that while we have plenty of records of levitation in the Occident, disconspicuity is mainly practised in the East. But in many respects the technique still needs improving—and at any rate, you wouldn't understand the first thing about it. . . ." He stopped, and his expression changed. "So why am I wasting my time with you? And how am I to know that you are not an agent anyway?"

Suddenly he seemed to be working himself into a rage, and Hydie became frightened. "Look," said Julien, without budging from the bed, "don't act like a lunatic. It bores me. Besides, the girl's got the money."

Boris looked at them irresolutely. As he stood staring at them the room gradually filled with silence, and street noises began to filter timidly through the window—a barge hooted on the Seine as it approached a bridge, and a passing lorry set the glass panes in vibration. At last Boris resumed his wanderings; he walked now with a slouch, on stiff legs. "Anyway, where have we got to?" he asked sulkily.

"Your efforts to obtain a transit visa through the invisible kingdom," said Julien.

Boris looked at him, startled. "That is rather well put," he said with grudging consent. "But I won't talk any more about the method. The details would bore you, and you lack the knowledge. It is all a matter of certain exercises—diet, posture, breathing, and the rest. All very boring—let it pass," he said, with a sweeping gesture, which he stopped in mid-air as his eyes caught on Hydie. "Absolute chastity is essential, though," he said to her meaningly. "And no day-dreaming. One hour of day-dreaming is enough to undo the progress of a month."

"How far have you got?" asked Julien.

Boris smiled at him slyly. "That's what you would like to know. But I can't talk about that. I would rather discuss the practical details. You see," he turned to Hydie, "for a while I thought I wouldn't need the money because I would travel on the train unseen; but that isn't feasible. The corridors on a train are narrow, so somebody is bound to bump into you and raise a hue and cry—and then the game would be up. Also, it is a long journey—more than ninety-six hours with all those frontier controls—and I must have a seat, if possible a sleeping berth, to remain fit. Do you think," he turned to Hydie timidly, "that second-class sleeping-car accommodation would be asking too much?"

Hydie shook her head.

"But it is a lot of money—nearly three hundred dollars."

Hydie nodded, avoiding his eyes.

"That is settled then," said Boris, trying to hide his satisfaction but actually grinning with joy. "You see, this way I shall be able to travel quite legally, on a tourist visa perhaps, and shall only go into disconspicuity after checking in at the hotel. In the hotel I shall make one or two final tests—ringing for tea for instance, and watching the waiter come in, look round the empty room, leave the tray with a shrug on the table and perhaps pinch a pair of socks out of my suitcase—who could blame him under the conditions in which they live? From then on the rest is child's play. . . ."

He remained standing in the corner next to the window and his gaze became vacant and withdrawn. Hydie moved in the rockingchair, and for a moment Boris' eyes seemed to focus on her. "You must go now," he said sternly. "You are disturbing."

"You should come with us for a walk in the fresh air," said Julien, rising from the bed.

Boris gave no answer. He stood rigidly near the window, in exactly the same position as when they had entered the room; his visitors had ceased to exist for him. As Hydie turned her head from the doorstep, his figure seemed for a second to dissolve into the curtain, and she gave a startled little cry. Julien, who had gone ahead, turned to her in the corridor. "What's the matter? Has the suggestion started to work?" he asked her, with a smile.

"I guess it's the hangover," said Hydie, closing the squeaking door of the room, with the immobile figure behind her.

"So that's that," said Julien when they got into the street. Hydie was so happy breathing the cold, fresh air that she felt no inclination to talk. After a while she asked nevertheless:

"Why didn't you warn me beforehand?"

"I told you that you would find him changed. But I did not know myself that he had gone completely off the rails. When I saw him the last time it was still in the balance. It must have happened during the last few days."

"What can one do about it?"

Julien shrugged. "Only the routine things. We shall have to get him into an institution where they will give him shock therapy or do a lobotomy, and he will either improve or he won't. If he does, so much the worse for him. I imagine it takes quite an effort to go insane, and I wonder whether one has the right to undo it all, against his will. But that's an old metaphysical teaser."

They crossed the Pont de la Tournelle to the Left Bank. It was no longer cold, and the sun had melted and dried the rest of last night's snowfall. A tug was slowly puffing up the Seine with two barges in her tow; the air was suddenly full of Sunday and false spring.

"Shall we go and lunch at a bistro? I would like to talk to you."

"I am expected to lunch at home," Hydie said doubtfully.

"Who can say 'no' on a day like this?"

"I can't," said Hydie. "One drifts. That's the snag with this town. One just drifts along the boulevards and cafés as in lotus-land."

"Only on the Left Bank," said Julien. "If our next conquerors would content themselves with the Right Bank alone, one could perhaps still come to an arrangement with them."

"That sounds about as reasonable as Boris' projects."

"My dear," said Julien, "why do you always provoke one to platitudes? Have you ever doubted that a hundred years hence they will discover that we have all been insane—not metaphorically, but in the literal, clinical sense? Has it never occurred to you that when poets talk about the madness of homo sapiens they are making not a poetical but a medical statement? It wouldn't be Nature's first blunder either—think of the dinosaur. A neurologist told me the other day that in all probability the snag lies somewhere in the connections between the forebrain and the interbrain. To be precise, our species suffers from endemic schizophrenia—that characteristic mixture of ingenuity and imbecility which you could observe in Boris. But Boris is only a slightly more pronounced case than the rest of us. Mediæval man thought he could buy divine indulgence for cash and argued about the number of angels that can dance on the point of a needle. The beliefs of our modern mass-movements are based on the same ingenuous imbecility. Our misfitted brain leads us a dance on a permanent witches' sabbath. If you are an optimist, you are free to believe that some day some biological mutation will cure the race. But it seems infinitely more probable that we shall go the way of the dinosaur. . . ."

"If that is what you are going to talk about during lunch," said Hydie, "I might as well go home to daddy."

"No," said Julien. "I have something to say to you—and it isn't a proposal either."

But he did not broach the subject until they were seated in the little restaurant on the quai and he had ordered their food. Then, after the first glass of wine, he said abruptly:

"So your break with Nikitin is definite?"

"Yes."

"How much do you know about his activities?"

"Very little. I never asked him any questions, and I wouldn't answer any about him, even if I could, is that clear?"

"Quite clear. I did not mean to ask you questions, but to tell you something about Nikitin which you might not know."

"I would rather you didn't," said Hydie, feeling suddenly sick with curiosity and apprehension. "I am neither interested in his amorous past, nor in the special work he was doubtless engaged in as they all are as a matter of course."

"But you have no idea what type of work it was?"

"No. Nor do I want to know, nor do I wish to continue this discussion."

"All right, my dear, don't bite my nose off. But you may ask yourself a simple question: why do I offer to give you facts about Nikitin now that you have broken with him, and why have I never offered to do so before?"

Hydie hesitated for a moment. "Maybe you knew nothing about him at the time. At any rate, it doesn't matter, and I told you I don't want to go on talking about it."

Julien carefully lit his cigarette butt, then said:

"I have known the facts for several months. The reason why I did not tell you while he was your lover should be fairly obvious. I was more or less in love with you and jealous of Nikitin; I could not afford to score by informing on him. So I avoided your company, and if you avoided mine it was partly because you were afread of what you might learn about him. And now, if you prefer it, we can talk about something else."

"All right," said Hydie. "I have never been good at pretending. Let's have it."

"The disarming thing about you is a kind of compulsive sincerity. It is part of your diet of self-punishment. Isn't it?"

"I thought you were going to tell me about the secret life of Fedya Nikitin."

"One moment before we come to that. I explained to you

why I did not tell you before. Why am I going to tell you now?"

"I don't know. Why do you think your motives of talking or not talking are so very interesting to me?"

Julien's face twitched. Then he said quietly:

"All right, here are the facts. . . ." He stopped, because Hydie had pulled her compact out and seemed entirely absorbed in making up her face. He squashed his cigarette in the ashtray—an exceptional gesture with him—and explained:

"Before they take over a country, they naturally prepare their lists for the first clean-up. As the numbers involved have to amount to a previously fixed percentage of the population, the task of selection is a considerable one. I won't bore you with details; the principle on which they work is roughly this. A number of reliable natives in various occupations and various parts of the country are assigned the task of drawing up lists of actual and potential Enemies of the People, Socially Unreliable Elements, and so on. These lists are compared and sifted on a higher level, for it is in the nature of the system that they embrace a too high percentage of the population. The final selection is made by punching-card machines. For instance, if a person's card shows (a) that he plays a leading part in the local fishing club, (b) that he has relatives abroad and (c) that he has served in the war with distinction, his card will automatically drop into a special tray and he is in for it. It is the only possible method, for the task is to eliminate all potential centres of resistance, the people capable of rallying others in one way or another—the 'activist element' as it is technically called. Political conviction plays only a subordinate part, for the primary aim is to eliminate the foci of all independent thought and action. Metaphorically speaking, it is necessary to pulverise the nation's spine, eliminate its ribs and break its bones, to reduce it to the level of an invertebrate organism, a kind of slug or jellyfish, before it can be digested. One may call it 'operation cobra.' . . . Fedya Nikitin is one of the higher bureaucrats engaged in preparing it for us; his job is to sift and check the elimination lists for the intelligentsia—artists, writers, men of letters, and so on. Needless to point out that if the French intellectuals working for his outfit had their way, nine out of ten of their colleagues and competitors would be shipped to the Arctic, including their dearest Party comrades. If you embark on this kind of thing there is no limit, and you run the risk that terror will degenerate into absurdity; the job of men of Nikitin's kind is to bureaucratise the terror, perfect the punching-card devices, keep an elaborate check on each other, and confine the absurd within reasonable limits. . . . What will you have with your coffee?"

The *patronne* had come out from behind the bar and waddled in her slippers to their table.

"What's wrong with my soufflé?" she asked Julien sulkily. "Your young lady has hardly touched it. Or is she not feeling well?" Her glance mechanically slid down to Hydie's stomach; when a young woman showed no appetite or looked as if she were going to be sick, her first suspicion was always that she was pregnant. Julien brushed her off with a joke and ordered two brandies.

After a long silence Hydie asked:

"How do you know?"

"About Nikitin? News gets around," he said vaguely. "Practically everybody in our circles knows about him. Among others, he was recognised by Boris. He has held similar jobs in other countries before."

"Do you mean," asked Hydie very quietly, "that Fedya had a hand in what happened to Boris' wife and baby?"

"Heavens, no—not directly. Nikitin had nothing to do with the landed gentry. The system is too vast and mechanised for such dramatic coincidences to happen. Haven't you noticed, my dear, in what undramatic times we live? Individual tragedies of the kind which made our grandparents weep, no longer occur. In tragedy there must be an æsthetic element. But there is nothing æsthetic about dysentery in labour camps, and nothing tragic about punching-card machines."

For a long time Hydie did not say anything. She lifted in an absent-minded way her glass of brandy, spilt some of it on the tablecloth, and put it down again without drinking. She looked at her watch, said in an aloof tone of voice: "I think I must go," then added in the same distracted, dreamy manner:

"But Boris is insane, so of course the whole story isn't true. How am I to know whether it's true?"

Julien blinked at her with a faint, compassionate smile.

"My dear, you know only too well. You have always known that it was one thing or another of this kind. Now drink your brandy, and don't look like that."

After another long pause, in which she went on playing absently with her glass, Hydie's lips began to quiver, and she asked:

"Is that why Boris always disliked me?"

"He knew that you had no part in Nikitin's doings, but of course . . ."

"And Vardi? And the people at Monsieur Anatole's?" Her voice began to rise to a higher pitch. "Everybody knew, didn't they? They looked at me and they knew and looked the other way. The girl who has body odour and nobody tells her." She spoke now in a loud, shrill voice, and people at other tables began to turn their heads. "Do I smell? Tell me, do I smell?"

"Now look," said Julien, "I've had enough with one lunatic this morning. Control yourself."

"And daddy knew too. That's why I haven't been asked to parties. Why did nobody tell me? Why didn't the family doctor tell me the facts about Body Odour and Personal Hygiene?"

"Because," Julien said, ignoring her hysterical manner, "because we live in a world which, though insane, is incorrigibly polite. Your father would of course rather shoot himself than interfere with your personal affairs. . . . Come, my dear, you need some fresh air."

"Wait. If that's what Fedya was doing, why don't the French police arrest him?"

Julien laughed out loud. "Arrest him on what legal grounds? Have you never heard of diplomatic immunity?"

Hydie briskly got up. "Nonsense," she said. The *patronne* eyed her anxiously. She signalled to Julien to get the girl out into the fresh air and pay the bill next time.

"All this is nonsense," Hydie repeated, walking so fast that it was difficult for Julien to limp in step with her. "You have either told me a pack of lies, or it is a matter for the police." She stopped a taxi, and was suddenly in such a hurry that she didn't offer a lift to Julien. He grabbed her hand, standing at the open door of the taxi.

"Where is the fire?" he said. "Are you running to the police? Don't make a fool of yourself," he repeated hurriedly.

"You insisted on telling me, didn't you?" she said in a harsh voice. "Did you expect me to keep it to myself and leave it at that?" She pulled the door closed with a bang and told the driver to hurry. The driver gave Julien a sympathetic wink and let the clutch in. It was obvious that he disapproved of Hydie picking a lovers' quarrel on New Year's Day, and particularly with a fellow with a limp.

While they were driving up the Champs-Elysées, Hydie made her face up for the second time within ten minutes, lit a cigarette and almost immediately threw it out of the window.

She felt compelled to keep her hands occupied and her body in some sort of action. She needed action, quickly, immediately, so that she should have no time to think. The thought of thinking itself was unbearable and made her head buzz with the kind of tantalising discomfort one feels when one has forgotten a name and tries in vain to recapture it. But she could not prevent herself from reviving last night's scene in Fedya's flat, and as his image in the new tie appeared before her mind's eye, she felt overcome by the same violent nausea which had sent her rushing to his bathroom. She moaned with physical misery, closing her eyes; when she opened them again she saw the driver watching her in the rear-view mirror. His quizzical expression reminded her of the look in the eyes of the *patronne* in the restaurant. Did everybody know about her? Was it really a kind of body odour? She dabbed a few drops of perfume behind her ears. She had had a new permanent wave the day before, and the smooth touch of her hair filled her with a new surge of disgust. Suddenly she thought of Boris standing immobile before the curtain, trying to dissolve in it. He too, knew, and he must loathe her more than all the others. For a few seconds she believed that the reason why Boris wanted to vanish was that he should not have to see her any more. She dug her painted nails into her palms, and forced herself to sit rigidly in her corner until at last the taxi stopped.

Her father was just finishing his coffee when she entered the dining-room. She had been so afraid that he would have gone out that she almost flung herself into his arms; only the feeling of her physical uncleanness held her back. During the last few weeks their relations had been strained. When she had come home late after an evening in Fedya's flat, she could not bring herself to call at his study to say goodnight; nor did the Colonel ever ask her "what she had been up to." But now she felt only an immense relief at his presence; and she was grateful because, though he must have seen at once in what state she was, he did not fuss, or greet her with worried exclamations. Only the French maid looked at her with impudent curiosity, just like the taxi driver and the *patronne* in the bistro. She remembered that the driver had not thanked her, though she had overtipped him.

"Could I talk to you in your study?" she asked the Colonel in a voice as steady as she could muster. While they remained in the dining-room they couldn't get rid of the maid. "Sure," said the Colonel. He picked up his coffee cup and, carrying it with him, preceded her to his study. While she blurted out her story, curled up in the farthest corner of the couch, he kept sipping his coffee without looking at her once.

"That's about all," Hydie concluded, lighting a cigarette with slightly shaking fingers. She had given him an abridged account of what Julien had told her, without omitting the fact of her affair with Fedya. "That's about all," she repeated. "As you see, I have behaved true to my mother's form. But that is no concern of yours. That part only comes in to complete the story. The reason I am telling you about this is to ask to whom I should talk at the Police. If I simply went to the nearest police post they would think I was mad."

The Colonel let a few seconds pass, then put the coffee cup down, dipped the ash from his cigar, and at last looked her straight in the face. His blue eyes were usually vague; Hydie could remember nearly every one of the few occasions on which their vagueness had disappeared. She lowered her eyes, fixing them on the tip of her shoes.

"I resent that remark about your mother," said the Colonel.

"I am sorry," said Hydie. "It's such a comfortable excuse for me, isn't it?" She was looking at her shoe, twisting her toes one way and the other, as if in pain.

"Right," said the Colonel. "As you said, your private life is no concern of mine. Even my superiors thought so when they refused to accept my resignation."

Hydie stared at him with such an expression of shock and terror that the effort to keep his voice and eyes steady became too much for the Colonel.

"You had to offer your resignation because of me?" she stammered, and at last she felt the relief of her eyes filling with tears.

"I guess that eventuality did not even occur to you," said the Colonel. "It is surely amazing how the business of searching one's conscience makes a person blind to other people's troubles." He paused, praying for his last remark not to sink in too deeply. "Now who put that crazy police idea into your head?" he asked in a dry voice.

She looked at him uncomprehendingly. "But surely it is a matter for the police?" Then a faint reflection of hope came into her eyes. "Or do you believe Delattre's story is just a lie?"

Again he let a few seconds pass, then he said:

"No, I don't believe that. As a matter of fact, the nature of Mr. Nikitin's activities is known to the services concerned, including the French. But that kind of thing has never been a matter for the police."

"But why?" Hydie cried with renewed exasperation. "Julien told me the same thing. I just don't understand it."

"I guess," the Colonel said wearily, "that it's always difficult to get proofs; then there is the question of diplomatic immunity, and the necessity to avoid scandals which might increase the international tension, and so on."

Hydie made a violent movement; she put her feet down and sat up straight on the couch. But she checked the sharp answer which was on her tongue, and said evenly:

"If it is a question of proofs, I can help. I have seen his notebook."

The Colonel looked at her coldly. "So what?" He had to make an effort to keep a note of contempt, almost of disgust, out of his voice.

"It was full of names—lists of names—with signs after them. It dropped out of his pocket at Monsieur Anatole's on Bastille Day when we first met him."

"And you picked up a stranger's notebook and read its contents?" he asked in undisguised horror.

"I gave it back to him the next day. But that isn't the point. I mean I *saw* that it contained lists of names."

"Look here," the Colonel said quietly. "Mostly when we talk there comes a moment when you explain that the things which matter most to me are 'not the point.' I guess we shall never see eye to eye on what the point of anything is. But for once I wish to make my point clear on the matter we are discussing. When you began to be seen going places with that guy Nikitin, it was intimated to me that I should warn you off. That I refused because I had no right to meddle in your life. Instead I offered to give up my job, as I have just told you. This I did in defence of your right to associate with the man of your choice, regardless of his country and politics. So long as I believed that you were in earnest about that guy, I had no right to reproach you with anything. But your present attitude frankly beats me. Yesterday you had a quarrel with your— lover; today you want to run to the police to denounce him because somebody told you something which you must have guessed all along. . . ."

"I guessed nothing. I knew nothing," cried Hydie. "I was blind, dumb, despicable, but not an accomplice. And if I don't do something now, I shall become an accomplice. Lord, can't any of you see that?"

"Well—no," the Colonel said coldly. "I can't see that. I can't see that it's your job to tell the French, who know the facts, how they should act on them."

"But they don't know. They can't know. They haven't seen a man going insane in a filthy hotel room, and they don't know that this is what will happen to them."

The Colonel squashed his cigar out and got up from the chair. "It's no good going on like this," he said wearily. "Maybe when you have calmed down we can talk again. But meanwhile . . ." He took a step or two towards her and laid his hand on her shoulder, but she withdrew from his touch with a frightened jerk. He looked at her helplessly. "Meanwhile," he repeated, more uncertainly, "maybe you will find out that sometimes an itch for a personal revenge can appear under the guise of some noble idea."

Hydie got to her feet. "That was about the meanest thing you have ever said to me," she said, suddenly calm.

"Well, you hate him, don't you?" the Colonel said, feeling that he was losing his grip.

"I hate him with all my heart, with my body and soul," she said slowly. "But I hate him because of what he does and believes and stands for. Just as I fell for him because—because he was sure of himself and had a belief, a certitude which none of you have. Because he is *real*, which none of you are. And now I know that he must be fought tooth and nail *because* he is real. But I guess you will never understand that. I guess," she repeated, taking a step toward him and fighting down an urge to let go and scream at him—"I guess you think I am just hysterical."

He looked at her helplessly, wanting to put his arm round her shoulder, but sensing at the same time that his touch might release some unpredictable reaction, let something loose which frightened him. "I guess you had better go to your room and lie down for a bit," he said quietly. But as she reached for the door, he stopped her. "And . . ." he said, controlling his voice; she turned her head with sudden hope and expectation. "Yes?" she asked.

"I only thought—maybe later on I could take you to a movie. . . ."

Her expression changed; he read the contempt and pity in her eyes, and turned slowly back to his desk, listening to her steps in the corridor as she regained her room. A few minutes later he heard the entrance door bang; she had gone out.

He poured himself a drink, and pulled out a leather-bound diary from the bottom of his desk. The last entry was dated more than three months before. He lit a cigar and wrote:

"January 1, 195–. . . . Bungled another chance to help H. To save somebody in danger of drowning you must know how to swim yourself. I am unable to make her out, but I can't help feeling that there is nothing much wrong about the girl except that she lives in these messy times, this age of longing. The bug of longing acts differently on different people, but we've all got it in our circulation. H. caught it when she ran away from the convent; so maybe when you get God out of your system something goes wrong with your metabolism which makes the bug more virulent. If that is the case, then this plague must have started in the eighteenth century, or even earlier, and now it is just working up towards its peak. And if it's allowed to take its natural course, the ravages will be worse than those of the Black Death . . ."

The Colonel re-lit his cigar, read what he had written, crossed it out, put the diary away, poured himself a thimbleful of brandy, and settled down to study a memorandum which outlined a British protest against the standardisation of the gauges of anti-aircraft batteries as detrimental to the economic interests of the sterling area.

8

A FLASH OF INSPIRATION

HYDIE lifted the glass to her lips with an affectedly calm gesture. Nobody was watching her except the fish in the neon-lit aquarium, and she felt perfectly calm in herself; nevertheless, she was compelled to demonstrate her sang-froid by the exaggeratedly rounded, measured gesture with which she sipped her Martini. The bar was nearly empty; Albert and Alphonse were taking advantage of the quiet hour to make up in whispered voices their monthly accounts. Tomorrow, having recognised her picture in the newspapers, they would tell their favourite clients with a pleasant and discreet little smile that *she* and *he* had been frequent guests at the bar, and that as a matter of fact, *she* had spent the last hour before the deed alone at the corner table next to the aquarium, sipping two dry Martinis, and looking "perfectly composed."

Hydie took her mirror out of the bag and, under the pretext of powdering her nose, studied her face in it. It looked no paler than usual; the faint dark shadows under the eyes were not sinister, merely piquant; the frightened flicker in the brown eyes only perceptible to herself; to anybody else her expression must indeed look "perfectly composed." This new mania of having to think of herself in phrases between inverted commas got on her nerves, but she could not help it. Since she had come to the decision that she must kill Feyda, she lived as if surrounded by mirrors. Though she felt calm, she must act her calmness; though she was amused when her father took her last night to a comic film, she had to act her amusement; though she enjoyed supper at Larue's with him afterwards, she had to act her enjoyment. And all the time phrases in inverted commas moved at the back of her mind: "the last supper"; "perfectly composed"; "nobody would have thought it." As she slipped the mirror back into her bag and heard its faint clink against the small revolver, she automatically had to think of "cold steel" and laughed out half-aloud—but audibly enough for Albert or Alphonse to look up with a pleasant questioning smile.

She looked back at him blankly, but her elation was gone and she felt a chill of fright. She took another sip at her Martini and the fright slowly ebbed away. She knew that it had been caused by the completely unfounded apprehension that people might read her thoughts and prevent her from carrying out the act. This was the only fear which had haunted her since her decision was made, and the reason why she felt that she had to act "being calm," though she had never felt inwardly more calm in all her life.

Since the solution had been revealed to her in a single, blinding flash, the world had become miraculously changed. Before, she had lived in a glass cage whose transparency had only enhanced her feeling of loneliness. Now the glass walls had changed into mirrors, and she was at last alone with herself. The people around her, even her father, had lost their reality, had no more substance than the anonymous chorus on the stage of a Greek tragedy. At moments their presence made her nervous because she felt herself reflected in their watchful mirror-eyes, and was forced to see herself as they saw her, and to think of herself between inverted commas. But these moments were transitory and of limited duration. Each time she shook herself free of the unreasonable fear of premature detection and failure, she sank as if by her own gravity into a blissful state of calm such as she had not known since her early days at the convent—until some trivial occurrence, like the barman's questioning glance a moment ago, ruffled the surface of her inner stillness and dragged her back into doubt and anxiety. Thus, for the last three days, Hydie had been living on two alternating planes: in the world of mirrors and inverted commas, and in that other world which was nameless, shapeless, and filled with a radiant stillness of flesh and mind.

She glanced at her watch: another half-hour to wait until seven, when Fedya got back from his office and she was sure to find him at home. She carefully sipped up the remaining drops in her glass and ordered her second and last Martini. She had decided long beforehand that she would have two, and no more, while "waiting for zero hour"; but it hadn't occurred to her before that in all likelihood she would never, for the rest of her life, taste a Martini again. She felt a dangerous pang of self-pity; and as Albert or Alphonse brought the slim stem-glass on a tray, with the floating single olive, the thin, cold walls of the glass faintly clouded, she saw the words "the last Martini" as if printed before her mind's eye.

She smiled at the white-coated, pleasant barman, and he smiled back at her, then returned with discreet, rubber-soled steps to his accounts, leaving her alone in her corner next to the aquarium with its fluorescent, gaping, goggling fish. Now she would never know whether it was Albert or Alphonse who had served her last Martini, and another of life's minor mysteries would remain unsolved—like the secret of that man or boy Marcel who kept forgetting his bicycle under Julien's window. Her eyes met across the glass wall of the aquarium the round, unblinking, Buddha-like stare of a fish with a beautifully iridescent body and long transparent fins like floating veils, and all the self-pity was gently drained from her: she was back in that other world of perfect, radiant stillness. She wondered, with a detached curiosity, whether these relapses into the mirror-world of vanity would still continue after she had killed Fedya and had irrevocably committed herself to the other reality. For no obvious reason she suddenly remembered Sister Boutillot, the rotund little French nun in the convent, and she knew that her question had been answered long before. On a certain autumn day they had been standing together near the pond at the end of the alley, and Sister Boutillot had said with her odd little smile: "You are in peace, you are perhaps in a state of grace, but this sentiment is liquid: now it fills you, now it turns out of you, through a puncture made by a little irritation, a tiny vanity, sharp like a needle. And voilà, the peace is finished, the grace is finished, the sentiment runs out glub-blubb, and back you are where you were, high and dry in the trivial existence. . . ."

They had often come back in their talks to this mysterious duality of experience—not the duality between flesh and the spirit, but the more vexing and incurable duality between the tragic and the trivial planes of existence. . . . "The passions, little one, the great purple temptations—bah! one knows how to treat them: there are reliable mé-thodes," explained Sister Boutillot. "But the little irritations, the little lacerations, the routine, the hum-drum, the imbecility of the good common sense—voilà l'ennemi! The devil can be vanquished, but what can you do against an incubus disguised as a provincial notary, perched in your heart, and ticking off its beats on an abacus as if it were a rosary? Ah, little one, you will find out that the real duel in you is between the tragic and the trivial life. When you are caught in the trivial life, you are blind and deaf to the Mystery; but then the tragic life can only be taken in tea-spoonfuls, except by saints. And even saints must continue the duel and must cry out again and again 'touché!' . . ."

She smiled mischievously at the desolate look in Hydie's eyes.

"Yes, even the saints find often that the rosary in their fingers has turned into an abacus. Thérèse of Lisieux was a very gentle little saint who never complained about the cold and the privations which killed her when she was only twenty-four; but she was almost driven to distraction by the rustling of the starched habit of a very venerable old nun whose place was always next to hers in the chapel. The devil is cleverer than you think, little one: he has littered the world with rustling sleeves, dripping taps, and little warts with three hairs on prelates' noses. The life on the trivial plane moves entirely between these furnishings; marriage and politics and the rest are merely enlargements of the wart on the prelate's nose. . . ."

Hydie smiled, remembering that Sister Boutillot herself had a tiny wart with exactly three hairs sticking out of it—though not on her nose, but on one side of her pretty, dimpled chin.

Yet, across the distance of all those years, the little nun had answered the problem which filled Hydie with so much apprehension: these disturbing relapses into the trivial world of barmen, mirrors and "last Martinis," during which her decision appeared suddenly questionable and fantastic. Now, having remembered that talk at the pond, she understood that she must accept these moments of defection, both before and after the act, as necessary and inevitable. Without them, it would almost be too easy. From the frog-perspective of the trivial plane, all decisions conceived on the other must appear as the crazy and absurd product of overstrung nerves. The flashes of tragic insight which had inspired saints and revolutionaries, from Brutus to Charlotte Corday, had always been acts of defiance to habit and common sense; and in between their rare appearances even the saints had to live in the dim twilight. Nobody could exist permanently in the rarefied atmosphere of a truth which defied common sense. The moments of truth, like those of ecstasy, were like short-circuits which made all fuses burn through. Afterwards, the darkness was only more intense—as it was just now. For at the moment, Hydie had practically forgotten the reasons why she was going to kill Fedya.

And yet, as she found glancing at her watch, there was only a quarter of an hour left. Fortunately, the reasons were all written down, briefly but neatly, in the letter to the Police which she carried in her bag. It contained a concise summary of Fedya Nikitin's mission: the selection of French citizens from the world of art and letters who were to be eliminated after the occupation. Then followed a laconic report on Hydie's efforts to draw the attention of the authorities to Nikitin's activities, and her complete failure to do so. Finally, the reasons which had decided her, in view of this official passivity and acceptance of defeat, to rouse the public from its apathy by a symbolic act of protest. French history abounded in examples of such symbolic acts, and of the healthy, inspiring effect which some of them had produced on the people's imagination. . . .

This mental recapitulation of the contents of her letter restored Hydie's calm. There was still about a half of the last Martini left in her glass. As she sipped at it carefully, she thought of her interview with the high-ranking official at the Ministry of the Interior which had convinced her that as matters stood, the only reasonable attitude was to defy the laws of common sense and reason—and the only escape from becoming a passive accomplice of the Nikitins, to kill and thereby immolate her father and herself.

Jules Commanche was a hero of the Resistance and held a key position in the French Home Security Department. Hydie had first met him shortly after her arrival in Paris at a reception of the Embassy, and had been impressed by his unconventional personality. He was a very tall, vivacious, sloppily dressed man still in his thirties, with the nervous eloquence of a young don not yet broken into academic routine. He had actually been a lecturer in archæology at one of the provincial universities, and had just published a much-discussed paper on "Artificial elongation of the skull during the reign of Pharaoh Akhnaton" when the second world war broke out. He fought with distinction, ran under the German occupation a secret radio transmitter for Allied intelligence; was arrested, tortured, sentenced to a long prison term, and after the liberation of France appointed Commissar of the Republic in an important provincial town. During the subsequent years of social strife and unrest he had shown himself capable of handling delicate situations with both tact and firmness; had been given a préfecture, then an under-secretaryship, and had finally been promoted, about a year ago, to his present post at the Home Security Department. In short, Commanche belonged to that new type of French official who had come out of the Resistance movement and who, because they felt their responsibility towards the State engaged or their ambitions kindled, could no longer turn back to their former occupations. Had there been more of them, they might have filled the sclerotic veins of the French bureaucracy with fresh blood; but their numbers were few, and their effect merely amounted to the injection of a stimulant into a moribund body.

When Hydie rang up the Ministry of the Interior, she had little hope that Commanche would remember her. To her surprise he did, and agreed to see her in his office the next day. Against the sacred traditions of French Ministries, he did not keep her waiting. His office was a large room with green padded double doors; its walls were hung with the hideous Gobelin tapestries of the Second Empire, along which stood busts in bronze, and spindle-leg tables with marble tops. Commanche rose briskly behind his forbidding desk, and shook hands with her in a manner which was both cordial and matter-of-fact. There were two deep leather arm chairs near the desk, but he pulled up another, armless one. "You look as if you preferred straight-back chairs," he said with a quick smile. "Don't look at the furniture, it isn't my responsibility. And now, what can I do for you?"

The directness of his manner reassured her, and she found it easy to talk to him. She told him in the simplest words about her liaison with Fedya, the story of the notebook, and the nature of Fedya's activities. She added that she had discussed the matter with her father, the Colonel; and as he did not seem to think it was any concern of his, she felt it her duty to report the facts direct to the French authorities.

While she spoke, Commanche's light-grey eyes had at first been fastened on hers, then had swiftly appraised her arms, legs, fur coat and remaining apparel; had finally returned to her face and rested there, first with attention, then with a half-amused, half-irritated smile. "Is that all?" he asked when she had finished.

Hydie nodded. She had not expected any dramatic reaction to her disclosures, but was nevertheless taken aback by his tone of voice.

"And what do you expect us to do about it?" Commanche said, almost rudely.

Hydie stared at him. "That's your affair," she said. "But surely you won't let him go on with this . . . with this appalling crime. . . ."

"Crime? To my knowledge Monsieur Nikitin has committed no crime against either French or international law."

"But I told you . . . I think you haven't understood. . . ." Hydie felt a growing helplessness, like being paralysed in a dream.

"I believe I understood you perfectly. You saw some jottings in somebody's notebook, which you assumed to be a list of names. Somebody else told you that he assumed these lists to have a certain purpose. You have no evidence that these series of assumptions are correct. And even if they happen to be correct, the drawing up of lists in a notebook for whatever purpose does not constitute a crime."

Hydie felt a fantastic suspicion arise in her. But was it so fantastic, and had the events of the last years not shown that the Nikitins had planted their agents everywhere? She had never quite been able to believe in these lurid disclosures, but now she was prepared to believe almost anything. In a surge of irrational panic, she glanced at the padded door with its silent green baize. Commanche watched her, and his amused smile became more pronounced. The faded Gobelins, with their hunting scenes of stags and wild boars being torn to pieces by ferociously leaping hounds suspended in mid-air, made the silence even more oppressive. At last Commanche seemed to take pity on her.

"No, Mademoiselle," he said, "it is not difficult to guess what you think, but I can assure you that I'm not a confederate of Monsieur Nikitin's—though there are no doubt a number of them in this building. If you had hit on one of them, it might have led to unpleasant complications for you. I therefore suggest that the sooner you forget about your—romantic adventure and the less you talk about it, the better for all concerned."

His rudeness helped Hydie over her momentary panic; humiliated and furious, she could almost feel herself bristle like the hunted stag on the tapestry.

"What exactly are you trying to hint at?" she asked, glowering at him.

A slight exasperation came into Commanche's face.

"But, Mademoiselle, you are not a child. Can't you see what will happen if Monsieur Nikitin's friends hear that you are going around telling stories about his notebook and so on? . . . Oh, I know you are not frightened"—he raised his hand to silence an interruption—"and I am not hinting at anything dramatic. But what would you say if one of our evening papers published a full-sized photograph of you under the headline 'A Piquant Scandal in the Diplomatic World—American Officer's Daughter Jilted by Commonwealth Attaché,' and so on?"

Commanche spoke in a quick, angry voice, but when he saw Hydie pale, his eyes let go of hers and fastened at a point on the crown of her head.

"I don't care," she said stubbornly.

"The point is not whether you care—though you do of course—but whether anything would be gained by a scandal. Do you think that after a scandal of this kind you would find anybody to believe in your accusations? People would naturally assume that you were trying to take your revenge on your former lover; they would talk of the hysterical imaginings of a jealous woman, and Monsieur Nikitin's friends would laugh their heads off."

Unconsciously Hydie had pulled her handkerchief from the

bag and was plucking it to pieces. Commanche watched her, waiting for her reactions. At last Hydie said:

"But all this is beside the point. You warn me not to talk about this matter to all and sundry. I didn't go to all and sundry—I came direct to you."

Commanche nodded quickly, as if he had waited for this answer and agreed with it.

"I appreciate that, Mademoiselle." His face had become a shade more amenable. "You haven't talked to anybody else?"

"Only to my father and to Julien Delattre, who explained to me about the lists."

"Delattre is a crank, but he is all right. We were *normaliens* at the same school. . . ." It was the first personal remark he had made during the conversation. Hydie quickly seized the point:

"Then you know that what he said about Nikitin is true. Why do you talk of 'assumptions' and pretend not to believe in them?"

Commanche looked amused again. "You are a very stubborn young lady. But whether I believe you or not is without interest. I told you before that all this is not evidence, and that even if it were evidence, legally there would be no crime. Not to mention such trifling considerations as diplomatic immunity, the international situation, and so on. . . . Really, Mademoiselle, I appreciate your gesture and—the way you must feel, but I can only repeat that the quicker you forget about the whole thing the better for all concerned."

He was obviously too polite to tell her that the interview was closed, but the tone of his voice and a slight tensing of his body as if preparing to get up, made his intention clear. Hydie had to force herself to remain seated. Her back rigid against the hard chair, she said in a dry voice:

"How can you, a Frenchman, say that it is not a crime when a man walks around marking down your compatriots with a pencil—like branding cattle for the slaughter-house? Don't you see—don't you *see* what is waiting for you?"

Commanche, who had half risen, let himself slump back into the chair. He no longer tried to conceal his exasperation.

"Are you really so naïve, Mademoiselle, as to imagine that we know less about these things than you do? Do you think we were unaware of Monsieur Nikitin's activities, or of your affair with him, if it comes to that? And as for your somewhat patronising remark about what is 'waiting for us'—myself, my family, my friends, in short, the French people—allow me to refuse to discuss it, in order to avoid embarrassing you."

"Me? I don't understand. . . ."

"You don't? Well, we both know what is waiting for *you*. A comfortable airliner when things get hot—and some nostalgic regrets for the sunny cafés on the Champs-Elysées. . . ."

He paused, noted with satisfaction that Hydie was squirming in her chair, and added with a kind of savage suaveness: "But as you will have such a thrilling last-minute escape, perhaps one of your fashion magazines will be asking you for a feelingly written article about the last days of France. . . ."

It was at that precise moment that Hydie had her flash of illumination. A moment ago, she had been squirming under the cold contempt of Commanche's words, and asking herself numbly why everybody was always so cruel to her. Then came the flash, the sudden understanding that Commanche was right, and that it was up to her to do what had to be done. As always in the case of an apparently insoluble problem, the solution, once found, appeared so self-evident that she could no longer understand why it had not occurred to her before. The pain and her humiliation ceased, as a wound suddenly ceases to hurt under the effect of a shot of morphia. Later on she remembered having read that people under torture sometimes had a similar experience, a sudden smiling insensibility and indifference to what happened to them. She knew that Commanche was in the right, but he could no longer hurt her. She rose, and saw her own figure dimly reflected in the window behind the official's desk. But the figure of the woman in the smooth fur coat appeared to her like the reflection of a stranger; and the strangest thing about it was that the pale, narrow face under the dark hair seemed actually to smile. This self-estrangement lasted only a few seconds, but Commanche noticed it and gave her a puzzled look.

"You are quite right," she said calmly. "I didn't understand at first, but now I do."

Her tone had so much changed that Commanche looked even more puzzled. She shut her bag and saw the bits of her torn handkerchief on her coat. She picked them up carefully, smiling without embarrassment. "How silly," she said, putting the bits into her bag. "It's just a nervous habit."

Commanche, who had come round the desk to shake hands and get rid of her, changed his mind. "I was very rude to you, Mademoiselle, but frankly . . ." he began.

"You were perfectly right," she interrupted him. "It was silly of me to bother you. I only thought . . ." She hesitated; what she had thought five minutes ago was now a matter of the remote past, and of purely academic interest. But she felt that for some reason she owed Commanche an explanation.

"I did not mean that if you arrested or expelled Nikitin it would make any difference in itself. I only thought that if the facts were made public, it would open people's eyes. It seemed to me that everybody was asleep. . . . Because it is all so fantastic, so hard to believe—as if a comet were approaching with its tail full of poison gas—I thought if people were to read it in black and white maybe it would shake them up. But I understand now that you can't do anything. . . ."

They were both standing; Commanche, who was two or three inches taller than Hydie, looked down at her with his half-tired, half-amused smile. His temper had gone as suddenly as it had risen; with one of his abrupt movements he reached behind him, swept some papers aside, and sat down on his desk.

"You say the people are asleep. Do you really believe that?" he asked.

It was now Hydie who wished that he would let her go. She wanted to be alone and think out the practical steps. Discussions in the abstract had lost all interest for her; she had heard enough clever talk from Julien, from Vardi, from all the clever people who all had their theories and philosophies and did nothing. But she respected Commanche because he had been imprisoned and tortured, and even more because he had remained, in spite of his important position, frank and unconventional.

"I don't really know," she said. "Sometimes I think everybody is asleep, or paralysed, and I alone am awake and see the comet approaching—but nobody will believe me. . . ."

Commanche made an impatient gesture. "I suppose you were brought up very strictly," he said. "You look like a Catholic. I remember somebody telling me you were brought up in a convent. Is that correct?"

Hydie, who didn't know what he was driving at, nodded in confirmation, impatient to go. But Commanche, after his outburst, seemed to be in a mood of nervous talkativeness.

"Do you think you were asleep in your convent?" he asked abruptly. "With your—intense sensitivity I am sure you were wide awake. But you closed your eyes and banished from your consciousness the most potent factor in an adolescent's life—sexuality. You managed to repress your awareness, and to pretend to be sleeping the sleep of the innocent. That is exactly what the people of the Occident do. They repress their awareness of the approaching comet. It has not been sufficiently realised that the political instinct-life of people goes as deep, and is subject to the same psychological laws, as their sexual libido. Like all vital instincts, it is irrational and impervious to reasoned argument. The political psyche of man has its primitive, savage id, and its lofty super-ego; its mechanisms for the repression of facts, its inner censor which prevents, more effectively than a State censorship, any unpalatable information from reaching the political neurotic's consciousness. . . ."

Though she had been impatient to go, Hydie found that she had sat down again on the arms of her chair. "But what is the practical conclusion?" she asked, trying to concentrate her thoughts.

"Mostly negative," said Commanche, who was evidently talking more to himself than to Hydie. It occurred to Hydie that this was always happening to her—whatever her sins and faults, she was a good listener. With an inward smile she imagined herself in the dock listening with an intelligent, attentive expression to the State Attorney asking for the death sentence against her. It was then that she saw herself for the first time in a situation between inverted commas.

"The negative conclusion is," continued Commanche, "that you cannot cure aberrations of the political libido by arguments. That, Mademoiselle, is why the so-called moderate Left with its purely rational appeal has failed. Before we can ever dream of a real cure, we must find out what it is that has gone wrong with the political libido of Europe. But for such leisurely, academic pursuits it is, alas, too late. . . ."

"Then what is the use of talking?" said Hydie.

"As you know, we French have an incurable passion for analysis," said Commanche with a look which made Hydie feel that in some subtle way he was still making fun of her; but she didn't care. "We just talk and talk, and in between we are invaded once in a generation or so and lose the best talkers in every family, and then we go on talking. For, unlike in your country, where one type does the talking, the other the fighting, with us it is the brilliant talkers who usually do the fighting and dying. We don't go in for your strong, dumb,

silent heroes. We are an incurably articulate nation. Our pro-
totype of a hero is Cyrano de Bergerac, who makes his thrusts
at the end of each strophe of a verbose poem. . . . But to
come back to our political libido. When does an instinct get
diverted into the wrong channels? When it is thwarted at its
source, or frustrated in its object. Now the source of all political libido is faith, and its object is the New Jerusalem, the
Kingdom of Heaven, the Lost Paradise, Utopia, what have
you. Therefore each time a god dies there is trouble in History. People feel that they have been cheated by his promises,
left with a dud cheque in their pocket; and they will run after
every charlatan who promises to cash it. The last time a god
died was on July 14, 1789, the day when the Bastille was
stormed. On that day the Holy Trinity was replaced by the
three-word slogan which you find written over our town
halls and post offices. Europe has not yet recovered from that
operation, and all our troubles today are secondary complications, a kind of septic wound-fever. The People—and when I
use that word, Mademoiselle, I always refer to people who
have no bank accounts—the People have been deprived of
their only asset: the knowledge, or the illusion, whichever you
like, of having an immortal soul. Their faith is dead, their
kingdom is dead, only the longing remains. And this longing,
Mademoiselle, can express itself in beautiful or murderous
forms, just like the frustrated sex instinct. For, believe me,
Mademoiselle, it is very painful to forsake copulation when
the mating season is on. And because it is so painful, the whole
complex is repressed. Only the longing remains—a dumb, inarticulate longing of the instinct, without knowledge of its
source and object. So the people, the masses, mill around with
that irksome feeling of having an uncashed cheque in their
pockets and whoever tells them 'Oyez, oyez, the Kingdom
is just round the corner, in the second street to the left,' can
do with them what he likes. The more they feel that itch, the
easier it is to get them. If you tell them that their kingdom
stinks of corpses, they will answer you that it has always been
their favourite scent. No argument or treatment can cure
them, until the dead god is replaced by a new, more up-to-date
one. Have you got one up your sleeve?"

"You said Delattre was a crank, but he says more or less
the same thing as you," said Hydie.

"Naturally," said Commanche. "We are of the same generation, and we both belong to the type of talkative men of ac-

tion. There are many more of our type—all brilliant, cynical, garrulous Latin talkers; but you shouldn't let yourself be taken in by appearances, Mademoiselle. When the comet appears, all our Cyranos will know how to die—not like your dumb heroes, but to die with a flourish. The world has never seen such a hecatomb of elegant deaths as France will produce when she finally vanishes from the stage. . . ."

He stopped; Hydie was embarrassed. However often he repeated that talkativeness and bravery might well go together in a Latin climate, she was nevertheless embarrassed by this verbal exhibitionism. Commanche's outburst was the more strange as he hardly knew her. Then it occurred to her that perhaps he too was going through some sort of crisis. Maybe the news was very bad again—she had not looked at the papers for days. The more reason for her to hurry if her act was to have any effect at all.

"Yes, Mademoiselle," Commanche went on, "when you and your compatriots—who are now so busy telling us what we ought to do—get into your airliners, Delattre and St. Hilaire and the rest of us will know how to make our own exits— with a flourish as I said, in the fastidious manner which goes so well with our national character. But if you ask me why I insist so much on the flourish, I will tell you in confidence that it will merely serve to cover our bewilderment. For you can only die simply and quietly if you know what you are dying for. And that is precisely what none of us knows. Ah, if instead of canned peaches and anti-tank guns you could ship to us some sort of new revelation. . . . Of course you will say that we should be able to produce at least that commodity ourselves. But the rub is, we can't. We are bled out, physically and spiritually. Our last message to the world was those three words which are on our stamps and coins. Since then, we no longer have anything to give to the spirit, only to the senses— our novelists, our poets, our painters, all belong to an essentially sensualist world, the world of Flaubert and Baudelaire and Manet, not to the world of Descartes, Rousseau and St. Just. For several centuries we were the inspiration of Europe; now we are in the position of a blood donor dying of anæmia. We can't hope for a new Jeanne d'Arc, not even for a young First Consul, not even for a Charlotte Corday. . . ."

His glance again circumnavigated her figure, appraising each detail with a swift, amused look. ". . . Now, if you were French, Mademoiselle, and if you lived two centuries earlier, and had been brought up in a provincial town on the works of Plutarch and Voltaire, you would make quite a convincing Charlotte Corday. . . ."

It was this remark of Commanche's which made Hydie feel for the first time that everybody could read her project in her eyes, and that she was surrounded by mirrors. She said with a forced smile:

"I would think it in very bad taste to kill a man in his bath tub with a kitchen knife."

The telephone which had been buzzing intermittently without Commanche paying any attention to it, started again. Commanche pressed a button, said "Yes, in two minutes," pressed the button again, and said in a changed tone:

"No, Mademoiselle, don't be misled by appearances. France, and what else is left of Europe, may look like a huge dormitory to you, but I assure you nobody in it is really asleep. Have you ever spent a night in a mental ward? During the Occupation, a doctor who belonged to our group got me into one when the police were after me. It was a ward of more or less hopeless cases, most of whom were marked down for drastic neurosurgical operations. The first night, when the male nurse made his round, I thought everybody was asleep. Later I found out that they were only pretending, and that everybody was busy, behind closed eyes, trying to cope after his own fashion with what was coming to him. Some were pursuing their delusions with a happy smile, like our famous Pontieux. Others were working on their pathetic plans of escape, naïvely hoping that with a little dissimulation, or bribery, or self-abasement, they could get around the tough male nurses, the locked doors, the operating table. Others were busy explaining to themselves that it won't hurt, and that to have holes drilled into one's skull and parts of one's brain taken out was the nicest thing that could happen to one. And still others, the quiet schizos who were the majority, almost succeeded in making themselves believe that nothing would happen, that it was all a matter of exaggerated rumours, and that tomorrow would be like yesterday. These looked as if they were really asleep. Only an occasional nervous twitch of their lips or eyes betrayed the strain of disbelieving what they knew to be inevitable. . . . No, Mademoiselle, nobody was really asleep. Remember that when you get home after your thrilling escape and write that feeling obituary for those of us left behind in the condemned ward. . . . Meanwhile, will you dine with me tomorrow?"

The unexpected conclusion sounded so abrupt and incongruous that Hydie was left speechless. The telephone buzzed again and Commanche said: "Yes, presently."

"Well, how about it . . . ?" he said with a swift smile. Hydie felt herself blush.

"Why do you want that?" she asked.

Commanche laughed. "We can analyse the reasons tomorrow—say at eight o'clock at Larue's."

Was that what he had been leading up to? Had he been making fun of her with all that melodramatic talk about the tragedy of his country—merely to make a pass at her? It made her shiver. Slowly she shook her head.

"No," she said. "Goodbye."

Commanche shrugged, without being in the least perturbed. He took her politely to the door, and as he opened its heavy padded wings, two ushers jumped to hold it open for her. "Thank you for your visit," said Commanche in the open door, shaking hands a shade more formally, but always with the same amused smile. "Au revoir, Mademoiselle."

Now, in retrospect, Hydie knew that she had been unjust to Commanche. His past record was an undeniable fact, and it was impossible for her to believe that he had not meant sincerely what he had said. If at the same time he had wanted to go to bed with her, that did not invalidate his sincerity. And yet she found it repellant that a man could talk about "dying with a flourish" to impress a girl—even if he really was going to die with a flourish. Of course he had an answer to that too —his Latin contempt for the "dumb, silent hero." But Hydie was not Latin, and though she knew that this was unjust, she still felt that Commanche's outburst of despair and the invitation to Larue's did not go together. It was all very confusing— but fortunately no longer of any real interest to her. And yet her talk with Commanche had been decisive, because it had shown her, with almost mathematical precision, that she must act herself, and that this was the only possible and honest thing to do.

She knew that she was no Charlotte Corday; she did not, like that exalted girl from the French provinces, expect a happy aftermath, "walking with Brutus in the Elysian fields." If she had to compare herself with anybody, she would rather think of that neurotic Jewish student between the two wars who had killed a German diplomat as a purely symbolic gesture, to attract the attention of the world to the plight of his kin. There had actually been two of those little students, both quiet, bookish creatures, and each of them had one day, probably acting under the same kind of simple inspiration as Hydie herself, gone out of his digs, bought a gun, and with trembling hands killed a man he had never seen before. And then there had been that Russian girl, not an exalted French provincial patriot but a rather mousy creature, a member of the Social Revolutionary Party, who had fired her gun at Lenin; and all those other learned, tea-drinking Russians, and the meek, bookish Jews, and the devout Moslems and mystical Hindus, and the verbose Frenchmen of the Resistance—they all had, at one time or another, discovered the value of the symbolic gesture, the ritual sacrifice, the ultima ratio of terror against terror where all other means had proved hopeless and sterile. Of course her act might also prove sterile, its results were unpredictable; but then who had ever known what interest a sacrifice will pay? When she came to think of it, her deed already appeared to her modelled on so many examples, and dictated by such elementary common sense, that there was really no reason to get excited about it.

The clock over the bar showed exactly seven. Hydie signalled to the barman for the check, trying to lift her finger as unobtrusively as Fedya used to do. To her surprise it worked. It was perhaps the first time in her life that she felt so sure of herself.

Her only regret was that her glass was empty. She had drunk the rest of her carefully hoarded Martini during her reverie, without paying attention to it. She felt a last pang of self-pity—she would have so much liked to sip the final drop with full awareness of the moment, and let its flavour linger on her tongue.

9

JUDITH AND HOLOFERNES

BECAUSE she wanted to be immune against surprises and unforeseen circumstances which might throw her off her balance, Hydie had mentally rehearsed a number of times her journey

to Fedya's flat, and what exactly she would say and do when
she arrived there. She had imagined what it would feel like to
be in the taxi and follow the familiar streets in dry, cold
weather, or through rain and slush; what she would do if the
taxi burst a tyre or bumped another car's mudguard, as so
often happened in Paris. She knew how often an elaborate
plan came to nought because of some such trivial accident.
For instance, if they bumped into another taxi, a policeman
might ask her for her papers and see the gun as she opened
her bag. Or the concierge in the block of flats where Fedya
lived might have been told by Fedya not to admit her. In this
case she would laugh, pretend that it was a practical joke on
Fedya's part, and bribe the woman to make her act as if she
believed it or as if she had not seen Hydie come in. But the
bribe must be neither too high nor too low, and she must not
fumble for money; so Hydie had laid aside a new thousand-
franc note for this eventuality in a separate pocket of her bag.

It was also just possible that Fedya was detained in his office and had not yet got back to the flat; in this case she would
wait in the little café on the opposite end of the street. Or somebody might be with him; then she would ask to talk to him
for a minute on the landing, and get it over there. It was all so
very simple that she wondered why lots of people did not keep
shooting lots of others all the time. If one thought of it, everybody was at everybody's mercy. This idea puzzled her for a
moment, while her taxi turned in the stream of traffic round
the Concorde, and into the Champs Elysées. Then it occurred
to her that she was in an exceptional position because she did
not have to bother to avoid being found out; to commit an
anonymous crime would of course be much more difficult.
After that, she felt a pang of guilt because once again she was
in a privileged position compared to the poor devils who had
to kill on the sly. When she discovered the absurdity of this
notion she gave a little nervous giggle and glanced frightenedly
into the driver's rear-view mirror; but he had not noticed anything.

Still, when they pulled up in front of the apartment house,
she had another slight attack of guilt because it was made so
easy for her—had she been planning a normal assassination as
other people did, she would have had to stop the taxi a few
blocks farther down and wear a veil or something over her
face. The little street was deserted; the weather was neither dry
and cold, nor rainy and sleety as foreseen in her programme:

there was a soft wind, mixing the dust which it stirred up with a few warm, heavy drops of rain. Why did one always imagine that there were only two alternatives, that things could only happen either this way or that way—that there would be a war or there wouldn't be one, that Europe would perish or be saved—and why did events almost invariably follow a third course? This again puzzled her, because she vaguely felt that it had a direct bearing on the act she was going to commit; so she fumbled with the money in her purse although she knew that she wasn't supposed to fumble. At last she found a few crumpled hundred-franc notes and pressed them without counting into the taxi driver's hand. The driver gave her the same curious look as all drivers and barmen had been giving her lately, although she knew that she felt and acted "perfectly composed." Anyway, it would now soon be over—the sooner the better. She hesitated for a second whether it would be wiser to walk once up and down the street and regain her breath; then she remembered that as she had come in a taxi there was no need for it. She pressed the buzzer of the glass-and-wrought-iron gate, the design of which she had always hated. The door clicked open; she was in a hurry now.

The concierge's office was to the right of the entrance passage. Hydie knew that she had to do something about that, but couldn't quite remember what; then she saw that she had forgotten to shut her bag after paying the driver. As she snapped it closed, she remembered the new thousand-franc note. She looked questioningly through the window of the office and saw Madame Bouchon, the concierge, sitting at her table peeling potatoes, with that horrible tomcat of hers on her lap. She too gave Hydie a curious glance, and looked as if she meant to say something to her, but apparently thought better of it, and with the ghost of a shrug went back to her potato-peeling.

As Hydie walked to the lift, clutching her bag, she wondered what the concierge had wanted to say. The lift-car had been left suspended on the fourth floor, which was Fedya's. Hydie pushed the button, but as the lift started its descent she changed her mind and began walking up the staircase. Once, when she had been late, Fedya had said that he had been listening for the whining sound of the lift for half an hour, each time hoping that she would be in it. It was one of the nicest things Fedya had ever said to her. To ride up now in the lift to his flat, announced by its familiar whine, was something she could not face; it would be as if she came under false pretences, under some treacherous disguise.

Though she was in a hurry now, she forced herself to walk slowly. This was the more indicated because her feet felt as if she were carrying lead in her shoes, and there was also a feeling in her spine as if some force were trying to drag her back. As she reached the first floor, she heard a door being shut on one of the upper floors and her instinct, or something familiar about the sound, told her that it was Fedya's door; then there were steps descending the staircase. At first she thought they might be Fedya's and her whole body went limp, because she had not rehearsed meeting him on the stairs and would not know what to do. But it was only a momentary panic, for as she stood half-slumped against the banister she realised with a great surge of relief that the steps were not Fedya's, only some woman's; the leisurely clop-clop of high-heeled shoes was unmistakable on the quiet staircase. Her body slowly regained its force because now she knew that everything would be all right; as she resumed her ascent of the staircase she scolded herself for being so silly and panicky. She reached the second floor, and the steady clop-clop above her came closer: then, turning round the next higher landing, a girl came into view and continued her leisurely descent toward Hydie. It was a slim girl in a fur coat; she had a dreamy, sullen look on her face, and she let her hand trail absent-mindedly along the banister. Hydie knew that she must have met her at some party, but could not recall her name. It had probably been at Monsieur Anatole's. When their eyes met, the girl gave her a slightly startled look; she seemed to wake up from a daze.

"Oh," she said. "Bon jour. . . . He's in." And, with a slight lift of her chin she indicated Fedya's door upstairs.

She stood about half-way up the flight of stairs, her hand limply resting on the banister, her index finger absent-mindedly drawing figures on its dusty surface. Hydie had come to a halt a few steps lower down. She was telling herself feverishly that the encounter did not matter and that she didn't care in the least whether she was seen or not; but this was an incident she hadn't rehearsed, so it was only natural that she didn't immediately know how to react. She stood undecidedly on the steps, clutching her bag, and she knew that it was essential to say something to prove that she was perfectly calm and composed.

"Haven't we met somewhere?" she said brightly, with what she hoped was a vague and ladylike smile.

"At Monsieur Anatole's," the girl said, watching her finger drawing figures on the banister. "I am Father Millet's niece."

"Oh—of course," said Hydie. She wondered whether it would be proper to mention her own name, but thought that perhaps this was not necessary. Then it occurred to her that as Father Millet's niece came from Fedya's flat, she was probably his new mistress; and if that was so then the poor girl must think that she, Hydie, was jealous or resentful. It was essential to dispel this misunderstanding and to put the girl's mind at rest. But on the other hand, she was in a hurry. It also occurred to her that as the concierge knew of all goings on in the house, this meeting explained why she had looked at Hydie so doubtfully. There were always unforeseen complications; she wished she had rehearsed meeting Fedya's new mistress on the stairs.

"Well—it was nice to meet you," she said at last. "I hope—I do hope we shall meet again." She spoke with warmth and emphasis to put the girl's mind at rest, hoping it was the right tone. With an almost beaming smile she took a step upstairs, clutching her bag. But the girl did not move, and kept drawing figures on the banister. "I wanted to ask you something," she said with her sullen pout.

Hydie was now almost level with her, but she was glad to stop; her legs were heavy again. "Oh, do," she said wearily.

"Somebody said you used to be in a convent," the girl said, without looking at Hydie.

"Oh, yes—a long time ago."

The girl kept staring at her hand on the banister.

"Is it very—difficult?" she said.

Hydie considered the question. "Difficult? No. . . . Not if you believe in it."

The girl nodded absently, as if confirming that this was what she had always thought. She lingered for another second, then said:

"Well—goodbye." She began to descend the staircase, her high heels making clop . . . clop each time they touched down on a step, her hand trailing on the banister. Hydie turned her head and watched her descend, remembering a little enviously that Monsieur Anatole always kept talking about her "enchanting posterior." Then, while the girl turned round the landing as if she were walking in her sleep, Hydie saw her in a new light: she understood that even Father Millet's niece had been bitten by the bug of longing.

There was now only one flight of steps separating her from Fedya's door. Hydie stopped, pulled the powder compact from her bag and made up her face. In the little mirror it looked pale, but calm. She was surprised that this surprised her. She asked herself whether she had really been so silly as to expect that something would be written on it. She dropped the compact back into her bag, where it again clinked against the gun; this time the dry, metallic sound sent a faint shiver down her neck and spine such as she used to get as a child when somebody scraped a blackboard with a long finger-nail. She closed her bag and briskly walked up the last flight of steps. Then, without giving herself time for further hesitation, she rang the bell of Fedya's door. While she pressed the button, she automatically ordered her face into a bright smile, as she always used to do before the door opened. She heard the familiar buzz inside; it seemed ages since she had last heard it, and yet it had been only a week ago.

Fedya was sitting in an armchair in his new dressing-gown, listening to the radio. He had been relieved that his new mistress had to leave so early because he wanted to do some thinking. He had noticed a certain coolness in Gromin's attitude to him—Gromin was his new boss, recently sent out from home—and this worried him. Gromin was a dour, short-spoken, uncultured man, who had never been abroad before—this fact in itself was significant. If they sent this type of person, who knew neither the language nor the first thing about the country, to such an important post, it showed that there was a new wave of distrust in the Service against those who had been too long stationed in Capua. And Gromin looked and behaved exactly as if he were the chief of a decontamination squad. Not that he was specially nasty to Fedya—Gromin seemed to make a point of being generally disagreeable to everybody and of treating the old hands as if they were all contaminated. It was just a nuance in their relations, an occasional glance or short remark of Gromin's, which had set Fedya worrying during these last few days. Before that, this nuance had either not been present, or Fedya had been too preoccupied with Hydie to notice it. He had only realised that something was wrong, or supposedly wrong, after the row with Hydie, when Fedya for a day or two had felt slightly shaken in his self-confidence, and consequently ill-tempered and suspicious.

But it was equally possible that it was all pure imagination, born from an uneasy concience. That he had an uneasy conscience was also a discovery of these last few days. There was of course nothing tangible to reproach himself with, nothing concrete which Gromin or anybody could hold against him. But Fedya's training had been a thorough one and he knew that the first stage in the process of contamination was rarely accompanied by concrete and tangible signs. He knew that for a citizen of the Free Commonwealth to live abroad was the same thing as for a healthy person to live in a colony of syphilitics. Every personal contact, the very air one breathed here, meant a constant exposure to infection. The first symptoms were easy to overlook, and once the poison got into one's blood-stream, it was too late. When that happened, it was only natural that the victim should be punished and isolated somewhere in the Arctic, to breathe the cold, pure air and to prevent him from contaminating others.

Fedya knew that it was mostly the fault of that spoilt, decadent creature who kept crying after her convent and behaving like a harlot. In short, she was a typical product of her civilisation and class, a carrier of the infection if ever there was one. It was she who had taught him to take a liking to bistros in a sentimental, petit-bourgeois way; to look down on Gromin, who had fought in the Civil War, because he drank red wine with his oysters; to prefer the works of decadent impressionist painters to the healthy and inspired battle pictures of Commonwealth artists. Worse than that, there had been moments when Fedya had been almost ashamed of being a product of the most advanced and cultured civilisation in man's history, and had felt an abject and treacherous admiration for the decadent world from which she came. True, this had only happened for a few short moments, and there was nothing tangible and concrete against him—but Fedya knew that it was treason nevertheless, and if called to account he would in all sincerity have to plead guilty and take what was coming to him. Fortunately it was all over now, and in its way it had been a valuable experience. At least he knew what they were like, those sick luxury products of a decaying class.

While Father Millet's niece was in the bathroom, getting ready to leave, Fedya turned the radio on louder and gave himself a drink. His thoughts had gone back to the Black

Town of Baku. If the Nobel brothers, who had once owned the refineries, had wives and daughters, they must have been exactly like Hydie. Yes, it had been a valuable experience, and fortunately it had come to an end just in time. It was equally fortunate that he had picked up this new girl to fill the gap. With her, there were at least no complications. She seemed hardly to be awake; even when he took her she remained passive and behaved as if the whole business disgusted her—which was much more proper and decorous than Hydie's shameless display. It was a mystery to Fedya how he had been able to stick that girl for almost four months.

He finished his glass and smiled uncertainly, for a disagreeable thought had occurred to him. He had just discovered that he had put up with Hydie for so long more out of kindness and pity than desire. And that of course was how the infection worked on one. To have one's fun with some desirable wench from the other camp was a perfectly correct way of acting—it was like looting the enemy's food-stores. But to develop petit-bourgeois sentiments in such a case was an extremely dangerous sign. . . . Well, it was over now; and soon everything would be over altogether. Capua was over-ripe to fall. Then all temptations and sources of infection would be eliminated for good. Then the new, clean, constructive life would start in the contaminated area. And yet Fedya could not help feeling an ever so slight pang of regret; it was this faint and uncontrollable reaction that worried him. For, no doubt, here was the reason for that coldness in Gromin's reaction to him. It was said that animals could smell that a man was afraid; and Hydie had once claimed that saints could smell the odour of sin. That was of course either ridiculous superstition, or there was some chemical explanation through glandular secretions and so on. But on the other hand, men like Gromin were something like the modern equivalent of Hydie's saints; and it was just possible that in some way they could smell it if a man was contaminated—even if there were no concrete and tangible signs. . . . Ah, it was time to finish with perfidious Capua, and make the world safe to live in. The only thing he regretted at the moment was those colourful fish in their fluorescent tank in the aquarium-bar. Inevitably, the tank would be smashed and the bar converted into a workers' canteen. That was of course as it should be, and the only thing wrong about it was that he again felt that ridiculous pang of regret. . . .

Fedya heard Father Millet's niece leave—without saying goodbye, as was her habit—and her steps recede on the staircase. To cut the vicious circle in which his thoughts moved, he gave himself another drink, and took a book from among the five or six volumes on the shelf over the couch. It was Marx's "Class Struggles in France," which he had not read since his University days. He leafed through the introduction by Engels and his attention was caught by its concluding passage:

> "It is now, almost to the year, sixteen hundred years since a dangerous party of revolt made a great commotion in the Roman Empire. It undermined religion and all the foundation of the state; it flatly denied that Cæsar's will was the supreme law; it was without a fatherland, international; it spread over all countries of the empire from Gaul to Asia, and beyond the frontiers of the empire. It had long carried on an underground agitation in secret; for a considerable time, however, it had felt itself strong enough to come out into the open. This party of revolt, of those known by the names of Christians, was also strongly represented in the army; whole legions were Christian. When they were ordered to attend the sacrificial ceremonies of the pagan-established church, in order to do the honours there, the rebel soldiers had the audacity to stick peculiar emblems—crosses—on their helmets in protest. Even the wonted barrack cruelties of their superior officers were fruitless. The Emperor Diocletian could no longer quietly look on while order, obedience and discipline in his army were being undermined. He intervened energetically, while there was still time. He passed an anti-Socialist, I should say anti-Christian, law. The meetings of the rebels were forbidden, their meeting halls were closed or even pulled down, the Christian badges, crosses, etc., were, like the red handkerchiefs in the Saxony of our day, prohibited. Christians were declared incapable of holding offices in the state, they were not to be allowed even to become corporals. This exceptional law was also without effect. The Christians tore it down from the walls with scorn; they are even supposed to have burnt the Emperor's palace in Nicomedia over his head. Then the latter revenged himself by the great persecution of Christians in the year 303, according to

our chronology. It was the last of its kind. And it was so effective that seventeen years later the army consisted overwhelmingly of Christians, and the succeeding autocrat of the whole Roman Empire, Constantine, called the Great by the priests, proclaimed Christianity as the state religion.

"London, March 6, 1895.   F. ENGELS."

Fedya sighed with contentment. That was the stuff—not bars, exotic fishes, sentimental bistros and crazy American heiresses. Here was solid substance, perspective, truth. He turned a page and started on Marx's text:

"After the Revolution of July 1848, when the Liberal banker, Monsieur Laffitte, led his godfather, the Duke of Orleans, in triumph to the Town Hall, he remarked casusually: *'From now on the bankers will rule.'* Laffitte had betrayed the secret of the bourgeois revolution. . . ."

There was an insistent buzz at the front door and Fedya became suddenly aware that it had been going on for some time. He cursed, wondering who the devil it might be, and went to open the door. When he saw Hydie standing outside, smiling brightly and at the same time chewing her lip, he had an impulse to slam the door and go back to his book. But he knew that would be uncultured behaviour, so he said "Ah—you have come back," as politely as he could, and stood aside to let her enter.

"I thought you would never open—but I knew you were in, so I waited," said Hydie, walking past him into the sitting-room.

"How did you know? I could have gone out for dinner," said Fedya.

"But I met Father Millet's niece on the stairs," Hydie said brightly.

Fedya looked at her suspiciously, fearing a scene of jealousy. He had once suffered such a scene from a temperamental girl in the Komsomol, and it had ended with the girl smashing his then most cherished possession against the wall—a glass paperweight with a picture stuck to its base which represented the shooting of the Communards in the Père Lachaise cemetery. This memory made Fedya take his stand in front of the radio with the chromium dial to protect this favourite among his acquisitions against possible manifestations of Hydie's wrath. But Hydie did not look as if an outburst were imminent; she was pale, almost white in the face, and she kept chewing her lip and looking at him with a strange, pensive stare as if she were seeing Fedya for the first time and trying to make out what kind of a person he was. They were both standing, and this got on Fedya's nerves because she was just a shade taller than he; when they walked in the streets it didn't matter, but standing like this face to face it made him uncomfortable. There was nothing he could do but ask her to sit down—resigning himself to some futile and embarrassing talk with recriminations and perhaps tears. But at any rate, he was decided to make it unmistakably clear that their affair was over, and no going back to it.

However, Hydie refused to sit down and merely shook her head at his invitation with a curiously slow, dreamy motion. Then she said, in the same absent-minded manner:

"I don't remember this dressing-gown—is it new?"

Unwittingly she had touched a sensitive point, because in his present state of remorse Fedya regarded his acquisition of the silk dressing-gown as another symptom of the contaminating effect of Capua. Had she come back to rub that in and rejoice at his weakness? If so, she had calculated wrongly, for at the first impertinent remark he would simply turn her out without ceremony.

"The old one was torn," he said drily. "But did you come here to see what dressing-gown I wear—or which persons visit me?"

Hydie looked at him with an uncomprehending, distraught stare—one could almost believe, Fedya thought uncomfortably, that she was blind; then, as his remark penetrated through the mist, she suddenly blushed.

"No—oh no," she stammered. "I really don't care, you know."

"Then why did you come back?" he asked with controlled impatience.

Hydie again stared at him in that disconcerting, absent way. "Because . . ." she said, and with fumbling, hesitant fingers she opened the clasp of her bag. She made a desperate attempt to pull herself together, but could neither say the words of the phrase she had prepared nor get herself to pull the gun out of the bag. Instead, to gain time, she got her powder compact out, just as Fedya had expected. She knew that he had expected it and that her mania to make up her face every five minutes when she was nervous, exasperated him; again she saw herself as he saw her, with all her thoughts and gestures mirrored in his eyes. But she felt unable to act otherwise than the way he expected her to act; besides, her knees were trembling and she felt the ground under her feet sway ever so slightly as if Fedya's flat were on the seventieth floor of a skyscraper. So she sat down in the armchair, felt with great relief her body relax on the elastic but firm support, and began to powder her nose, smiling at him over the little mirror of her compact.

"Because . . ." she heard herself say, "because I wanted a drink. . . ."

Fedya turned on his heels without a word, got the bottle and poured her a small drink.

"More," said Hydie. "You did not use to be so niggardly."

"If you drink you will again make a scene," said Fedya. "I must go out in ten minutes."

"Just a little drop more," said Hydie.

He gave her a look of cold, polite contempt and added a few token drops to her glass. Hydie drained the glass avidly. She had made a mistake in limiting herself to two Martinis at the bar. Now she was hopelessly bogged down on the plane of mirrors, dressing-gowns, powder compacts and trembling knees. She had been unable to utter her prepared phrase, much less to pull the gun out of her bag—chained by mind and limbs to the trivial plane, the words and the gesture appeared unimaginably absurd. Where was the power to lift her back again into the inspired sphere where the absurd became reasonable and logical? Inconsequentially a line of poetry drifted through her mind: *And the nightingale is dumb, And the angel will not come.*

"If you feel not well, I shall take you home in a taxi," said Fedya.

A hideous suspicion had occurred to him: perhaps she was pregnant and had come to tell him. Hydie could see the idea as clearly written on his face as if she were reading it in print. Without thinking, she said:

"And what if I really *am* pregnant?"

She saw his eyes narrow, and not only his manner, but his whole hard, sinewy body become stiff and formal like a traffic cop's who, holding up a driver for harmless speeding, discovers that the car has been stolen.

"If that is so, it is no concern of mine," he said precisely.

"No? Isn't it?" She no longer had to think; the conversation rolled on by its own gravity, as it were.

"No," said Fedya. "I cannot know—how many others there have been."

"Oh," said Hydie. "Of course not." She felt herself smile and noticed with wonder that the insult did not hurt her, that she experienced the same blissful insensitivity to pain as when Commanche had been lashing out at her. She opened her bag, put the powder compact in its place, and her hand touched the gun. Its touch was solid and friendly, and something in her said "now." She let her hand rest on the gun in the bag and saw that Fedya's eyes were resting on the bag and that the colour of his eyes had changed. She felt that "now" like a physical force acting on the muscles and joints of her fingers, and at the same instant she had the curious sensation that the centre of her consciousness had been propelled out of her body and was watching the scene from a remote distance, through the wrong end of a field-glass. This distant observer registered the solid touch of the gun on the fingers, and the rub of the clasp of the bag against the wrist; but it had also power to influence the automatic sequence of events and to transmit, by remote control, as it were, the order: *"not now. Not in anger."* This was strange, for apparently there was no anger present in the nerves of her body. It was merely her detached awareness which suspected that traces of anger must be lurking somewhere. Then Fedya's voice came, travelling through space like a disembodied echo:

"Don't do foolish things, please."

He advanced one step, with the slow, damped movements of a diver walking on the bottom of the sea, then stopped because the gun was now pointing at him. Apart from that curious change in the colour of the eyes, his hard and yet boyish face showed no emotion or anxiety. Now he again moved slowly forward, and the detached part of Hydie's mind registered with interest that her body shivered with revulsion at his physical nearness. She slowly shook her head, hardly perceptibly, but it was just enough to make him stop and stand still; the effect was the same as when he raised a finger at the waiter in a bar. This seemed rather amusing for some reason, but again Fedya's voice interfered:

"Why do you want to do that?"

He spoke in his normal voice, but it sounded remote and

muffled, as if she had stuffed wax into her ears. Her own voice sounded equally unreal:

"But you know why."

Her mind had no part in this silly conversation between two divers moving cloggedly and yet weightlessly at the bottom of the sea. Her mind was floating over the surface, observing through layers of liquid, listening to the muffled echo of their voices.

"Because you are pregnant?"

"No. You know why. Your lists."

Suddenly Fedya understood. The boyish look went out of his face. It became grey and very tired, the face of a weary, middle-aged factory worker or mechanic. All the tension seemed to have gone out of his muscles. He licked his lips, and said at last in a flat voice:

"Oh—that. Then we must talk. But first we will have a drink."

Again she slowly shook her head, and again he stopped moving and stood still. Then he shrugged, turned his back on her, walked the two steps to the couch and sat down.

"You wanted to talk," Hydie heard herself say. She saw him reach for his glass on the table next to the white ebony radio, drain it slowly, put it back on the table and turn the radio off. Only the sudden silence told her that it must have been on all the time, playing some dance music.

"Why are you not afraid?" she heard herself say in the silence.

. . . How terribly stupid, thought Fedya when he turned the radio off. It happened sometimes that a man ruined his career or became a traitor because he was in love with a woman. He had never been in love with this girl, and yet she had destroyed his future. She would never shoot with that ridiculous gun, but she knew and would talk and cause a scandal. Even if she didn't, the fact that she knew was in itself enough to make him unfit for the Service. There was only one honourable and correct solution: to confess everything to Gromin. Then he would be demoted and sent to some camp in the Arctic, either as a prisoner or as a guard. In both cases his career was finished. The idea was partly bitter, partly comforting. He could almost feel in his nostrils the biting, cold, clean air spiced with the smell of furs, snow and timber. He would either fell the timber or guard others felling it. In both cases the timber would be floated down the river, cut in the sawmill, used to serve in the hatch of a ship or to hold the roof over a working family's head. It was not a bad cure for somebody infected by the foul air of Capua, and not a bad solution for the son of Grigor Nikitin.

"Why are you not afraid?" he heard Hydie ask, in that infuriatingly dreamy voice. He had never loathed anybody as he loathed her at that moment. He was stupefied by the idea that he had ever desired this girl with the ungainly legs, or been impressed by her airs. It was really too stupid that she of all women should be his ruin. Then a new idea came to him, and his eyes lit up as they always did when he found the unexpected solution of a puzzle. Perhaps it was not a stupid coincidence after all, and the girl was an instrument of destiny— that is to say, he corrected himself, of the logic of History. She had proved his unworthiness, his vulnerability to temptation—and at the same time she had shown him how trite and stale those temptations were. He gave a short laugh; then said, in answer to her question:

"It is no good explaining why I am not afraid. That you will never understand. . . ."

He saw that she gave no sign that she had heard him, and thought that she must be under some sort of hypnotic trance. He remembered that when she had come into the room he had been afraid that she would smash his precious radio. He smiled and, leaning forward in his chair, took the light ebony case from the table. He briefly caressed its smooth surface, played with the knob of the luminous dial, said, "Look, that is why," and hurled the case against the wall. It made a pitiful clattering noise as the valves broke, the chassis twisted and the frame split into pieces; then there was silence and Fedya looked at the wreckage with a bitter smile.

"Why did you do that?" asked Hydie, whose eyes had followed his movements quietly, without emotion or surprise.

"That," said Fedya, "I did to answer your question. I liked that radio—but it was not important. I like this dressing-gown, but it is not important, and when I shall go away I shall burn it or perhaps give it to the concierge. We like these things and you like these things, but for you they are everything and for us they are of no importance. They are like toys—one plays with them, one throws them away. Nothing is of importance, only the future. That is why I am not afraid."

He got up. "Now we have talked enough, and you must go,"

he said, walking toward her in the hope that she would get up too, and that he could take from her the stupid revolver lying at the arm of her chair. But once more she shook her head, and he knew by instinct that he should not attempt to reach for it any more than one should try to take a bone from a dog. He did not care much whether she shot him, and she would probably miss anyway. But it was in the interest of the Service to avoid a scandal if possible, so there was nothing for it but to humour her until she got back into a normal state and could be got rid of. He got himself another drink and sat down on the arm of the couch, wondering how he should set about it. Then he heard her ask:

"What happened to Leontiev?"

His thoughts were on the Arctic, on the silence of the vast snowfields and the rhythmic sound of the felling of timber—as if a swarm of great woodpeckers had invaded the virgin forest. It was not a bad solution.

"He is going to be extradited," he said absently.

"Why?"

"It was found out that he had done dirty things before he left—embezzled money and denounced innocent people to the police. His wife committed suicide for shame."

There was silence again. Then Hydie gave a little sigh, and asked in that strangely remote voice which was at the same time dry and softly compassionate:

"Do you know when you are lying, Fedya, or don't you know any longer?"

Fedya had never slapped a woman's face, but at that moment he would have given much to be able to do it. What held him back was not that stupid revolver, but his duty to prevent a scandal. That at least had to be avoided at any cost. He summoned all his patience and self-discipline for a last attempt to bring her back to reason. He forced himself to make his voice patient and gentle; and, after the first few words, its sound made him indeed regain his calm—and even feel a kindly pity for the unhappy, fat-legged girl.

"Listen, please," he said. "We have talked about these matters often before. You don't like that we make scientific studies of human nature like Professor Pavlov. You don't like revolutionary vigilance, and lists on the social reliability of people, and discipline, and re-education camps. You think I am brutal and ridiculous and uncultured. Then why did you like making

love with me? I will tell you why and you will understand. . . ."

. . . That part of Hydie's mind which kept behaving like a
detached observer watching the scene from a distance, registered that Fedya was talking with great sincerity. It further
registered that there was a tone of quiet resignation in his
voice as if he had given up a cherished hope, as if a spring
had broken in him; and also, that by force of sitting so unnat-
urally erect for so long, her own legs were tingling with pins
and needles.

"Then why did you like making love with me? I am not a
tall and handsome man. . . ." His voice, which came muted
through space and silence, sounded a little embarrassed, and
his face was actually blushing, so that the freckles under the
taut cheek-bones became more visible. ". . . There are no tall
and handsome men who come from the Black Town in Baku,
because there were few vitamins in the food around the oilfields. So it was not for this that you liked to make love with
me. It was not physical. It was because I believe in the future
and am not afraid of it, and because to know what he lives for
makes a man strong. For a person like you, who once also believed in something, that is more than sex appeal. . . . Of
course many ugly things are happening in my country. Do
you think I do not know about them? I know them better than
you do. But what good is sentimentality? It does not help, and
it corrupts. And what difference will it make in a hundred
years that there is a little ugliness now? It always existed. In
a hundred years there will be no ugliness—only a classless
world state of free people. There will be no more wars and no
more children born in Black Towns with big bellies and flies
crawling in their eyes. And also no more children of the bourgeoisie with crippled characters because they grow up in a
decadent society. . . . You are unhappy, no? Why are you
unhappy? Why do you always long for that convent? Because
your parents and your teachers could give you nothing to replace that superstition. Everybody in your world is unhappy.
Everything here is infected with unhappiness. It is like syphilis. So it must be burnt down like an infected slum and a new
house built in its place. In a hundred years humanity will have
a new house which is clean and healthy. But for that we must
fight and win, and fighting is always ugly. . . . I am not
handsome, but you have felt attracted to me because you
know that we will win and that we are only at the beginning—

and that you will lose because you are at the end. You feel that because you know that we have an idea and a plan, and you have no plan and nothing to oppose it. . . . That is why I was not afraid of your little revolver, because you can't have the courage to shoot me. To kill, one must believe in something. If you were pregnant, you could perhaps have killed me. But for politics, for ideological reasons you cannot do it, because there is nothing in the name of which you could do it. To kill, one must have a clean conscience. That is why I can kill, and you can't. . . ."

He stopped, realising that this was not at all what he had meant to say. He heard Hydie's voice:

"Why do you want me so much to kill you?"

He stared at her uncomprehendingly. Her hand was now on the gun and her expression had changed: she looked as if she had suddenly woken up. She was no longer a distant observer. The scene had risen from the sea-bottom to the surface, the room was no longer silent, she heard them both breathe and their voices were rasping; her heart was again drumming painfully and there were pins and needles in her leg. The touch of the little revolver was comforting, a current of strength seemed to flow from it into her arm, and again something in her said "Now."

"Oh, Fedya . . ." she said, and pressed the trigger, thinking "now—not in anger." Nothing happened; she had forgotten to release the safety-catch. While she fumbled with it, Fedya jumped, then the shot went off with a loud report and Fedya, looking very surprised, slumped down like a big stuffed doll before her armchair. She had to extract her feet from under him, then she walked to the door—limping because of the pins and needles.

She stood on the landing and pressed the button of the lift. The staircase was quiet, then the lift-cabin began to mount with its familiar, high-pitched whine. As she stood waiting for it, her mind was blank and empty.

She passed the window of the concierge and saw a cardboard sign hanging on it: "Gone out—back in ten minutes." Mme. Bouchon's horrible tom-cat rubbed its back against her legs, obscenely raising its bushy tail. She found a taxi and gave the driver her address. In the cab her head began to ache, and she thought of her father and knew that she would willingly face any torture to make her senseless act undone. Then she felt unaccountably happy and knew that it had been the only sensible act in her life. Then this certitude evaporated as if it had never been there, and she fell back into a despair so bottomless as she had never thought within the capacity of human experience.

10

MONSIEUR ANATOLE'S FUNERAL

IT had been Monsieur Anatole's wish that everybody in the funeral procession should travel in horse-drawn carriages.

"I shall not be in a hurry," he had written in a postcript to his Will, "so why should others be? I wish that the guests at my last reception, where for once they will be able to talk without imposing on me the boredom of listening, should be spared the heartless rattle of internal combustion engines turning in low gear, and should enjoy instead the sight and smell of horses, fittingly adorned with black plumes and ribbons in their manes." But he had also hastened to add:

". . . this wish should not be interpreted as a reactionary gesture, for as a believer in the idea of continuity, I accept motor cars as the necessary though malodorous vehicles of Progress. A funeral procession, however, is not an occasion for the display of streamlined expediency, and a horse's fart will be a more welcome salute to my coffin that the splutterings of a choked exhaust pipe."

Thus, on that brilliant February morning A.D. 195–, pregnant with the first intimations of spring and with unconfirmed rumours about a surprise descent of parachutists in the Rhone Valley and several Channel ports, a long procession of carriages, drawn by one or two horses, set out from the Quai Voltaire towards the cemetery of Père Lachaise. It was headed by a magnificent hearse with walls of polished glass surrounding the coffin covered by mountains of wreaths and flowers, like a hot-house on wheels. Hidden in all this tropical vegetation travelled Monsieur Anatole's shrivelled little body with his black skull-cap, his white silken eyebrows and yellow goatee, like a malicious lemur; his thin lips still curved in the curious smile which had formed as he uttered his famous last words:

"*Quelle surprise. . . .*"

He had said them after he had apparently stopped breathing, with Mlle. Agnès already holding the traditional mirror
before his face, and his eyes had opened for a second, then
closed. The nature of the surprise which had so startled Monsieur Anatole was the subject of lively controversy; some said
it was the effect of seeing his face reflected in that critical moment in the little mirror; others, among them his nearest
friends, that he had carefully prepared this effect and chosen
his last words so that they were simple, quotable and eminently puzzling; while still others clung to a more mystical
and optimistic explanation.

This latter opinion prevailed among the guests at the funeral party who, in view of the alarming rumours, felt in dire
need of some mystical comfort. Most of them had brought
their anti-radiation umbrellas, which for some time had been
out of fashion, and had stood them discreetly next to the
coachman's brake; and now and then a top-hatted man of
letters would glance at the Geiger-counter on his wrist, pretending to measure the time it took to get across Paris in a
horse carriage. The ladies, as usual, were less concerned, unable to appreciate a menace which was not tangibly present to
the senses, and more interested in the presence of the photographers and newsreel-men who lined the route of the procssion
along the quays. Without doubt, Monsieur Anatole's funeral
was a picturesque social event which would fill the illustrated
papers—provided that their next issues still appeared.

The procession followed the quays of the Left Bank—past
the Academy which had never elected Monsieur Anatole
among its members; past the Palace of Justice where he had
been sentenced to six months prison for distributing pacifist
pamphlets during the first war; past the restaurant to The
Golden Drop where, at small expense and with much pleasure,
he had acquired his cirrhosis of the liver; past the long row of
bookstalls where he had collected his first editions, old maps
and engravings of young ladies with dimpled buttocks and rosy
breasts; past the Latin Quarter with its busy bistros, blasé
students, lazy cats and shady little hotels where, more than half
a century ago, he had laid the foundations of the prostate
trouble which was in the end to kill him; past the Petit Pont
where the ancient road from Rome to Flanders had pierced
the waterway of the Seine, where the North had become
wedded to the Mediterranean, and produced that unique civilisation of Cartesian hedonists of which Monsieur Anatole had

probably been the last representative offspring. The four black
horses drawing the hearse nodded with resigned wisdom as
they jogged along; their bay and chestnut lay-cousins showed
their enjoyment of the unexpected gala-outing by frequently
opening their neat rectal rings and dropping perfectly-shaped
spheres of honey-coloured dung. The sparrows in the naked,
silvery branches of the plane trees along the quay hurried to
the rare feast while the golden balls were still fuming in the
frosty sun; the top-hatted men of letters sat erect in their
coaches fidgeting with their black cotton gloves and enjoying
themselves with grave miens. But the procession only got into
its real stride when, past Notre Dame, the smooth asphalt gave
way to cobble-paving; now the wheels struck up their cosy rattle, the horses' shoes once again drew sparks from the worn
cobble-stones, and carriages fell into a soothing vibration
which brought the smell of dust and harness and faded per-
fumes out of the creaked and battered leather seats.

After following the Seine, the cortège turned into the Boulevard Henri Quatre, then solemnly rattled round the vast Place
of the Bastille. As their carriage passed the hideous July
column erected in the place of the ancient gaol, the Colonel
and Hydie both thought of the fireworks they had watched
from Monsieur Anatole's terrace on the last Bastille Day, just
over half a year ago. It was then that the whole tragi-comic adventure had started, with a chance encounter of Hydie's bare
elbow and Fedya Nikitin's nose. She could still almost see the
faint trickle of blood, glistening a gory purple in the light of
the spluttering Catherine wheels.

"It is all over now," said the Colonel without looking at her,
and hampered by the presence in their carriage of the young
American, Albert P. Jenkins, Jr., who had been sent over on a
war cemeteries project and had been a frequent guest at
Monsieur Anatole's.

But of course both Hydie and her father knew that it wasn't
over and never would be. Tomorrow they would leave for
home on a streamlined Clipper, just as Commanche had fore-
told, though for different reasons: the Colonel's resignation
had been accepted and all that remained for them to do was to
vanish from the scene swiftly and discreetly. His superiors had
been very decent about it and assigned him to a new job back
in Washington; everybody had been so humiliatingly decent
and discreet. If she had managed to kill Fedya properly instead of bungling the job by just wounding him in the loin,

they couldn't have hushed it up and the whole thing would perhaps have made sense after all. As matters turned out, it was merely an embarrassing incident, and both Commanche's department and the Commonwealth Embassy, each anxious for its own reasons to avoid a scandal, had hurriedly agreed to regard it as the act of a hysterical and jealous female which concerned neither the police nor the public. There had been no prosecution, not a word in the press, not a question asked; Fedya had been whisked away home, and Hydie and her father were going home too, and the incident might never have happened. Had she killed him, her father would have been ruined and Fedya would be dead and Hydie herself in prison, waiting to be tried; and yet it would probably have made sense on that different plane where deeds are measured on a different scale. Now, after this pitiful anticlimax, she was forever banished from that exalted sphere, and condemned to live in a portable glass cage again.

"It's all over now," the Colonel repeated. "Day after tomorrow we shall be home. . . . I thought perhaps you might feel like taking a job."

"I thought so too. I am glad you mentioned it," said Hydie sagely.

The procession turned into the Faubourg St. Antoine and her eyes beheld, in the nostalgic agony of parting, the scenery of the street: the old houses, each with its personal odour and secret, the trees in their white, silvery nakedness, the concierges in slippers, staring at the funeral from the doorways under the long balconies with their horizontal flights of sooty iron grilles; the whole, unique mixture of Mediterranean sloth with Nordic diligence and thrift. If Monsieur Anatole there in front, rolling along in his ambulant greenhouse, were capable of feeling, he would probably feel the same bitter pang of departure. Already the trees and shops and mangy cats and shabby cafés had a tinge of unreality to them, as if the present were merely a memory, issued from the homesickness which would start the day after tomorrow, when the plane touched down at the airport of Washington, D.C.

At the approaches of the Place de la Nation the procession came to a halt, for a huge demonstration was moving down from the workers' suburbs of Belleville and Menilmontant. They were marching six and eight abreast, their front ranks mainly composed of young men and girls with short hair and bright eyes; but interspersed among them were tough characters of a different type, in bulging leather jackets which looked as if they were lined with steel rods or knuckle-dusters or guns. Over their heads floated streamers in bright red with black lettering, displaying slogans like "DEATH TO THE WARMONGERS," "LONG LIVE THE COMMON-WEALTH ARMY OF PEACE," "THE WORKERS OF PARIS WELCOME THEIR LIBERATORS," and so on. Some of the streamers carried crude paintings of the leaders of the Government dangling from gallows; others featured huge, smiling portraits of the late Father of the People with his arm around his successor's shoulder; still others, the red dove of peace carrying a hammer and a sickle in its beak.

In the third carriage behind the hearse, Monsieur Touraine, the editor, and Monsieur Plisson, the Man of Letters, were contemplating the demonstration. Monsieur Touraine had put his umbrella in front with the coachman, but Monsieur Plisson's stood next to his leg, his black-gloved hand resting on its handle. His face looked grey and shrunk, and he was nervously rubbing the grey spats on his insteps against each other. "Do you think it is true about the parachutists?" he asked.

Touraine shrugged. "The reports are confused. The last news was about some suspicious fog moving along the Channel, but this is the foggy season anyway."

The Man of Letters' face seemed to shrink even more. "Do you believe an identity card made out in a different name is sufficient protection?"

Touraine shrugged again. "Why should you need that? They won't do anything to you."

"How can one know? I have lent my name to a number of committees and cultural organisations."

"My dear friend," said Touraine, "if I were a bachelor like you, with no family and responsibility, I wouldn't worry. But as it happens, I have a wife and two children, the elder one just starting school—not to mention the responsibility for the biggest evening paper in the country."

He fell silent and they both watched the demonstration approaching through the large Avenue Philippe Auguste. The three outlets from the square leading towards the centre of the town—the Boulevard Diderot, Boulevard Voltaire and the Rue du Faubourg St. Antoine in which the funeral party stood stuck—were blocked by cordons of mounted police. As the head of the demonstration emerged into the square, the young people marching in its ranks greeted the police with laughter, whistling and shouts. A police officer rode towards the centre of the square with the obvious intention to parley with the leaders of the demonstration, but as stones and bricks began to fly towards him, he hurriedly turned tail. At the same time the demonstrators broke rank and invaded the square which a moment later became a cauldron filled with a milling, boiling mass of people, with banners and streamers swirling over their heads as if they were being turned round and round by a whirlpool in a sluggish current. Now and then the pulsing central mass shot out a tentacle of a score or so of toughs against one of the three police cordons, but quickly withdrew it again in view of the bared sabres of the police. Meanwhile, stones kept flying in all directions; a brick smashed through the glass wall of the hearse—which had come to a halt just behind the line of police horses barring entry into the Faubourg St. Antoine—and settled peacefully among the flowers on Monsieur Anatole's coffin. As if this outrage were too much for them, the police now charged into the centre of the square, dealing flat sabre blows right and left with obvious relish on running people's heads and shoulders, regardless of age and sex. The central mass of the demonstration heaved towards the outlet into the Boulevard Diderot whose police cordon had not charged; and as the flood approached, this cordon opened up in the centre, swinging back like the two wings of a lock-gate, and let the running crowd pass. The whole manœuvre had probably been planned to divert the demonstration into the channel which provided the least direct approach to the centre of the town, and towards other prepared police barriers. In a short while the square was empty except for a few wounded demonstrators, who, after being kicked for a while by the policemen, were being thrown into black ambulance cars with barred windows; and except for a horse lying on its back, surrounded by another circle of police staring at it with grieved solicitude. The whole encounter had lasted less than five minutes.

Monsieur Plisson gave a sigh, and settled back on the worn leather seat of the carriage. Neither he nor Touraine had commented on the scene they had been witnessing; now the Man of Letters resumed the conversation where it had been broken off:

"What do you intend to do, then?"

Touraine shrugged again.

"My dear friend, in all revolutions and upheavals there are

imbeciles who are sacrificed like that horse over there. What matters is to avoid being one of them."

"But how is one to avoid it?"

Touraine thought of his house in Morocco, and the small two-engined plane ready at Villacoublay. Madame Touraine had insisted that they should leave at once, but if afterwards the crisis turned out to have been one more blind alarm, he would be called a coward and be forever covered with ridicule. If, on the other hand, he sent his wife and kids ahead to safety, there was no guarantee that the plane would be able to get back, and he might be stuck. As for sending them by boat, he did not dare to take the risk in view of the rumours about the Channel ports. By instinct he preferred that they should all stick together, but the nightmare of it was that nobody could tell which exactly was the right moment to take the decision and abandon all: flat, furniture, job, social position—the fruit of a lifetime of intrigue, pushing, humiliation and honest toil. His boy was five, the girl seven; a single error in timing and they were all lost. And there was also Josephine, the French poodle, expecting her first litter next week. How could he explain his dilemma to an imbecile like Plisson? He said in a cheerful voice:

"Nothing turns out quite as bad in reality as one imagined it. One should not believe in all the tendentious rumours about the Commonwealth regime. After all, they were our allies in the last war. I, for one, have never indulged in atrocity-mongering, and as far as my limited influence over the paper went, it has always observed an attitude of strict objectivity. You will be the first to admit that. . . ."

Monsieur Plisson nodded gravely:

"I myself have never directly engaged in politics and have always kept an open mind about the social developments in our time. . . ." They were both silent for a while, slightly embarrassed, slightly bashful, and both reflecting bitterly how little one could trust one's neighbour in these days.

Touraine sighed. "I suppose there are always possibilities of coming to an arrangement, provided one succeeds in proving one's desire for honest co-operation. What matters is to avoid at all costs that acts of irresponsible provocation should occur. Whatever the motive of such romantic gestures may be, it is always the whole community that pays."

Monsieur Plisson nodded. "It happened the last time. To be quite frank, I was opposed to conspiracy and violence even then. If the legends are discarded, the results achieved were pitifully small, and the suffering inflicted by provoking acts of retaliation enormous. Another bleeding of the country on that scale would be impossible to endure. The only important thing, as I see it, is to preserve the substance of the nation."

The police gave the hearse the sign to proceed, and slowly the funeral got moving again. The two men fell back into silence, and Touraine once more went over the whole weary argument with himself whether to leave at once and give up everything, or to wait and risk the closing of the trap. The arguments for and against were balancing each other, and in this deadlock Josephine's litter suddenly assumed an inordinate weight, like the last straw which breaks the camel's back. Plisson's phrase about saving the substance of the nation still rang in his ears. His two kids were part of that substance; but that again was an argument which cut both ways where his dilemma was concerned. Why indeed not wait until the puppies were born, an event which the children awaited with such excitement? It was as good a time limit, and as rational an argument, as any other. After all, the Romans decided their plans of campaign by observing the flight of birds, or throwing a sheep's offal over their shoulders.

The carriage behind Monsieur Touraine's was shared by Julien and Father Millet. The Father had donned for the occasion the coarse saffron cowl of his Order which, enveloping his bulky frame in statuesque folds, was extremely becoming—especially in the setting of a horse-drawn carriage. The Father's huge posterior and the folds of his habit occupied three-quarters of the carriage seat; in the remaining quarter sat Julien, leaning into his corner, his game leg stretched out between them. As they were traversing the square, a wounded demonstrator was shoved by two uniformed men into the ambulance. The casualty was a boy of about seventeen; thick, oily blood was oozing from his ear which was neatly cut into two halves; he was unconscious, probably owing to concussion or skull fracture. Father Millet snorted with disgust.

"Each time I see our police in action, I am tempted to become a Communist," he said.

"What will you be tempted to become when you see the Commonwealth police in action?" asked Julien.

"Either a victim or a desert father on a small oasis. I liked that article of yours."

"Your idea of an oasis is probably different from mine," said Julien.

"We'll see," said Father Millet.

The procession followed with a leisurely rumbling of its wheels the Avenue du Trône, then veered left into the Boulevard de Charonne. As it turned the corner, they could see the hearse with a neat hole in its glass wall, from which cracks radiated in all directions like the rays of the sun on a child's drawing. A slight jolt, caused by some unevenness of the cobble-paving, made a loose slab of glass fall out and splinter into fragments in the gutter.

"Hearses should be made of unbreakable glass," said Julien.

"That is an eminently timely suggestion," said Father Millet. "Do you know that the police have gone completely off their heads, and the Government too? They have arrested my niece."

"What on earth for?" asked Julien.

"Apparently she has had an affair with some Commonwealth agent. If they arrest all the other people with whom she has had affairs, I shall rejoice in an un-Christian manner. Were you by any hazard among them?"

"No," said Julien. "Nor was that unhappy Pontieux. They have arrested him too."

"That is a different matter," said Father Millet, suddenly grave and pontifical. "He had a truly pernicious influence on the younger generation. In my eyes he is the symbol of the intellect's betrayal of the spirit."

"He is just a clever imbecile," said Julien. "It wasn't his fault if people took him seriously. He was more surprised about it than anybody else." He smiled, then continued: "The funny side of it is that his wife has always been a real, honest-to-God Commonwealth agent, a fact which poor Pontieux never guessed—and that she, of course, is free."

"You don't say," said Father Millet, shocked. "In times of crisis they have an infallible instinct to arrest the wrong people."

"You are still an innocent, Father," said Julien. "How could they hope to keep their jobs under the new regime if they arrested the rising stars of tomorrow? Look at the carriage behind us. . . ."

In the carriage behind Father Millet's travelled the poet Navarin and the physicist Lord Edwards. When the police charged with their sabres into the demonstration on the square, Edwards, who had never seen such a thing happen, grew red in the face with indignation.

"Let's go and fight the bloody swine," he said, tugging the poet by his sleeve, one leg already on the step of the carriage.

Navarin had to put up a mild struggle to hold him back by pulling with both hands at Hercules' jacket, while the physicist's enormous feet under the baggy striped trousers hung out of the door. Fortunately the battered running-board broke under his weight and this settled the issue, for Edwards, having lost his balance, allowed himself to be dragged back into the seat, where, after a few breathless puffs, he subsided into silence. Gradually, however, as the procession got going again, he seemed to recover his calm under the soothing influence of clattering hooves and rumbling wheels; and as they turned the corner of the Avenue du Trône, he asked in a changed tone:

"So what are you going to do?"

As Navarin looked at him with an uncomprehending smile, he added in a grunt:

"I mean if you are invaded."

The poet arched his eyebrows in surprise at the Englishman's awkward manner of formulating the question, and answered in a tone of explaining to a child that the earth is round:

"In the case of conflict, which could only be caused by Imperialist provocation, the duty of every democratic-minded person is to support unreservedly, unhesitatingly and unconditionally the Commonwealth of Freedomloving People."

"Hm," said Hercules. He said nothing for a while, only uttering some puffs and snorts; then unexpectedly he wagged a finger in front of Navarin's face and grunted:

"I call that treason."

Navarin thought he had misunderstood Edwards, whose French accent was abominable.

"I beg your pardon?" he asked, with his ravaged cherub's smile.

"I call that treason," Hercules the Atom-Smasher shouted over the rattle of the wheels; then with a deep, contented sigh which seemed to release his chest from some long-standing oppression, he settled back into his corner, and decided then and there to go once more into that wretched question of the expanding universe; but this time in the light of purely mathematical evidence.

Navarin, after the first shock, came to the conclusion that the only possible attitude to take in the face of this outrageous and unexpected defection was, short of getting out of the moving carriage, to subside into a stony silence. He edged away from Edwards as far as the restricted space permitted, maintaining his fixed smile, and suddenly a long-forgotten story came back to his mind. In the early years of the Revolution a newspaper-cutting was shown to the erstwhile Father of the People. It contained a short news item according to which, during the British General Strike, police and strikers had played a soccer match which the strikers had won. The shrewd old leader had promptly declared that the British were a hopeless case from the point of view of the World Revolution, and had stopped the subsidies to their Party. . . .

They were indeed, the poet reflected, a hopeless people, together with the rest of the Anglo-Saxons and with Protestants in general. The new creed could only take firm roots where the old one had never been whittled down by Puritanism and Reformation; among peoples accustomed to absolute, unquestioning submission to the hierarchy of the Holy Church, Roman or Byzantine, whose ends justified all means employed on the road to salvation. That was what cranks like Edwards would never understand, nor the foolish strikers who played soccer with the police, nor their more foolish police who let themselves be beaten by the strikers. They were a people of cranks, non-conformists and schismatics, descendants of that arch-schismatic, Henry VIII. When he came to think of it, Edwards, with his shaggy head and enormous paunch, looked rather like him.

Suddenly, as the horse jogging in front of them lifted his tail, Navarin had an inspiration. He would write a play about Henry VIII with obvious modern parallels, showing how that obscene Blue Beard's heretic defection, caused solely by his disgusting promiscuity, had been at the root of all the evils of war and dissention which had befallen Europe since. The more Navarin thought of the idea, the more he liked it. It would be his first play to be performed under the new régime. The subject would appeal to healthy national sentiment by bringing back memories of the English invasions of France, and it would by-pass all delicate problems arising out of certain aspects of the situation. . . .

Smiling his cherubic smile, Navarin felt almost grateful to Edwards, whose heretic outburst had inspired his idea. His only regret was that in the future stimuli of this kind would exist no longer.

Two carriages farther ahead, Commanche had just finished telling Georges de St. Hilaire why he had resigned from his job.

"At least I am free," he said. "Now we can start all over again, like the last time. I suppose you have a place for me in your outfit."

St. Hilaire nodded, and for a while they talked about arms-caches, liaison and other technical matters. At the entry to the Boulevard Menilmontant the procession again came to a halt, for some men in Basque berets and with automatic rifles had started tearing up the pavement to erect a barricade. When they saw the hearse, however, they waved it on, and even re-placed a few cobbles to spare it too rude a jolt. The procession slowly clattered on, with more glass fragments falling out of Monsieur Anatole's greenhouse.

"Those were our chaps," said St. Hilaire. "Not many, but tough." He yawned, his whole face contorted in a grimace.

"The funny thing is," said Commanche, "that I too feel more bored than anything else."

"Needless to say, ours is a boredom of the second order," said St. Hilaire, whose manner of speech had become, with the approach of action, surprisingly lucid and simple. "It is the boredom derived from anticipating the hangover after victory. The thought of the memoirs I am going to write afterwards makes me shudder."

"You can rape victory only once; the second time she is no longer a virgin," said Commanche gloomily.

"As for the memoirs," said St. Hilaire, "they will of course either be called: 'The Dignity of the Gesture' or 'The Challenge of Destiny.' Good—the details we shall settle later."

"What I don't understand," said Father Millet, as their carriage rumbled past the nascent barricade, "what I shall never understand is what makes a person like you carry on. If you don't believe in a transcendental justice, in ultimate punishment and reward, what prevents you from becoming an op-portunist like Touraine? After all, if you eliminate the divine factor from the human equation, his attitude is completely reasonable and logical. For me it is of course easy; having staked everything on the Absolute, I can never get either bored or fed up. But to go on fighting your ding-dong battles for some elusive relative values, or a lesser evil, seems to me a pursuit as remarkable as futile."

"My dear Father," said Julien, grinning, "you will always remain an incorrigible totalitarian at heart. I am as tired of your clever dialectics as of Pontieux's, so let us call a spade a spade: what you ask me is the unconditional surrender of my critical faculties, 'to buy protection' as the mobsters say. Forgive me for putting it so crudely, but if I have to choose between one regime of terror which menaces me with eternal damnation if I don't play ball, and another which merely threatens me with thirty years in a re-education camp, I shall obviously choose the latter. In the Arctic there is at least always the hope of an amnesty or a change of regime, both of which are excluded from your system."

Father Millet fingered the cord on his robe in genuine distress. "I feel sorry for you," he said, with a mournful sigh.

"You need not bother, I feel quite sufficiently sorry for myself. Believe me, it is not always easy to resist the temptation to creep back into the sheltering womb and be warm and cosy, submerged in what you so aptly call in your baptismal rites the 'immaculate uterine font of divinity.' And believe me that I envy with all my heart those colleagues of my craft and generation who, in middle age, acquire the true faith as others acquire ulcers."

Father Millet raised his hands in horrified protest, but Julien went on unperturbed: "You need not be shocked, for if all our experiences leave physical traces in our memory, you may as well regard your faith, or any other, as a kind of chemical precipitate. Some of these faith-encymes have a poisonous, others a soothing effect, but all of them function independently of our reason—which is why homo sapiens is essentially schizophrenic in his mental structure. Alas, my poor Millet, your treatment produces at best a harmless brand of schizos, performing their curious rites in specially reserved corners of the ward."

"You are in a worse state than I thought, Julien," said Father Millet. "If you allow me to put matters into equally crude and chemical terms, your whole system is poisoned by the absence of Grace."

"That may conceivably be so," said Julien, "but:

"Thine absence is a void which thy presence cannot fill,
Thine absence is a wound which thy presence cannot heal . . .

"I wrote that once to a girl, at a time when I still wrote poems, but it fits the case under discussion. There was, however, an English mystic, who put it much better: 'The vision of Christ that thou dost see—is my vision's greatest enemy. Thine has a great hook nose like thine—mine has a snub nose like to mine. . . .'"

The extinct cigarette, stuck to Julien's lip, bobbed up and down as he talked, and as he paused it remained pointed at Father Millet. He threw it out of the carriage, and said:

"No, my dear Millet, your hook-nosed solution is out of date for me and my like. Those who are under the curse of honesty to themselves must remain mangy lone wolves with nowhere to huddle for warmth. But don't let's be so arrogantly sentimental. I guess the earth was always full of lone wolves in times like ours, when civilisation is at a loose end between a dying world and the birth of a new one. The best one can hope is to build a few oases."

"I fear that sounds too allegorical to me," said Father Millet, "and not much of a constructive programme. If you mean by oases something like the catacombs of the early Christians, or the mediæval monasteries—they all had a programme and a creed."

"I don't believe anybody has ever produced a constructive solution while History was passing through the hollow of a wave. The greatest genius could not have found a way out of the predicament of the Roman Empire in the fifth century A.D. Programmes are not made in the laboratory; they ferment like wine in the wood. I have a hunch that the time is not far when a new spiritual ferment will arise, as spontaneous and irresistible as early Christianity or the Renaissance. But meanwhile I have no programme to offer; and yet I won't have any of your patent medicine."

The procession rattled along the Boulevard Menilmontant, and the massive stone walls of the cemetery came in sight. Julien shifted his stiff leg.

"Your oasis will be a chilly refuge," said Father Millet. "It sounds rather like an Eskimo hut, built of slabs of ice in a desert of ice."

"The other day," said Julien, "I found in a bookstall on the quays an old copy of the *'Alchemist's Rosarium'*. It says that the philosopher's stone can only be found 'when the search lies heavily on the searcher.' But it also says: 'Thou seekest hard and findest not. Perhaps thou wilt find if thou doest not seek.' I shall carve both maxims into the ice wall of my igloo."

"That still doesn't amount to much," said Father Millet. "It still doesn't explain why you should take sides and get yourself involved in one scrap after another, instead of acting wisely like Touraine. If you have nothing to hold on to, in the name of what can you blame him?"

"That brings me to the third maxim for lone wolves," said Julien. "We must learn again, my dear Millet, the lost art to blame nobody but ourselves. *Tout comprendre, c'est tout pardonner* is a woolly phrase that doesn't lead you anywhere, because it automatically includes your own actions into the pardon. The correct phrasing should be: *Tout comprendre— ne rien se pardonner.* . . . To comprehend everything, to forgive oneself nothing."

"That's better," said Father Millet. "But it is a hard creed and an arrogant creed."

"*Tout comprendre, ne rien se pardonner,*" repeated Julien. "In my submission this maxim solves several hoary dilemmas implicit in the human condition. The details we shall settle later, as our friend St. Hilaire says."

In the first carriage behind the hearse travelled Mlle Agnès and Dupremont the pornographer. Dupremont's place should of course have been occupied by the deceased's son, Gaston. But Gaston the rake had spent the night with his new mistress and failed to show up in the morning; so at the last moment before the procession started Mlle Agnès had invited Dupremont, whose vehicle had not turned up in time, to share her carriage. They were an ill-assorted couple, the elderly moth-like maiden and the elegant novelist with his dark fringe-moustache and slightly uneven eyes; they both felt ill at ease and found little to say to each other.

At last, as the procession rounded the Place of the Bastille, Dupremont took heart and remarked:

"I can imagine how you feel."

Mlle Agnès answered without a moment's hesitation:

"No, you can't. I am very glad."

Dupremont was dumbfounded and, being a very shy person, could again think of nothing to say. It also occurred to him that in the course of the many evenings he had spent at Monsieur Anatole's, he had hardly ever heard Mlle Agnès' voice. At least he could not remember that it had such a fresh, clear ring to it.

After a short silence, Mlle Agnès spoke again:

"Do you remember that evening when Monsieur Leontiev came to see us?"

"I remember very well," said Dupremont.

"Do you remember what he said about that new sect?"

"I do," said Dupremont, and his heart gave a jump.

"He said this sect believed that if people could liberate themselves from fear, all forms of tyranny would collapse. And that only those are free from fear who have lost everything. He also said they believed that while one remains attached to a wife or parents, one always trembles lest they come to harm through one's actions, and therefore must leave them as Jesus cast off his mother at Cana. . . . I thought that very reasonable."

Dupremont fingered the narrow fringe over his lip, which had grown moist with excitement.

"I thought so too," he said.

". . . But I did not have the force to leave my father. Now I am free," Mlle Agnès concluded, her cheeks faintly colouring as if by the blush of a moth.

Filled with the wild elation of the timid, Dupremont thought how full of surprises this world was even for a middle-aged pornographer in search of his road to Damascus. For a long time now he had known, though he had been reluctant to admit it, that Father Millet had let him down; to try to lead people to their salvation via the *bidet* was an admittedly clever scheme, but it left him more and more frustrated and unhappy. Ever since that evening when he had heard Leontiev expound in his clipped, soldierly manner the beliefs of the sect of Fearless Sufferers, he had felt that here at last was something at the same time mystically inspired and eminently reasonable—quite apart from the keen and profound attraction which all self-flagellatory and mortifying practices exerted on his mind. But then Leontiev had disappeared; and Dupremont had been too shy and undecided to seek him out before it was too late. Only this morning, when the first rumours about the parachutists and the fog over the Channel had come in, Dupremont had thought that in the struggle against such hopeless odds, the methods of that obscure sect would probably be as efficacious as any. And now, thanks to Gaston the rake's ignomonious absence from his father's funeral and to his own carriage not turning up, he had at last found the very contact he was seeking. For evidently Mlle Agnès was already in touch with the local branch of the sect—provided, of course, that such a thing existed.

"I knew that you were interested," said Mlle Agnés.

"How did you know?" asked Dupremont, mopping his damp brow with his silk handkerchief.

"I knew."

She spoke with the brisk authority of a hospital nurse. It was obvious, Dupremont thought, that the sect had its own sources of information; it had perhaps many members already, and its invisible observers everywhere. And perhaps Mlle Agnès, that colourless shadowy figure, was one of the few just in Israel for whose sake Sodom might have been spared. She had served and borne her cross unselfishly and unquestioningly, though many would say that her self-sacrifice was caused by neurotic attachment; but that was beside the point, for motive did not enter into the question of value.

What was the next step expected from him? He did not dare to ask her any direct question for that was against the etiquette of conspiracy; the correct method was to wait patiently until one was approached. His glance brushed by chance Mlle Agnés hands, which were folded in her lap. She wore black mittens such as Dupremont had only seen worn by maiden aunts in the days of his youth; and on her left ring finger, just behind the finger-nail, there was a small patch of sticking plaster. It seemed to him that he had noticed several patches lately on people's hands: was it a secret sign of recognition?

Or was it all fantasy, a play of his imagination? . . . When would he know?

Mlle Agnès, who must have become conscious of his looking at her hand, shifted it onto the seat of the carriage.

"At any rate," she said with her faint, moth-like smile, "at any rate, one may hope that Monsieur Leontiev's journey to us, in spite of its very tragic end, has not been entirely in vain."

As the procession, following the deserted Boulevard de Menilmontant, approached the cemetery walls, the horses pulling the hearse quickened their pace. Perhaps to them the smell of the cemetery was as to other horses the smell of the stable, or perhaps they were frightened by the sudden emptiness of the streets; at any rate, they actually broke into a kind of trot, most unfitting for a funeral procession. To curb them, the black-liveried coachman in front had to pull the reins with all his might, leaning over backwards like an oarsman near the finish of a race, while all the time more fragments of glass were falling out of the hearse and breaking on the pavement with a high-pitched tinkling which punctuated the echo of the muffled rumbling of the wheels.

Shopkeepers were everywhere pulling down their shutters; from the apartment windows came the rattle of Venetian blinds being let down; the concierges were pushing the heavy carriage gates closed while scanning the skies—in which one or two low clouds had appeared—with uncertain looks of fear and defiance. There was no longer any traffic in the streets; the only pedestrians still about were housewives hurrying home with their provisions, with long sticks of bread jutting out of their shopping bags. Only the bistros on the corners were full, the customers all crowded together at the bar like people sheltering from a cloudburst. The sky, however, was clear and transparent with the pale February sun—except for those few, low, plume-shaped clouds, whose appearance seemed to attract so much attention among the crowds in the bistros, and even among the members of the funeral party—for their heads could be seen popping out of the carriages, with necks contorted and faces turned upward.

Hydie was too much absorbed in her own thoughts to notice the change of atmosphere in the street, and the Colonel deliberately chose to ignore it. He was thinking, once again, that it was truly amazing how the preoccupation with one's conscience made a person deaf and blind to other people's worries—for Hydie had not even asked him what had happened to his list of Frenchmen who were to be evacuated in the operation called "Noah's Air Convoy." That list had weighed on him heavily during these last six months; selecting one man meant condemning another, and he had felt like Flavius Josephus when Titus had granted him the privilege of choosing seventy men to be taken off their crosses among the seven thousand defenders of Jerusalem who had been crucified under the city walls. The Colonel felt a cowardly relief at the thought that the responsibility was no longer his; besides, the whole project had already come to nought, because it was impossible to evacuate the families of the selected men, and most of these had refused to leave without them. Yet during all these months Hydie had not asked him once about his lists—busy as she was with getting herself from one squalid mess into another, and acting out her absurd melodrama. How could a person of her intelligence have failed to realise that American girls were not cut out for the part of martyrs and saints? American womanhood had produced no Maids of Orleans and Madame Curies, no Krupskayas or Rosa Luxemburgs, no Brontë sisters and Florence Nightingales. Perhaps because they were too busy writing syndicated newspaper columns and playing bridge; perhaps because they had been granted equal rights without having to struggle for them, and the competitive urge was lacking. It was a matter which he must think out some day; but meanwhile his poor girl was eating her heart out because she could not walk with Brutus in the Elysian fields.

The silence in the carriage became oppressive, and the Colonel turned to Albert P. Jenkins, jr., who, perched on the collapsible seat opposite Hydie, was watching every detail of the passing street scene with the earnest application of a field anthropologist.

"What happened to that war cemetery project?" he asked.

"It's off, sir," said Jenkins. "I was switched to a new project some time ago."

"What sort of new project?" the Colonel asked absentmindedly.

"A field research project into the courting patterns of the French urban and rural population, according to social categories and geographical regions."

The Colonel smiled wryly. "Is that our most urgent job at the moment?"

Jenkins took his glasses off and began to rub them thoughtfully. "It is rather important, sir. The last time the most frequent single cause of friction between our troops and the local population was the ignorance of the troops of French courting patterns. Second in importance came divergencies in the male drinking patterns. Our poll ratings show that the resentment caused by friction of this kind has a decisive political effect, and that in the case of nearly eighty per cent of the subjects questioned this resentment outweighed the appreciation of military and economic services rendered."

"So you think," said the Colonel, "that the army should

introduce training courses in French courting patterns for all enlisted men?"

"Yes, sir," said Jenkins, blowing on his glasses. "Incidentally, such courses might have a wholesome effect in certain cases of battle fatigue."

The hearse had passed the cemetery gates and the horses, feeling at home in the broad chestnut alley lined with family vaults in stone and marble, had calmed down to a dignified pace, nodding their plumèd heads and keeping their bowels respectfully tight.

"The implication of the project, sir," said Jenkins, jr., "is that, the last time we came in, we were without appropriate knowledge of the courting habits, drinking patterns, party structures and idiosyncratic traditions of the populations concerned. This unpreparedness was mainly due to our mistaken assumption that Europe was capable of running itself. As this assumption turned out to be demonstrably incorrect, it is evident that this time we have to come adequately prepared for the task of integrating Europe into a structure of lasting stability and thus preventing a third—sorry, sir, I mean fourth —global disturbance."

"My God, young man," said the Colonel. "How can you talk about our looking after Europe when we haven't yet learned to look after ourselves?"

Jenkins displayed a smile-pattern of large teeth which, though uneven, were kept under proper dental care.

"The task of holding a baby which they have not asked for falls usually to the inexperienced of immature age. It can also be shown by way of analogy that insufficient experience in running one's own affairs is no obstacle to efficiently running the affairs of others."

The Colonel shook his head. "The way you talk one would think that running Europe is just another war cemetery project."

Jenkins gave a last rub to his glasses, tried them on and remarked:

"The two subjects, sir, appear to have an intimate logical connection."

The procession entered the cemetery through the main southern gate facing the Rue de la Roquette. Just before the gate, on the corner of a little street appropriately named Rue du Repos, a small crowd of workmen stood in the open door of a café, watching the sky. They stared indifferently at the battered hearse which had begun to shed some flowers and leaves of evergreen through the breached glass wall onto the pavement, then again lifted their faces to the plume-shaped clouds in the sky to which were now added a few white, horizontal streaks of vapour. Their expressions varied between fear, doubt and grinning incredulity; but behind their eyes, unknown to them, there had appeared some grey, primeval glint, like the flicker of a candle at the bottom of a cave. Thus, Hydie thought, must mediæval crowds have stared at the sky Anno Domini 999, waiting for the Comet to appear.

And yet, driving down the main alley of the cemetery towards the monument of the dead, everything within sight, from the old chestnut trees to the stone angels kneeling with folded wings in front of the family crypts, seemed to confirm Monsieur Anatole's cherished belief in con-ti-nu-ity. The very man himself after whom the cemetery had been named, Père François de La Chaise, was a symbol of that continuity; a nephew of the father confessor to Henry IV, he became confessor to the Fourteenth Louis; a Jesuit and lecturer in philosophy, he took an active part in the intrigues between the Montespan and Madame de Maintenon; supported the King in his squabble with the Pope, but used his influence with the Pope to moderate his wrath against the King; remained a devoted friend to Fénelon, the writer, even when the latter's Maximes incurred papal condemnation; and fell conveniently ill each time he disagreed with Louis, which circumstance enabled him to refuse to grant absolution. In short, he was truly a man after Monsieur Anatole's heart.

Following the itinerary which Monsieur Anatole had drawn up with his own hand, the long procession wound its way through the narrow circular avenues, paying homage to the glories and follies of the past: past the crypt of Abelard and Heloise, the graves of Molière and La Fontaine; past Sarah Bernhardt and Marshal Ney, past Balzac and Victor Hugo, past the alien guests of honour, Wilde and Gertrude Stein. There were monuments to the victims of the first and second World Wars, and of the Franco-Prussian War; and there was the bleak, naked wall spattered with bullet marks, against which the last resistants of the Commune had been lined up barefoot and shot.

". . . The two subjects, sir, seem to have an intimate connection." What were the subjects Albert P. Jenkins, jr., had been talking about? Hydie had not followed the conversation, but the last phrase had somehow remained in her ear. To her, the only intimate connection of Monsieur Anatole's funeral was with those who could not participate in it. She thought of her first meeting with the Three Ravens Nevermore on Bastille Day; now Boris had gone mad, Vardi had been hanged after confessing that he had planned to poison the people's water supply with germs of bubonic plague, and Julien had become a lonely, bitter man, wrapped in the hair-shirt of his solitude. Leo Nikolayevich Leontiev, Hero of Culture and Joy of the People, was either already dead or felling trees in the Arctic forest, perhaps even in the same camp where Fedya stood guard at the machine-gun turret. Which of his five expressions would Fedya wear, staring into the dusk of the Polar night—the guarded look with all shutters down, or the sexy look remembering the hours spent on the couch of the little flat with Father Millet's niece . . . ?

And the living—those who were still alive and free today, were watching for the appearance of the Comet, and they were all sick with longing. There was Monsieur Dupremont, riding in the first carriage, longing for a penance which nobody would inflict on him; there was Hercules the Atom-Smasher, longing for a universe whose laws were the same for stars and men, and were open to the mind's understanding, and could be summed up in simple words as in Plato's day. There was St. Hilaire, who believed that man's only answer to destiny was the gesture for gesture's sake, and Commanche, preparing to die with a flourish but not knowing what he was dying for. They were all sick with longing, even Fedya and Father Millet, both waiting for their own variant of the Kingdom of Promise, and wondering why it was so slow in arriving; even Monsieur Touraine, longing for the security of bygone times, when a man could cultivate his weedy garden and elbow his way to success, with no greater worries than the boy bringing bad marks from school. . . .

Her thoughts travelled back to Sister Boutillot standing in the alley which led to the pond, where the autumn breeze swept the leaves towards her feet, her lips carefully forming the words: "My flesh also longeth for thee, in a dry and weary land." Oh, if she could only go back to the infinite comfort of father confessors and mother superiors, of a well-ordered hierarchy which promised punishment and reward, and furnished the world with justice and meaning. If only one could go back! But she was under the curse of reason, which rejected whatever might quench her thirst without abolishing the gnawing of the urge; which rejected the answer without abolishing the question. For the place of God had become vacant, and there was a draught blowing through the world as in an empty flat before the new tenants have arrived.

As the procession reached the appointed site, the air-raid sirens began to wail. The guests alighted from the carriages, checking their Geiger-counters, clutching their umbrellas, and fingering their faked identity cards. The siren wailed, but nobody was sure: it could have meant the Last Judgment, or just another air-raid exercise.

SIGNET GIANTS

Complete and Unabridged—Only 35 cents each

THE AGE OF LONGING

Arthur Koestler. Koestler's most powerful novel since *Darkness at Noon*. A brilliant picture of Europe under the threat of total enslavement and the fate of two lovers who symbolize the conflicts of their time. (#S985)

MISTER SMITH

Louis Bromfield. The story of a man in desperate revolt against a "perfect marriage" and a stifling way of life. By the author of *The Rains Came*. (#S954)

THE WOMAN OF ROME

Alberto Moravia. A beautiful woman dreams of a decent life, but is caught in a net of passion. (#S844)

THE SKY IS RED

Giuseppe Berto. The desperate life and loves of four teenagers in a bombed-out Italian town. (#S971)

JUDGMENT DAY

James T. Farrell. The climax of Studs Lonigan's wasted life —the exciting finale of a modern masterpiece. (#S875)

THE STRANGE LAND

Ned Calmer. A savage novel of the men and women who fight, love and die in war. (#S851)

ARCH OF TRIUMPH

Erich Maria Remarque. A love affair full of passion and torment. (#S796)

THE STUBBORN HEART

Frank G. Slaughter. The big bestseller about stormy Reconstruction days in the South and a young surgeon fighting for his ideals. (#S956)

BACK STREET

Fannie Hurst. The famous story of a woman who sacrifices respectability for the sake of the man she loves. (#S961)

POSSESSION

Louis Bromfield. The engrossing story of a small-town girl who won wealth and fame in the glamorous international world of music. (#S979)

BERNARD CARR

James T. Farrell. A rebellious young writer finds love in Greenwich Village. By the author of *Studs Lonigan.* (#S893)

NATIVE SON

Richard Wright. The distinguished contemporary classic about a man against society. (#S794)

THE TROUBLED AIR

Irwin Shaw. A stirring novel about a man's struggle with the evils of our time, by the author of *The Young Lions*. (#S931)

THE PROMISING YOUNG MEN

George Sklar. Temptation and corruption beset a young man's quest for quick glamorous success. (#S924)

SIGNET DOUBLE VOLUMES

Complete and Unabridged—Only 50 cents each

NO STAR IS LOST

James T. Farrell. "The best of James Farrell's books," *Time Magazine* says of this story of Danny O'Neill's Chicago family. By the author of *Studs Lonigan*. (#D946)

LIE DOWN IN DARKNESS

William Styron. An outstanding novel about a tortured girl and the people and events that lead her to the brink of despair. (#D967)

THE SEVEN STOREY MOUNTAIN

Thomas Merton. The spiritual autobiography of a young man who withdrew from a full worldly life to the seclusion of a Trappist monastery. (#D929)

MOULIN ROUGE

Pierre La Mure. The colorful true-life story of Toulouse-Lautrec, painter and tragic lover of Paris' most exciting women. (#921AB)

A WORLD I NEVER MADE

James T. Farrell. Danny O'-Neill's raw, earthy life in a South Side Irish family, by the author of *Studs Lonigan*. (#D926)

THE RAINS CAME

Louis Bromfield. The Pulitzer-Prize-winning novelist tells an intriguing story of unforgettable men and women in exotic India. (#904AB)

THE NAKED AND THE DEAD

Norman Mailer. The literary sensation of our time—the brilliant best-seller about a handful of men on a Pacific Island. (#837AB)

KNOCK ON ANY DOOR

Willard Motley. A powerful novel—the dreams, frustrations and crimes of a slum youth who died in the electric chair. (#802AB)

THE YOUNG LIONS

Irwin Shaw. Irwin Shaw's great bestseller. A moving panorama of war reveals the stories of three soldiers. (#D817)

FOREVER AMBER

Kathleen Winsor. The fabulous story of Amber St. Clare, who by her wits and beauty became a favorite of Charles II. (#809AB)

STAR MONEY

Kathleen Winsor. A beautiful young author zooms to success, but loses the one thing that made life worth living. (#868AB)

TO OUR READERS: We welcome your comments about any SIGNET or MENTOR Books, as well as your suggestions for new reprints. If your dealer does not have the books you want, you may order them by mail, enclosing the list price plus 5c a copy to cover the mailing costs. Send for a copy of our complete catalogue. The New American Library of World Literature, Inc., 501 Madison Avenue, New York 22, N. Y.